A PERFECTLY PARANORMAL VALENTINE

A PERFECTLY PARANORMAL ANTHOLOGY VOLUME 1

HELLUCY HOWE   LEISL LEIGHTON   MARNIE ST CLAIR
SAMANTHA MARSHALL

LOVE PNR? JOIN OUR PERFECTLY PARANORMAL PARAMOURS FACEBOOK GROUP

If you want to get to know the Perfectly Paranormal Anthology authors a bit more, get sneak peeks of what's coming up as well as giveaways, special offers and just some PNR fun, then join our Perfectly Paranormal Paramours Facebook Group.

Find us here:

https://www.facebook.com/groups/251663560162131

CONTENTS

FILIGREE AND FATE

HELLUCY HOWE

FILIGREE AND FATE

Tales from the Fae Court
Book One

~

Hellucy Howe

❀ Created with Vellum

ABOUT FILIGREE AND FATE

Who'd have thought coming face to midriff with an Unseelie lord would end up with everyone covered in garden mulch?

When famed fae-artist Lady Zhulija Aphiski is asked to make reception decorations for a notable Unseelie family wedding, she is attacked by racial bigots at the initial consultation, and that's despite having a safe pass from fae royalty. Injured and insulted, she rejects the contract.

Not expecting Lady Zhulija to be assaulted in his own home, infamous Unseelie Lord Dario Eribifax immediately recognises his 'true mate'. How on earth can he convince her to accept both him and the contract for his sister's wedding – especially when she has yet to recognise their fated connection?

The Valentine's Day wedding of his sister and her fiancé is ten days away. Desperate to regain Zhulija's help, and earn her affection in the process, Dario appoints himself her personal assistant. What could possibly go wrong?

DEDICATION

I give thanks to my fellow anthology authors for sharing the wild trip:

Leisl, Marnie, Georgia

and Samantha, who refused to give up on me.
Sam, I love you.

ZHULIJA

Zhulija drifted down to the Eribifax mansion's welcome garden and closed her wings, noting with pleasure how many of the plants in this botanical nook mirrored her own. How naive of her to think the greenery would be different on this side of the river; plants were plants whether you were Seelie or Unseelie.

After twitching at her flutter-skirt, checking her bodice laces were still secured in a neat bow and assessing the safe attachment of her basket cover, she moved up the steps to the imposing front door, rapped the knocker and waited. The shape of the knocker called to the artist in her. Leaning closer, she traced the shape of the Dark Crimson Underwing Moth from which the Eribifax family had sprung, her fingers moving over the striations of the wings.

The door opened and she came face to midriff with a fae-male. A jolt shot up her fingertips as they moved across taut muscles. She snatched her hand back.

"By Old Lady Willow!" Zhulija straightened, cheeks blazing. "I do beg your pardon!"

"Are my muscles to your satisfaction, Lady?" A knowing smile revealed the fangs flanking his otherwise even front teeth. His lingering glance assessed her from head to toe, a widening grin causing dimples on his honey-coloured skin.

"I was studying your unusual knocker." Her flush deepened, but she refused to lower her gaze. "I have an appointment with Lady Erib-ifax, and I'm carrying a safe pass granted by the queens, which, I assure you, I had no intention of breaching." Her words died away as her focus locked on his deep grey eyes. She fell into a fathomless, comforting mist; it wreathed her, welcomed her, smoothed over her with soothing warmth and … Zhulija jerked and blinked.

"Come right in, pretty fae-lady. Your caresses didn't offend me in the slightest and our safe pass is intact. I'm very glad you found us." He bowed, arm sweeping an invitation.

The old fable of the spider inviting the fly into its parlour assailed Zhulija. "Oh, but I didn't mean to, um, stroke you, I just …" Stopping, she swallowed. "Again, sir, my pardon." Stepping past him, she heard the deep breath he drew. Like he was scenting her; how peculiar. Turning to face him, she lifted her chin. "Thank you, my appointment is with the Lady Catocala Eribifax."

Eyes soulful, his hands-to-chest motion was pure theatre. "I'm crushed, my Lady. I've been waiting for you forever."

"Oh, but I …" The ridiculous man was flirting with her. She clasped her basket tightly. "I really am here to see Lady Catocala."

"Of course, Lady Zhulija." Her doorman indicated the side table. "We can put your basket there as soon as I shove that ugly cande-labrum aside." The reception hall calmed with earthy tones. Dark green marble tiled the floor, and there was a creamy green, marble side table against one wall, graced by a gold candelabra. Beige velvet drapes flanked the windows either side of the doorway.

She stiffened. "You … you knew who I was all the time!"

"But, of course. A visit from a Seelie lady via our joint queens' promise of safety is an interesting event." A tilt of the head accompa-nied his roguish smile. "Forgive me if I offend, but constant conversa-tion about the upcoming wedding can pall on one." He winked. "And people with appointments have a name." He gripped the basket handle. "Allow me."

Zhulija's hand shot out, covering his on the basket. "Oh, no, it's perfectly fine."

His hand remained, and those downcast stormy eyes assessed her fingers on his skin before dark lashes lifted to impale her with heat. "Are you sure?"

He tugged.

She tugged back. "The basket contains samples to show Lady Catocala."

He cocked one eyebrow, staring. She shivered, but refused to be cowed, allowing her claw-tips out to infinitesimally pierce his flesh. At that, his hands slid away.

A smile broadening his firm lips, he turned. "This way to the old lady."

Shaking her head, Zhulija followed him down the hall. He didn't wear a uniform, so maybe he wasn't staff, but if he wasn't staff, then …

He leaned into an open doorway without bothering to knock. "My latest fan to see you, Mother."

"Really, Dario, your manners are execrable." A ruby-haired woman in a sparkling, violet robe sat at a desk. A pearl comb secured her up-do. "I doubt she is any fan of yours."

Face hot, but with a better understanding of his disrespect, Zhulija eased past the chuckling, tautly muscled Adonis filling the opening. "Thank you, Lord Eribifax." She closed the door in his grinning face.

"I apologise for any offense my son has given, Lady Zhulija."

"None taken, Lady Catocala." Zhulija smiled and accepted the seat the Unseelie matriarch indicated.

"Let's get started then, shall we?"

Removing the basket cover, she lifted out her samples, naming them as she placed them on the desk. "Filigree baskets to be filled with a plant, some macaroons, wrapped lollipops or chocolates, little pots of nectar, honey or jam, or whatever else you might like. Blown-glass bowls to be filled with sand and flowers or floating candles. Smaller bowls can be made with flat surfaces to sit on tables or with hanging loops. Samples of handmade papers for invitations and place cards.

Here is a filigree tube able to take one flower stem as a lady's brooch, or a buttonhole for males."

Lady Catocala reached for a lacy metal basket. "Such beautiful work, my dear." Her glance contained a sting. "I wonder that a renowned artist like yourself would stoop to crafting fripperies for weddings."

"The first wedding was a favour for a close friend." Zhulija smiled through tight lips. "Making lots of little bits and pieces is a way to relax whilst practicing my skills and thinking about my next major project. I find the muse works as it will."

"Yes, yes, I'm sure it does." Lady Catocala rotated the filigree basket. "Would you mind if my daughter Vinaya views your samples?"

"Not at all." Zhulija smiled. "I was surprised not to see her with you – it's her wedding, isn't it?"

Lady Catocala waved a hand as if to swat an insect. "Indeed." She lifted a handbell and melodic chimes echoed through the room. Moments later, the draperies behind the desk rustled apart to reveal a sliding door. A younger version of Lady Catocala danced through.

Vinaya Eribifax was smiling. Her wine-coloured hair tumbled over her left shoulder in waves, and a deep-teal robe offset the grey eyes and honeyed skin tones common to the Eribifax family.

"I'm so excited! Such a pleasure to meet you, Lady Zhulija. I love your work and to have you as my wedding consultant is simply wonderful. We weren't sure if you would agree, you know, since you're Seelie Lepidopter-fae and we're Unseelie, but here you are." The girl paused for breath, her wings flaring to reveal upper halves in shades of black, silver and cream and underwings of crimson edged with black. Vinaya clapped and reached for the samples. "Ooh, look at these delightful baskets – I can just see them on my tables." She did a tiny sidestep. "Or wait, no! The glass bowls are delightful – can you create different colours in the glass, Lady Zhulija?"

"Yes." Zhulija made a note on her pad. "And the filigree baskets can be gold, silver, bronze, rose gold or copper. The papers can be whatever colour you choose."

"Do you write out the invitations and place cards yourself?" Lady Catocala steepled her fingers.

"No, but one of my sisters is a calligrapher. We often work together."

"Hmm." Lady Catocala watched her daughter, a genuine smile gracing her lips. "This is your choice, Vinaya?"

"Oh yes." Lady Vinaya did a pirouette. "I love Lady Zhulija's work. May I have the baskets in rose gold and hanging bowls in rose and lavender? Also, the filigree floral holders in rose gold? They'll look lovely on dove-grey formal coats."

As they worked out the particulars of the order, Zhulija retrieved the filigree flower holder, and tucked it behind her ear as she often did with a pen or paintbrush, clipping it to her hair to secure it. Other pieces she wrapped and tucked into her basket before re-tying the flight cover.

"It really is delightful having you decorate my wedding," Vinaya enthused. "Mycostat, my fiancé, will be so thrilled."

"That's wonderful." Zhulija smiled. "In the meantime, I'll begin crafting the items. Here's my card should you need to contact me for any reason."

"Thank you, I'll take that." Lady Catocala extended a hand. "Here's mine."

Zhulija was stooping to collect her basket when the door to the hall flew open, bounced off the wall and a fae-male wearing a uniform in Eribifax colours rushed in.

"Brax!" Lady Catocala glared. "What's going on? You dare interrupt?"

"My apologies, Lady Catocala. I didn't realise …" The fae-male saw Zhulija and his eyes narrowed. "She's here! The Seelie thief threatens the ladies."

As he leapt towards Zhulija, another two fae-males raced into the room. The sense of their malice swamped Zhulija in a wave of breath-stealing grey fog; a complete contrast to the warmth of her earlier welcome. She backed away from the hard fingers reaching for her, flailing at them with the basket. "I have a safe pass!"

The men paused.

"Brax?" One of the followers grabbed Brax by an arm.

"You can't believe a thief!" Brax shrugged off the restraint and charged again.

"What do you think you're doing, Brax?" Lady Catocala stood. "Unhand Lady Zhulija immediately!"

Brax ignored her as he reached out.

Zhulija's back met a wall; she couldn't avoid the reaching hands. She was jerked off her feet and forced to the floor. The hard surface smacked her forehead, shoulder and hip, before someone rolled her, face down and dug a knee into her back. The force was so intense, it caused her breath to shoot out in a winded croak. When the pain in her head chose that moment to surge, her mind fuzzed like dandelion puff balls caught in a tornado.

"Check the basket." The voice of Brax barely penetrated as she fought the dull bands around her chest, sabotaging her ability to breathe. Zhulija was helpless to resist her basket being wrenched over her wrist, but fresh pain freed the frozen muscles of her lungs and she gulped at air like a landed fish. An agonised cry left her at the new and fierce torment of her arm being thrust behind her back and forced upwards.

"Stop, I say, stop!" Lady Catocala's anger snapped like a whip.

"Dario, come quickly!" Vinaya cried.

Zhulija tasted blood, heard the sound of glass breaking – her samples? Helpless, breath rasping, she struggled, moaning as her arm was pushed towards the back of her skull and hot needles exploded through her shoulder. Footsteps thundered nearby.

"What in blue blazes is going on?" Dario roared over the din.

"We've an intruder, my Lord. A Seelie thief. She has your missing pen tucked behind her ear."

"You have my invited guest!" snarled Lady Catocala. "This is an outrage! Release Lady Zhulija at once!"

"Let her go!"

"But my Lord—"

"I said let her go!" Dario's hiss was a knife on whetstone.

The pressure on Zhulija disappeared. Her all but numb arm smacked to the tiled floor, the impact adding to the burning agony of her muscles. She couldn't stop the sob escaping.

"Lady Zhulija?"

Panting, lips trembling, she met the concerned gaze of Dario. "W-what's h-h-happening?"

"I'm so sorry they've hurt you, sweet lady." His eyes wandered over her face, before focusing somewhere near her left ear. Louder, he said, "A mistake has occurred, but I can see why they think you're a thief."

"Dario, are you mad?" Lady Catocala spat out. "There's no way that Lady Zhulija is a thief; she's been with either you or me the entire visit."

"Mother, a moment please." He reached out with gentle fingers to unclip and withdraw Zhulija's filigree flower holder from behind her ear. "I can see this isn't a pen – what is it?"

"A filigree flower holder!" Vinaya snatched it from him, then crouched to check on Zhulija. "Are you alright, Lady Zhulija? This is just awful."

Zhulija struggled to sit; the burning in her right arm and shoulder was excruciating. Dario reached to help, but she slapped his hands away, wincing as she clawed her way to her knees. Her eyes registered the remains of her samples, her smashed basket with the flight cover in tatters. A pulse of outrage brought tears to her eyes. Breath shuddering, wincing, she struggled to her feet.

"Lady Catocala, Lady Vinaya." She swayed, voice shaking. "Please accept my regrets, but I'm sure you'll understand my inability to fulfil your commission."

Lady Catocala flinched, her mouth taut. "I must apologise for this fiasco, Lady Zhulija."

Vinaya was crying. "Oh, Lady Zhulija, I had so wanted … I'm so sorry."

"As am I. Good day." Every step Zhulija took hurt her aching body, but she pushed herself towards the front door, determined to remain polite.

"Wait!" Dario called.

"I don't think so, the safe pass was a lie and trusting it was a fool's choice."

Someone grabbed her arm and Zhulija's hurt morphed to rage. Hissing, she slapped her other hand upon the aggressor, her thoughts full of broken glass and smashed filigree.

"Aargh!"

"Dario, what happened?"

"She burned me."

"I'll get her, Lord Dario!"

"No! Leave her be, you've done enough damage."

Cradling her abused arm, Zhulija fled the chaos. Colliding with the door jamb, she blinked at the tears obscuring her vision as she staggered outside.

Diplomatic relations be damned – she had to get away.

Had to find safety.

She just needed a moment …

2

DARIO

"**M**ab's tits!" Dario stared at the crisp filigree pattern seared into his honey-hued skin.

"My Lord, we can't let her get away with that." Brax jerked a thumb at his helpers. "We can make her pay."

"NO!" Dario lunged in front of them, fangs bared.

"But my Lord Dario ..."

"This house has fought for equality between the Seelie and Unseelie fae for generations – I'll not have your bigotry ruining it." Dario's voice deepened to a growl. "In fact, if any of you touch her, I'll rip your wings off."

The trio of footmen shrank from him, mouths gold-fishing.

"And I'll use those ripped off wings for wallpaper!" Lady Catocala swept forward to cradle Dario's hand. "You could get this magically healed or keep it and have a lovely scar. I'm sure it's painful." Her lips firmed. "Serves you right. I can't imagine you thought Lady Zhulija a thief." She snatched the filigree holder from Vinaya. "This looks nothing like the pen I gave you – which is on my desk, by the way. I borrowed it, and if you'd just bothered to ask around, this nastiness could've been avoided."

"I never considered Lady Zhulija a thief. All I did was curse when I couldn't find my pen," Dario shook his head. "I didn't tell anyone to start a fae-hunt."

"Did you hear that, you stupid creatures?" Vinaya smacked Brax across the arm. "If I wasn't a lady, I'd be tempted to punch you all."

The other two footmen backed hastily away.

Lady Catocala's hands flashed to her hips. "Stop that at once, Vinaya."

Vinaya threw her hands in the air. "But everything is ruined!"

Dario pinched the bridge of his nose. "What's ruined, Vinaya?"

"My wedding on Valentine's Day." She glared. "Lady Zhulija had just agreed to make the reception decorations. I couldn't wait to tell Mycostat but now it's all spoiled. You and these oafs have ruined my wedding!"

Dario shook his head. "I had nothing to do with it." He assessed his stinging hand, liking the pattern, resistant to the idea of a healing. Maybe cold water would help.

"I'm afraid it's worse than that," Lady Catocala said.

Dario's gaze shot to her. "What do you mean?"

"Our idiotic footmen just assaulted Lady Zhulija Aphiski, who, I'm sure you know, is a daughter of Seelie Duke Papillion." She glared at the errant footmen. "Feuds have started with less provocation. How long do you think before it escalates to a full-blown Seelie versus Unseelie war?"

Dario closed his eyes. "Bat turds."

Vinaya's fangs flashed. "You'd better fix things for my wedding, Dario."

"For Mab's sake! I need to fix more than your wedding." Dario wheeled and pointed. "You three wait in my study. We'll talk about this fiasco later." He strode towards the front door.

"But Dario, you can't just leave!" Vinaya wailed. "Where are you going?"

"To find a way through this imbroglio; something I can't do if I stay here."

Dario slammed the front door, then paused to massage his temple. What a troll-be-damned mess those blasted footmen had created.

He'd have to fly to the Papillion Estate, seek audience with Duke Papillion and offer reparations. Would the Duke be amenable? He really needed to work on Lady Zhulija first. Would she be willing to see past both the injuries and the insult? He shook his head recalling her courage – distressed and injured, she'd still politely told them all where they could stuff themselves. He grinned. He'd liked that. She'd been injured, her clothing torn and rumpled, but she'd zapped him and swanned off like a princess.

Dario froze mid-step below the colonnaded veranda as he grappled with the extreme notion that he was attracted to her.

PEERING OVER THE HEDGE, Dario relaxed – she hadn't left. She'd fanned her sooty wings, with their splashes of green, cobalt, violet, cream and white, but she was yet standing in the welcome garden. He basked in her beauty, limned against the bright sky.

"Lady Zhulija." Was that frog croak his voice? He cleared his throat.

Snapping her wings shut, Zhulija faced him, black and violet hair fluttering about her shoulders. "What do you want now, Lord Dario? Haven't your people done enough to me?" The pearlescent caramel skin of her cheeks revealed a darkening blemish, tear tracks, and green-speckled violet eyes dull with pain.

Dario clenched his fists. Forget attraction – it was too mild a word for the feeling inside him. "Lady Zhulija, I need to apologise for the actions of my staff."

Zhulija crossed her arms. "You need to apologise, do you? Lady Catocala and Lady Vinaya were full of apologies. I'm a bit over them."

He closed his eyes for a moment. "I know, but it's all I have right now. I'm devastated you were assaulted and accused of theft over a misunderstanding."

She huffed a laugh. "A misunderstanding? That's what you're going with? I'm not sure I can accept that explanation, or your apology. Your people attacked me unprovoked. Is it because I'm Seelie fae? Do they still hold a grudge from the fae wars? They didn't know me, or what I was doing in your home, nor did they care. I even had the safe pass and it meant nothing."

He walked closer. "You have no idea how much I regret their actions. I can assure you they'll be dealt with."

She took a pace backwards. "Stop there."

He stopped. "I mean you no harm, Lady Zhulija. They thought the pen stolen, when in fact, my mother had borrowed it."

"I don't understand." Her hands spread. "What's so important about a pen, anyway? Apart from the gold?"

He grimaced. "It's an heirloom gifted to my grandfather by Nuada Silverhand of the Irish Tuatha de Dannan, centuries ago."

"The gift of a king." Zhulija nodded. "I can understand the concern, but not their attack. It wasn't necessary to hurt me and smash my belongings."

He winced. "Correct, and one of the reasons I'm apologising."

"One? Oh, I get it." She snorted. "Not only will your Queen Maerovana and my Queen Dianathke be angry, you're worried about offending the Duke of Papillion."

"My concern is for you." Even as he spoke, he was staggered to the depths of his Unseelie soul by how true that was. Dario wanted to cuddle Zhulija, smooth her hair, kiss the silvery path of her tears, nuzzle the bruises, lick her lips, kiss her until neither of them could remember their own names. It was both bewildering and overwhelming. He fought to understand; he had never cared about any of his past dalliance partners – what was different about Zhulija?

"Thank you for your concern."

"Your mouth looks swollen? Did they hit you there too?" He eased a step nearer.

"My mouth?" She frowned. "I've been biting my lips; it helps distract me from my shoulder and arm pain. I'm too sore to fly and I want to go home."

"Let me help you." Did he sound too eager? "I'll fly you home." A second infinitesimal step.

"I don't think so." She shook her head. "I might not survive if your help is anything like what happened earlier."

"Sorry can't possibly encompass the true depth of my feelings." Dario's desperation grew. "I'm not the one who hurt you. Please let me fly you home. While we're flying, I'll grovel some more."

A weak gasp of laughter from Zhulija. "Grovel? You? I don't think you're the grovelling type."

Dario sidled closer. "Will you please accept my apology, Lady Zhulija? Allow me to fly you home?"

She ignored his request, but her gaze pierced him. "Tell me why you're apologising?"

"For your treatment by my footmen, your injuries, your pain." He eased a little closer.

"That's all?"

He flung his arms wide. "Mab's tits, woman! What more do you want?"

She reached up and tapped the tip of his nose. "Better language for a start. And what about my samples? My basket?"

Closing his arms tightly around Zhulija, Dario fought a triumphant grin as he spread his wings and leapt skywards. "I apologise for your samples and your basket being broken. I'll even apologise for my language."

She gaped. "Are you ill?"

Laughing, he headed for the river. The Rubiconia was the Seelie/Unseelie border, its water neutral territory. "No, just trying to distract you, and it worked. I'm flying you home, aren't I?"

Zhulija looked around. Their kind were as comfortable in the sky as on the ground. She sagged. "You win. Thank you for flying me home." Her words were silk soft, gentle as a whisk of fur.

The urge to protect her firmed inside him. "Do you accept my apologies, Lady Zhulija?"

"Are you going to keep plaguing me until I do?"

"Definitely." He made his words a caress of velvet. Silvery, deep and rich.

Zhulija shivered, avoiding his eyes. Tightening his arms, he admired the black and purple colours of her hair, the sweep of lashes on her cheek and the shape of her ruby lips as he flew over the Rubiconia River border. He registered the neutral Isle of Garadenya to their right, bifurcating the river for a furlong, with its castle-fortress that had been empty for several generations. It was not much further to the Papillion Duchy with its sweeping willows around a wide, shallow lagoon.

"Should I land outside the gates?"

She was frowning. "Is it okay for you to be in Seelie territory?"

"Fortunately, our queens wrote the safe pass as a two-way permit."

Her glance was unreadable. "Could you set me down outside the green gazebo this side of the forest?"

"Across the boundary but not right to the front door? Won't that sound an alarm?"

"Not while I am with you. I wish to go to the gazebo – it's my studio."

"Ah, your studio." Dario nodded. "Of course. I know you'll want to start on my sister's wedding decorations straight away, but don't you think you should rest for today?"

"What?" Zhulija gaped at him. "You know I'm no longer doing Vinaya's wedding."

"You refused the commission because of the attack on you. I've apologised for that. Profusely. I've grovelled. I've flown you home safely. I plan reparations. Couldn't you change your mind about Vinaya's wedding?" He dropped down to a smooth landing next to the gazebo steps.

She stared at him, before shaking her head. "No, the whole idea was a mistake."

"Please?"

She frowned, still shaking her head.

"Pretty please?"

"I. Said. No." Her lips were a straight line.

"Why not? Didn't I apologise prettily enough?" He fluttered his eyelashes. "Please, beautiful maiden, I—"

"Alright!" She rolled her eyes. "I accept your apologies, but I won't change my mind about Vinaya's wedding."

"I didn't just give you half of an apology." He cocked his head. "Are you afraid? I pledge your full safety. I will even be your bodyguard to ensure it."

A wrinkle of her nose. "Nothing you say will alter my decision."

"Damn." He ran a hand through his tricoloured hair. "What about something I do then? Something to make up for the damage to you and your property?"

Zhulija stamped her foot. "What part of 'No' don't you understand? Is it the N? Or is it the O? You couldn't say or do a single thing to make me change my mind."

He grinned as her opposition triggered an unexpected blossoming inside his soul, which caused his previous attraction to be trumped by primal recognition. He'd more than met his match, he'd met his true mate. "Challenge accepted, sweet Zhulija."

"What? What challenge?"

His wings spread. "Besides, you owe me for burning my hand."

A blaze sparked in her eyes. "*I owe you?*"

"I'm so glad you see things my way." He winked, his psyche ablaze with joy. "I'll be back, my Lady Zhulija. Prepare to make wedding decorations. I'll tell Vinaya you're on it." Flexing his wings, he left the ground.

"You're not listening to me!"

Dario grinned as he looked down. "Your voice is a delight, I'll be happy to listen to it forever." Dipping his wings, he wheeled towards the river.

"You arrogant Unseelie oaf!" Zhulija's scream drifted to him. "What's wrong with you? We'll see about a challenge! I'll sort you out, you just wait!"

He was so looking forward to that.

ZHULIJA

"Good evening." Stepping into the dining room, Zhulija tilted her head to disguise the bruising on her left cheek, certain it blazed like a star. Her siblings were already seated at the table. She braced for interrogation.

"Punctual as always," Lyssica said, winking. Janeska grinned over her glass of sherry-nectar, Tindresse waggled her fingers and Armelle blew a kiss.

"At least we can eat now," groused her eldest brother, DeMaksim.

"Just because you're a bottomless pit." Treymeron moved nimbly to avoid his brother's fist.

"DeMaksim Aphiski!" Their mother, Duchess Azura, turned from the window where she was standing with Duke Yanvian to glare at her eldest son. "Your siblings are to be protected, not preyed upon."

"Yeah, don't 'prey upon' me, DeMaksim," jibed Treymeron, grinning. "Don't you know I'm vulnerable?" He chortled as DeMaksim flipped him off behind their mother's back.

"Vulnerable!" Janeska and Tindresse both hooted with laughter, then hi-fived each other.

"You're about as vulnerable as a porcupine," Armelle shook her head.

"And just as cuddly, I hear." Lyssica wrinkled her nose.

"What?"

"Really?"

"Who'd you hear that from?"

Lyssica waved a hand airily. "I never divulge my sources, darlings, but I hear Chinoserie Douglas was unhappy."

"Chinoserie Douglas?"

"You were trying to cuddle Chinoserie Douglas?"

"No!" Treymeron grimaced and made a gagging noise. "Don't be ridiculous."

"I'll tell her you said she's ridiculous," Lyssica threatened.

Treymeron pointed at her. "You do and I'll tell Grenade Helioze you reckon he has a wart on the end of his nose."

"You lying piece of ..."

"That's enough!" The whiplash of Duchess Azura's voice silenced them.

Zhulija watched her mother's threatening gaze move across the angelic, innocent visages of her siblings. Who were they trying to convince?

Zhulija wasn't surprised when her father crossed the room to put an arm around her shoulders, but the pressure caused her to wince.

"Are you alright, Zhu?" His concern warmed her.

"Of course." She didn't turn her head.

He scanned what he could see of her face, then nodded. "Let's join our wild bunch and eat dinner, hmmm?"

Duchess Azura glided over. "There you are, Zhu."

"Hi, Mama." Zhulija twisted to keep her mother on her right. After a cheek kiss, the Duchess grasped the hand held out by her consort and they moved to the table.

After they were seated, Zhulija served herself food from the platters being passed and pretended to eat, the chatter of her family flowing around her like a comforting blanket. She listened to DeMaksim reporting on estate management lessons and Armelle talking about her music students, but the conversation faded into the background as she played with her food. Chewing hurt her bruised face, plus her wrenched right arm and shoulder made controlling cutlery awkward.

Duke Yanvian tapped a fork against his water glass. "Quieten down, please. Your mother and I wish to hear how Zhulija's meeting turned out."

"Yes, were the Eribifax Matriarch and her daughter impressed with your samples?" Duchess Azura turned an expectant smile on her youngest child.

"Oooh." Janeska winked. "Did you see that dreamy Lord Dario Eribifax, by any chance?"

"Dreamy?" Treymeron chuckled. "Have you missed the fact that he's also called the Unseelie Beast? He's reputed to be vicious to enemies."

Duchess Azura frowned. "Not now, Trey."

Zhulija attempted a smile. "Yes, they were impressed, and yes, I saw Lord Dario. It was strange crossing the Rubiconia to Unseelie territory, but nothing happened."

"Really." Duke Yanvian sipped his wine. "So, where'd you get that bruise?"

She forced her eyes wide. "Bruise? I have a bruise?"

He snorted. "Unless you're going to suggest that's paint on your face?"

"Oh, this little mark?" Without thinking, Zhulija raised her left hand, forgetting how sore she was. She flinched.

"Zhulija? What happened?" Trust Maman to notice.

She sighed. "I fell." Mostly true. "Tripped on a rug I hadn't noticed. Hit my cheek and landed with my right arm twisted behind my back." Zhulija played with her fork. "Knocked the wind out of myself, wrenched my arm and my shoulder." Flipping her good hand palm up, she glanced from one family member to another.

"You're a terrible liar, Zhu." DeMaksim shook his head. Next to him, Tindresse's eyes were rolling and, in her peripheral vision, Armelle and Lyssica were nudging each other.

"Do you know you babble when you're inventing a story, Zhulija?"

Duke Yanvian tilted his head. "It gives you away every time, no matter how plausible your fabrication."

Defeated, Zhulija closed her eyes.

"What really happened?"

"I …" A tear trickled.

Her mother poured tea into a fluted cup, spooned a little nectar into it and passed it across the table to her. "Why don't you explain what occurred at the Eribifax Estate, Zhu honey?"

Tea was her mother's answer to all the world's ills. Zhulija dashed the lone tear from her cheek, claimed the cup and sat, staring into the golden liquid.

"Zhu?"

"It started off well." She crumpled a napkin.

"So you've said." Duke Yanvian stirred his own tea.

"That's truth." Zhulija touched the cup to her lips but the tea was hot. She put it down. "My muse was fascinated by the door knocker design, I bent to study it. I was running fingers over it when the door opened and then I was stroking a man's stomach."

Her siblings howled with laughter.

"That poor butler." Janeska laughed, clapping her hands.

Zhulija shook her head. "It was Lord Dario, not the butler."

"Dario Eribifax answered his own front door?" Treymeron goggled at her. "I'd never do that."

"You don't do much of anything." Tindresse made a face at him. Trey answered with a rude finger gesture.

"Tindresse! Treymeron!" Duke Yanvian glared at both of them.

"Did you trace out his six pack while your hand was glued to his tummy, Zhu?" Armelle giggled into her hand.

"I explained and apologised." Zhulija's face was burning.

"Look at you blush." Lyssica's green fingernail pointed. "He must be even dreamier up close and personal."

"Lyssica, that's not ladylike." Duchess Azura tapped Lyssica's hand with a teaspoon. "Please behave."

"Zhulija?"

Her father was giving her 'the look'; Zhulija knew there was no escape. "Lady Catocala and Lady Vinaya were thrilled with my samples. They offered a contract."

"You do lovely work, Zhu." Janeska smiled. "They'd have to be mad, or stupid, if they didn't want to hire you."

"Very true," agreed Duke Yanvian. "Go on."

Unhappily, Zhulija related the events.

"What!" Her father's roar was so loud the windows rattled. "They attacked you?"

She cringed, unable to distinguish her mother's words when noise from her siblings drowned everything else out. "Please stop." She covered her ears. "Let me finish."

Her father thumped the table until all sound ceased. "Keep it down."

"Continue, Zhu." Her mother's voice was butter soft. She patted her husband's forearm.

"Lady Catocala and Vinaya called for Lord Dario."

"What did he do?" Duke Yanvian's face was thunderstorm dark.

"He made them stop." Zhulija rubbed her nose. "Then helped me roll over and saw the filigree flower holder in my hair."

"Oh, Zhu," DeMaksim murmured. "You always tuck that sample behind your ear."

She nodded. "Lord Dario knew straight away it wasn't his pen and I hadn't done anything wrong. He showed it to his footmen, but the damage had been done."

"Your injuries?"

"And all my samples smashed." Zhulija sniffled. "I wish my power was more than artistic so that I could've defended myself against those judgmental trolls."

DeMaksim's hiss was a sizzle of cold water on hot stone. "Defensive power isn't all it's cracked up to be, Zhu, and your art is a fae treasure."

"The whole business is outrageous." Tindresse's teaspoon clattered in the saucer. "They hurt you; something needs to be done."

Treymeron grinned, rubbing his hands together. "We're going to war against the Eribifax!"

"Don't be foolish, Treymeron!" Duke Yanvian glared. "We're not going to war. We'll request an apology and reparation."

"Lord Dario apologised several times and has offered reparation." Zhulija's voice cracked. "Please, no fighting. I couldn't bear it."

"There'll be no war." Duke Yanvian frowned at his youngest son.

Her mother smoothed the damask cloth. "Did you accept his reparation offer?"

"Not exactly." Zhulija's head began to throb as she stumbled through her edited explanation.

"So Lord Dario apologised profusely, assisted you home, then took your negative response as a challenge to be overcome?" Duke Yanvian's brow furrowed. "An interesting man. One I will be speaking to, particularly since the two-way safe passage agreement was breached on its first usage."

"Oh, but Father ..."

Zhulija's father speared her with 'the look'. She swallowed.

"This is a serious matter, Zhulija." Duke Yanvian's eyes never wavered from her own. "You were assaulted despite our safe pass, jointly approved by Queen Maerovana and Queen Dianathke. The ramifications threaten all Lepidopter-fae; these actions need careful finessing to avoid a pointless war."

She quivered. "I know."

"Ssh, Sis. It'll be okay." DeMaksim's gentle hand on her shoulder was comforting, but still painful.

"I-I ..." Zhulija's gulping sobs escaped despite her best efforts. Duchess Azura was there in an instant, gathering her into a warm cuddle. Her sisters clustered about, stroking her hair.

Duke Yanvian cleared his throat. "And the contract for the wedding supplies?"

Red-eyed and weeping, she met his expectant look. "I-I repudiated it."

"That's my sister!" Treymeron crowed, pumping his fist.

"B-but I w-wanted it!"

Her mother kissed her temple. "We know you're keen to consult for an Unseelie family; a resumé highlight for certain."

"Lord Dario kept asking me to reconsider."

"And will you?" Her father pursed his lips.

"Lady Vinaya chose nice pieces for her reception. I'd like to."

"How about Lord Dario? Is he a nice piece?" Grinning, Janeska patted Zhulija's cheek.

Zhulija stiffened, colour flowing from neck to cheeks.

"Oooh, she's blushing!"

"What's he like, Zhu?"

"Is he strokable?"

She recalled the electrical jolt of that first touch and something roared a protest inside her. Zhulija flicked her gaze from sister to sister. "Keep your claws off him."

DARIO

Winnowing fingers through his hair, Dario released a pent-up snarl. "Before we start, let me remind you all that, as Queen Maerovana's appointed representative in this demesne, I have the power to use whatever means I deem necessary to access the truth of any crime. Those powers include truth reading, physical persuasion and incarceration." His molten gaze pinpointed each fae-man in turn. "Now, explain to me why molesting a Seelie lady of impeccable birth and reputation, who held an authorised safe pass into our lands, was considered an intelligent move."

"You said your pen was missing." Brax wrung his hands. One of his helpmates flinched, the other closed his eyes.

"Did I say it was stolen? Did I tell you to attack an innocent guest?"

"You've ruined my wedding!" Vinaya wailed from her window seat next to their mother.

"Be quiet, Vinaya!" Lady Catocala sighed.

"Brax?"

"I was trying to help, my Lord."

"Creating a diplomatic incident is helping?"

Brax held his hands out. "I didn't know who she was!"

"How is that relevant? You're saying if you'd known her identity, events would have been different? In what way?"

Brax stared at him, opened his mouth, closed it, then shrugged.

"Jern? What do you have to say for yourself?" Dario focused on the next man.

"My Lord, I can only apologise." Jern was pale and quivering. "When Brax said a nasty Seelie woman had gotten in, stolen your gold pen and was holding the ladies hostage in the anteroom, I leapt to assist him. I wasn't aware he'd lied."

"What?" Dario's brows shot skywards. "That's what he told you?"

"Y-yes, my Lord." Though pale, Jern met Dario's blazing eyes.

Thrusting out a tendril of mental energy, Dario assessed the man's mind. Truth. Tapping his claw-tips on the desk, he looked for the third footman. "Corab, come out from behind Brax."

Adam's apple bobbing, Corab sidled into view. He stood tall, the bloom of youth still in his cheeks. "Sir, me Lord, I thought as I was helping. Mr Brax told me the same as Jern here and I-I ..." His lip quivered, but when Dario mentally truth checked, his version of events was solid.

Dario's eyes narrowed. "Anything to add Brax? Care to explain why you bamboozled Jern and Corab with a pack of lies?"

"I was only telling them what I'd heard."

"Heard from whom?"

Brax's eyes shifted away. "I can't rightly remember, my Lord."

"How convenient." Fuming, Dario conducted a truth search through Brax's public thoughts and found the fae-man's mind to be a seething morass of jealousy and hatred. Digging a little deeper, he discovered a strong belief of Seelie inferiority and bitter disagreement that the civil war of the previous generation had ended in a truce. He didn't sort through it all, but the reasons for the lies were obvious.

"My Lord, I apologise and I promise to do better."

"Better?" Dario slammed his fist on the desktop. "You're very lucky you didn't do any worse, Brax. You're a traitorous, conniving liar who committed unprovoked assault on a royally approved guest." His teeth clenched. "I refuse to employ such a person."

"She's just a woman, my Lord. A Seelie woman at that." An ingratiating smile. "A written apology will surely suffice."

Grinding his teeth, Dario shot around the desk and grabbed his prey by the throat. "She's not just a woman, you bigoted, overzealous idiot! She's my woman and you hurt her." Dario shook him. "Never mind you're making a mockery of the queen's orders, in an action capable of restarting the war!"

Brax's eyes bulged as Dario's clawed hand dug into his throat. He gurgled something.

Hair a fiery nimbus, Dario bared lengthening fangs.

"Dario!" Lady Catocala poked him in the back with her cane. "Back down. You can't shred the lackwit until Queen Maerovana is consulted about the violation of her personally signed safe pass."

Roaring, Dario flung Brax away. The fae-male sailed backwards to smash into the wall. The smell of urine wafted. Dario's vicious glare swivelled to encompass Jern and Corab. Jern was gasping and Corab shaking, but neither of them cowered.

"Remember they were manipulated, Dario."

Swallowing, Dario closed his eyes, fought the out-of-control rage.

Lady Catocala tapped her cane. "Jern and Corab, you've been misled by a traitorous liar, so we'll give you a second chance. Return to your duties. Please request Suitilay to attend us."

"Yes, my Lady." Jern turned from Lady Catocala back to Dario. "Nothing like this will ever happen again, my Lord."

Dario, in the middle of a breathing exercise, only grunted.

Corab never took his eyes from Dario. "Thank you, me Lord. Me life is yours, Sir me Lord."

"How right you are." Dario opened his eyes. "Don't disappoint us again." But it was not Corab's life he hungered for. Claws scraping the desk, Dario focused his eagle-sharp attention on Brax. The fae-man gulped, but stood stone still. Wise prey.

Suitilay appeared in the doorway. "Your will, Lord Dario?"

"This creature dishonoured the safe pass I secured from our queen by attacking an honourable Seelie lady without provocation. He also concocted a tale of falsehoods to convince two of our junior footmen to join him. Prepare him for transport."

"Ah, of course, my Lord, you wish the queen to interview him." Suitilay nodded. "Very appropriate."

"Go to Queen Maerovana?" Brax shivered.

"Aye." Dario's tongue swept his fangs. "I'm sure she'll be interested to hear how you made her into a liar. Don't you think, Brax?"

"No! I thought you'd—"

"You didn't think at all!" Dario thumped his fist on the desk. "You've failed to justify your actions to me, now you can explain yourself to Queen Maerovana. Tell her how you defiled her given word and threatened centuries of accord between the Seelie and Unseelie Lepidopter-fae."

"She has no mercy!" Brax backed away but stilled at Dario's animalistic growl.

"You think I have? After you besmirched the reputation of Family Eribifax and hurt my woman? I've not been named the Unseelie Beast for nothing. If there's anything left of you after our queen's through with you, I'll be happy to show you why." Dario's hair glowed like a furnace. "Take this scum-larva away please, Suitilay."

"As you wish, my Lord Dario." Suitilay fisted his chest.

"But she'll kill me!" Brax gripped fistfuls of his hair.

"And if war results from your behaviour, I'll string my bow with twine made from your guts!" The windows rattled with Dario's roar.

"Allow me to remove him from your presence, my Lord Dario." Suitilay dug twig-thin fingers into Brax's collar and yanked the footman off-balance. Brax's heels drummed on the tile as he was dragged from the room.

"Oh, and Brax?" Dario bellowed. "Just in case it wasn't clear – you're excommunicated from the Eribifax Family. We'll not be associated with treason." He listened as the wails faded down the corridor. When a slamming door cut off the irritating noise, he was flooded with vicious satisfaction. He ignored the shuffle of feet from behind him – there were plans to make, people to see ...

"Dario?" Lady Catocala used her cane as a cattle prod.

"Ouch!" He rubbed his hip. Turning his head, he gave his mother the evil eye.

"Turn that burning glare off." She prodded him with her cane again.

He blinked, sighing as he reined his powers in. "Yes, Mother?"

"You handled that well."

He shook his head. "I was so close to sinking in claws and fangs, I could taste him ..."

"But you didn't. Under the circumstances, no one would have blamed you."

"Circumstances?"

"You called Lady Zhulija your woman, more than once. Is that truth? Lady Zhulija is your mate?"

His eyes widened. "Blue blazes!" He sagged against the nearest object as dots connected in his mind. "Of course she is. That's why I was so drawn to her, why her welfare was so important to me, and why her scent was so thrilling. Mab's tits! But how does an Unseelie/Seelie connection come to be? What is Fate playing at?"

"What delightful irony!" His mother's brilliant smile was unexpected but genuine.

His eyebrows shot up. "You don't mind her being Seelie?"

"I'm not the treasonous bigot that useless wight is." She snorted. "Moreover, your father didn't fight and lose his mind, in a war aimed at uniting the two halves of the fae into a whole, because he believed in prejudice. It's more relevant if I ask; do you mind?"

He pictured Zhulija, and a smile creased his face. "No, she's a delight. Why would I care?"

"I'm glad you don't." Lady Catocala huffed. "There are still too many pockets of rebels and troublemakers for my liking."

Dario's mouth flat-lined. "Which is why the border watch is vigilant and why I ordered them to show no mercy."

"In any case, congratulations!" Lady Catocala shifted forward. "I'm more than thrilled you've found your mate. True mates are rare and precious, no matter the source. Does she know?"

"Not yet as far as I'm aware."

Lady Catocala wagged a finger. "Well, remember, under fae-law you can't take away her right of choice by telling her."

"I know, but it's not a law I ever expected to be subject to."

Vinaya did a little pirouette. "Dario, it's wonderful! Your children will be half Seelie and half Unseelie, just like the original Valentine!"

His eyes widened. "The original Valentine? What in the name of Queen Mab are you talking about?"

"Valentine was the child of a Seelie/Unseelie relationship and was constantly persecuted. Seelie fae hated his Unseelie blood while Unseelie fae hated his Seelie blood. He should have become a Lost-soul fae but instead campaigned his whole life for acceptance and love for everyone, regardless of race or creed. He was the first Neutral Fae. He and his loving consort died within hours of one another; it's said they couldn't face the world without the other half of their soul. In their memory, the legendary Queen Morgana created Valentine's Day. It's such a romantic story! That's why Mycostat and I chose Valentine's Day for our wedding gala."

Dario groaned. Romance. He would have to do romance. He wasn't sure he knew what that was.

SNAPPING HIS WINGS CLOSED, Dario strode boldly to the guard house at the gates of the Papillion Estate. He flexed one hand as the breeze ruffled his shoulder-length hair clear of his face before tickling the pointed ears common to all fae. Pointing artfully in multiple directions, the attractive, youthful, just-out-of-bed hairstyle caused people to underestimate him. Time spent considering what to wear had resulted in charcoal leather form-fitting trousers, tucked into his favourite, calf-high boots. He flicked a flower petal from the sleeveless silver tabard that accentuated his muscular frame from shoulder to thigh and displayed the emblem of Clan Eribifax across his chest. The ensemble reflected his wing colouration and was completed by a low-waisted charcoal belt, supporting two well-used short swords on either hip. Anyone viewing those would be reminded that he was also known as the Unseelie Beast; not one to be trifled with. The darker charcoal cloak flowing from his shoulders rippled like low-lying thunder clouds.

Two guards stepped forth to cross swords in front of him. Another pair waited a couple of paces further back. He did the expected and stopped.

"Lord Dario Eribifax. I don't have an appointment with Duke Papillion, but I believe he will be keen to meet with me."

"Your Lordship." The blonde guard bowed. "We'll have to check with His Grace. Apologies for the delay."

"I understand." He did. Perfectly. His own guards would react in similar fashion if a Seelie Lord, or any stranger, showed up at his gates; otherwise, they'd be failing their responsibilities. He watched the four guards whispering amongst themselves before one spread his wings and sped towards the manor.

He neither spoke, moved nor relaxed as he waited. Two of the guards tried to watch him but couldn't hold his stare. They kept swallowing, shuffling their feet and glancing at their leader – the blonde who had spoken to him. That one maintained a watch that went past where Dario stood, feet firm, eyes intent.

Although the blonde appeared to be ignoring him, Dario sensed that his attention was as equally on the Unseelie lord waiting at the gate as it was on the path that vanished into the forest nearby. Likely suspicious of an attack, finding it difficult to believe that an Unseelie fae-lord was brave enough to visit alone. If the tables were turned, Dario would be the same.

Facing the estate, Dario was first to see the messenger returning.

"Open the gate! His Grace confirms his appointment with Lord Eribifax."

Dario felt a mirthless smile tugging at his lips. Oh yes, Duke Papillion certainly wanted to see him.

~

THE DUKE WAS WAITING in his office, along with a younger fae-male. Dario looked for signs of Zhulija's heritage and identified it in hair and eyes. Unlike Zhulija, the green in Duke Papillion's eyes was dominated by violet striations, whilst his black hair was sprinkled with both blue and violet splotches. The younger male, with his identical features and colouring, looked to be a son. Dario discounted the pair being together as a show of force; he was unexpected, no matter what they told staff.

"Thank you for agreeing to see me, Your Grace." He swept a deep bow. "Lord Dario Eribifax at your service."

Duke Yanvian nodded. "Well met, Heir-Lord Eribifax." He indicated the younger male next to him. "My eldest, Heir-Lord De Maksim Aphiski." Dario met icy eyes set in a fierce frown. They exchanged polite bows despite the anger vibrating from Heir-Lord DeMaksim.

"I thank you for seeking me out, Heir-Lord Eribifax, since we have serious things to discuss. I assure you, if you hadn't arrived here within a four day, I'd have come looking for you." A wintry smile. "Which wouldn't have been pleasant."

Dario bowed again. "I understand such feelings, Your Grace. I tender my deepest apologies for the terrible wrong done to Lady Zhulija and beg your forgiveness."

"You understand?" Duke Yanvian's lips twisted. "Have daughters, do you, Heir-Lord Eribifax?"

Dario winced. "Um, no, Your Grace, but I have a sister." He sighed. "I'd be just as horrified and angry were similar treatment meted out to her. Again, I apologise. I seek to make reparation for the ill behaviour of my household. I'm empowered to speak on behalf of my mother, the Matriarch Eribifax."

"And how is the delightful Lady Catocala faring?"

"Well, Your Grace."

"And the miscreants who visited this gross misconduct upon my youngest daughter?"

"Dealt with, Your Grace." Dario detailed the interview he'd

conducted and the results. His barely tamped fury surged beneath its shield and the crimson in his hair fired to an iridescent blaze.

De Maksim's eyes went wide.

"You sent the ringleader to Queen Maerovana?" Duke Papillion blinked. "I'd not expected that, Heir-Lord Eribifax."

Dario's low snarl vibrated in his throat and prowled the room. "He was also disowned by the Eribifax Family. My father fought beside you in the war to unite the fae and I'm equally as passionate as he was. I went to great trouble to secure Lady Zhulija's safe pass from the queens, affording her as much protection as possible from those pockets of resistance wishing to fracture our peoples and reinstate the old cultural barriers. The dishonour was treasonous, and Family Eribifax is loyal to its queen."

"Your father was a fearsome warrior and a delightful friend. I mourn his passing." Duke Papillion raised an eyebrow. "As for you, I'm impressed that the son of my old friend is dedicated to upholding the values his father held dear. Your prowess in confronting the rebel factions is widely renowned."

"You do me too much honour and I thank you for those cherished words about my father." Dario bowed." Shall we now talk about the point of my visit?"

Duke Papillion nodded. "Let's sit first, shall we?"

Dario accepted DeMaksim's offer of a chair. "We're agreed that Lady Zhulija was wronged, that my family owes her an apology plus reparations and that I'm correct in coming to see you." Dario ran a hand through his hair. "I've punished the offenders, apologised several times to both Lady Zhulija and yourself and commenced reparations …"

"Commenced?" The Duke's eyes fastened on the filigree scar decorating Dario's hand.

"I offered help when she was in pain." His memory of her suffering still filled him with anger. "I flew her back here."

"So you did," Duke Yanvian agreed. "Then tried to coerce her into making artwork for your sister's wedding as if nothing had happened."

Dario frowned. "Coerce?" He shook his head. "Now there, we disagree, Your Grace. I requested she consider changing her mind about repudiating the contract – yes. I'm still trying to please my sister, who insists her wedding has been ruined, after all. But I only asked after I'd apologised that number of times and assisted Lady Zhulija home. I'd already promised reparation and still plan to keep that promise, no matter what she decides."

"Hmmm. If I accept all that, Heir-Lord Eribifax, may I ask what you have in mind for reparations?"

"Of course, and I will answer as soon as I have my plans fully prepared. At the moment, I foresee a number of items spread out over a period of time. Perhaps flowers to start with, as is fae tradition. My sister's wedding is planned for Valentine's Day, and whilst reparations for Lady Zhulija are high on my priority list, so is a family wedding in two seven-days' time. As a family fae-person, I trust Your Grace understands."

"Is Lady Vinaya difficult then?"

Dario's grimace was rueful. "More like spoiled, Your Grace."

For the first time, the second Papillion Family male proved himself to be more than a statue. He snorted. "We've a few spoiled family members too. I commiserate, Heir-Lord Eribifax, and thank you for your care of my youngest sister."

"I'd like to believe any decent fae-male would be pleased to help a lady in distress, and yet, someone my family considered a decent fae-male behaved like a cave-troll to her." His lips wrinkled in a fang-revealing growl. "I wanted to rip him to pieces."

DeMaksim cocked his head. "Yet you sent him to Queen Maerovana?"

Dario snorted. "My mother intervened."

A laugh escaped DeMaksim. "Ah yes, mothers." He nodded in complete accord.

Even Duke Yanvian's lips were twitching.

"Please, call me Dario." He smiled. "Both of you. I believe we'll be seeing more of each other and Heir-Lord Eribifax is such a mouthful."

"Very well." The Duke nodded. "You may call me Yanvian; I'm sure

DeMaksim agrees to our informality. I wish to be kept fully informed of events, and based on my memories of your father, I look forward to our future association. You're welcome here at any time."

"Thank you." Dario sighed. "I'll do my best to meet your expectations."

"I'll break out the whisky-nectar then, shall I?" DeMaksim reached for ornate glassware.

Their acceptance had relief sweeping through Dario in a tidal wave. Now he just had to convince Zhulija.

ZHULIJA

"What do you mean you had a meeting with Heir-Lord Dario Eribifax? Where and when?" Zhulija glared at her father. "I can't imagine any scenario where you'd chance meet an Unseelie lord."

"No chance meeting." DeMaksim swirled his glass of whisky-nectar. "He came here."

"*You* were there?" Zhulija's anger simmered.

Her brother shrugged. "You know Father and I work jointly running the estate." He sipped from his glass. "I don't do that from my bedroom."

"Lord Eribifax told the gate guards he had an appointment with me." Duke Yanvian smiled. "I admired his effrontery and acknowledged the appointment because we needed to talk about your assault whilst in his care."

"He was angry about it." DeMaksim whistled. "His hair lit up like a firestorm and his growling raised hairs on the back of my neck." He rubbed his nape. "You should've seen him." He shook his head, lips stretched into an admiring smile. "A worthy foe."

Zhulija's finger stabbed the air. "You're right, DeMaksim, I should've seen him." The finger swung. "Why wasn't I called to the meeting, Father?"

Duke Yanvian flexed a hand, palm upward. "I'm your father. It's my duty to care for you."

"And as your older brother ..." DeMaksim saluted her. "Between Father and I, we had you covered."

She ignored her brother. "How old am I, Father?"

"Twenty-eight." His brow wrinkled. "Why?"

"We're adults at 25, yes?"

His frown eased. "Yes, of course, but you're a fae-female, dependent on me and ..."

"Father, I'm no child." She bared her teeth. "If you cut me off financially, I could support myself through my art career. I continue to live here because I love and respect my family and don't see a need to move out." Her scowl flicked between them. "Yet it's clear neither of you consider me an adult worthy of respect. You're talking about me like I'm a thing instead of a person."

"Hey!" DeMaksim frowned.

She rounded on him. "Did you suggest I be asked to the meeting?"

"No." He backed up at Zhulija's incendiary glare. "Sorry."

Duke Yanvian spread his hands. "Zhulija, I simply accepted his apologies on your behalf and agreed to his offer of reparations. Although those are yet to be determined."

Zhulija gasped. "You accepted his apologies on my behalf? What part of me being a full-aged adult did you miss?"

"Well, none." Her father smiled, yet his eyes were hawk sharp.

"Don't try to play me, Father!" Betrayal tasted like bitter ash.

"I think you're being a bit dramatic, Zhulija." His smile turned toffee brittle.

"That's very condescending, Father!" Her hiss did justice to a kettle on the hob. "Let me show you how dramatic I can be." Her hands tensed into claws as she reached for a goblet of whisky-nectar to drown him in.

Her father put one hand up. "I thought I was acting in your best interests, Zhulija."

The nasty taste became a vile tide sweeping across her tongue to choke in her throat. "I don't see it that way!" Zhulija flung the goblet contents at him. Around the room, everything loose shot into the air, swirling and hovering. Pens, papers, tumblers from a desk. A carafe, napkins, a salver from the table. The avalanche of items hurtled at Duke Yanvian and De Maksim in the wake of the thrown goblet.

Duke Yanvian's eyes widened. "Demon spit! I thought avalanche abilities had been bred out!"

DeMaksim's jaw dropped. "What's going on?"

The cloud of disparate items rained forcefully onto the two fae-males.

"Ouch! Zhu, cut it out!" De Maksim crouched to avoid a tray.

"Zhulija! Stop this at once!" Duke Yanvian roared, batting at paper confetti. Both men raised their hands in self-defence, twisting and shrinking as they tried to avoid the barrage.

"I have no idea where that came from, but I'm according you the respect you've shown me!" Zhulija's voice echoed from all corners of the room; issuing from glass shards as a tinkle, from metal as a tinny screech, from paper as a sibilant hiss, from pens as a spatter of sparkling multi-coloured inks, which shaped her words in the air to glow like a display of fireflies. Gathering herself, Zhulija reined in the power she was startled to discover crouching white-hot inside her body, dropped her hands and glared at her father and brother.

DeMaksim sprawled on the floor, legs outstretched, propped up by arms rigid behind him. His face bore a few cuts and streaks of blood spotted his clothes. Duke Yanvian crouched nearby, similarly bedecked with cuts and specks of blood. They gaped at her like startled deer.

She swallowed, staring down at her hands, searching for traces of the power which had surged from them.

"Holy snapping swamp turtles!" Treymeron crowed from above them. "What in thunder was that, Zhu?"

Raising startled eyes, she saw Trey, her mother and all of her sisters leaning over the second-floor balcony.

"I d-don't know."

"Oh goodness!" Her mother's hands flew to her cheeks. "I haven't seen a display of avalanche power since my great-great-grandmother passed."

"That's all you can say?" Duke Yanvian's mouth thinned. "After Zhulija attacked us?"

"Serves you both right." The Duchess Azura wrinkled her nose. "She had cause. You were out of line excluding her from the meeting. Even Lord Eribifax should have requested her presence."

"Lord Eribifax did the right thing coming to see Father." DeMaksim wiped at a blood spot.

Snarling, Zhulija levitated a tray to thump into the back of his head. He fell forward to smack his face on one upraised knee. "Swofgtrh!" He cursed as fresh blood spattered.

"I deserved to be part of it, you misogynistic prig!" Zhulija's rage simmered. "Father, in future, I wish to be consulted about anything that relates to me. Are we clear?"

He was nodding when a knock sounded and the door opened to frame their major-domo, Entanglit. He offered Zhulija a tray containing a bouquet of flowers accompanied by a card. "From Heir-Lord Dario Eribifax for you, Lady Zhulija."

She snatched the card and read: "Pretty flowers for a pretty Lady. A small token of my apology. Dario." His signature was an elegant swirl. "Pretty flowers for a pretty lady! He sends me this banal, toad-eating smarm?" Her screech caused the debris of her 'avalanche' to stir in rustling threat.

Entanglit's eyes bugged at this unusual response to what he considered a respectable floral offering.

Zhulija flung up her hands; DeMaksim ducked. "I'm battered and bruised. I was treated like some sort of criminal. My hard work has been smashed into shrapnel and he sends bloody flowers as if I'm a pampered layabout? I'll show him flowers! Give them here!"

Mute, arms outstretched, Entanglit proffered the tray.

"Wait, Zhulija!" Duke Yanvian struggled to his feet. "Flowers are a tradition—"

He stopped at her furious glare.

"Flowers are meaningless. A gesture made by a coward who can't even be bothered to speak to me in person. We'll see about that!" Rage a living thing, Zhulija snatched up the bouquet and departed in a whirlwind of airborne wreckage.

∿

BLAZING ire helped Zhulija overlook the bruised soreness of her body; enough for her wings to carry her across the Rubiconia River into Unseelie territory for the second day running. The Eribifax guards raised a hand in greeting as she approached, but she didn't stop. Zhulija aimed for the Eribifax welcome garden, touched down and surged along the path. Stones from the rock garden flanking the walk swirled up around her like an honour guard. Stopping on the veranda, she flexed her claws and sent the airborne rocks careening into the imposing front doors. Clatter! Bang! Thump!

As soon as the rain of rocks stopped, the door swung open to reveal the head of Suitilay the butler. His wary expression altered to startlement as he beheld Zhulija. His mouth opened.

Zhulija wasted no time. "You tell that damned haughty lord and master of yours that he can take his useless flowers and shove them where ..."

The door was wrenched wide to showcase the fascinated features of Lord Dario Eribifax. "Yes, Lady Zhulija? Where might I put the flowers that I thought were a good start to my reparations?"

"You think these stupid flowers are a suitable start to reparations I wasn't even consulted about?"

"I visited your father and I understand it's common to apologise with flowers."

"I was attacked and my belongings smashed!" She vibrated with rage. "I'm not a simpering ninny to accept a pathetic bunch of common flowers to make up for such gross criminal behaviour." She slashed the bedraggled bouquet through the air. The absorbed fae-men contemplated the broken-stemmed, wilted flower heads, almost devoid of petals after their rough flight.

Dario offered a tentative smile. "Put like that, I can see I made a mistake."

"Oh, how clever you are!"

The smile on Dario's lips froze. Next to him, Suitilay winced.

"Perhaps—"

"You have the unmitigated gall to make arrangements with my father as though I'm a child, then send me flowers. You should have sent the gods-be-damned things to him! Of what use are they to me? All they do is send a message that you don't take me seriously because I'm female. You've disrespected me and murdered some poor innocent blossoms. It's like you're offering me a pat on the head. Shall I simper and flutter my lacy handkerchief?"

He tilted his head. "What—"

"You deserve to be strangled with the blasted handkerchief! I was the one assaulted! I'm the one whose belongings were destroyed! As an adult, I deserve to be the one whom you address with details of reparations. Not my father. Not my brother. Nothing is agreed upon until I say so. Got it?"

Dario didn't take his eyes off her. "You've made things crystal clear. In my defence, I just wanted to surprise you."

"Grrr." She ripped off one of the remaining flower heads and flung it at him. It hit his shin and dropped to lie on the veranda at his feet. "Surprise!"

He sighed. "I'm sorry that the flowers weren't to your taste. Any hints as to what might be?"

Hissing, Zhulija raised taloned fingers, swirled them and performed a flinging gesture. Flowers, leaves and twigs from the nearest garden beds rose in a cloud, circled, then pelted towards a startled Dario. He dove sideways to land supine on the decking, where he curled himself into a ball and cocooned himself in his wings.

With great presence of mind, Suitilay retreated inside and slammed the front door.

Shaking, Zhulija directed her avalanche of garden detritus towards Dario's altered position and watched in furious satisfaction as it pelted down on his foetal cocoon with stinging ferocity. She waited until her storm settled. Waited until Dario cautiously flipped his wings back to clear the debris. Waited until he sat up. Waited until his gaze tracked down his garden-bedecked lower limbs, across the veranda and down to where she stood at the base of the steps. Waited until he met her eyes.

That was the moment she flung the bedraggled remains of his pathetic bouquet with violent force. The few limp stalks hit him in the chest, then dropped to his lap as he sat gaping at her.

"I present you a bouquet of flowers in delighted thanks for your thoughtful consideration. I believe flowers do well in a vase of water." She'd altered her voice to a girlish coo.

He goggled, opened his mouth, closed it.

"You look like an ornamental goldfish." Zhulija wrinkled her nose at him before stalking away. Head high, body stiff with anger and pride, she rounded the corner of the track to the welcome garden, ensured she was out of his sight, then stopped. Sagged as her fulfilled anger died away, and pain from wrenched and bruised muscles reasserted itself. Flying here had been a fool's move, but anger had bolstered her, heating her insides like the small furnace in her studio. Now those feelings were ashes, and she didn't know where she'd find the strength to fly home again. On top of that, it dawned on her that, after her vengeful performance, she was stranded in Unseelie lands without friends.

She bared her fangs. "Bat turds!"

Tears flowed.

6

DARIO

"Wow." Brushing the garden refuse from himself, Dario shook his head. Zhulija had put him in his place … hard. He grinned; his true mate had fangs and talons and wasn't afraid to use them. Things were looking up.

Behind him, the door opened. He turned, expecting Suitilay, but it was his mother, frowning at him.

"What was that about, Dario?"

He waved a hand. "Just getting to know each other."

"What an unusual dating style you have."

Dario glared. "I made a mistake." His lips twisted. "Lady Zhulija came over to point out that error."

"Really." Lady Catocala studied her son as if he had lost his wits. "It must have been an extreme mistake for her to undertake such a flight after yesterday's attack. You flew her home because of her injuries, didn't you?"

His eyes widened. "Blast and damn!" Whirling, he leapt off the veranda and sprinted down the path. The welcome garden came into view, appearing empty behind its hedged border. He slowed. She must have departed after all. Concerned for her welfare, unprepared for the volume of disappointment swamping him, Dario stopped, hands on

49

hips. He'd just decided to take wing when the sound of a sniffle reached his ears. Standing on tiptoe, he craned his neck.

There sat Zhulija on the smooth lawn, hugging her legs, her face buried between her knees. The peach-coloured fabric making up the panels of her skirt pooled around her, reminding him of a draping of loose flower petals. The glorious, black-splashed violet hair he wanted to stroke trailed in ringlets down her back, over a fitted, sleeveless cherry velvet bodice with matching boots. Her feet were drawn up like sentinels as she leaned into her cradled knees and rocked slightly.

With great deliberation, Dario scraped a foot through pebbles lying loose on the path. Zhulija stiffened. A lightning flash later, she'd rolled to her knees and used her hands to propel to her feet. When he strolled through the gap in the hedges constituting the gateway to the welcome garden, she faced him, arms akimbo.

He stopped a little distance away. "I deserved the treatment you just dished out."

Zhulija stared, his blunt admittance appeared to disarm her. "I'm glad you understand. "Tears were drying on her cheeks, but she'd ignored them. Having just learned something important about his mate, Dario decided to do the same. "What reparations can I offer that you would be willing to accept, Zhulija?"

"Do you have any healing abilities?"

He shook his head. "I wish I did; I don't like that you're in pain." He might be able to sort something out though – there was a relative of Mycostat who did potions.

She sighed. "I can't craft things properly, or with any great speed, whilst I'm healing."

"Are you saying that you'd be willing to make items for Vinaya and Mycostat's wedding?"

"Perhaps the decorations for an Unseelie wedding would be an interesting addition to my achievement list." She shrugged, then winced. "Also, I wish to re-create my samples at some point."

Dario seized the olive branch. "What if I arranged for you to have an assistant?"

She cocked her head. "You'd do that?"

"If it'd help, it's a small thing I can do for both you and Vinaya."
Dario watched as she tapped the toe of one cherry velvet boot on the
grass. The movement fluttered the petals of her skirt. He allowed his
gaze to wander up her shapely hips to the front-laced bodice
caressing her waist, before it widened to curve around her bosom.
Higher, the creamy honey of her skin appeared lickable, her elegant
neck waiting to be nibbled upon, her lips … pursed with disapproval.
His eyes shot up to meet hers, the violet orbs were shooting daggers.
He essayed a weak smile.

Zhulija's hands went to her hips. "I. Am. Not. Your. Dinner."

He swallowed. Tried to look contrite. "Sorry." He wasn't. She was a
delicious vision he would remember in his dreams later. "We've
agreed you'd accept an assistant. What else?"

"I will need some supplies."

"Just tell me what you want and I will organise it." Did he sound
too eager?

"A moment while I think." Her eyes became unfocused, she
brought her hands up and used the fingers of one to count
points off on the digits of the other. Her lips moved, words
falling soft as floating gossamer. "Pretty sands for the tinted
glass, wax for candles, gold and copper for filigree work, tiny
coloured feathers …" Her hands dropped; she looked towards
him again. "I'll need to work out my list and get it back to you.
That will be the first thing I do in the morning. Please ensure
that my assistant arrives ready to start at half an hourglass past
dawn."

He bowed, entranced. "As you command, my Lady."

"I appreciate that you're willing to do this."

"My honour demands it, but it also pleases me."

"I thank you."

He wanted it clear between them. "You're accepting both my
apologies and my reparations?"

"Alright, okay, yes!" She glared. "You really are persistent, aren't
you?"

"Part of my delightful character."

She snorted. He watched her glance around, hated when her bearing changed from crisp command to a droop.

"May I fly you home once more?"

Zhulija considered him. "As part of the reparation?"

"Pfft." He flicked dismissive fingers. "More like common courtesy. Proper reparation is yet to come."

Her lips pressed together. "Now why does that sound ominous?"

Dario dusted a leaf from his hip. "I have no idea."

She contemplated whatever was behind him, not meeting his gaze. "I imagine you've worked out I'm too sore to fly."

He thought her pride adorable, but knew better than to tell her. "Don't worry, it'll just appear as if I'm ensuring your safe passage through Unseelie territory after yesterday's imbroglio."

Zhulija brightened. "Of course!"

Dario smiled, a hackle easing, widening of his lips. Any Unseelie fae would recognise his repeated actions as marking his territory. So primitive. He couldn't wait for Zhulija's reaction when she found that the Unseelie were much more rough-hewn than the Seelie fae she was accustomed to.

ZHULIJA

Cradling her mug of mint tea, Zhulija walked through the meditation garden as she made her way to the studio. The fountain splashed in the early morning light, a constant pacifying murmur. She passed the twins, Tindresse and Janeska, as they performed the graceful twirl of their exercise routine, raising her mug in salute as she progressed along the stepping stones in the path of enlightenment. Reaching the little rock shrine at the end of the path, she laid a leaf as her daily offering, before sidling around the shrine to pass under Old Lady Willow and onto the first bridge in the water garden. The ponds were all shallow and bedecked with lily pads and she admired the various colours of the lilies in bloom as she crossed the series of connecting bridges linking the sections of gravel paths. Beyond the water garden, the rambling roses of the cottage garden spread over the pergola, framing beds of hollyhock, foxglove, catmint, delphinium, phlox, peonies and cosmos, amongst others. Zhulija loved how they grew in a carefully cultivated wilderness of scented beauty.

Zhulija often winged her way over the top of all the gardens, but the passage through was a calming, energising ritual with frequent inspiration for her muse and today she felt in need of being soothed.

This second day since her assault, the pain of her injuries was at an excruciating high; bruises blossoming in abstract purple flowers on her skin. Flying would've added to the agony and the stroll was loosening her sleep-stiffened muscles.

When her gazebo studio appeared against its forest backdrop, Zhulija was ready to meet Lord Eribifax's promised assistant and begin the planning of their work activities. Nobody waited on the steps. She frowned. Reliability was important, something she would emphasise to Lord Dario the next time she saw him.

Like right now.

Her mouth fell open as Lord Dario Eribifax turned from the top level of the veranda, where he'd been peering through the reinforced windows of her studio, and waved.

"A fine morning, Lady Zhulija."

Her heart rate increased. "Why are you here?"

"I said I'd arrange your assistant." He spread his arms. "Here I am."

"You're my assistant? What do you know about artwork?"

He shrugged. "Probably not a lot, but I'm a fast learner and very good at organisation."

She scrunched her nose. "Organisation of what?"

"Supplies, for a start." He beamed, beckoning high over her shoulder.

Completely puzzled, she turned. Hovering nearby were sixteen fae-males, each carrying large tubs emblazoned with the words 'Bollidee's Garden Supplies'. She must have been deep in thought to have not seen them sooner.

The leading fae-male winged closer. "Good morning, Lord Eribifax, where do you want the sand?"

"Sand?" Was that breathless squeak her voice?

"Just here, thanks." Smiling, Dario gestured to the ground at the base of the steps.

"Right you are."

A cascade of garden sand was delivered. The next fae-male added the contents of his tub, followed by another.

Zhulija watched in growing horror. "What is this sand for?"

"Glass making!" Dario raised his hands wide and high. "I thought I'd get a head start and surprise you. I arranged it with the gate guards." He waggled his fingers, grinning as he waited for her approval.

The contents of the last tub rained down upon the veranda, showering both of them with a strong and steady stream of grit. It saturated Zhulija's hair, trickled down her neck and struck her face in stinging particles. She couldn't see Dario, but she could hear him spitting and cursing.

"Oops! Sorry about that – a handle broke! Thanks for the order, Lord Eribifax."

By the time the air was clear enough to see, the deliverymen were gone.

"By Old Lady Willow!" Zhulija spat sand out of her mouth and contemplated her tea mug. It was now overflowing with tea-saturated sand. Her gaze swept the mess of sand cocooning them shin deep on the veranda, touched on the larger sand dune below, then met the crestfallen eyes of Dario.

He grimaced. "Sorry, that didn't turn out as I planned. It was going well before the last tub."

"You think so?"

"You don't sound pleased."

"I'm still coming to grips with all this sand, not to mention being covered with it." She gritted her teeth; particles of sand crunched and rolled. Working her tongue, she spat again, her anger rising.

"I didn't know there would be quite this much – it'll last you a while."

"Oh yes, it will. Forever, in fact."

A frown twisted his face. "What do you mean?"

Zhulija swiped more gritty grains from her mouth. "I mean that I don't use this type of sand – it's far too coarse. I've no use for it, so even forever is too short a time."

Dario's mouth fell open. He looked carefully around, taking in all of the mounded sand. "You – you don't use this sort of sand?"

"No."

"Oh." He took another look. "Not at all?" One hand covered his mouth.

She could see he was beginning to understand. "Not at all."

He bowed his head, turning aside. His shoulders shook.

Her anger gave way to uneasiness; surely he wasn't crying? "Dario? Are you alright?"

"Nnnh!" His snort echoed off the glass windows. Seconds later, he was roaring with laughter, hands dropping to his knees to support his unsteady frame.

"I don't think it's funny!" Zhulija's temper rekindled. "Look at this thrice-damned mess! It's all over us."

He pointed at her, seemed about to say something but a fresh paroxysm of mirth doubled him over.

"I hate sand in my clothes!" she hissed.

"No use!" He was howling like a fire-wolf.

Craning her neck at the sound of wings, Zhulija saw what she expected to see. Flying low above the trees, two gate guards, her father and both of her brothers burst into view in response to the estate breeching alarm.

"Zhulija, are you okay?" Duke Yanvian called as he landed. "Who attacked you?"

She clenched her fists. "My new assistant, Lord Dario, arranged for a blasted order of scum-sucking sand!"

"Sand?" DeMaksim back-winged. "Are you planning a new garden?"

"No, damn it!" She swallowed, drew a breath. "He ordered sand so that I – we – could make glass. He said he'd explained things to the gate guards."

Treymeron scratched his head. "Never seen you use any sand like this before."

She glared. "That's because I don't."

"Why is Lord Dario your assistant?" Her father was tapping fingers against his thigh.

"I didn't know he was until this morning."

The Duke switched his gaze. "Dario?"

He was sitting in their sand pit. "I couldn't find anybody on short notice."

Not laughing now, are you? Zhulija's satisfaction was short lived as more sand trickled down her back.

Her father gestured. "Whose idea was it to, ah … wear the sand?"

Dario's mouth twisted. "The handle of a sand tub broke."

DeMaksim chuckled. "So, you received a delivery of sand you don't use, ordered by an assistant you didn't know you had, and it was dropped all over you by mistake."

Zhulija's glare drilled holes. "I knew I was getting an assistant!"

Duke Yanvian rubbed his mouth. "You just didn't know who." There came a snigger from one of the guards at the back of the group.

Zhulija seethed while the males exchanged loaded glances.

"Oh, this is the best!" Trey crowed. "I'd love to have seen the sand storm falling on you!" Seconds later, all men succumbed to glee. The two guards were holding each other up as they laughed.

It was the last straw for Zhulija, the reins on her rage broke. A tornado of sand shot into the air from around her, spinning out to sting everybody. Laughter switched to protest.

"Hey!"

"Zhu, stop."

"Zhulija! Cut this out right now!"

Leaving the flying sand to its own business, she marched into the forest and returned to the house for a shower. A vigorous application of soap, a cloth, and a cascade of warm water later left Zhulija clean and refreshed with not a grain of sand in sight.

LATE MORNING FOUND Zhulija inside her studio assessing supplies and making notes. Knocking interrupted her. She emerged from her store room to find a very sheepish Dario with his face pressed to the glass. Crossing to the door, she unsnapped the lock and slid it open.

"Yes?" She crossed her arms, wincing as the action pulled at the pain in her shoulder.

His smile was lop-sided, his hair a gorgeously contrived mess. "May I come in, Zhulija?"

She frowned. Why'd he have the gall to look so yummy while she struggled with injury and annoyance?

"I've brought lunch." He held up a basket.

"Any tea?"

He looked hopeful. "A thermos full."

With a huff, she relented. "Lunch and tea sound wonderful. Come in." As he passed her, Zhulija saw that he was wearing DeMaksim's clothes. "You've had a shower."

He cast her a speaking glance. "There was a lot of sand in unmentionable places."

Her face burned. "So I discovered."

Sighing, he placed the basket on her design table. "I'm sorry about that. I thought I was being helpful."

She flung her hands wide. "I understand, but Dario, it would've been better if you'd asked what was needed."

"It was meant to be a surprise."

"You certainly achieved that."

He winced. "But not in a good way." He shook his head. "You must be cursing my family for everything we've put you through. I can't say, or be, sorry enough."

She softened. "Let's sit and share what you've brought."

"Wait." He delved in his pocket. "I meant to give you this first thing, but, well … sand." He thrust a corked bottle at her. "It's a herbal healing elixir. I got it from Mycostat's mother – she's a potion maker."

Zhulija accepted the bottle but eyed it doubtfully. "She doesn't even know me. Why would she send me a healing potion?"

"Because Vinaya, Mycostat and I asked. Vinaya actually begged – she's set on having you make decorations for their wedding and Rympala will be Vinaya's mother-in-law." He opened his hands, palm up. "It will help you, Zhulija, I promise."

Concerns allayed, Zhulija uncorked the bottle and poured its contents into a glass Dario produced out of the lunch basket. A pleasantly herbal scent assailed Zhulija's nostrils as she raised the glass for a cautious sip of the thick, dark green liquid. She enjoyed the taste, hoping it worked to heal equally as well, and drank until the glass was empty.

"Here." Dario handed her a plate with a large slice of buttered nut bread, two hard-boiled eggs, some cheese and several strawberries. A mug filled with steaming tea was set in front of her before Dario settled into another chair and tucked into his own plate of food.

"What sort of sand do you use for your glass making?" He sipped from his mug.

"Oh, I use very fine river sand. I collect it from the Rubiconia myself." Zhulija chewed on nut bread before swallowing. "I visit a number of sites because there are different coloured sands. Some-times I dye the colour into it myself, but only if I have to. The colours Vinaya chose I already have."

Dario grimaced. "I've only myself to blame for that stuff up."

She pointed a strawberry at him. "Plus, Father, DeMaksim and Trey will all be gunning for me when I go back to the house for dinner."

He shook his head. "Don't worry, they'll leave you alone."

She blinked. "That's delusional. Yesterday I pelted them with orna-ments and today it was a storm of sand. They won't be happy."

His smile was devilish. "Maybe not, but we all deserved it. I told them they'd have to go through me to get to you."

"Oh!"

He winked. "Can't let any more harm come to my favourite wedding designer, now can I?"

Zhulija's smile was weak. "No, no, of course not." His favourite wedding designer – the term sounded friendly and business-like.

"How's your lunch?" His lips stretched into the smile of a business-like friend.

"Just dandy." The food soured in her stomach as she experienced an epiphany. She didn't want a friendly business-like smile from Dario – she wanted to be the object of a white-hot, panty-melting smile.

She wanted him, full stop.

8

DARIO

The sun was high when Dario arrived for their second workday. Later than he'd planned, but Eribifax Estate business neither disappeared nor completed itself. Entering through her open studio door, Dario went looking for Zhulija, surprised to find that the further he progressed, the more space he discovered. Of Zhulija herself, there was no sign. He spied more rooms opening off the main one, a lofty ceiling and … was that a second level?

Scratching his head, he checked the distant door. He was in a gazebo. He knew he was. Scanning the place with mage-sight showed him the shimmer of plum-splat, the magical colour that accompanied enchantment casting. He whistled. An enchantment this large was unusual – the Duke either loved his daughter very much or had a pet leprechaun. Maybe both. Well, she wasn't here, but with an open door, she couldn't be far. He re-traced his steps, searching as he went.

Finally spying a note on Zhulija's desk addressed to him, Dario opened and read it. *Collecting things in the forest. Won't be long. Make yourself a cuppa.*

He decided to wait until Zhulija returned so they could enjoy a cuppa together. In the meantime, he'd observed several baskets of very twiggy branches. Time to make himself useful. He began to break the wood up and stack it in the fireplace. When the grate contained enough kindling for a fire, he filled the wood box next to the fireplace with more. By the time Zhulija returned, he was very pleased with his efforts.

"Good morning. I've got the tea mugs ready." Dario grinned at Zhulija. As he committed her windswept hair and prettily flushed cheeks to memory, a yearning to kiss her filled him. He restrained himself, knowing it was too soon.

Her return smile was akin to a blossom reaching for the sun. "There you are, Dario." She carried another basket of twiggy branches.

"Good, you have more work for me." He rubbed his hands together. "Although there's plenty of kindling from those other baskets that you left here."

She frowned. "Kindling? What?" She walked her basket to the work table, looking bewildered. "Where are the other baskets of twig trees?"

He nodded. "That's what I'm talking about. I saw you'd collected fodder for the fire, so I broke it all up to save you the trouble." He indicated the loaded fireplace and overflowing wood box.

Zhulija stared hard, swallowed and sank into the nearest chair. "Y-you broke them all up for the fire?"

"Yep!" Dario beamed.

She dropped her forehead into her palm. "They were the basis for the feather trees Vinaya has selected for part of her wedding decorations. I spent all morning looking for just the right-shaped pieces."

"Oh." Dario's smile faded. "Sorry."

Her smile was weak. "Never mind. Plenty more in the forest. I'll just go back and get other pieces."

"I'll come with you. Two of us will get it done faster, right?"

"Right."

He followed her, feeling like an idiot. Several hours later, he was an exhausted idiot. The pieces were required to look like little trees with lots of evenly spaced branches. Many of his finds were rejected because the branchlets weren't similar in size, shape and colour. By the time they'd collected enough for the wedding order, Dario had found only one that was acceptable to Zhulija. They'd walked around in circles, back and forth through the forest, in their relentless hunt for the damned bits of wood. Who knew selecting twig trees could be so difficult?

~

DAY THREE WAS warm and sunny with gusts of wind. Dario was delayed by a messenger from his queen, requesting a full account of the attack on Zhulija. His queen being unhappy about the violation of her promise of safe conduct for Zhulija was no surprise, nor was the knowledge that she wanted detailed facts to concoct a punishment befitting the crime. Brax would suffer. The knowledge supplied Dario huge satisfaction; it served the sod right. Aware Queen Maerovana would send a dispatch to her Seelie royal counterpart, explaining her word was still trustworthy, his response was very detailed. Even though they were cousins, Queen Dianathke would draw as much enjoyment from seeing Queen Maerovana squirm as possible, and every ounce of humiliation Queen Maerovana endured, she'd take threefold from Brax's hide.

Climbing the steps to the closed studio door, Dario looked through the window to ensure Zhulija was inside. She was bent over a table sorting items into piles, so after a brief knock, he slid the door aside. "Good morning, Zhulija."

The wind chose that moment to whoosh into the studio with frolicsome glee, whirling fluffy bits off her table into a dust devil.

Zhulija flung herself over the table. "Quick! Close the door!"

Mouth agape, Dario stared at an eddying storm of feathers. Pretty, tiny, bright-coloured feathers. They spun everywhere in a crazy swirl, a lighter-than-air blizzard, with Zhulija stuck in the middle. Gulping, Dario slammed the sliding door. In his haste, he tore it from its doortrack and barely stopped it from crashing to the floor. Gripping with both hands, wiggling and juggling, he finally got the sliding panel back onto its runners. Only then could he close it. With sinking heart, he turned, knowing he'd worked too slow.

"By Old Lady Willow, Dario!" Zhulija stood, arms akimbo as she glared at him. "The feathers are everywhere."

He sighed. "My apologies, although I don't see how I could have done anything to stop that from happening."

"You could have waited until I told you to enter." She was scowling.

"Yesterday, you said I could knock and walk in. I did. What more do you want?"

"For my assistant – that's you, I believe – to get here on time?"

He refused to be side-tracked by his admiration of her fierce spirit. "I'd love to be at your beck and call, Zhu, but I do have other demands requiring my attention. I'm doing the best I can. Now, let's re-gather the feathers. With both of us separating them into whatever piles you want, it won't take long to get them organised."

"My feather tree is awful!" Dario threw his hands in the air. Feathers fluttered in wild spirals of fluff. One stuck to his bottom lip; he sputtered and swiped at it. He glared as Zhulija fought a smile.

"It's repairable."

Thrusting hands into pockets, Dario angled away to find himself scowling at a series of glass statues arranged on one of the myriad shelves in Zhulija's studio. Frozen in their intricate poses, the statues ignored him. The figures of a male and female dancing were captured in sweeping, swirling elegance. Each pair blown in a different colour glass, the couples showcased stages of the dance as they flowed, dipped and twirled. Eyes moving down the line of dancers, Dario felt awe seep through him. He recognised the dance from the arrangement of line, shape, flow and colour in Zhulija's work. So beautifully crafted they appeared to be moving.

"You've created them dancing the Rhynfallia."

"Oh, you recognise the Rhynfallia?"

He nodded. "Hard not to with romantics in the family. Vinaya and

Mycostat didn't plan a Valentine's Day wedding by accident." He flicked a glance at his pathetic tree.

Her fingers twitched at feathers – here straightening, there adding more string. "I imagine they're going to dance the Rhynfallia at their wedding then? Do they know if they are 'true mates'?"

Turning back to her glass-work, he bent, studying one of the statues in detail. "No, they chose each other normally, but when they perform the Rhynfallia in full, they might find they are. Vinaya would be ecstatic. Doesn't matter that falling in love can occur without 'true mate' recognition."

"It's what most fae want. Probably because they see a true mating as a certain thing." Zhulija tilted her head. "I've always wondered how Valentine and his mate Rhynfallia knew what dance moves to make, way back then."

"Maybe she invented it." He shrugged. "It is named after her."

"Yes." Scissors snipped behind him. "We know, now, that dancing the Rhynfallia reveals 'true mates' to each other and the completion of it will bind their souls if they are. It's even been said performing the Rhynfallia is like a game of chance – is your partner your mate, or just another dance partner?"

Dario grimaced. "I've heard some men label it entrapment. Caught whether they want to be or not."

"They have a choice." Zhulija's voice was tart. "Nobody forces them to partake of the dance. Besides, if they end up mated, it's their true mate. Why would they have issue with finding their beloved? Doesn't everyone yearn to find the fate-chosen, other half of their soul?"

"You'd think so." Dario craned to follow the flow of radiance high-lighting the next set of dancers. "Maybe men just don't like admitting to being romantics. I know I don't." He twisted so that he could see both her and the statues, comparing her innate grace to that same quality in her work.

"Not very macho, you mean?" She turned the tree to a different area and added another feather.

"Many men won't admit to feelings." He grunted. "Whatever the reason, lots of people still dance at least part of the Rhynfallia. Can't find yourself mated if you don't finish the dance, no matter who your partner is."

"And, at some point, mates still have to do the traditional exchange of blood, the public claiming amongst witnesses, and the acceptance marking, fated or not." Zhulija laughed. "Still, it's hard to avoid dancing the Rhynfallia since it's played at every ball, and everyone adores it. I've seen same-sex pairs dancing it more than once."

"So have I." He grinned. "Some of those same-sex pairs find themselves mated too. We both know it's not because they can't find a partner of the opposite sex."

"That's true." She nodded. "Is that your way of telling me you prefer men to women?"

He choked as he met her gaze. "Mab's tits no! Whatever gave you that idea?"

She giggled. "Nothing. It was fun watching your reaction."

"Well, I like women. A lot." His gaze swept over her. "Lately, there's one particular woman who's piqued my interest." He took a step closer.

Zhulija moved around the table and pushed the feather tree he'd been working on towards him. "Ta-da! Your tree looks great now – it only needed a little more attention to detail." She flipped a hand palm up at the arrangement of twigs and feathers, smiling at him.

"Thank you for rescuing it." Dario wasn't sure if she was concentrating deeply or ignoring his advance. He studied her, noting the flags of colour darkening her creamy caramel complexion. Not unaware of him then. "You're having to do that a lot. I'm not much of an assistant, am I?" He placed the tree on the desk and folded his arms.

"Don't be put off, you're doing marvellous." Zhulija smiled encouragingly.

"Oh come on." He snorted. "First, there was the sand fiasco. Then I broke up all of the twig trees you'd painstakingly collected and put them into the fire pit because I thought that they were kindling."

Her smile was bright. "We collected more twig trees."

"After that, I opened the door and let the wind in while you were sorting feathers." He wrinkled his nose. "I'm sure I still have a feather stuck in one nostril."

She laughed. "The look of horror on your face was funny."

"On *my* face?" He shook his head. "I think you mean on yours. Seeing you fling yourself over the table far too late to stop the flight of the feathers was a sight to behold."

"Oh yeah? What about you, ripping the door off and struggling to get it back on its runners?"

Dario chuckled. "In that case, I'd say we both win the ridiculous crown." His smile faded. "I'm hindering you, aren't I?"

"You just need practice, Dario. Besides, you're wonderful company, and it's been lovely getting to know you." Colour rising in her cheeks, Zhulija gestured to the pots of twiggy branches and the piles of shaped and coloured feathers. "Now come on, they won't make themselves."

"A pity. Damn tree things." Dario wiped his hand across his mouth to hide his ecstatic grin. She really, truly liked him. He wanted to leap for joy.

"What was that?"

He spoke louder. "Just saying they're pretty grand tree things."

"Let's hope Vinaya and Mycostat think so."

9

ZHULIJA

Dawn streaked the horizon as Zhulija wiped perspiration from her brow and contemplated the table full of glass pieces resulting from her night's work. She was grateful her ability to magically manipulate heat enabled her to create in glass and metal. Maman claimed ancestral dragon blood – something Zhulija was sceptical of. Whatever the reason, she could generate extreme heat but no flame. She'd gravitated to working metal and glass at night because the fae of her inner circle were sleeping and safe from the intense temperatures needed to sculpt those materials. She was also less likely to be interrupted.

Turning one glass hanging pot between her fingers, she checked for trapped air bubbles, satisfied when there were none. Naturally, each piece had been checked before being annealed but she still preferred re-checking afterwards. The blown-glass balls were so pretty in the peachy colour that passed for rose gold. They only needed hanging strings before they were ready for storage on the wall-mounted rope harness.

Zhulija removed a reel of finger-width, lavender silk ribbon from a cupboard and laid it on the table. Attaching the triple hanging ribbon-cords would be Dario's job when he arrived. She yawned, rubbing her eyes. It was several hours before Dario's usual start time; she could indulge in a nap and dream of him – a gorgeous man she struggled to keep her eyes away from and couldn't wait to see again. Yawning again, Zhulija settled herself comfortably on her daybed and drifted off.

It seemed no time at all before someone shook her awake.

"Wakey, wakey, Zhu."

Armelle's voice impinged on her semi-conscious state. Zhulija cracked an eye open; all her sisters hung over her like Old Lady Willow's drooping branches.

"Maman guessed you were here when you didn't appear at breakfast."

"We thought we'd bring some."

"Breakfast, that is."

Sighing, Zhulija opened her other eye and summoned a smile. "Thanks, I'm starving."

She was tucking into a bowl of berries with cream when the door whooshed aside to frame Dario. Zhulija's mouth watered as he strode in, his gorgeously windswept hair adding to his bad boy appeal. His large, muscled form was encased in a grey tabard, black trousers and well-worn, calf-high, black leather boots.

He cast his cloak over the back of a chair. "Please tell me we aren't making more feather trees today, Zhu. I'm over them." Sighting her sisters, Dario skidded to a halt so fast Zhulija wondered if smoke was rising from his boot heels. He cocked an eyebrow. "Hello, ladies."

"Good morning." Four voices chorused like birds tweeting in the dawn.

Zhulija waved; her mouth was full of berries.

"Lovely day." His smile upgraded him from gorgeous to breathtaking. Zhulija was glad to be sitting down – he made her weak in the knees.

"Wow!" Janeska shook her head.

Lyssica sauntered towards Dario, a shark scenting blood. "I'm Lyssica." Her voice was a purr. "That's Armelle to your left and behind Zhu are our twins, Tindresse and Janeska. You must be Lord Dario

Eribifax." Her smile gleaming, she tucked a loose strand of dark hair behind her ear. "Zhulija's our baby sister, you know." Her lashes fluttered.

Zhulija glared at her sisters whilst chewing a strawberry.

Dario bowed, his eyes flicking over them. "A pleasure to make your acquaintance, ladies." His gaze returned to Lyssica. "Something in your eye, Lady Lyssica?"

"Perhaps you could remove it?" Lyssica cooed, leaning closer.

Hand tightening on her spoon, Zhulija wondered whether cream curdled as quickly as her feelings. Lyssica was an accomplished flirt; the 'something in my eyes' routine was a patented move. Zhu's annoyance flared – after she'd warned her sisters away, they were here making trouble.

"My apologies, Lady Lyssica, but my fingers are thick and clumsy. One of your sisters is a better choice to poke around a vital organ like your eye."

Zhulija's spoon jerked in her bowl, flicking a blueberry into the air. Her smile blossomed as Dario swept around Lyssica, caught the errant blueberry and popped it into his mouth. "Yum." He winked. Behind him, Lyssica scowled at his back.

Resolve firming, Zhulija stood. "Thanks, Lyss, I might be the youngest, but you've missed the fact that I've grown up." She knew, right down to the soles of her fluffy slippers, that her sisters were visiting to satisfy their curiosity about Dario. Was the baby comment meant to put her in her place, or warn Dario away? If they thought she needed protection, they were way off track. Were they trying to show her Dario was fickle and fancy free?

Dario's hand wave encompassed the group. "Are you ladies here to work then?"

Armelle wrinkled her nose. "By Old Lady Willow, no."

"We came to check on Zhu after she pulled another all-nighter." Janeska patted Zhulija.

She jerked away. "Quit that! I'm not a pet."

Tindresse added more berries to Zhulija's bowl. "Eat these up – you need the energy."

Zhulija's glare cut like a dagger. "I can look after myself. We spoke about this a few nights ago – if you recall?"

Lyssica ignored her. "Do you work out every day, Lord Dario?" Voice dripping with admiration, she reached towards his chest. "You have amazing muscle definition."

"No." Face expressionless, he stepped sideways to avoid her fingers.

"Your colouring is wonderful." Armelle pouted her lips. "I've always adored red, black and silver grey together. I'm sure your wings are very pretty."

Dario's lips twisted into a sardonic grin. "Are my eyes sparkly silver too? Perhaps red to indicate lust, or anger?"

Lyssica barrelled on despite the acidic response. "Do you style your hair or is it naturally that wild?"

Tindresse clapped her hands. "It looks silky – may I touch?"

Dario folded his arms. "No."

Janeska took a step, but Zhulija dropped her bowl on the table and grabbed her sister's arm. She opened her mouth—

Dario's voice was splintering shards of ice. "Let's be clear, ladies. I'm not interested in spreading my wings to show off my colours, or in having my muscles stroked, and if anyone touches my hair, I usually break their fingers. I'm not here to socialise. I came to assist Zhulija with her crafting. You read me?"

"Oh, but Lord Eribifax—"

"Not clear then." He squared his stance as if preparing for a rough and tumble. "Listen up. I've no wish to offend, but none of you interest me apart from being Zhulija's sisters." His glare swept over them. "In that position, I'll accord you the respect that you accord me. Got it?"

Zhulija grimaced. "Alright, dear sisters, I've had sufficient to eat so please take the dishes back to the kitchen as you go. Thanks for thinking of me. Don't come back." She snatched up the carry bag, thrust her bowl and spoon inside, then swept across the room to hold it out.

Tindresse took it, her smile wry. "You're spoiling our fun, Zhu."

"No fun here. Take yourselves elsewhere, we've work to do." She met the eyes of each of her sisters, baring a warning fang. "Leave. Now."

"Fine." Lyssica shrugged, but a flush mantled her face and neck. "I'm sure we'll see you later, Lord Eribifax."

"See you at dinner tonight, Zhu." Armelle offered Dario a weak nod then followed Lyssica.

"Are you sure, Zhu?" Janeska cocked her head.

Zhulija's lips wrinkled, revealing both fangs. She hissed.

"Ookay." Janeska and Tindresse hastened past Dario.

The door shut with a crisp snick.

Dario raised his eyebrows. "Was that a test of some kind?"

"My sisters checking up on me. I apologise for their behaviour."

His expression remained neutral. "You wanted to see how committed I am, then?"

"I did not arrange that sisterly drama." Zhulija's brows drew together. "And, committed to what? Assisting with Vinaya and Myco-stat's wedding pieces?"

His lips thinned. "The wedding pieces – yes, of course."

She nodded uncertainly – were they speaking of the same thing? "Well, we are on a time-line."

"So we are." His smile was harsh. "Is that why you worked all night?"

"Partly."

"The other part being that you don't trust me not to muck things up somehow?"

She shook her head. "No. Blowing glass is tricky, needs complete concentration and at night my family are asleep, so no interruptions."

Dario massaged the bridge of his nose. "No interruptions by me, you mean?"

"That's not what I'm saying." Zhulija rolled her eyes. "You know you're easy on the eyes, milord – another distraction I can't afford when blowing glass."

He brightened. "You feel uneasy around me – I understand that. You were attacked in my home, I orchestrated the sand fiasco, the branch disaster and the feather storm. Add my pathetic attempts at feather trees and you probably thought I was a sure bet to wreck the glass blowing somehow." He winked. "Me being such a distraction and all."

She ignored her blazing cheeks. "You're a distraction for any red-blooded fae-girl, but again, this had nothing to do with you being gorgeous and everything to do with the privacy I need for glass blowing."

He nodded. "Okay, but you're more to me than just a 'red-blooded fae-girl' and I'm the biggest distraction you'll ever have. You know that, don't you?"

Zhulija tipped her head to the side. "What in the name of the Queendom are you talking about?"

His lips twisted. "Fine, play innocent, but we both know the truth." He spun towards the door. "I need air." He strode out.

Anger bubbled to life – how dare he walk out on her without proper explanation! Bursting on to the veranda, she found Dario stalking to and fro, muttering to himself. "You stop right there!"

He whirled, eyes phasing through silver and black to crimson. "Give me a good reason."

Zhulija blinked. With deliberate steps, she closed their distance to tap a fingertip on his chest. "Listen, it's no lie that I blow glass at night, alone. You don't have to flatter and flirt with me – it makes me uncomfortable when it's not true."

"Flatter and flirt? You think I'm playing you?"

She waved a hand. "That business about attraction between us." She shrugged. "You and I both know you're handsome and I realise from the looks you've been dishing out lately that you find me good looking enough to notice – but you must have tonnes of far more suitable Unseelie ladies at your beck and call. I have no wish to be a curiosity for you to bed and set aside."

"A curiosity? You think this is a casual attraction?" He glowered. "You insult both of us. It's fortunate I know the truth between us."

Zhulija sighed. "We're back to that truth business again? I told you – my night work has nothing to do with lack of trust."

His lips flattened. "Wrong truth, Zhu. You're being deliberately obtuse. The one I'm talking about is something we both recognise on a gut level but you won't admit and I can't tell you without breaking fae-law."

"By Old Lady Willow's roots! This is bloody ridiculous. I've no idea what you're blathering about. Why can't you just get to the point?" She jerked on his tabard, digging her claws in, dragging him down until they were nose to nose. "Explain it to me, Dario. Now!"

The gust of his cold mirth bathed her. "As you command, darling!"

She had no time for breath, only shock, when his mouth sealed her own; his lips moving, deliberate, intent, delicious. Unable to resist, Zhulija pushed up to deepen the inexplicably wonderful contact. She thrilled as Dario's arms encircled her, dragging her hard against him. Mindless, she lifted her legs to wrap around his hips, locking them behind his back. He jerked against her, their fangs clashing, tongues twining, lips moving slickly. She writhed to get closer still, sliding her arms up his marvellous chest and about his neck. Her talons scraped his scalp, clutching at strands of silky mane. His wildly aroused growl reverberated inside their mouths. Zhulija lapped it up, revelled in him; sank into his flavour of sunny forest glades, the air after spring rain. He was as decadent as molten chocolate swirling on her tongue; she couldn't get enough. The taste, the sensations, his stroking, soaked into her parched soul, just as surely as their veins flowed blood …

Blood? Zhulija jerked her head back to stare at Dario. He panted, eyes kaleidoscopic with flaring patterns of argent, ruby and ebony flame. Her tongue touched her bottom lip, tasting the shared slick of blood as it blended deliciously in her mouth. She could feel her fangs throbbing, see Dario's, gleaming white behind his blood-painted lips.

"Y-you kissed me!" Her tongue snaked out, slid over wet lips before flicking across to share his, another taste of nirvana between them.

"Just as you kissed me." He grinned, eyes burning. "Everything about you says you yearn to do it again." His voice dropped to a growl. "As do I."

She swallowed, unable to deny it. "I need to think."

He shook his head. "Tut-tut. Thinking is over-rated, Zhu." His fore-claw stroked her cheek. "With thought, we talk ourselves out of so many truths. Feel this thing between us; feel, as well as think. Add our emotions, the way we've touched, the flavour and mix it well. Recognise that it's not simple lust. Therein lies your answer – our answer." His lips caressed her trembling mouth again, before sliding to kiss her cheek, eyebrow, forehead. Bewilderment flooded as he set her away, holding her tight just until her shaky legs supported her. "If you trust me as you say, you'll work it out, sweet Zhu. I can't be any clearer without breaking fae-law." He backed a few paces, meeting her stunned gaze with those wild, kaleidoscoping eyes before arcing his striated wings and arrowing skywards.

CLUTCHING her hair with clawed fingers, Zhulija sensed wildness rising. Shivering, she stared until Dario faded from view, then screamed to the empty sky.

He, a known ladies' man, had rejected her sisters, threatened to break their fingers, gotten annoyed at what he called 'her games', revealed hurt feelings at perceived slights, become angered at what he saw as lack of trust, and yet, kissed her into yearning craziness …

Why?

What did he want from her?

He talked in riddles. What must she recognise? How did you combine emotion, touch and flavour with thought? Logic and sensation were oil and water.

If he was right and she had the answers, he must already know them …

She couldn't ask him, but others had visited her studio.

Fanning her wings, Zhulija sped homewards to face her sisters on the breaking waves of her wrath.

Ignoring the guards angling towards her from their gate duty in response to her screams, Zhulija aimed for the French doors and burst in from the gardens. Gathered for lunch, her family whirled from the buffet at her volcanic eruption into the room. Her father, brothers, even her mother had assumed defensive stances in front of the girls; they relaxed upon recognising Zhulija.

Her mother stepped forward with arms outstretched. "Zhu! Is something wrong?"

Ignoring her mother, she aimed a claw-point at her sisters. "What did he mean?"

"Ah, what did he mean by what, Zhu?" Armelle spoke softly as if sensing something was not right.

"By what he did? By what he said?"

Armelle cocked her head. "You mean in rejecting Lyss's advances?"

Side-tracked, Zhulija's frozen gaze swung to Lyssica. Her mouth wrinkled in a snarl. "You attempted to seduce him."

Lyssica backed up. "I wouldn't have really. I was protecting you, Zhu!"

"You all tried to steal him!"

Janeska raised her hands, palms out. "No, we were testing him, Zhu, seeing how committed he is to you."

"He thinks I don't trust him."

"Do you?" Her mother.

The savagery swirling inside her hesitated; she tilted her head. "Yes!"

Duke Yanvian pointed. "Why is your face covered in blood? Is it yours?"

"He – I – we …" She swallowed, brought fingers to her lips. "We kissed. Our fangs cut, the blood belongs to both of us."

"What?" Duke Yanvian let loose a roar of outrage. "That Unseelie jackal had the gall to kiss you and exchange blood? I'll have his guts for boot laces! I'll rip that pretty boy hair out strand by strand! I'll—"

"You won't touch him!" The guttural thunder of Zhulija's voice was emphasised by an airborne cloud of objects, rattling into her personal halo. She raised claws sparking purple, her hair billowing as if in a gale.

"No, Zhulija!" Her father froze. "No, no, you're absolutely right. I won't touch him. My apologies for threatening him. No one in this room will touch him without your permission. He is safe and, and, welcome in our home."

The words settled, felt right. She glared at her siblings; they all looked away. Whispered words in her mother's calming tones drifted her way.

"There's no threat, Zhu. Stand down, relax and feel safe knowing that Dario is yours alone."

The breath caught in Zhulija's throat. "Mine? Dario is mine?" Items dropped as Zhulija's palpable shock undermined her use of power.

"Of course he is, sweeting." Duchesse Azura smiled warmly. "That's what this is about. The intense attraction, the newly revealed power, the exchange of blood between you – you're mate-claiming Dario Eribifax. And he, you."

"Mate-claiming." Zhulija let the phrase roll through her. "Oh! We're true mates! That's what he couldn't tell me." She caught her mother in a wide-eyed stare. "It's against fae-law; he must think I'm a total idiot."

Duchesse Azura opened her arms. "I doubt it, sweetling. He'll be waiting for you."

Gulping, Zhulija ran into that soft, warm, tried-and-true embrace and snuggled in.

"Well, thank the gods!" Duke Yanvian sagged. "But an Unseelie son-in-law." His groan was heart-felt. "DeMaksim, some whisky-nectar, please?"

"Can I have some too?" Treymeron sidled up to his brother. "I'm overcome with angst."

DeMaksim set out a row of tiny glasses. "Push off, Trey."

But after he poured, he handed everyone a restorative glass.

DARIO

Dario tapped a pen on his desk-pad, concern eating him up inside. Another day over with no message from Zhulija. He'd given her an ultimatum – painted himself into a corner. Why hadn't she answered? He flung the pen to the desk, splattering ink across the open document.

"Mab's tits!" Snatching up a sponge, he dabbed at the mess.

"Really, Dario." His mother frowned from the doorway. "Your face is black enough to give the staff nightmares."

"Sorry." He wasn't. He wanted to rip the document into tiny pieces and scatter them; swear until his voice deserted him; fling black shadows until people understood that he was the nightmare.

"Excuse me, your Ladyship." Mycostat eased around Lady Catocala and plunked a glass into Dario's hand. "Try this."

Dario drained the shot of whisky-nectar like spring water. Mycostat refilled it from the bottle he held, watching Dario scull it again.

"Dario! Go easy on that." His mother caned her way into the office. "We don't need you drunk as well as lovesick and sense scattered." She relieved him of the sponge and wiped up the ink.

Mycostat snorted. "Relax, your Ladyship; it takes a lot to get Dario mellow. I've never seen him drunk."

"Nor will you." His father, haunted by memories of the war, had coped by drowning himself in alcohol and had been killed while too drunk to defend himself. A mistake Dario had vowed never to make. He deliberately ignored the rest of the accusations his mother voiced.

Vinaya sailed in. "I've made us a huge pile of sandwiches." She plunked a small plate containing a lettuce leaf and four points of a single sandwich on to the smeared pages. They all stared at the pathetic offering.

"Naya, that wouldn't feed a rabbit." Mycostat rubbed Vinaya's back. "Nice thought though."

A breath of laughter escaped Dario. "I'd hate to see your version of small if you consider that paltry offering a huge variety."

Suitilay arrived, pushing a cart containing two much larger trays of sandwiches and a third tray of cake. The trolley's second shelf bore the tea urn, cups and fixings.

It was Vinaya's turn to laugh. "Ha! Tricked you. There is a lot of sandwiches. I just allowed Suitilay to bring them."

"At least he can be trusted to have *your* back." Dario couldn't resist the verbal jab.

Suitilay looked down his nose. "I fail to see how leaving myself open to a rain of garden refuse could further my unquestionable allegiance to the family. It was aimed at you, my Lord, and you deserved it."

"Touché!" Dario's right hand flipped palm up. Everyone laughed.

With a bow, Suitilay withdrew, leaving them to the picnic.

~

THE BUTLER RETURNED a half hour later. "My Lord Eribifax, you have visitors."

"Show them in." Dario was afraid to hope.

Suitilay pushed the door wide. "Your guests, Heir-Lord DeMaksim Aphiski, Lady Lyssica Aphiski and Lord Treymeron Aphiski." Both fae-males carried crates and Lady Lyssica had a basket athwart one arm.

For a moment, Dario stared in frozen shock. Then his wits and manners reasserted and he introduced everyone.

Lady Catocala nodded. "Charmed to meet more of the Duke and Duchess Papillion's brood."

"I'm sure the pleasure is ours." DeMaksim bowed over the crate he held.

"Can we put these down now?" Treymeron asked. "This member of the brood is tired."

"Mycostat, would you please help Lord Treymeron?" Dario moved to assist DeMaksim.

"Sure." Mycostat put down half a sandwich and crossed to help with the load.

Treymeron smiled across the top of the crate. "So you're the groom whose wedding these baubles are for."

"Baubles?" Vinaya clasped her hands. "Oh wow! Lady Zhulija came through. That's wonderful, isn't it, Mycostat?"

"Absolutely." Mycostat watched Vinaya prying at the crate lids.

"Like this." Treymeron showed them how the covers unlatched.

"I've a reel of lavender silk ribbon for the baubles – they'll be suspended from the ceiling," Lady Lyssica said to Vinaya. "That was one of Lord Dario's planned jobs, but he didn't finish."

"Oh, that's alright." Vinaya smiled. "I can do that. I'd love to. You won't mind missing out on that, will you, Dario?" She aimed a cheeky grin at him, but it faded as she saw the way Dario and DeMaksim were eyeballing one another.

Locked in his staring match with DeMaksim, Dario's eyes burned as they begin kaleidoscoping.

"If you hurt her, I'll kill you," DeMaksim lisped around enlarged fangs.

"I plan to love her, not harm her." The red heat flashed from Dario's eyes and up into his hair. He growled.

"Wow." DeMaksim chuckled. Did his skin look scaly? "You have it as bad as she does. Wonderful."

A growl vibrated from Dario. "Where is Zhulija? Why are you here instead?"

"She's finishing some items." DeMaksim's fangs had reverted to fae-normal, just small top ones. "Without your assistance, she needs to work harder to complete the wedding paraphernalia."

Dario frowned. "That's a weak excuse. If she doesn't want—"

"Zhu needs time to process, think and make her decisions, and if you're smart, you'll allow her to have it. She's an emotional whirlwind. Father threatened violence against you, which had her setting up to attack him. He backed down, apologised and promised no harm would come to you."

"She defended me? With that tornado of stuff she conjures?"

DeMaksim's grin was beatific. "It was brilliant, although terrifying when it happened. Maman calls it avalanche power – an old, recessive family trait."

"I know how he feels." Dario shook his head. "Poor Duke Yanvian – I wonder if he needed to change his underwear?" The two fae-males locked eyes in mutual understanding and burst into laughter. Dario sighed. "Okay, I'll wait for a sign from Zhu."

After a searching glance, DeMaksim nodded. "She said to tell you there's a gift."

"A gift?"

"It's Valentine advent five-day. I believe that she has a few more planned." DeMaksim was grinning. "Lyssica, give him the first gift."

Lyssica's hand appeared over DeMaksim's shoulder, holding out a mid-size rectangular box wrapped in gold foil and tied with a bow. "From Zhu."

Accepting the gift, Dario moved to his desk, unwrapping the package with slow, shaking fingers. She hadn't given up on him.

"Hurry up Dario! I want to see." Vinaya was dancing in anticipation.

"It's my present." Dario held his breath as he drew off the lid and pushed aside the tissue paper. Inside lay a gold filigree pen. Jaw dropping, he stared. Was it? He lifted his scarred left hand to compare … yes, the pattern was identical. He laughed so hard he fell off the chair.

His guests weren't allowed to leave until he'd wrapped up the

Eribifax heirloom pen as Zhulija's return gift. By then, they were all laughing.

~

THE NEXT DAY, DeMaksim and Trey were accompanied by Armelle. Their crates held the feather trees, which were unpacked to the accompaniment of laughter as Dario related how he had chopped the first branches up for firewood.

His Valentine advent gift from Zhulija was a smaller version of the round glass bauble vase that had been made for the upcoming wedding of Vinaya and Mycostat. It contained sand and a small bouquet of flowers. He understood the reference to the ill-fated posy he had sent, which she had re-delivered in pieces, accompanied by part of his garden. His Zhulija was certainly getting her pound of flesh. He loved it.

Suitilay smirked at seeing the gift in pride of place on Dario's desk. "I believe Lady Zhulija's a fitting match for you, my Lord."

Smiling, Dario continued to stare at the little vase. This time, he'd prepared his return gift in advance. He refused to tell Armelle that a trio of rare burgundy blood roses, a gift fit for his queen, nestled inside the gift box. He wondered what Zhulija would make of it.

~

WHAT SHE MADE of that Valentine's Day lead-up gift was her own version. A single burgundy blood rose in blown glass.

Dario's hand trembled as he held it. Zhulija had probably stayed up, just for him, the previous night making it.

"Wow, Dario." Vinaya sounded awed. "That is so-o beautiful!" She paused in unpacking her filigree flower holders to admire it.

It was a work of art revealing the hand of love in its glistening perfection. He laid it reverently back in its silken nest and arranged the box where he could see the rose at will.

Which was often.

The return gift he entrusted to the basket held by Janeska was a box containing an antique key with a silk bow through its top loop. There was nothing to tell Zhulija what it was for. If she accepted him as her mate, he'd show her the beautiful gazebo remodelled to mirror her studio. No discussion had occurred between them about a mating, never mind living arrangements if their mating came to pass. In truth, he'd no idea what Zhu thought. Aware of their significance to each other, he'd come to terms with the possibility of spending time in both realms – that was doable while he was only Heir-Lord. After seeking advice from his mother, he'd advised Queen Maerovana of events, pointed out ramifications, even dared to make suggestions. Her answer, the response of a dangerous fáe-woman who was a law unto herself, had yet to come.

DAY four's wedding finery proved to be filigree baskets with brackets for place cards, cushioned by sponge leaves in DeMaksim and Treymeron's crates.

Tindresse carried a basket containing several packages layered in soft leafy coverings. She presented the basket to Dario. "Today's Valentine advent gift from Zhu, your lordship."

Dario unwrapped the series of glass statues he'd last seen gracing a shelf in Zhulija's studio – the beautiful frozen couple in their intricate poses, dancing the sweeping, whirling Rhynfallia. Each set was a different hue of glass, while showcasing progressions of the dance as the pair glided, angled and spun. In admiring the procession of dancers, Dario experienced a repetition of the awe that had swept him at his first viewing. He recognised anew the dance from the exquisite positioning of line, form and colour in Zhulija's artwork.

"By Queen Mab!" Lady Catocala caned closer for a better look. "Those statues are superb, Dario."

"Lady Zhulija is a true artist." Vinaya crouched for a closer view.

"I didn't think she'd ever give those away." DeMaksim was shaking his head.

"Hope you've got something good, Lord D." Trey grinned. "Hard to counter these."

In answer, Dario handed over a large envelope.

"A card?" Trey mocked. "That the best you can do?"

But Mycostat whistled. "That's no card – that's an invitation to Queen Maerovana's birthday ball tomorrow night. She was born on Valentine's Day eve and holds a ball every year; she handpicks all the guests. It's said to be amazing."

"You were invited, Dario?" Lady Catocala looked pleased. "What an honour. Where is she holding it this year?"

"On Garadenya Island in the Rubiconia River." Dario was relieved. His queen had replied to his missive with a pile of invitations. "We're all going, Mother. Me, you, Vinaya and Mycostat." As she gaped, he turned to DeMaksim. "I also have invitations for your entire family." He produced a second envelope. The Aphiski contingent were equally startled.

Lady Catocala's hand firmed on her cane. "Well, that explains why it's on the river isle – neutral territory."

"Yes, a deliberate choice." Dario winnowed a hand through his hair. "Queen Maerovana's cover note said she wants to meet the lady whose safe pass was violated and all parties concerned."

Tindresse's hands flew to her mouth. "Oh goodness, everyone will need a special outfit!" She chivvied her brothers out the door as fast as possible.

"She's right. We've no time to waste! Come on, Vinaya." Lady Catocala grasped her daughter's arm and dragged her off.

Mycostat poured himself some whisky-nectar and topped up Dario's glass. "Mab's tits. It always comes back to clothes." His expression was morose. "They'll be after us next."

"We both have new outfits for your wedding, in two days' time." Dario saluted his future brother-in-law. "Can't get more perfect than that."

Mycostat sighed. "Dario, that's genius, but the women won't let us get away with it."

Dario pursed his lips. "I'd better ask Suitilay to request the presence of the tailor with some outfits then."

"Now? You think he'd come here now?"

"He'll come." Dario's smile revealed his sharp fangs. "We have an understanding."

ZHULIJA

Garadenya Isle blazed with light. Zhulija marvelled at how night's darkness fled before the false daylight provided by myriads of festive lanterns strung from every tree and pole. She tapped one foot to the strains of music drifting out of the fortress as she stood in the receiving line with the rest of her family. The music was entwined with infectious sounds of gaiety, announcing the progress of Queen Maerovana's Valentine birthday ball to anyone with ears. Waiting for the queen's major-domo to announce them, Zhulija smoothed shaky hands down the pearl-sprinkled, fitted lace bodice of her dark cherry gown and fluffed the tulle layers frothing over the satin underskirt. Black lace gloves without fingertips encased her hands, a perfect frame for the sparkling silver points of her polished burgundy fingernails. Even her extruded claws had been painted burgundy and silver in case a claws-out event occurred. Flexing her fingers as the line moved forward, Zhulija kept eyes on her parents and simply alternated her black cherry satin boots in their wake. Around Zhulija, her sisters were twittering with excitement, ignoring their brothers who brought up the rear of their family cavalcade.

"The Duke and Duchesse of Papillion, Heir-Lord DeMaksim Aphiski, Lady Lyssica Aphiski, Lady Janeska Aphiski, Lady Tindresse Aphiski, Lord Treymeron Aphiski, Lady Armelle Aphiski and Lady Zhulija Aphiski." Listing them in birth order, the major-domo's sonorous voice rolled like an ebbing tide over the clamorous sea of people in the great hall. He spoke quietly to her father, who nodded before escorting her mother downstairs to the main floor where they stopped. DeMaksim's hand under her elbow helped Zhulija's confidence as the siblings followed. A tall female-fae with lemon-speckled, dark teal hair approached in a swirl of marigold satin to speak to their parents. Zhulija could hear nothing of her speech over the revelry.

"With that gorgeous colouring she has to be from the Zygaeniday family." DeMaksim's smile was predatory.

Zhulija kept her voice as confidential as her brother's. "You'll have time to socialise later."

He grinned. "Looking forward to it." A squeeze of his fingers urged her to follow their parents and the Zygaeniday lady. The Aphiskis were guided between bouncing brownies, gyrating gnomes, undulating dark elves, dour dwarves with gnarly beards and cackling pointy-hatted witches. Zhulija was startled when a puca winked its velvety black eye and rattled its chains in her direction. Occasionally, a light elf shone amidst the ocean of dark fae.

Resplendent in their finery, enthroned side by side on a dais, were the two queens of the fae world: Seelie Queen Dianathke, and her Unseelie counterpart, Queen Maerovana. Their proximity revealed the familial heritage of their shared great-grandfather, King Oberon. It was apparent in blue eyes and the similar cast of honey-toned features, but where Queen Maerovana was a busty golden blonde, Queen Dianathke had rich chocolate hair and a lissom build. No one disputed the loveliness of either queen, or their reputations of ruling with a firm hand backed by strong individual magics.

At this first meeting, Zhulija had envisioned the Unseelie queen would be dark featured, like the reputation of the Unseelie fae, and the Seelie queen would be correspondingly fair and pale. At her thought, both queens focused on her, smirking. Seconds later, Queen Dianathke's chocolate hair became ash blonde while Queen Maerovana's hair turned midnight blue. Zhulija froze.

"Tut, tut, Lady Zhulija." Queen Dianathke retained her lazy smile, but Queen Maerovana's gaze was eagle intense.

"Apologies for not guarding my public thoughts, your majesties." Zhulija dropped into a deep curtsy. "I meant no disrespect."

The Seelie queen continued to smile. "That, we could also tell, Lady Zhulija."

Duke Yanvian frowned. "Forgive—"

Queen Dianathke shook her head. "Not now, Yanvian. We will talk later."

Tight of mouth, Zhulija's father bowed, but his eyes flashed Zhulija a warning as he stepped back.

Flowing to her feet, Queen Maerovana glided down from the dais to confront Zhulija. Her well-built shape was more buxom up close, whilst her hair continued to shade from midnight through all shades of blue, to blonde and back in a continuous pattern of colour and light. Bright blue eyes were dagger sharp with the force of her power and presence. Zhulija swallowed under the queen's pin-point focus.

"So, you're the girl causing me to hold my birthday ball in this out of the way place." Her voice rang bell-like across the great hall causing a silence that spread like ripples in a pond, until the entire hall was cocooned in quiet expectation.

Zhulija swallowed. "I beg your majesty's pardon, but I'm not sure what sort of impact I had on the situation. I had no idea where your birthday ball was being held until I received an invitation yesterday."

The queen nodded. "Oh yes, I'm sure that's true, but Dia and I have been hearing lots about you."

"You have?" Zhulija wasn't certain whether to be alarmed or not. When Queen Maerovana began to circle, Zhulija turned with her, attempting to maintain eye contact. She wasn't certain she wanted the Unseelie queen behind her. A tinkle of laughter came from Queen Dianathke, still seated on her dais throne.

"When a request came from the Eribifax family for a safe pass into Unseelie territory for the youngest daughter of a Seelie duke, I was naturally curious. I asked Dia what she knew about this Lady Zhulija Aphiski, who was suddenly of high interest to some of my people. Dia explained that you were an artist who makes wedding decorations as a side business. I had thought an artist who must make trinkets to survive couldn't be a very good artist, but then Dia showed me a few, acquired pieces of your work. They're better than good, they're beautiful. Tell me why a gifted artist feels the need to make wedding paraphernalia?" Queen Maerovana stopped moving to stand side on to both the dais and the bulk of the great hall.

Zhulija shrugged. "It helps my thought processes. Wedding pieces were amongst my first efforts; now I've made most of the items often enough that I can still think and plan my major artworks without being idle. I suppose you could say it's creative doodling."

"Interesting." Queen Maerovana pursed her lips. "Once I saw your artwork and understood why the Eribifax family wanted your visit, I decided to grant the pass. I didn't expect you to be any trouble, but that was proved a fallacy when my pass, my word of protection, was dishonoured by a footman on the Eribifax Estate." She shook her head. "I was pleased Heir-Lord Eribifax sent him to me, not easy for him under the circumstances, but I had a lovely time questioning the treasonous creature." She shook her head sadly. "Where do these crazies get their ideas? Have you ever wondered, Lady Zhulija?"

"No, your majesty. I haven't come up against anyone like that before."

"Fortunate girl in your sheltered life." The Unseelie queen made a moue. "I have been unlucky enough to meet more than my fair share. This particular one was most upset that you had escaped him and very angry that you had burned Heir-Lord Eribifax. He believed you should pay." She snorted. "Pay for being Seelie instead of Unseelie? He ignored our common heritage. Foolishness." Queen Maerovana's fanged smile was viciously pleased. "He has discovered, the hard way, my lack of tolerance for fools."

Uncertain of the conversation's direction, Zhulija stayed silent.

"I was fascinated when I heard Lord Dario still bore the scar from your burn instead of having it healed, as he easily could have done." Queen Maerovana cocked her head. "Did you find it strange, Lady Zhulija?"

"I haven't given it much thought, Your Majesty." Zhulija curled her fingernails into her palms, wondering where Dario was. "I am unaware of the Eribifax family's skills."

"Of course you are." Queen Maerovana nodded. "I contacted Lady Catocala for details and her response intrigued me enough to continue our correspondence. Imagine my surprise when I discovered one of my justifiably feared, and trusted, Unseelie lords had offered his own services as reparation for the wrongs done to a duke's youngest daughter. Few people would understand why he was doing the reparations with his own hands, but Dia and I were convinced there could only be one reason."

"My Queen, Queen Dianathke, I greet you both." The sound of Dario's voice was wonderful. He swept a deep bow. "If you would allow the indulgence, I believe it's my turn to speak with Lady Zhulija."

Zhulija looked across to the stunningly handsome fae-male who she had finally understood was her mate. As usual, his shoulder-length tricoloured hair was angled in multiple directions and he wore the Eribifax family colours. His form-fitting trousers were charcoal leather, snugged into calf-high black boots, while his sleeveless silver tabard, fitted over a crimson silk shirt, was complemented by a low-waisted black belt, from which hung two short hip swords. His dark grey eyes were full of warmth; his smile stroked her skin.

Zhulija reached for Dario's hand and ran her fingers across the filigree scarring. "Why didn't you get this burn healed?"

"It bothers you, Zhu?"

"I've never before hurt someone that way."

"I should hope not!" Dario grinned. "You marked me, as true mates do. I was yours on the first day we met, even if you considered it to be only a self-protective act. You mate-claimed me; there was no way I was going to have the mark of my beloved removed."

Zhulija's palms flew to her cheeks. "You knew? Way back then?"

"I did, though I confess I thought a gentle Seelie lady couldn't be strong enough for the Unseelie Beast." He reached, clasped a hand and drew it from her face. "You soon proved me wrong." Keeping her hand in his, Dario dropped to one knee. "I'd like to tell you I'm very much in love with you, Zhulija Juniper Aphiski. Would you be willing to fulfil our mating and share your life with me?"

"Oh! Oh, yes, Dario. I'm in love with you. Of course I will." Zhulija swept close to Dario and pulled him up for a kiss. A delicious meshing of lips to rediscover his flavour of sunny forest glades tangled with the aftermath of spring rain. His arms snugged around her, their mouths briefly parting, before reconnecting to lick deeper into their kiss. Zhulija was so wrapped up in Dario, she forgot where they were.

"Ahem!" Queen Maerovana tapped both of their arms. "True mates are always a delight. Too bad there aren't more such unequivocal unions. Tell me, Dario, have you marked Lady Zhulija in return? Not yet? What about the sharing of blood? You've completed that? Good. You've been marked, but she hasn't, you've shared blood, you've accepted each other here, in public, as true mates, In that case, I believe it's time for dancing."

"Dancing? Now?" Zhulija, eyes only for Dario, identified the indignant voice of her younger brother.

"Yes, now, young Lord Treymeron Aphiski. Now is the perfect moment." Queen Maerovana turned to wave at the musicians. "Play the Rhynfallia for Lord Dario and Lady Zhulija."

Zhulija stared up at Dario, wondering how she could be so lucky.

His smile was a thing of love and wonder. "The Rhynfallia – you will dance it with me, won't you, darling?"

"I'd be delighted." She swung into his arms for the first few steps as the music cascaded around them. Separating to fingertips, gazes connected, they moved in graceful arcs to the lilting melody before parting to retreat in a smooth but intricate foot pattern, to circle one another in lithe fluidity, swirling to the music with a supple agility that elicited "wows" from the riveted watchers. As they danced, dipped, twirled and spun, Dario and Zhulija had eyes for no one but each other while they performed the ancient fae mating ritual, which was only ever a total success for true mates.

The music rose to a glorious crescendo as Zhulija came once more into Dario's arms for the closing rhythms of the ceremonial dance. The moves of the Rhynfallia routine were so finely structured that a finishing point could be predicted once the later stages were completed. Zhulija and Dario flowed through their final elegant glide into the penultimate moment, where their wings spread in arcs of brilliant colour. Spinning Zhulija back over one arm, Dario bent to kiss her. His hand on her neck eased up to caress the sweep of her hair before flowing back to stroke her nearest wing.

Overflowing with love and joy, Zhulija felt a heat trailing over her brow, following Dario's palm to her wing, then spreading across from one wing to the other. He was marking her in his own way, just as she had done. "How did you mark me?"

His eyes brimmed with love. "I've put a dash of my family's crimson colour in your hair and altered the cobalt markings of your wings to also be crimson."

"Lovely." Her mind began to buzz, as if someone spoke just outside the correct wavelength. Unconcerned, Zhulija drew Dario down for another kiss, just as a hand landed on each of her shoulders. Startled, she drew back; Dario had also jerked, but his grip on her tightened as they both sought the cause of the unwelcome interruption.

Queen Dianathke stood to one side, a hand on each of them, with Queen Maerovana on their other side in the same position. The two queens spoke as one, their combined voices rolling like thunder through the great hall.

"I accept the true mating of Lady Zhulija and Lord Dario, and from this day forth, claim them both as my subjects. They have marked each other, exchanged ritual blood, declared their acceptance of each other as true mates and danced the Rhynfallia to its shared conclusion. They are one in our sight and our service."

The buzzing in Zhulija's mind crystallised into clarity as soon as the two queens finished the marriage declaration and fell silent. Her thoughts were invaded by a shout: *"Zhu's mine and I'm hers!"* She winced, followed the line of speech back to its source.

"Dario?"

Zhulija? You can hear me!" Her mind rang with the power of his internal voice as Zhulija nodded. Dario hugged her tight.

Beside them, Zhulija saw the two queens share a satisfied smile.

12

DARIO

"Dario, can you believe the queens gifted us Garadenya Island?"

Zhulija and Dario stood in the turret's highest room overlooking the driveway. Said driveway and its flanking grounds hosted a chaotic spread of fae – dancing, laughing, screeching and yodelling at the moon. No one seemed to care who was Seelie and who was Unseelie.

"No, I didn't expect something as wonderful as that." Dario breathed in an exquisite lungful of honeysuckle and Zhulija. At the end of the driveway, the estate gates opened to the centre of the bridge across the River Rubiconia. Turning left led to Unseelie territory and right to Seelie lands. The queens' generosity, coupled with their joint claim of ownership of both Zhulija and himself, meant both of those directions led to home. They were no longer simply a Seelie lady and her Unseelie lord, they were both. "It comes at a price though."

"One we agreed upon." She turned her head to meet his eyes. "You don't regret becoming agents for the combined crown of the faelands? That we are the border force for both Seelie and Unseelie?"

"Regret it?" Dario shook his head. "Absolutely not. It was a brilliant manoeuvre. They've been unable to decide how to deal with this castle athwart the river on no-man's land for centuries. Our mating will help to bridge the cultural divide between the Seelie and Unseelie sects, making the term 'no-man's land' obsolete. As a group, our joint families make this region strong and none of us want to see any resumption of the inter-fae wars of 50 years ago. Our queens know we're loyal to the Linked Crowns because they saw inside our minds at the conclusion of our Rhynfallia."

"As we did each other." Stretching, Zhulija pressed a kiss to Dario's lips. "Will you mind not inheriting the Eribifax Estate? Now it's been transferred to Vinaya and Mycostat after Lady Catocala?"

He sighed. "I cannot deny I love that estate; I grew up there, it was my home and I will miss it. Just as you will miss the home where you grew up."

She tapped his nose. "What about the reparations I am owed?"

Dario flung his arms wide. "You have me; I'm your reparation."

"That's all I get?" Zhulija pouted.

His mouth dropped open, then closed with a snap as she dissolved into laughter.

"Cheeky little minx." He was grinning.

"I'm releasing you from the debt."

Dario wrapped his arms around her again. "Zhu, my sweet, I'll happily spend the rest of my life ensuring you achieve appropriate reparations."

She frowned. "What's your idea of appropriate?"

"I'll let you know when we reach that point." He rubbed his thumb along her bottom lip. "But here, we won't have to buck years of tradition. It's exciting that as the first Duke and Duchesse of Garadenya, we can create our own traditions, find our own way."

"I like the sound of choosing our own path to the future. Shall we start now, beloved?" Looking at him from under her lashes, she licked his thumb, then sucked it into her mouth.

"What a delightful idea, my darling." He slipped his thumb free to taste her lips again. Moving on, he kissed her cheek, her eyelids, her brow; slowly ran his hands down her back to her waist and paused. "Have I told you how delectable you look tonight? I adore the way the top of this dress cups your breasts, then spreads into that puffy high and low skirt over your sexy heeled boots … I want to peel the top down, flip the skirts up and have you lock those boots around me."

"Oh! Goodness. There's my beast." Zhulija's cheeks swamped with colour.

"You're blushing, sweetheart." He nibbled a soft kiss to the side of her neck, then hesitated. "Would I be wrong in thinking you innocent in the art of love and sex?"

"Not wrong at all. There was no one I was attracted to."

"Erm. Okay." Dario's throat rippled. "I can go slow, but ah, how slow would you like? What if I … Do you know … Perhaps I should explain …" He floundered to a halt as she let out a happy trill of laughter.

"Oh Dario." Zhulija nuzzled his jaw. "I know how everything works; I just need a little practice."

Grinning, he opened his arms wide. "Here you go. I volunteer for practice." He choked when his novice mate flattened her hand against his erection and rubbed, feeling and shaping with a firm grip. He pushed into her grasp as pleasure flooded him. "Uh, wow. Perhaps we should move on to something else."

"Y-you don't like my touch there?" Zhulija caught her bottom lip under her fangs as she studied him from under her lashes.

"I like it too much, Zhu." His confession rewarded him with her sunny smile. "Continue and I would finish very quickly. I want us both fully engaged here."

"What do you suggest then?"

He reached for the buckle of his sword belt. "Let's work together undressing. Look how my belt releases." He re-clasped it and let Zhulija undo the tricky buckle before placing his sword belt carefully against the wall. He stripped off his tabard and tossed it, after her nimble fingers made quick work of the triple-grouped side strings.

Shown the hidden ties of his shirt, Zhulija released them, allowing the shirt to gape as she patted his chest. Reaching around her, Dario grappled with the hooks of her gown. Becoming distracted when she rubbed her hands across his abs, stroked his nipples, then kissed and licked from one side of his chest to the other, he shivered.

She sighed. "Mmmm."

Growling, he clenched his hands in the fabric of her dress. "Wait." He was panting. "I don't want to rip this gorgeous outfit." She giggled, but stilled while he freed the gown. It slithered from her body to the floor, a dark cherry froth of lace, tulle and satin.

"By Queen Mab's … um, er …" Dario was riveted to the mouth-watering sight of his mate wearing her boots, tiny red lace underwear and no bra.

Zhulija was cupping her bare breasts with a wicked grin. "No dead queens here, last time I looked. I believe these are my breasts, Dario, I hope they'll do instead." There was her cheeky, under-the-lashes glance again. He loved it.

"You're so beautiful you put the moon to shame – who needs Queen Mab?" He fitted his own fingers around her stunning breasts, thumbed the hardened nipples, before lowering his head to nuzzle, lick and suckle until she was gasping and mewling in his grasp. He dropped one hand to cup her sex, pushing at her underwear until Zhulija helped him dispense with them. Separating her legs, Dario felt Zhulija arch upwards to meet the fingers he slid into the heated, luxurious wetness awaiting him.

"Dario, oh!" Writhing in his arms, she rubbed her breasts against his broad chest and moved around his massaging fingers. When her mouth flowered hot against his, their bodies snug, he took the opportunity to lower her to the soft velvet coverlet spread out and waiting. He crawled over her and his fingertips went back to working between Zhulija's outspread legs. Kissing her breasts again, he took turns drawing the tips into his hot mouth. She was shuddering in delight as his lips traced a smouldering path down her sweet body. Rimming her belly button with his tongue, tracing kisses over the line of one hip, he continued downward to the pearl centred above the entrance to her sex.

She went wild as he licked and sucked the hard little nub, his fingers still circling, dipping and massaging her inner passage. She bucked under him, then lifted her hips to grind against his marauding mouth and skilful hand. His tongue kept flicking and swirling until she exploded into a shivering, shaking, gasping paroxysm of pleasure. He continued to kiss and lick and love her through the aftershocks, until she stilled, eyes closed.

Rolling to one side, Dario finished removing his boots and trousers.

"Dario?" Zhulija stirred, opening one eye.

"Just taking the rest of my clothes off, darling." He returned, sliding up and over her body, taking pleasure in the friction of his chest against her swollen breasts. "Are you okay, my sweet Zhu?"

"Yes, let's do this; I need you, Dario."

Their mouths met, her tongue there to greet his. *"With pleasure, my Zhu."*

He rubbed his erection against the damp swollen folds between her legs, eased himself inside her gorgeously firm channel. Shivering at the marvellous sensations of tight, wet heat, he pushed forward and felt the gasp of breath explode from her mouth when her innocence gave way. Dario paused, deepening their kiss, sliding his hands up to play with her nipples and give her the time to adjust, even though it was torturous to stop so close to nirvana.

"This feels amazing, Dario."

Zhulija finally reached to cup his bottom and urge him on. Unable to stop himself, he thrust until his erection was totally swallowed and they both cried out in wordless delight.

"Are you okay, sweetheart? Any pain?"

"I'm fine, better than fine. More please."

Wasting no time, Dario pulled back then pushed forward again. Zhulija rose eagerly to meet him, tilting her hips so he slid even deeper. They gasped and Zhulija flexed the muscles of her sex around his erection, wiggling beneath him in playful experimentation. That wrecked Dario's control. His next thrust was faster, the pleasure escalating each time he drew away and plunged back to fill her. They rocked in a sea of overwhelming sensual enthusiasm, grappling to keep each other close, to love each other more, until Dario stiffened, feeling a roiling tsunami sizzle out from the base of his spine. He exploded in fierce thrusting pleasure, against her, inside her, surging to a completion he'd not expected in his wildest dreams. He felt Zhulija's muscles clamp tightly around him, before a low gasping cry left her lips and she joined him, shaking with her own release.

"HAPPY VALENTINE'S DAY, MY DARLING." Dario leaned in to kiss Zhulija on the lips, just as Vinaya and Mycostat completed their wedding ceremony with a kiss. His sister and Mycostat were definitely in love, but they didn't have the 'true mate' connection that he and Zhulija had found. True matings were rare; everyone rejoiced when they did happen, but love matches were equally accepted, and Dario was happy for Vinaya and Mycostat. They'd still dance the Rhynfallia but they wouldn't be rewarded with the divine inner connection he and Zhu had found.

Zhulija cocked her head. "I am curious about one thing."

"Only one?" He waggled his eyebrows. "The world is full of curiosities." He bent, chuckling as she poked his ticklish ribs; something she'd discovered during the night. He'd found a few interesting erogenous zones on her body also.

"It's the gift of the key you gave me." She raised her own eyebrows. "What's it for?"

"Ah." He nodded. "Come, I'll show you." He escorted her from the rose garden, around the back of the Eribifax mansion and along a path between a pair of tall hedges. To one side of a small lake, a gazebo glistened. "Your key opens this replica of your gazebo studio. I had it constructed for your usage when you were here."

"You believed I would move here after our mating?"

He shrugged. "I wasn't sure. I knew we would have to work hard to cope with the Seelie/Unseelie aspect of our relationship, so I thought that we might alternate between here and either your father's property or somewhere of our own in the Seelie lands. I was going to discuss it with you in order to achieve mutually acceptable arrangements."

Her face softened with love for him. "Could you be any more perfect?"

Colour darkened his cheeks. "I'll do my best."

"Too bad my new studio is now in the wrong place." Her mouth drooped.

"You still need a studio." Dario grinned. "I'll have no trouble getting it transplanted to Garadenya Island, my love."

"Oh, yes!" Zhulija clapped her hands. "That's wonderful."

He cupped her chin in his palm. "Promise me one thing."

"And that would be?"

"We come from different worlds, so from time to time we will experience difficulties."

She nodded. "I can't argue with your logic."

"Promise me we will always talk things through, find answers we can both relate to."

"Yes, I agree to that." She tilted her head to kiss his fingers. "A wonderful idea, my Unseelie Beast."

"I pledge you the same, my Seelie Darling."

Her smile warmed his heart. He kissed her ravishing mouth until they were both panting.

She licked her lips. "I have an idea."

He eyed her, wondering how soon they could return home for more loving; he felt in a constant state of arousal around her. "Yes?"

Zhulija reached into the valley between her breasts and withdrew her key. "Let's go check out my gazebo. We can test how well the door locks." She winked at him. "From the inside."

He reached to run a finger along her bottom lip. "What a delightful idea."

"I thought so."

Grinning, Dario swept his mate up and settled her into his arms as he raced for the gazebo.

The End.

♥

AUTHOR'S NOTE

Dear Reader,

Thank you for reading Zhulia and Dario's story. I hope you enjoyed it. If you'd like to find out what happens next, then I recommend Cherith and DeMaksim's story!

Find it in:

A Perfectly Paranormal Halloween

Reader reviews are wonderful, so if you did enjoy the story, please leave a review. It will be gratefully appreciated.

If you wish to know more about me, I have a website:

www.hellucywrites.com

ABOUT HELLUCY

Meet Hellucy Howe, a Book Dragon who teethed on romantic fairy tales and went on to voraciously devour anything paranormal. Writing was also second nature but became something to do in secret when the stories of her young child mind were ridiculed. Homes were populated with books and hidden caches of story notebooks inspired by a fertile brain and a massive creative streak.

She became a Professional Reader and a Closet Scribbler, convinced no one would want to look at the mad ramblings of someone who hates getting dirt under her fingernails and knows ironing was invented as a torture method.

Nowadays, Helen loves inventing paranormal and fantasy romance from the comfort of her cosy study with a hot cup of tea beside her laptop and her little spaniel, Lexie, snoring at her feet. With her anthology contribution of 'Filigree and Fate', Helen was dragged kicking and screaming from her closet, into the deer-in-headlights world of being a Real Author.

And if you want to get to know the Perfectly Paranormal Anthology authors a bit more, get sneak peeks of what's coming up for the APP Anthologies, as well as giveaways, special offers and just some PNR fun, then join our Perfectly Paranormal Paramours Facebook Group.

Find us here:

ACKNOWLEDGMENTS

With sincere and profuse thanks to my fellow authors, Leisl, Marnie and Sam, for their assistance, technical know how and continuous encouragement. You're all very wonderful to work with and I'm blessing my lucky stars to have been included in the group. The publication of our anthology, with my story included, is a dream I'd never expected to achieve – so glad to be proved wrong!

LOVE CURSED

LEISL LEIGHTON

LOVE CURSED

A Gods Cursed Novella
Book 1

❧

Leisl Leighton

Published by Leisl Leighton as Permien Press. For more information, email: leisl@leislleighton.com

First published 2021 in the A Perfectly Paranormal Valentine Anthology. Rewritten and republished 2022 as a single title novella by Permien Press.

Cover design – Samantha Marshall; Editor – Marnie St Clair

ISBN: Ebook: 978-0-6451089-5-8; Print: 978-0-6451089-6-5

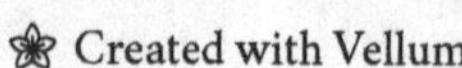 Created with Vellum

ABOUT LOVE CURSED

A love across time, cursed to stay apart ...

Coven librarian, Juliana Stevens, jokes about being cursed. Cursed to fail at love, to fail her family, to fail at being a witch. But after finding an old diary that speaks of Gods and witches and an ancient Love Curse, she starts to realise it isn't a joke: she truly is cursed.

Even worse, if she does not go to Rome, uncover a secret spell, and be in the exact spot the hex was bound by midnight on Valentine's Day, her soul will continue to be cursed forever. Oh, and she must do it all with her soulmate who was bound by the same spell to never reveal himself to her, too.

Valentine's Day is supposed to celebrate Happy Ever After, but if Jules can't manage to access her magic and find the man she's been kept from for thousands of years, it's going to be Happy Never After forever more.

To my Mum and Dad – you made me believe I could write and get published and let the stories in my heart take shape. Love really can do impossible things.
Thank you.

CHAPTER 1

"Would you like a drink, Julianna?"

"Umm …" Jules blinked rapidly at Simon. Was she supposed to say yes, or no? The information on first dates she'd looked up online hadn't covered this scenario. It was at times like this she really wished she'd inherited her mother's talent for reading minds – although, if she'd inherited her mother's talent, she wouldn't be here. But longing for magic was as useless as longing to have her parents back, so she pushed that thought away as quickly as it had come and tried to read the answer in Simon's eyes.

He began to tap his foot when she didn't answer immediately, then said slowly. "A drink?" His eyes widened a little as he waited for her response.

Did that mean he wanted her to answer yes, or no? Hells, she was so lost.

"Oh, for Goddess-sake! Are you thirsty or not?" the voice in her head snarled.

She wanted to ignore the voice – it didn't seem particularly happy she was here – but it had a point. Her mouth was incredibly dry, so … "Yes? Please."

Simon smiled and stood. "Gin and tonic with a twist of lime good for you?"

Yuk. But would he offer that if he didn't think it was the right drink for this situation? Probably not, so … "Yes please."

A slight nod and another smile.

Another good guess. This was going great even if she did have to drink gin.

"I'll be right back. Make yourself comfortable."

She nodded, even though there was no chance she'd ever be comfortable on this particular sofa. It was overstuffed, hard and for some strange reason, covered in plastic.

Well, if he truly wanted her comfortable, maybe she didn't have to stay seated.

Jules stood, making a little ripping, sucking sound as the bare part of her legs separated from the plastic – why was it so hot in here? She shouldn't have worn this cream wool dress with its capped sleeves and pretty lace collar. Grandmama always said good wool was cool in summer, warm in winter, but right now, Jules simply found it stifling. But there was nothing else in her wardrobe that was date worthy.

She quickly sniffed at her armpits, hoping the hotness didn't equate to smelly sweat. Thankfully, all she smelled was a faint whiff of her deodorant. Thank the Goddess for that!

Maybe if she walked about a bit, it might help. Waving her hand in front of her face like a fan, she made a little turn around the room. Surely it wasn't rude to look around? She should have done a more thorough job when she'd researched date etiquette. But most of it had been about what date you could first kiss on and what date you could go to second base, who should pay if you went out and so on. Nothing was discussed about a first date where the guy cooked for you at his family home.

It was okay though. She hadn't yet given away that this was the first time she'd been on a date – pitiful given she was 28 – and Simon didn't seem to want to chuck her out right away, so that was a good sign. In fact, it seemed like the date was going well.

Date.

Her lips twitched into a smile and, clenching her hands to her chest, she did a little spin on the spot.

She was on a date. An actual date. And her date was making her dinner.

Would he kiss her? She hoped so. Or maybe not. Hells, she didn't know. But it was nice to think there was a chance of something like that happening even if she didn't particularly long for it to happen in the usual tingle-in-the-tummy, curl-the-toes kind of way.

Was that what she would feel if he kissed her? Or would his kiss be more like when Aunt Ophelia kissed her? The old woman had this thing about kissing on the lips which was a bit odd in a family not given to demonstrative hugging and kissing. But it wasn't even the kissing on the lips that was so bad, it was the fact Aunt O's lips were a curious and shudder-inducing combination of parchment dry yet somehow always sticky. Probably had something to do with the ten-tonne of lipstick she wore. Or the never-ending supply of lollies she munched on.

Thankfully Grandmama had stopped Aunt O from kissing Jules; or touching her as she had a want to do – she was a bit of a close talker – many years ago because her sensitivity to magic had got to the point it was noticeable, and, *"We must never let anyone else know of your affliction before we've found the cure!"* her grandmama had always lectured. Jules had always hated that lecture and not just because it was kind of pointless – it wasn't like she was about to go running around telling everyone about her affliction especially given who her family was and what it could mean if certain people in the community found out. No, she'd hated it because the great Violetta Stevens, grand Matriarch of the Stevens family and Melbourne Coven Leader, had kept her hope alive for so many years with her talk of a cure. But there was no cure. No hope. She would always be like this. And if her Grandmama couldn't face the truth of that, well, at least she could, no matter how much it hurt.

And, if she were to look on the bright side, Grandmama's protectiveness and the affliction had saved her from Aunt O's kisses, so, it wasn't all bad.

Although, right now, given nobody but Bas had touched her for years, she almost missed Aunt O's disgusting kisses.

Hells. She did want Simon to kiss her, if only for the aching need inside her to be assuaged. And if anyone could do it, it should be him. She hadn't had any unfortunate reactions to being in this room with him for the ten minutes they had sat chatting – well, he chatted and she listened. He did seem to love talking about his work; and she had to admit it was interesting hearing about the potions he created with the little bit of magic he had access to. Not that he'd put it like that. He'd made it sound like his magic was grand, but she knew better. She wouldn't be here if it was.

But that was by-the-by. Hearing about the kind of magical work he did filled in some gaps she didn't know she had in her knowledge base. The books and grimoires she worked with and catalogued in the Coven Library under Stevens House didn't mention small household spells like the ones he seemed so proud of. But the best thing was, that even though he spoke about magic, and she'd known coming here that he had access to very little, there didn't seem to be any around him at all. She hadn't even felt a tingle from him when he'd sat on the couch right next to her after taking her cardigan. She also hadn't felt a tingle of anything else looking into his handsome face with his hair slicked back like some mobster from the twenties and a superior smile twitching on his lips as he bragged about his latest stain-removal feat.

Probably not a great sign given this was a date, but beggars couldn't be choosers.

The Council would never countenance her dating anyone outside of the magical community but given her affliction, she couldn't date anyone inside of it, so she'd always been stuck. But after hearing Grandmama complain about him and his family and their ebbing magical abilities and how the rest of the Council were on a mission to oust families that were not pulling their weight, she knew this could be her chance.

She might not want another date with Simon – especially if he kept looking at her as he'd done when she'd arrived, like he was about to win a prize. He had no idea she was no prize despite her family name and their standing in the magical community – but she wasn't about to explain that to him. It certainly wouldn't be a tick in the right column at this early stage.

"Here you go, my dear. Let me know if it's too strong."

She took the proffered drink and sipped obediently, trying very hard not to gag as the horrid taste of juniper and alcohol filled her mouth. Thankfully, he'd made a very weak gin and tonic, so she was able to swallow it and not spray the mouthful all over his beautifully pressed suit. "It's lovely," she said, smiling up at him.

"You know, gin is what prostitutes used to drink. It was cheap and rotted their brains, so their job was at least bearable."

She widened her smile, still trying to ignore the voice in her head. Not that ignoring it had ever done any good. The voice came to her more and more this last couple of years. Perhaps her affliction was also driving her insane.

"You're saner than he is. Do you think he thinks looking at you like that is charming?"

Oh Goddess. Simon *was* looking at her funny. Did she have a maniacal grin on her face? She pressed her lips together and looked away, her gaze lighting on the humongous and ugly portrait that hung over the mantlepiece. "This is … astonishing."

Simon's gaze immediately swung to the portrait. "Yes, isn't it? We're very proud of it. Mother commissioned it a few years ago and Armando Sinclair himself came to do the drawings. He's a 'normal' but is very talented."

She nodded knowingly even though she had no idea who Armando Sinclair was – obviously someone well-known in stuffy circles going by the expression on Simon's face and his air of general satisfaction as he gestured at the portrait. "It's very … lifelike. I almost feel like your mother's eyes are following me." She hid a shudder.

"Yes, it's a feature of Armando's work. He likes to draw the viewer into the painting. See how the smile on her face almost says, 'come to me'."

"More like 'run far away, little peasant'."

Jules choked back the urge to laugh as she said to the voice in her mind, "*Not now, please. You can talk as much as you like later. Just not now. I don't want to ruin this. If things go well, I'll have a date on Valentine's Day. I might not ever get another chance.*"

An aggravated sigh was her only answer.

"*Thank you.*"

"*You won't thank me if you stay much longer with this pillock.*"

She clapped her hand against her mouth to stop the snort of laughter from erupting.

"Julianna? Are you okay?"

"I'm fine. Drink just went down the wrong way."

He frowned at her. "Perhaps I did make it a little strong. Here, let me fix it."

He took the drink from her – she hoped by some miracle he might not bring it back – then just as he went to turn, a bell sounded from the next room.

"Ah, our dinner is ready. Let me show you to the table and I'll get it for us."

She allowed him to take her elbow and lead her into a formal and very stuffy blue and gold dining room – Goddess! Did they think they were living at the Palace at Versailles? – and then stood as he pulled out a chair at one end of the table.

"Sit here and I will be right back with our Pasta al tomato and our Salad al Verde."

"*What language does he think he's parroting?*"

Jules held onto her snort only as long as it took the door to slap shut behind Simon.

"*He's an idiot,*" the voice said.

"*Be nice.*"

"*Hard to in the face of such idiocy. You can't seriously consider going on another date with him?*"

"*Maybe.*"

"*Well, then, you'd be the idiot. Especially given the fact you have someone so much better waiting in the wings.*"

Jules snorted. "*If that were true, I wouldn't be here.*"

"*If only you could see. He's waiting there for both of us. He's—*" The voice cut off with a choking sound as pain, sharp and icy, spiked through her head.

"Ow!" she gasped, clutching at her head as the kitchen door swung open and Simon entered with a tray covered with a large and very shiny metal cloche.

"Ta-da. Our dinner is served." Thankfully he was too busy looking at the cloche to notice she was in pain.

She quickly dropped her hands and said, "Yummy," trying her best to cover the fact her eyelid was still twitching from the pain echoing through her head. Perhaps she should go and get her head scanned – these attacks were getting worse and worse.

"*It won't help,*" the voice said, the sound of it not much more than a whimper.

"Shut up and go away."

"I beg your pardon?" Simon had stopped a few feet away from the table, his handsome face marred by outraged surprise.

Damn it. Had she said that out loud? "Sorry," she said quickly. "I was talking about my phone. I must have left it on in my handbag in the other room."

"Your phone? I can't hear it ringing."

"Oh, can't you. Well, that's good then. Shall I help you with this?" she said, standing so abruptly she knocked the chair over.

"Careful!" Simon shouted as she made a grab for it, catching it before it hit the floor. "Mama would be extremely annoyed if those chairs were damaged. She hunted for months for just the right shade of blue in the tapestry seat and just the right honey in the wood and ended up getting them shipped from a monastery high in the Austrian Alps. They are very expensive."

She gingerly put it back in place. "If they are so expensive, should we even eat in here?"

"Of course. Where else would I entertain Julianna Stevens, granddaughter of our Coven Leader?"

"Where else indeed. And please, it's Jules."

"Really?" His tone and the tightening of his mouth suggested what he really meant was 'It's so … common'. But to his credit, he rallied, and with a nod to her seat, said, "Sit please … Jules. Let me serve you then we can chat and get to know each other better."

She sat back in the chair very carefully and waited as Simon served the pasta – tomato and basil from the smell. He grated parmesan over it without asking her if she wanted any – she did, but twice the meagre amount he'd put on – then placed it down in front of her with a flourish. He then served her a small plate of salad – a few lettuce leaves with a few pieces of tomato and basil and way too much balsamic dressing from the smell and the drenched look of the leaves – and then, after serving himself, took a seat at the other end of the twelve-seater table.

"Bon appetito," he said and tucked in.

"*Idiot*," the voice muttered, making her snort just as she lifted her first mouthful to her lips. A piece of tomato-soaked pasta dropped from the fork, hit her breast and ran a snail-trail down the front of her cream dress.

"Damn," she muttered.

"Oh, you are a klutz," Simon said. "But here, let me fix that for you. I've been working on a new cleaning spell for just this occasion."

"No, don't—"

But it was too late, he'd released the small spell. It hit her square in the chest, fizzed around her for a moment as if it wasn't going to work and then,

BANG!

Her allergy to magic reacted forcibly. The table in front of her blew up and she was thrown back by the force of the explosion, tomato pasta and salad flying everywhere. She hit the wall with a loud smack of breaking plaster, wood and crockery. Her head hurt from where it had impacted with the wall, but that pulse of pain wasn't as bad as the smarting cuts that sliced her skin everywhere the magic touched her or the nausea roiling in her stomach. She slid down the wall and fell onto her hands and knees, heaving everything she'd eaten in the last half day onto the floor. Somewhere in her mind she was conscious of a voice screaming obscenities.

She managed to look up and across the room.

Simon was trying to extricate himself from a tangle of broken chairs while swearing and screaming like a banshee.

She pushed groggily to her feet and staggered over to him, wanting to help, muttering as she went, "Sorry. So sorry. I didn't mean to ... I can't help it ..." She managed to help him get free of the chairs.

Simon rolled to his side, pushed to his feet and staggered away from her. "That was you?"

"Yes. In part. I'm allergic to magic," she blurted out.

"You ... what? You're magically disabled?"

"Oops. Cat's out of the bag now. Too bad, so sad."

But she barely heard the voice in her head because Simon was looking at her like she was some kind of monster. "A witch who is allergic to magic? Why ... Your family should never let you out of the house! It's criminal. I would never have ... look at what you've done!"

Face hot with her anger and chest heaving, she couldn't stop herself from saying, "It was partly your fault. You shouldn't use magic on others without first asking permission."

"I ... You ..." His mouth opened and closed like a guppy, bits of pasta and tomato falling from his head as he shook his fist at her. "It wouldn't have been a problem if you weren't an abomination. Get out! Get out of my house. I will be seeking reparations from your grandmother, that I promise you. You haven't heard the end of this!"

There were things she should have said to him – he was being very rude when it was half his fault – but what was the point? She wouldn't win him over and besides, her grandmama would cover this up by fixing the damages and wiping memories. She only wished Violetta could wipe her memory because she'd love to forget this disaster. And the dream she'd had that for this once, she wouldn't be alone and loveless on Valentine's Day.

Jules turned, shoulders slumped, arms wrapped around herself. She should have known better than to try for something close to normal. She grabbed her bag from the other room, limped out the front door and only hoped she wouldn't bump into anyone she knew before she could get home and out of her tomato, basil and blood-soaked dress and have a shower. It was going to be embarrassing enough having to explain this to her grandmama without having to deal with anyone else seeing her as well. And Bas wouldn't be pleased. She'd have to avoid him until morning when he was back in his cat form. Pity. She could do with one of his hugs right about now but that would have to wait until tomorrow night when he was in his human form again and she'd made certain he wouldn't go after Simon.

Her lip wobbled and she swiped at the tears that fell down her cheeks. Why did her life have to be so complicated and difficult?

Thankfully, the voice remained silent. Good. She really couldn't deal with it right now.

CHAPTER 2

"**B**astien? Where are you?"

"Shh." He poked his head out of his room to wave Tamuel, his cupid 'brother', in from the hallway. Despite being blind in his human form, he could still see the cupid's aura shining in the darkness of the hallway due to the enormous power he held, jewel bright with greens and purples and yellows and vibrating outwards. "Tighten your hold on your powers. Jules is asleep in the room next door."

"At this hour?"

"She went to bed early with a headache. I don't want to wake her."

"No. I imagine you don't."

He nodded at his old friend. There was no way Jules could know what they were up to. Too much was at stake if they wanted this to work.

And he needed it to work. He'd lived without hope for so long. The unbinding of the curse that had made his life a living hell for almost 2,000 years had seemed nothing but a pipe dream for so long.

A pipe dream tied to a small loophole once every 200 years on Valentine's Day Eve.

A loophole that had seemed beyond his grasp when one after

another reincarnation of Lianna barely acknowledged he was alive, let alone had the curiosity to question the nightmares they endured and the fact they reacted badly to magic. They'd just … accepted, Lianna's spirit pushed so far down inside them by the curse that he could do nothing about the silent screaming he sometimes thought he heard from her.

But Jules was different from all who came before, and her birth and the fact Tamuel had found the journal had—

"Where do you want me to drop the boxes?" Tamuel asked.

"In the library—no! Don't use your magic here. You'll hurt Jules – I can't believe you'd forget."

"I didn't forget. But she's not in this room – you never said she was *that* sensitive."

Bastien shrugged. Violetta could barely even touch her grand-daughter now for fear of Jules's magical sensitivity reacting to the power just under her skin. He never thought he'd be grateful the curse had taken his power, but at least it allowed him to touch her. She was rarely ever touched by anyone anymore. "It's been getting worse."

"A sign?"

He shrugged again. Tamuel's guess was as good as his. "We also don't want Violetta sensing you were here when she gets back. She's not expecting you to arrive with the shipment until next week – you're supposed to be stuck in Rome." Tamuel's well-constructed role of magical artifacts dealer, Tomaso di Erosi, alongside a friendship he'd struck up with Violetta and her deceased husband many years ago, had helped as a cover for why he was around so much, but it wouldn't explain why he was here now at this hour or why he had the journal they needed Jules to 'find'.

"Here – take my arm. I'll lead you downstairs," Tamuel said.

Bastien brushed his friend's arm aside. "I might be blind in this form, but I know my way around this house and the library better than you – I have lived here ever since Tamara Stevens built it 150 years ago."

"Of course. Lead the way."

He made his way out into the hall, down the stairs, across the foyer to the door that led to the library that lay in secret underground caverns deep below Stevens House. He led Tamuel down the four flights of stairs, their footsteps echoing off the stone walls and arched ceiling. The sound changed as they stepped into the huge library at the end of the stairs, disappearing in the high arches of wood and stone overhead and the stacks that filled the multiple rooms that made up the library.

He didn't bother to turn on the lights in the massive chandeliers overhead. He certainly didn't need the light to get around and Tamuel had the eyesight of a cupid so didn't even need to use his magic to light his way.

As he moved into the cavernous space of the library, there came a rustling from the far corners and a rushing pressure – the ghosts of Stevens House coming out to protect what was theirs from intruders. "It's just me," he said. They immediately settled down and went back to whatever they did when they weren't haunting someone or protecting the library.

"So it's safe to teleport the boxes in now?" Tamuel said, bringing Bastien's attention back to the job at hand.

"Yes. There's enough stone and dirt between us. Jules won't be affected. And any leftover magic will be syphoned into the magical ark that Violetta created to protect Jules from the latent magic in many of the books, so she won't sense you used any down here."

"Clever." There was a light thump as the load of boxes filled with old books, journals and manuscripts landed at the base of the steps. Good. Jules wouldn't miss them there. "What now?"

"Unpack half of the top box and put the books on the kitchen table in a pile with the journal on the top."

"The kitchen table?"

Bastien nodded. "Jules won't be able to ignore them. And when she sees the age of the journal, she won't be able to stop herself from reading it before she does anything else."

"Are you certain?"

Bastien raised his brow. "Does a cat love cream?"

"I don't know – do you?"

"Ha." He didn't bother mentioning that when forced into his cat body during the day, he never touched dairy – it made him feel a little ill now like it would a real cat. Not a good sign at all.

"Here, hold the journal while I take care of the rest."

Tamuel pushed an old leather-bound manuscript into his hands – Jules would be horrified neither of them were wearing cotton gloves to handle it. Even so, his fingers tightened around the soft leather binding. "Hello, old friend."

He'd spent many hours watching Esta write this journal, listening to her ponder what to put into it about the curse and what had happened to him and Lianna. It was meant to be a bridge between him and the Stevius family after she'd gone, to explain the curse – a curse that cruelly stopped him from talking about it and what had happened – and to ask for help in finding a way to break it.

But this journal was more than that. It was a history of their love.

Esta had written about how he and Lianna had met, how it had been love at first sight, how, despite Lianna's vows and his job as a cupid, neither of them had been able to do anything but give in to their desires. With one meeting of gazes in that crowded marketplace, he'd known she was his soulmate and they were destined for each other.

A fact that had made him the happiest cupid alive.

Until Clodia had used it against them to curse them.

If not for Esta, he would have lost himself to madness. But Esta had come back in secret after the dust had settled and found him, taking him to her family. Even so young, she'd had the power to bind him to her sister to keep him safe. The only thing she couldn't tell him was what had happened to his son. She went back to serve out her time with the Vestal Virgins, always on the lookout for information about the baby, but never found anything. He assumed the baby must have died in the explosion of power, his soul and body mercifully taken to the heavens. It was an eternal grief, one that the years had only dulled.

Years later, when Esta had finally been released from her 30 years of service, he'd thanked her for all she'd done by vowing to always be a guardian to her and her family. Not a selfless vow given he wanted to be close when Lianna was reborn into her family line as all witches were every few hundred years.

Unfortunately, knowledge of why he was cursed, and how he came to be bonded to the Stevius family, died with Esta's great-great-granddaughter when the journal he now held in his hand was lost in a house fire – or so he'd thought. Hope had died, little by little with every century that passed and nobody questioned what forced him to live as a cat by day, blind man by night or caused him extreme pain if he ever tried to talk about any of it. Pain that only got worse if he ever tried to be more than a guardian towards Lianna's reincarnations.

Life had become monotonous and hopeless until Tamuel found him a century ago and told him he wanted to help. He would never have thought a fellow cupid had it in them to care about anything other than their job, but Tamuel had proved to be different. He'd said that all curses were a horrifying cruelty, a wrong that needed to be righted if they could. Not only that, but he'd also had much to say about how wrong it was that Eros had never tried to break the curse binding his son – and one of the greatest cupids of his time – keeping him from his soulmate.

It had given Bastien hope; hope that had grown with Jules's birth. It was like Lianna was more alive in her than ever before. And somehow, he was more than a guardian to her. They were best friends.

It would be different this time. It had to be.

He took in a deep breath. "This is going to work," he said to Tamuel.

Tamuel put his arm around Bastien's shoulder. "Yes, it is. I'm certain of it. It's long past time this curse was ended."

Bastien swallowed hard. "Yes, it is."

Tamuel squeezed his shoulder and then turned back to his task. A few moments later, he asked, "Does it matter where on the table I put these?"

"No. Anywhere will get her attention. She has this thing about books and food—" He whipped around at a sound coming from upstairs, his hand going out to slap against Tamuel's chest. "Did you hear that?"

"What?"

There was another shuffling thunk and a curse. "That. Jules. She's moving around upstairs."

"How can you tell it's her? I can barely hear anything."

"She just swore under her breath."

"You really do have the hearing of a cat."

"Can you finish up down here without me?"

"I think I can manage such a difficult task by myself," Tamuel said.

Bastien ignored the sarcasm and ran to the stairs.

"Wait!" Tamuel called out.

He stopped. "Shh. She'll hear you."

"Sorry."

"Well? What did you stop me for?" He really needed to get upstairs. Jules sounded like she was limping. And was that blood he could smell? And tomatoes? What the hell?

"The journal." Tamuel held out his hand, pointing to the book clutched against Bastien's chest.

He couldn't believe he'd forgotten he held it. It would have been a disaster if Jules had seen it in his arms. The curse would never let him hand over information to her so easily. As it was, even helping Tamuel to set up the journal for Jules to find caused a burning sensation in his chest that wasn't exactly pleasant. "Here." He put the journal down on top of the boxes Tamuel had magicked in minutes ago then took the stairs two at a time.

He burst out of the stairwell into the foyer and stopped. Jules wasn't in the foyer – there was no sign of her blue and green aura with its dark heart of amethyst glowing in the cavernous space. But she was close. Her presence called to him like a beacon, especially when something was wrong.

And there definitely was something wrong.

CHAPTER 3

The scent of blood and tomatoes – and basil – mingled with the scent of vanilla and cinnamon that was purely Jules. It led towards the back of the house; not upstairs like he'd expected.

He moved quickly down the arched hallway, his feet padding softly on the polished floorboards. He followed the scent into the kitchen, circling around the large island bench and past the table, heading towards the laundry – and cursed when he tripped over something on the floor.

A handbag by the sound and feel of it. Strange. Jules had been brought up to always be neat and tidy so that the map of the house in Bastien's head wasn't disturbed by anything being out of place. The fact she'd just dropped her bag in the middle of the floor wasn't good. Also, why would she need a handbag if she'd just come down to the kitchen from her room to get something to eat? Had she been out without telling him?

His worry spiked. He picked the bag up and put it on the table, his hand coming away wet. He lifted it to his nose – tomatoes, basil and a hint of blood. "What the hell?"

"Hello?" Jules's voice wavered out of the laundry. "Is that you, Bastien?"

"Yes." He was long past being surprised that she could sense him in the same way he sensed her – another difference with this incarnation. "What's happened? What are you doing down here? You went to bed with a headache. I thought you were asleep."

"I spilled something on myself." Her voice was muffled then became clear. "I'm just putting it in the wash. You head up to bed. I can deal with this."

He got to the door just as the washing machine started up.

"If you spilled something, why can I smell blood?" He stopped in the doorway, taken aback by her aura – it was unsettled, vibrating wildly, colours flashing randomly as if she'd been shocked. That only happened when she was exposed to magic. "Jules. What the fuck happened?"

"Shh," she said, rushing towards him, her aura pulsing faster and incredibly bright – so bright he could see the entire outline of her body, including the wild mass of her curling auburn hair that swung down her back rather than being caught in the tight bun she usually favoured. "Stop shouting. I don't want Violetta to wake up."

"Your grandmama is out."

"Oh."

"What happened?"

"I don't want to say right now."

"Why not?"

"Because …" She flapped her hands around, the movement clearly visible inside her aura. "Because …" He knew her well enough to know she was trying desperately to think of something to tell him that wouldn't make him a) worried; b) get angry; or c) get her into trouble with her grandmama.

"Jules. You know I can see your aura, right?"

She slouched and made a squished sound of frustration. "Can explanations wait until after I've had a shower? I'm covered in pasta sauce—"

"And blood."

"And blood," she groaned. "You know, it's not fair you still have the senses of a cat even when you're in your human form."

"It makes up for the blindness."

She swore under her breath and touched his arm. "I'm sorry. That was mean of me. It's just—"

"You're in pain."

"Yes. And I wish you hadn't caught me like this."

She gestured again and he thought at first she meant covered in pasta sauce and blood, but then realised she must be standing there in only her underwear because she'd put her clothes into the washing machine. Swallowing hard against the familiar but inconvenient desire that surged through him, he said roughly, "Right. Shower and change, then explanations."

"If you insist."

"I do if you don't want to get Violetta involved."

"No, I do not. But please, promise you won't lecture me. I already know what I did was stupid."

He snorted. "I'll try."

He followed her upstairs and sat on the edge of her bed as she disappeared into the ensuite with her pyjamas. He wished now he hadn't insisted on moving his bed to the room next door years ago. He'd been happy to be there for her when she was young, but as she grew into adulthood, it was too hard. Courtesy of the curse, she just couldn't see him as anything other than a friend, and it was a constant ache, especially at night when he lay awake keeping watch over her as she slept.

He'd asked Violetta to make up some lore about him that said he must sleep elsewhere when his witch reached a certain age, and thankfully, Jules had swallowed it. Even so, there were times that he did stay in here with her. Especially when the nightmares made her scream and cry. Nightmares she could never remember once she woke but that he knew were memories of the last few months of Lianna's life and her death. Those nights, when he came in to hold her and stay with her to help her fall back to sleep were both the best and worst nights of his life. So close, and yet so horribly far away from what he knew they could be.

Given all that, it was absurd that sitting here now while she showered felt too intimate.

He shifted to the floor.

After ten minutes, the bathroom door opened, a cloud of steamy air billowing out into the room alongside the scent of vanilla and cinnamon – and a little citrus tonight. And underneath, the faint smell of blood. She'd obviously been exposed to magic. But how? The magic Tamuel had used would have been shielded by the layers of rock and soil between the house and the library, so that couldn't be it. "How badly did the magic lash you? Do you need to be bandaged up?"

"No. The cuts aren't bad."

"Cuts?"

She sighed and sat on the bed beside him, crossing her legs to face him. "I wasn't asleep in bed like you thought. I lied about the headache."

"Why?"

"I had a date."

"What?" The pain of that statement jagged through him, but he swallowed it down. "Who? Did you go to a magic club? Is that why you were bleeding? You know this is exactly why you can't go out with anyone in our community—"

"Whoa – you promised no lectures."

"Sorry – it's just ... I didn't expect you to do something like this."

"What? Try to be happy? Try to find love?" She sighed, her aura sparking around her in agitation. "I'm lonely, Bastien. The only friends I have in my life are you and grandmama and while I treasure both of you in my life, it's…"

"Not enough."

"Yes."

Oh Gods. If she only knew he was her soulmate, the one who loved her best in the world and that she loved him; was meant for him. But he couldn't tell her. Even thinking of it made pain stab through his head. He hid the pain though and reached out for her hands, holding them gently in his even though touching her always brought with it an aching pain of loss – his loss, her loss – and a simmering anger he'd never been able to put aside.

Fuck Clodia and her curse. If he ever got his hands on her, he would do worse than kill her, he would … He sighed internally. It was useless to rage about what he would do because he could do nothing – even if she wasn't long dead, his powers were bound by the curse.

Hopefully, once Jules had found the journal, he and Tamuel had planted, and read what was inside, she'd remember what she needed to do to break this curse. But he couldn't tell her any of it. All he could do was be here in whatever way she needed – and right now, she needed her friend. So, he swallowed the pain and asked, "Who is he?"

"Simon Smithson-West."

"Smithson-West? The cleaning specialist family Violetta was going on about last week because their magic is waning?"

"Yes. His magic is particularly weak so I thought he would be safe."

"Jules, you know better than that. No magic is safe."

"What am I supposed to do? Go out with a human?"

"Of course not." It was against their laws. Humans couldn't be trusted with knowledge of their world – too many bad things had happened in the past when they had become aware magical people and creatures lived among them.

"So, I'm just … what? Meant to live alone forever?"

"Jules." He pulled her forward and she tumbled against him, her arms going around him, holding tight. "I didn't mean—"

Jules shook her head against his chest. "No. Don't worry about it. It's not your fault I'm an abomination."

He stiffened. "Abomination?" He pulled away, wishing to all the Gods he could see her face because her voice was expressionless. "Who told you that? Simon?"

"He was angry—"

"That doesn't excuse him calling you that or using his magic on you." Of course that's what had happened – nothing else explained the blood and pasta sauce that had been all over her. "I'm going to kill him."

"No." She gripped his arms as if she really thought he was about to go and follow through on his words. "He's not worth it. Besides, he got punished enough with the backlash. It ruined his entire dining room." She snickered. "He'll be using his powers to clean that room for the next few weeks."

"Good." It wasn't enough. Not nearly enough. But there wasn't really anything he could do. It wasn't like he could realistically go around to the warlock's house to teach him a lesson – he couldn't go anywhere without a Stevens, tied to their bloodline like he was. And Jules would hardly drive him over there so he could castrate the bastard as he deserved. Abomination! He deserved more than castration, the donkey's arse!

"Why did he use his powers on you?" It wasn't something a powered person would usually do without permission – certainly not on someone from their community. The ramifications of doing so had caused blood feuds between families in the past, exposing them to humans – which was why it was pretty much outlawed to use magic on anyone without permission.

Jules sighed. "We were having dinner at his house – he cooked tomato and basil pasta. I dropped some on my cream dress and he offered to use his latest cleaning spell to fix the stain."

"He did more than offer."

"Yes, well, it's apparently a specialty of his and he was pretty enthusiastic and wanted to help and let the spell go before I could stop him." She screwed her mouth to the side again. "If you think about it, it was kind of gentlemanly."

Bastien snorted. "Even if that were true, from the sounds of it, he wasn't gentlemanly afterwards."

"Well, it's kind of understandable. The backlash that destroyed his dining room threw him across the room. He was hurt and upset, even more so when I blurted out my apologies about my magical allergy. He … lost his shit."

"Jules." He wanted to pull her back into his arms but she sat stiffly, holding herself apart – holding herself together? He could see in her aura the hurt she felt. He sidled closer and began to rub her back as she always liked, but she winced and he quickly stopped. "Sorry."

She grabbed his hand, pulled it back towards her. "No, don't stop. That felt nice."

"But you're hurt." It must have been bad for the backlash to have caused cuts on her back too.

"I'm fine. Just papercuts really. They'll heal in a few days. Just hold me until I fall asleep. Please?"

He did just that, lying down so she could cuddle into his side, and stroked her hair. He hoped she'd fall asleep well before sunrise when he'd need to leave her before the change took him over. She must have been tired because her breathing slowed within minutes, the tension easing out of her body as she fell asleep.

Soon, he'd be able to do this every night. She'd find the journal tomorrow and read it and then she'd know she was cursed, would know he was tied up in that curse too, and she'd want to break it. And even though it was cutting it close, with only thirteen days until Valentine's Eve, he knew she could do it. Not that there was any other choice – they couldn't have given her more warning than this or the curse could try to stop them. It had proved to be just that insidious over the years.

Thirteen days until they were both free.

Thirteen days until he could tell her everything he'd held inside for too long and share with her what had been stolen from them almost two millennia ago. For too long, Valentine's Day had signified a happy never after for them. But this year, he was certain it would be the first day of happy ever afters from here-on out.

It had to be.

CHAPTER 4

*J*ules yawned widely as she made her way down the stairs. She was so tired, even though she'd slept well until Bastien had left her this morning. That's when the nightmares had come. She shuddered just thinking about them. They sucked all the life and light out of a room.

Hang on. That wasn't a metaphor. There literally was no light around her.

Her foggy mind went into instant alert as it registered the stygian darkness.

Her breath, a heavy pant, echoed off the grey stone walls as she tried to swallow down rising panic, caught statue-like between one step and the next.

Don't be silly. It's just a stupid childhood fear.

"No it's not. No it's not. The nightmare's real. We're being buried alive."

She clutched her throat. *"Stop it. Stop it. That's not happening. It's not real."*

"But the dark! We hate the dark."

"Shut up. Just shut up and stop panicking and we'll be okay." Stupid internal voice! If it wasn't being sarcastic and unhelpful, it was filling her with unreasoning panic.

One step at a time – that's all she needed to reach the light switch at the bottom of the stairs.

And breathe. Breathing would be good.

She took a big breath. Then a step. Then another.

Her grandmama had obviously forgotten to turn on the lights when she came down earlier to do the magical part of her research before Jules started her hours in the library. She was usually so good about turning the lights on, even though she could use her witch lighting to light her way and didn't need the electric lights like Jules did. Violetta must have been super pre-occupied to have forgotten.

"Use the torch on your phone."

"I forgot to charge it last night. It's still in my bag in the kitchen."

"Oh, Goddess. Did the ceiling just move down a bit?"

"Shut up."

She really needed to do something about her internal voice. Only crazy people talked to themselves as if their internal voice was a different person.

"You're crazy to be walking into that darkness."

She ignored it and reached out, only a little relieved to feel the cold stone under her palm. She pictured the arcs of stone and wood that made up the ceiling. How high and solid they were, how when the lights in the sconces on the walls and in the chandeliers were on, the underground space felt airy and spacious despite the crowded stacks.

Keeping her hand on the wall, she carefully made her way down into the Coven library.

She loved the library.

"When it's lit."

She shuddered and made herself think about the work she so loved: working with her grandmama, upholding their family's grand tradition as keepers of the greatest works of magic in the Southern Hemisphere.

As she took the turn into the last stretch of steps, there came a rustle and whispering from the dark cavernous space below.

"What's that? Is the roof caving in?"

She swallowed hard. *"No."*

"Are we sure it's not the ceiling caving in?"

"Absolutely. You know it's just the family ghosts. They're harmless."

"That's what you think. Ghosts are never harmless."

"Well, they've never hurt me."

Bastien chose that moment to rub against her leg. She couldn't see him, his black fur at one with the darkness surrounding her, until he looked up, his peridot-coloured eyes a bright glow in the dark. Seeing them helped her fear retreat a little. She smiled. "I'm okay. You go and turn the kettle on for me."

He made a meeping sound and took off, taking his night-glow eyes with him.

"That was a mistake."

"No. I can do this." Just two more steps to the library floor, a few paces along the wall towards the kitchen to reach the light switch and …

"Yaahhh!" She tripped over, pitching forward to land smack on something that crumpled under her weight but had sharp edges that dug into her leg and side. "What the ever-loving—"

"Julianna dear, are you okay?" Her grandmama's voice came from deep within the stacks.

"I'm fine."

"Sorry, I forgot to turn the lights on. Be careful of the boxes at the bottom of the steps. We had a delivery from Tomaso last night and I haven't had a chance to move them."

"Right. Thanks."

"Could have had that warning 30 seconds ago!"

She pushed upright from where she'd landed on top of a box, rubbing her jeans-clad thigh where a bruise was likely blooming. Oh well, it would just add to the pinprick bruises she had all over her torso from last night.

"We promised Bastien we weren't going to think about that idiot again."

"Yeah, I'm trying not to."

"Try harder. Remember that he called you an abomination and magically disabled."

"He wasn't wrong."

"Coming from someone whose claim to fame is stain-removal spells ... really!"

"Yeah. But ... I'd so hoped to have a date for Valentine's Day finally."

"That won't happen until we overcome the curse – ow!"

She winced and rubbed her forehead wondering over her internal voice's use of the word 'cursed'. A Freudian slip? Had she subconsciously realised something her conscious hadn't?

Nah.

There was no way she was cursed – even though it would certainly explain a thing or two about her life. But it was ridiculous. Who would bother cursing her?

Not that she wanted to be cursed. Poor Bastien went through hell twice every 24 hours because of the curse that had been placed on him by some mysterious witch many centuries ago before he'd been taken in by her long-dead ancestor. Of course, the only reason they knew he was cursed was because curses were Violetta's research specialty. Nobody in the family had ever questioned what made Bastien turn into a cat during the day or why he was bonded to their family. He was just a family fixture. But Violetta had figured it out when she was in her teens and had worked since then trying to learn everything she could about curses to help him. So far, she'd discovered a curse could only be removed in three ways according to the lore – by the original castor; by finding a loophole within the original casting (there were often loopholes, according to Violetta); or by discovering where the spell was cast and casting a spell that was its opposite on a significant anniversary of the original casting.

Apart from that, all information about Bastien's curse remained elusive and the curse itself made it impossible for him to talk about the details.

But if anyone could find a way, Violetta would. Jules was certain of it.

She wished she could be the one to help him. More than wished it. Every part of her ached with the need to do something to ease his torment and find a solution, but apart from research, what could she do? It wasn't like she could help unbind the spell. Even if they found it, she would have to be a truly powerful witch to be able to unbind a curse that had lasted for centuries and she was far, far, far from that. She might be the most talented archivist and translator the Coven had known in over a century, but in truth, she was only a burden. If her grandmama hadn't spent so much time trying to discover why Jules was allergic to magic, then maybe she would have been able to discover how to help Bastien.

She sighed. Gods, she wished she could be the one to help him like he had always helped her. He was the only one who could from the moment her parents died in the car accident. The only one who could hold her when things got too much. Of course, there was a limit to even that because he had to leave her when his transformation drew near or hurt her with the magic of it. Without him, she felt lost and alone.

She'd hoped to change that with someone like Simon who might be able to be there for her in ways Violetta and Bastien couldn't.

But hoping and having were two very different things, as she'd been violently reminded last night. It seemed that love, like her magic, was something that remained out of her grasp.

She blinked rapidly, chewing on her lip. She wouldn't cry. Crying never made her feel better. Only work did that. Getting lost in a translation or cataloguing job always made the blues fly right away.

"To do that, you need to turn on the lights. Please."

"Right."

Grimacing, she patted her hair to make certain it was still in its neat bun, then ran hands over her favourite flower-print shirt with the capped sleeves to tuck it back into her jeans – damn. Was that a tear? No, just a loose button. Phew. She did it up, then backed carefully away from the mess of boxes she'd fallen over and felt along the wall.

The light switch was here somewhere.

There.

Light sprang to life from the wall sconces and chandeliers made from old twisting driftwood. Their bulbs lit up the arches of stone and wood with a cheery golden glow. She smiled, breathing in the smell of books – dust and leather and something else that made her yearn to learn everything she could from the words inside.

But before she could get on with her translation work, she needed to deal with the stack of boxes she'd tripped over.

She righted the fallen boxes, noting one of them was open. Half the books were missing from the box. "Damn it." Why couldn't the interns do what they were told? They knew not to unpack the boxes. Violetta had to check the new acquisitions for dark magic and then Jules had to sort them into piles – what needed to be translated, what could be catalogued and shelved, and what needed to be handled with kid gloves – literally.

Where could they have put the items they'd pulled from this box?

The kettle chose that moment to whistle. She turned to the kitchenette.

Stopped.

Bastien stood on the table sniffing at a stack of old books that had been piled there.

Bloody interns. "I don't care if Trevor and Marie are distant family, I'm going to kill them."

CHAPTER 5

"Who are you killing this time, dear?" Violetta asked, sticking her head out from the end of the stacks nearest the kitchen.

"Trevor and Marie," she grumbled, gesturing at the books that should never have been put on a surface people ate and drank at.

"Before you go about finding them and killing them, do you mind turning that kettle off and making a cup of tea?"

"Fine."

"I'll be right out. I just need to find one more thing." Violetta disappeared back into the stacks again.

Jules picked up Bastien, gave him a quick cuddle then made a pot, letting it steep as she got out Violetta's favourite bone-China teacup and a mug for herself. She quickly poured herself a tea, added two sugars and a good dollop of milk before her grandmama could see and give her the 'tea lecture'.

Turning back to the table, she eyed the books on the edge of it warily. Inched closer. She didn't feel any magic coming from them.

"That doesn't mean anything. Be careful."

Her internal voice was right. Some magic was tricky, especially dark magic.

"You shouldn't have unpacked them without me," Violetta said as she came out of the stacks. Her immaculate grey bob swung beside her still-lovely heart-shaped face, her dark brows furrowed as she joined Jules at the table. "Even though Tomaso said there was no magical texts, you know I like to check. I don't want you being hurt like last time."

"I didn't unpack them. Trevor or Marie must have done it last night before they left."

"It can't have been them," Violetta said, pouring herself a cup of tea. "The shipment didn't arrive until well after we'd all finished for the day." She tipped her head in that considering way of hers and moved closer to the stack of books and manuscripts, her long violet skirt swaying gently around her legs, the pearls and crystals around her neck making a little clacking sound as she walked.

"Your mother moved like that. Like a dancer."

"Did she? I can't remember that."

"Did you say something, dear?"

"Nope." She sipped her tea as her grandmama gave her the gimlet stare that made people tremble in their boots.

She looked down at her feet.

"You're wearing sneakers, not boots, so you're obviously safe."

"Thanks."

Violetta, eyebrow raised in a perfect arch, returned her attention to the books. "Who could have put these here? I didn't do it, did I, Bastien?" He shook his head. "I didn't think so, but it's good to be sure. You know how distracted I can get when doing my research. I wouldn't put it past myself to start unpacking the boxes without realising it." She tapped her chin in thought then said, "Why are you rubbing your hip like that?"

She turned to see Violetta frowning at her. "I didn't see the boxes and fell over one."

"Then why did you say you were fine? Honestly, Julianna, it doesn't do anyone any good when you lie about getting hurt. Do I need to call Doctor Pilar?"

"No! I'm fine." The last thing she needed was Doctor Pilar coming over and seeing the cuts and scratches all over her torso. He'd tell Violetta and then she'd get The Lecture. Although, she would definitely get The Lecture when she told Violetta about what had happened last night. She wished she didn't have to tell her grandmama about the embarrassing event – it was bad enough Bastien knew – but if she didn't want it getting around that she had no magic …

"It's lucky your grandmama is excellent at forgetting spells. Hopefully she'll wind a little something extra into his that will make him cower every time he so much as sees tomato or basil again."

"I don't want her to punish him."

"It's no less than he deserves."

"You don't mean that."

"Of course I do."

An image of Simon cowering before a stand of tomatoes at the supermarket spun into her mind, but no matter how gratifying it would be to see it, she couldn't allow it. What had happened wasn't truly his fault. It was hers. She'd been the one too desperate to find love. She had to face facts – it just wasn't going to happen for her. She had her grandmama, Bastien and her work. That would have to be enough.

She met Violetta's gaze and told her what had happened.

"Julianna! You should have told me the instant it happened. Not only should Dr Pilar have been called last night, who knows how many people Simon has told by now!"

"I doubt he's told anyone apart from his mother. The clean-up was extensive. Besides, I think he was hoping to blackmail you with the knowledge, so that wouldn't work if he told people."

"Julianna, that's not the point."

"It's exactly the point."

Violetta glared at her. "Well, I'm calling Dr Pilar just to check you out."

"Please don't. Bastien helped fix me up last night—"

"Bastien knew!" she said, glaring at the black cat winding around Jules' feet.

"I said I'd tell you this morning. And I have. You can now go and wipe Simon's memory – his mother's too if needed – but please don't do anything else. It was my stupidity that caused the problem. So please promise you won't do more than wipe the event from his memory." She stared down her grandmama's gimlet glare.

"Very well," Violetta said after a long, tense moment. "I will figure out the best spell and take care of it this afternoon."

"Thank you."

Violetta went to reach out but pulled her hand back before it could make contact. "Are you certain you're okay?"

"Yes. Please don't worry." She tried a smile, but it came out a bit wobbly, so she turned her attention to the books on the table. "All I want to do is get stuck into these. They look fascinating." She took a step closer to the end of the table the books were stacked on, tripped over the edge of a rug and lost her grip on her tea mug. It soared out of her hand, the tea flying out of the mug right towards the stack of old manuscripts, journals and grimoires. "No!" she cried as she hit the edge of the table.

"Watch out!"

Jules knew the cry wasn't for the books. She threw herself sideways, landing hard on the floor on the other side of the table as Violetta thrust her hands out, a small amount of power sparking around her. Jules pushed up and crawled around the kitchen island, trying to get further away from the magic that, even though minimal, was a thousand needles pricking her skin. Her stomach heaved.

She grasped for the bin just in time, vomiting up all her breakfast.

"Julianna, I'm so sorry. Are you okay?" Violetta stood above her, hands half stretched towards her.

"Yes. Yes. Don't worry about me. See, not even bleeding." She held out her arms. "I'm fine." She wiped her mouth. "What about the books?"

Violetta's mouth worked for a moment before she gave a little nod – thank the Goddess she wasn't about to carry on apologising about using magic around Jules. "I saved them." Violetta pointed across the room.

Jules pulled herself up and leaned, trembling, against the centre bench. Tea was splattered across the table, dripping off the edges, but thankfully the pile of old and fragile grimoires, journals and books had been transported across the room and sat in two piles on Jules's desk in the far corner of the room. "Thank the Goddess. I thought I'd ruined them. You see, that's why you never put books on the kitchen table!"

"Are you sure you're okay, dear?"

"Your transportation spell was minimal, so I'm fine. Stop fussing." She waved her hand and moved out from behind the centre bench, almost tripping over the rug just beyond it. Before Violetta could say anything, she said, "I just need to clean up here and then get back to work. I gather since you put those on my desk, there's no magic in them."

"I don't feel anything – which matches with Tomaso's assurances. You'll be safe from them at least."

"Grandmama."

Violetta's nostrils flared as she turned away and gestured to the boxes at the base of the stairs. "I didn't realise Tomaso was sending so many," she said airily. "They'll keep you busy for a while.

"I can't wait," she said, meaning it more than she'd ever meant it before. She needed to be distracted from the disaster that was her love life.

Violetta helped her clean up the mess of tea. Mindful that the older witch watched every movement, Jules hid the twinges of pain pinging all over her body. Finally, with a suppressed sigh, she rinsed the cloth then headed to her desk.

"Well, I'll leave you to it then. I've got a few things I want to finish here before I go and deal with Simon and his mother."

Her tone was so ominous, Jules felt compelled to say, "Grandmama, you promised."

Violetta sighed. "I know." She picked up her tea and walked back towards the stacks, her purple skirt swishing around her knees, crystals and beads clicking and clacking in an almost hypnotic rhythm as she went.

Bastien jumped up onto the desk and rubbed against Jules, meowing at her. Giving him a long stroke from head to tail, she turned to the books on her desk. "So, Grandmama is doing her work, how about I get stuck into mine?" Bastien meowed at her in response. She really wished she could hear him like other witches could with their Familiars – but she was not a normal witch, nor was he a normal Familiar – but it seemed to be an enthusiastic meow. "Which one should I start with?" He patted the oldest-looking journal on top of the pile to the left. "Good pick." It was the one she was most drawn to – its age calling to her along with the ancient Roman letters scrawled on the front.

"My Life of Magic in the Service of Vesta by Esta Stevius of the Vestal Virgin Coven," she translated.

Vestal Virgins! Oh Goddess!

A frisson of excitement chased over her skin. Shivering a little, she pulled on her cotton gloves before taking the journal to place it gently on the cradle in front of her.

"Now, what secrets do you have to tell me?" she whispered as she opened the leather-bound parchment.

Bastien, rather than sit in her lap as he usually did, perched on the desk, his gaze on the journal as if he meant to read along with her. She stroked her hand over his back as she started to read, but after a few pages, forgot all about him, lost in the unfolding story before her.

Images formed in her mind as she read, so real it was almost like she'd been there and seen it herself.

"You have."

"What?" Her heart thumped hard and fast in her chest.

"Read on."

"Okay."

Jules turned the page carefully, the cotton gloves startlingly white against the yellowing pages of parchment.

Her breathing came in little gasps as her eyes scanned the words, her brain doing an automatic translation.

Her nightmares. Her dreams. They were all here. On the pages of this ancient journal. How could that be?

She turned another page, her lips moving now as she whispered the words before she'd even translated them in her mind. She knew. She knew this. She'd heard it before over and over in her nightmares. She'd never remembered it until now, but she knew it was true.

The horror as Lianna Stevius, Vesta's chosen vessel for the powers she wished to give to humanity, was torn from her lover, from her child, cursed and buried alive.

She didn't need to read the words to know that was what had happened – she'd woken screaming from the horror nearly every night of her life, the memory of dirt raining down, choking her, darkness smothering her, gasping for breath until … until there were no more breaths.

Even though she knew where the story led, she couldn't stop herself from reading the words Esta Stevius had written 2,000 years ago about the punishment that turned the servant into a cat who'd been so kind to her and Lianna.

His name had been Bastieno.

Bastien.

Oh Goddess. Was this why he was cursed? Because he'd helped a Vestal Virgin be with her lover?

A Vestal Virgin whose memories had played in her dreams and nightmares all her life.

That could only mean … "No," she breathed, unable to believe it.

"Believe it. It's true."

"Lianna?"

"Yes."

She winced as pain spiked through her eye. But she couldn't stop herself from reading because she couldn't believe what was in front of her eyes.

The curse. Esta had written it down. She read it, lips moving over the words. Her skin prickled and hairs rose all over her body, but she couldn't seem to stop.

Bastien howled and struck out at her hand as she went to turn the page, then leaped at her as she rocked back in shock, his movement enough to make her chair roll back from her desk to smack into the wall a metre behind her.

"Julianna!" Violetta's voice, a panicked cry, rang out from deep in the stacks. The sound of running echoed hollowly, coming closer until Violetta burst out of the end of the stacks in the middle of the room, eyes wide, face filled with fear as she raced over to Jules. "Julianna. I felt magic. You're bleeding."

Jules looked down at her hand where a line of blood welled across the back of her hand. "Bastien swiped at me. He stopped me from reading the curse in that journal." She gestured at it, her mind swirling with images from her nightmares and dreams.

"Memories. Not dreams."

Violetta gasped. "Oh, my Goddess. Where did you get this?" She snatched up the journal. "Did you read this?"

Jules nodded slowly, still so shocked that she wasn't bothered by the fact Violetta had picked up the ancient journal without gloves on. "I don't understand. It's the dream. The nightmare. The one that's tormented me ever since I can remember. It's written in there. How can that be?"

Violetta's large name-sake eyes slowly rose to focus on her. "I was right. You *are* cursed, my dear."

"What? How did she know that?"

Violetta's words – and those of her internal voice – snapped her out of her stupor. "Don't be ridiculous. How can I be cursed? Who would bother to curse me?"

Violetta tapped the journal. "It's in here. I've only ever remembered the latter parts of my life as Esta – my most recent reincarnations are far clearer – but now, seeing this, I remember more. I know who you are."

Bastien made a sound of surprise, his head snapping up to stare at Violetta as if seeing her for the first time.

"He recognises her."

"Oh Goddess. Oh Goddess. It's true."

"I knew your soul was old. I just didn't realise how old. But this explains so much. I always wondered why you couldn't remember at least part of who you'd been – it's highly unusual for a reincarnated witch or warlock not to remember at least some of their past lives."

"No." Jules pushed up from the desk, took a step back. "I'm not an old soul. I don't carry that kind of power."

"Yes. You do. And you are. You were Lianna Stevius. And Bastien was …"

"The servant who helped the demi-god and Lianna be together."

Violetta frowned at her for a moment but then said, "Yes. I remember now. It's why he's always been bound to our family like he has. Why his curse has lasted this long. But now you've found this, now you remember – we can free you both."

"How?"

"Go to Rome. Unbind the curse."

"What? How? I can't go to Rome."

"But you must." She tapped the journal. "You know how curses work. We don't have the original witch who cast it. But we do have the words and three souls who were there – and now you remember, we can find where it was cast and undo the evil that was done so long ago."

"But don't we have to do it on an anniversary?"

"Yes."

"But when is that?"

"It's all in here. You just read it."

"Not that bit!"

Violetta flipped open the journal and pointed at the date written on the page at the start of the section Jules had just read. "If I know my ancient Roman calendars right – and I do – the anniversary is on the thirteenth of February."

"Valentine's Day Eve? But today's the second. That only gives us not even two weeks!"

"Then you better hurry up and pack. I'll book your flights to Rome. Bastien and I will meet you there. Come on, hurry up. We don't have time to waste."

CHAPTER 6

$\mathcal{J}$ules thrust the shutters open and looked out at the plaza below, busy with people returning from a day of work or sightseeing, and now looking for a place to eat. She couldn't believe she'd slept the day away due to jetlag – why hadn't anyone woken her? They had so few days as it was with her having to figure this all out by midnight on Valentine's Eve – talk about cutting it close! Why couldn't she have found the journal a year ago? Violetta hadn't seemed terribly worried about losing another day when she'd checked on her an hour ago. She'd said they couldn't find the exact place the curse was cast down in the Forum until after all the tourists were back in their hotels and *pensiones* for the night.

Well, her grandmama might not be worried, but she was. It was now the fifth, which meant she only had a week to find where the curse was cast and figure out the bits that were missing from Esta's journal so that they'd be successful on the night. The young Vestal witch had been so traumatised that there were parts of what Clodia had done that she didn't remember, like how the High Priestess had managed to bind and hold a demi-god and a witch with the powers of a Goddess.

Jules was certain those were some important bits of information they'd need to discover if they wanted to break the curse. Not to mention what had happened to the demi-god who was supposed to be her soulmate and forever love and where they could find him.

Pain stabbed her through the eye and she clutched her head.

"You can't think about him."

"Really?" It still blew her mind to think the voice she'd heard all her life was an ancient part of her reincarnated soul. *"Anything else you want to tell me?"*

"I'm trying. But the curse doesn't allow me to tell you much."

"Well, if you can't help me, how am I meant to discover any of what I need to know?"

Silence greeted her question.

"This is going to be such a disaster," she said out loud.

The shouts of the vendors in the marketplace a few streets away lifted to her. The musical Italian echoed off the cobblestones and ancient brick walls, mingling with the honking horns and the distant roar of cars, trucks, buses and whizzing mopeds. Normally, it would have called to her, making her smile at the incongruity of the ancient mixed with the new, but she was too worried to be charmed.

Although, maybe a walk and a little explore before she was needed tonight would be a good way to work through her thoughts – and work out the kinks she'd gained from the horror that had been the almost 50-hour flight here. Multiple delays and four stopovers – really, she'd have to make certain she booked the home-leg. Violetta had booked her flights while Jules read the journal, grappling with the fact she was the reincarnation of Lianna Stevius and was cursed.

Of course, her grandmama had no idea about booking plane travel given she always used her magic to transport herself places – like she'd transported herself and Bastien here after dropping Jules at the airport. Another reason to hate her non-magical status. Something that would hopefully be fixed once she had vanquished the curse. Perhaps wandering around the ancient city might jog some memories or enable the voice to tell her more.

Thankfully, she was free to do so. Tomaso had smoothed things here with the Roman Coven and there were no restrictions to where they could go or what they could do. He'd also organised accommodation and so on after Violetta had called him to tell him about what they had discovered. Jules had been surprised to hear Violetta had shared so much with him, but then again, he was one of her grandparents' oldest friends. Apparently, she'd met him when she was little, but she couldn't remember. She was looking forward to meeting him now, though, but he had been off talking to contacts, trying to get some older maps of the Forum to help them find the exact spot the curse was cast. And now, according to Violetta, he was at the Forum scoping out where the security guards were as well as trying a few different cloaking spells they could use that wouldn't affect Jules. They really couldn't let anyone see what they were doing down there.

Violetta had gone down to the Forum by herself every night since arriving here to jog memories of her life as Esta.

Maybe she should do the same.

"You already know what you need to know."

"Do I?"

"You know the players and the words of the curse. Work backwards from there. Remember all you've seen."

"My nightmares and dreams? You know I can't access them."

"Try."

She closed her eyes and tried to think back to the horror of images she'd woken from a few hours ago, but they remained as elusive as always. *"I can't do it. Why do you expect me to do what Bastien and Violetta are failing to do?"* Bastien couldn't talk about that night – every time he tried, he suffered horrible pain that caused blood noses and bruising if he persisted. And Violetta also seemed blocked from a great deal of Esta's memories.

"At least she's trying."

"That's not fair. I'm trying too."

"Not enough. Don't you want to free yourself? Free Bastien?"

"You know I do." She would do anything for him.

He had to be freed of the curse. Nobody but the ancient Gods would think he deserved to go on being punished for helping Lianna be with her lover. He deserved everything good. He certainly deserved more than to be locked to her friendship and service. He deserved to be lo—

Pain spiked behind her eye and she let out a hiss, pressing her finger against the orb.

The door opened behind her and she turned, hand still to her eye. "Bastien," she said, a smile widening on her face. He'd just showered after his change, his short black hair still a bit damp with comb marks in it. He'd dressed in a favourite soft blue t-shirt – had it always highlighted the breadth of his shoulders, the muscles in his arms and chest like that? – and a worn pair of jeans that sat low on his hips and looked a little looser than they had when she'd seen him wearing them before she'd left to catch her flight. Had he not been eating enough? His change always used up so much energy. She'd have to make certain he took better care of himself now she was here. "I was wondering where you were. I expected you to come back right after you changed."

"Sorry, I was held up." A strange expression crossed his face. Come to think of it, he looked a little grey.

"Are you okay?"

"Absolutely. I'm a little hungry though. Do you want to come down to the kitchen while I get something to eat?"

"Sure." She moved away from the window. "Is Grandmama or Tomaso back yet? I want to ask them if they've found any more information about Lianna's lov— Ow!" She grabbed her head, staggered, then sat with a plop on the bed.

"You really need to get a hang of these curse-rules."

"You think?"

"Jules!" Bastien raced across the room to her. "Are you okay?"

She dropped her hand and forced a smile. "I'm fine. See. I obviously can't think about either of us deserving lo—" It hit her so hard this time she was flung backwards, the bed thankfully making a soft landing. "Ow. Damn it to hell and back."

"How are we supposed to do this if we can't even think about what we can't think about?"

"Don't ask me. I've never been able to figure it out. Ow. That hurts!"

BASTIEN SAT on the bed beside Jules, not quite knowing what to do. She hated anyone fussing over her but Gods, how he hated seeing her in such distress. He touched her arm. "Jules?" When that didn't get a response, he tangled his fingers in hers, pulling her hand away from her face then stroked her forehead until the tension he could feel there softened.

She let out a little sigh, tilting her head into his caress. "What would I do without you, Bastien?"

He wished he could tell her that she'd never have to find out.

She sat up slowly and sighed. "You've endured this for almost 2,000 years. How have you stayed sane? I've only known about my curse for three days and I feel like I'm going to lose my shit any second."

"You're stronger than you think."

She sighed, the sound full of unsaid things that made him wish once again that he could drag Clodia to Tartarus and hand her over to his great uncle to receive the reward she so richly deserved for doing this to them. He wanted to tell Jules how special she was. That he was certain she would be the one to discover how to break the curse. It wasn't just that she shared her full name – Julianna – with his Lianna – all the reincarnations were named Julianna, a strange twist of the curse. It was everything else, including the fact she had preferred to be called Jules, stamping her difference from the moment she could talk.

Keenly intelligent with a thirst for knowledge that shaped everything she did, she was far lonelier than any version who'd come before because she seemed to be far more aware of all that was missing in her life. It was like she could feel the power trapped deep inside her – asking her parents and Violetta from the age of four why she couldn't use her power and not being content with their answers. She'd researched and researched and researched – to no avail, of course. Nothing was written about the curse she was under and the curse itself made it difficult for her to think of other things that might tip her off as to what the issue was.

But even the fact she questioned had given him hope.

Then there were her dreams and nightmares. She could never talk about them, but he knew they were memories from things she said while in the grip of them. None of the others had ever had any kind of access to their past lives' memories.

Also, she looked eerily like Lianna in a way none of the others ever had, right down to the heart-shaped face, the auburn hair with the white streak and the green flecks in her topaz eyes. And there was the fact that none of the other incarnations had ever responded to him like she did. He'd only ever been a guard or sentinel with the others. But with Jules, from her earliest years, he was a companion, teaching, guarding, listening. Then, as she'd moved into adulthood, he'd become her friend. Her best friend.

Her only friend.

But for him, she was so much more than just a friend.

He loved her so much. So deeply. More deeply than he'd ever thought he could. It was a living hell not to be able to tell her.

Jules sighed again, the sound full of a deep sadness that made his heart ache.

He would be happy to ride out this torment if only he could comfort her properly. If only he could make her sadness fade away and fill the space with happiness, fulfilment and the love she deserved. The love she'd had within her grasp and would still have but for the wickedness of a witch who'd grasped for power that wasn't hers and had lashed out with a curse in an act of possessive revenge.

Jules knew of the curse now, knew of Lianna's demi-god lover – but until the curse was broken, she would never see that he was the lover and that he treasured her more than he'd treasured anything in his long life. That she had never been, and would never be, alone.

He squeezed her hand in the absence of the words he longed to say, the words she longed to hear. She sniffed and moved her hand to rub at her face.

She was crying?

"Jules? Why are you crying? You know you can do this, don't you? I believe in you. We all do."

She sniffed again, then leaned against him, her head on his shoulder. "I know. It's not that so much as …" She took in a deep, shuddering breath. "This is going to sound so selfish and horrible, but I just realised that if I do succeed, you won't be with me like this anymore. What am I going to do without you?"

What? He pulled back to look at her aura – it was a bit muddy and thin, as if she was pulling it into herself in protection. What was going on in that intricate mind of hers? "What are you talking about?"

She stroked her finger down the side of his face. "You were bound to my family – to me—" She coughed. "Because of the curse. But once it's gone, you'll be free. You can go and live your life however you choose." She turned and cupped his face. "And I want you to go. I want you to be free to live the life that was taken from you all those years ago. To have everything you lost. And I promise, I will make sure you have everything you need to do whatever you want to do. You deserve far more out of life than to be tied to me and my family for a moment longer. It's just, I'm going to miss not having you as a friend anymore. Not like this anyway."

What the ever-loving-fuck? She thought he'd leave her? But before he could disabuse her of that notion, she barrelled on.

"I'm sure it will be a relief not to be tied to me anymore. And you don't need to worry about me – if you are – because if my magic is freed as you all think it will be, then I'll need to learn how to use it. Bit pathetic to go back to school at almost 30, but beggars can't be choosers, right? At least, on the bright side, I'll be able to start to date within the magical community. Maybe fall in love and have that love returned." She winced. "That'd be nice, right?"

What? She wanted to fall in love with someone else? Had she forgotten about her demi-god lover – him – and that they'd finally have a chance to be together?

But of course, that was just his wishful thinking. Despite the fact Jules was so like Lianna in looks and, in some degree, temperament, she was very different from her in other ways. She was a modern woman in a modern world. She wanted love, but she also wanted many other things – Lianna had been perfectly happy to think only of their life together, the children they would have, the home and family they would build. Jules had her work and it was very important to her. And with her magical powers in her control, she'd naturally want to explore what she could do within her career path without being encumbered by someone her soul had loved in some distant past.

He'd always thought she would just want what Lianna wanted. But that wasn't true.

She might not choose him at all.

The thought sliced through him, hard enough, painful enough to make him jerk back.

"Bastien? Are you okay?" She steadied him. "I knew you lied to me last night when I arrived. The changes are getting worse, aren't they? It's why you took so long after your change to come in here, isn't it?"

"It's fine. I—"

A knock at the door pulled him from his depressing thoughts.

Power sang to him from the other side of the door.

Tamuel.

"That must be Grandmama." Jules jumped up from the bed before he could stop her – couldn't she feel the difference in power between the cupid and Violetta?

"I'm ready, Grandmama—" The words died on her lips as she opened the door, stumbling back a few steps. "Who are you?" she asked, her voice tight, pained.

"*Tamuel! Mind your power,*" Bastien said through their cupid mind-speak.

The cupid bowed, his aura pulsing then pulling back towards him. "I'm sorry. They told me you were sensitive but I didn't realise how much. Forgive me?"

CHAPTER 7

The suave elderly gentleman sauntered into the room, causing Jules to stumble away from him.

She backed up until she hit the wall. How had she not noticed the difference in power radiating through the door? Violetta was powerful, but nothing like this. And even though this man had pulled it back, her skin still prickled.

"Who is he?"

"I don't know."

"He feels ..."

"Familiar."

"Yes."

She watched him warily as he crossed to shake Bastien's hand. "You're looking a bit grey, my friend."

"You know each other?"

"We're old friends. Aren't we, Bas?" His accent lilted like the Italian ones lifting from the plaza below her window, but with a slight difference in cadence. She struggled to look away from him, especially when he caught her gaze with his twinkling black eyes. Her skin prickled with the danger evident in him. Someone with that much power would always be dangerous to her, no matter their intentions for good.

"Touch him."

"Are you crazy? He's too powerful."

"He won't hurt you."

"Tomaso di Erosi, at your service," he said, extending his hand.

"Don't touch him," Bastien snapped, moving between them.

"Aw, Bas, don't be like that," he said, pulling his hand back. "I won't hurt her. That's the last thing I want."

"Then you should keep your power to yourself like you've been told."

"True." Tomaso laughed out loud, the sound ringing in the air, twining around Jules, making her want to laugh with him. There was something that felt … familiar about it. Like the laughter of a friend you hadn't seen for a while.

"May I?" He gestured to the chair at the desk, but before she could even nod, he'd walked over to it. He unbuttoned his immaculate steel-blue suit blazer, exposing the snowy white and expensive-looking shirt underneath, its two top buttons undone to show off the strong column of his tanned neck and a few inches of chest, and sat down. He ran his large hands along his suit pants and looked up at her, black eyes twinkling as if he were overjoyed.

His salt-and-pepper hair was cut short in a way that showed off the strong waves. His eyebrows were thick, black and straight, yet didn't overwhelm the strong patrician lines of his face. There was something oddly familiar about him – maybe because she had met him when a toddler, even though she couldn't remember – something that made her want to draw closer, to touch him.

"Then touch him. Take his hand."

She took a few steps towards him. "Nice to meet you finally. Grandmama has spoken about you a lot over the years."

"As she has you." His smile widened. "She has kept me up to date with your progress since I met you when you were but a babe."

"Really?"

"But of course. Your little problem has been a particular fascination." He rubbed his hands together. "Breaking such a powerful curse – what a feather in my cap that will be."

She frowned at him. "This isn't a game to me."

His smile disappeared, his gaze intent. "I can assure you, it's not a game for me either. I take this very seriously. But to be involved in such an endeavour after so many years of ... boredom. You have to excuse my excitement."

She nodded, even though it seemed a bit weird to be excited about all this. Terrified, worried, angry, frustrated – all good. Excited – not so much.

"So, shall we be friends?" He held his hand out.

"Tomaso!" Bastien snapped again. "Stop it."

"It's fine," Jules said as she moved past Bastien to stand in front of the other man. "I can't feel anything from him now." It was strange, given how much power she'd felt only moments ago. And she really did want to touch him because there was something ... unreal about him. Something she felt touching him might reveal.

Warily, she grasped Tomaso's hand.

Her jaw slammed closed and her fingers spasmed around his, tightening. Oh Goddess. She'd made a mistake. She braced for the slashing pain as her body rejected his magic.

It didn't come. Instead, the room swirled around her as images flickered to life in her head. She pitched forward, falling, falling ...

She opened her eyes with a start to look up into a face that was bewilderingly familiar.

It was her face, she realised with a start. Although there were slight differences in the nose and skin colour, the arch of the brow.

Wetness landed on her face. Was it raining? One of the drops rolled across her cheek and into her mouth – salty. Not rain, tears. The woman who looked like her, who held her, was crying.

The image flipped and suddenly she was no longer looking up at the woman but was the woman looking down at the baby in her arms. A baby still covered in the mess of a fresh birthing.

"My baby boy."

She lifted a trembling hand, stroking down the side of the baby's face, her vision starring. Pain, grief and an overwhelming love stole her breath as she stared at the new-born in her arms. "Please. Don't blame him for my transgressions. He's an innocent," she whispered.

The baby gurgled and she bent to kiss his beautiful forehead, to breathe in the scent of him, but Clodia was already there, reaching to take him. Lianna tried to hold on, to keep him with her for a moment longer, but the High Priestess turned away, pushing the baby into little Esta's arms. "We will need his power. Put him in place in the pentacle." Esta hesitated. "Do it now, girl, or I will use all your power and I will not be gentle about it."

"No!" Lianna cried, trying to move, to reach out to her new-born son. The golden bands on her arms tightened and weakness overwhelmed her so she could barely breathe.

Across the pentacle, another voice cried out. "Don't do this, Clodia. My aunt can't possibly want this."

Sebastio. He was here? How had Clodia bound him? This wasn't possible – was it? She scrabbled onto all fours, trying to peer through the night, but she couldn't see him, could only hear him as he continued to yell at Clodia, voice ringing with panic and rage as he fought against whatever held him here.

Clodia did not have the power to bind a demi-god for a few minutes, let alone the three weeks it had taken her pregnancy to come to fruition, her demi-god-warlock son growing inside her even faster than any of them had thought possible. It must be that blood-red gem Clodia had been wearing since the night the High Priestess had captured them.

The bands on her arms tightened again, taking more power, more energy. She screamed.

"Lianna!" Sebastio called out. "Stop it, Clodia. You're hurting her."

"Do you think I care?" the High Priestess shrieked. "She broke the law. Committed treason. For this, she deserves to lose all her power and more."

"Because of you. You gave her no choice."

"She always had a choice, and she chose to lay with you over her vows, over her obligations to Vesta and to Roma."

"You cannot do this. The Gods will not allow such hubris."

"My hubris? What about yours? And if they were so concerned, surely your father would be here now to stop me."

Sounds of struggling. "I will make you pay."

"You and your army of cats."

Lianna gasped. What did she mean? Sebastio was a cupid, a son of Eros of the Greek Pantheon, not Bastet with her army of cats in the Egyptian Pantheon.

Clodia's cackle filled the air as she lifted her arms and began to incant her spell. Lianna cried out as more power was pulled from her, twisted and warped to obey Clodia's will and not her own. Across the pentacle, her servant, Bastieno, cried out in pain and disappeared from her sight. No. No.

Sebastio yelled, still trying to stop the mad High Priestess, but there was no point. She'd wanted this all along. She'd made certain Lianna was found guilty of treason. The priests of Roma and her fellow Vestal priestesses had helped Clodia further bind Lianna's powers and kept her imprisoned until the birth of her baby. Of course, they thought she had months to go until that time, but Clodia had other plans. She needed this all to come to fruition before Lianna's service in the Vestal Virgins was over – she'd admitted as much when she'd hidden Lianna away from everyone to hide the speed of the pregnancy. Now Lianna realised she'd sped things along not only so she could steal Lianna's Goddess-given powers while she still had access to them through the arm manacles, but so she could use the birth energy to further her schemes.

"Please, don't use my babe. Not like this."

"I will use him however I wish. He is here, after all, because of my plans; my needs. And he is far more powerful than I ever dreamed. That power will make all the difference."

Oh Gods. She thought the High Priestess was going to bind the baby's magic to her like she had Lianna's, but this was even worse. Clodia was going to use the baby's power as well to help steal her powers and there was nothing she could do to stop her. She would be dead soon. Clodia didn't even have to kill her. By Roma's laws, for her treason of breaking her vows, she would be shoved into an underground cell, big enough to be considered 'accommodation', with enough food and water to last for a few days as per Roma's laws. The entrance to the cell would be sealed and filled with dirt. She would suffocate long before she would starve. And she had no magic and no way to help herself. Or her baby. Or her Bas. "My Goddess, help us."

"She will not come to you. You have broken her laws."

She didn't care. She didn't care. This wasn't right. But it was no use. All she could do was cry out, "I love you, Sebastio. Remember I love you, always."

"I love you too, Lianna. Always."

"Save our son. Make sure he knows he is loved."

"I will try." There was something wrong with Sebastio's voice, it was strained and higher. Was he going to disappear like Bastieno? "Don't leave me, Sebastio! Don't leave me!"

"He will be near but always far, never to know your love again," Clodia shouted. "As you will never know his."

The High Priestess raised her hands higher, wind whipping around her now, the cries of their baby and Sebastio drowned by the howls of the dark power that threatened to steal everything Lianna held dear.

Clodia's gaze met Lianna across the pentacle. The jewel in the necklace she wore glowed darkly red, pulsing like a heart. Lines of dark-tinged red light shot across the five points, lighting up the lines of the pentacle the High Priestess had dug into the grass. Lianna screamed as it shot into her, but her scream was cut off as it squeezed around her chest, lifting her into the air. Light from the glowing pentacle blinded her.

Clodia laughed, the sound a shriek in the wind that tore at Lianna's *stola* and cut gashes in her skin as she hung above the magical inscription for elemental earth – earth that was soon to be her grave.

Clodia's mouth twisted and she cried out,

"I bind your love into my curse

You will be as a blind man dying of thirst
Reaching for that which lays so close at hand
Love slips through your fingers like grains of sand
Forever hidden from you, forever lost
Until you agree to pay the ultimate cost
I bind you and your lover into this curse
Always to be near but powerless to reverse
Animal to human, hidden from sight
Two centuries between to mourn your plight
I bind you both three times three times three
All power to me, so mote it be."

There was a roar and a flash of light as the curse hit Lianna square in the chest. It knocked her out of the reach of the pentacle and into the pit behind her. She landed with a thump, gasping for breath. Dirt started to rain down on her. She tried to stand, but couldn't, so flipped over and crawled into the cell as dust filled the air around her, making it hard to breathe. Then she hit a wall. The cell was smaller than she'd thought it would be. She groped in the dark. There was supposed to be a pallet and food and water. She found the pallet but no bundle. There was no food or water. Clodia wasn't even holding properly to their law. She wanted Lianna to die sooner rather than later, because then, and only then, could she fully take possession of Lianna's power.

Lianna sat on the thin pallet, wrapped her arms around her legs and put her forehead on her knees, trying to slow her breathing and not cough as the only entrance disappeared in a tonne of dirt. She tried to pull at the golden armbands, free herself from their binding as she'd tried to do every day since they were captured, but they refused to budge even though they no longer burned into her flesh.

It was over. It was over. Her only hope was that Sebastio wouldn't meet Bastieno's fate, whatever that had been. Hoped that he would free himself soon so he could rescue their son and take him far away from this place of despair.

She coughed, hardly able to breathe in the dusty air. She wished she could believe she'd meet them someday when her soul was reborn and they'd find their love again, but if she had it right, the curse had bound her soul so she would never know her love until … until she'd paid the ultimate cost. Wasn't this the ultimate cost?

She sat there, rocking and trying to figure it out, until the air ran out. Her eyes closed as fog and darkness followed her down, down, down …

CHAPTER 8

*B*astien sat beside Jules for two days and nights, only leaving her side when the change took him over. Violetta and Tamuel came and went after they'd spent time in Jules's vision with her – something both had the power to do – one she kept living repeatedly in her mind as if looking for something.

He didn't know if she'd found that something, but Tamuel and Violetta had seen valuable information that had been missing until now; insight into Clodia's use of the HeartsBlood Gem – an ancient and powerful gem rumoured to have been cut from the heart of an ancient Goddess. It was the reason Clodia had managed to bind him so he couldn't fight back. She'd also used it to push more power into the armbands she'd put on Lianna as a child that had allowed her access to Lianna's powers. However, something had gone wrong in her use of it that night and her plan had backfired. She'd lost control of Lianna's power at her death, rather than becoming mistress of it.

The information was a double-edged sword though – they would now need the gem to help break the curse. But Tamuel was certain he'd seen something about where it might be in the Roman Coven's library.

Bastien just hoped he was right.

Jules whimpered. He grasped her hand. It was cold. Too cold. "Come on, Jules. Wake up." He smoothed the mass of her silky curls back from her face then took a chance and kissed her forehead. Pain lanced through his eye, but he kissed her again.

The door behind him opened.

"Did you find it yet?"

"Not yet, but we will," Tamuel said.

Violetta's presence prickled over his back as she came to stand behind him. Her power felt edgier, a little less controlled than usual. But that was only to be expected, he supposed. If he still had access to his powers, he imagined they'd feel edgier too, given how worried he was about Jules. Even so, he said, "Careful with your power."

"How is she?" Violetta asked, pulling her power back.

"She's cold and struggling to breathe."

"She should wake soon then."

"She better." She might be reborn again in the future, but she wouldn't be Jules. And he loved Jules, his love for her deeper, sweeter, stronger than ever before. It killed him to think she might not love him back, but better she be alive and in love with someone else, thinking of him only as a friend, than to not be in this world at all.

He didn't want to live in a world that she did not live in. He'd had to do that too many times already, but this time, he feared, he wouldn't survive the loss.

"I think she's coming around," Violetta said. "Her lids are fluttering."

Jules sat bolt upright with a loud gasp. She tore her hand out of his, her movements frantic as she struggled to breathe.

"Jules, it's okay, you can breathe. You can breathe." He grabbed her shoulders, moving along her arms to her hands – they were at her throat, scrabbling. He pulled them away and held them.

Violetta said in a low, calm voice, "Bastien is right, Julianna dear. You are free of the vision. Just breathe. Breathe. Focus on my voice, on Bastien's touch, and breathe. In, then out. Slow. Nice and slow. Yes, that's it. That's my girl."

Her hand brushed past him, as if she wanted to touch Jules, but she pulled away before she did. "That's a girl. That's better," she said. "Open your eyes. Can you see me?"

"Uh-huh."

"Can you see Tomaso?"

"Yes."

"And Bastien?"

Jules twisted then gasped. "You changed clothes?"

He nodded, smiling, throat too full of relief to allow him to speak.

She stiffened. "How long have I been out?"

"It's the evening of the seventh."

"No!" She jerked, her hands twisting out of his grip. "I've lost two days?"

"Shh, shh," Violetta said. "You must stay calm."

She didn't – her agitation and distress were hot jabs against his skin. He pulled her to him, tucking her head under his chin, hand stroking over her back. She felt too thin – the vision had taken too much out of her. "It's not lost," he whispered against the crinkling curls of her hair that tickled his chin. "We know so much more now. It has helped. Your vision has helped."

Slowly, she began to soften in his hold, her breath slowing and deepening.

"She died. Lianna. So lost and alone."

The heartache in her voice made him want to weep. "I know." He cupped her face and lifted it up, pressed his lips against her forehead again despite the pain it caused him. "But she's not alone now. We're all here."

"That's right," Tamuel said. "And we're going to put an end to this. And then you can be with your love. You just have to believe."

"Yes." She didn't sound too thrilled. She swallowed hard, pulled back a little. He let go of her but she gripped his hands, held on. "I couldn't see him. I still don't know who he is."

"That's okay," Tamuel said. "I—"

Bastien said quickly, "We can cover all of what we have discovered after we get some food into Jules. You must be starving."

She nodded slowly. "I am hungry."

"Then let's go get you something to eat. The rest can wait." At least, it had to, until she'd had a chance to recover. Right now, she felt too much like she might slip away from him.

~

Jules ate her pasta hungrily, eating almost as much as Bastien did – he'd not eaten properly after any of his changes because he'd been worried about her, so he was like a bag of bones. She was glad to see him making up for some of that now.

As she ate, Tomaso apologised to her. "My powers were pulled back, I assure you. I had no idea just shaking your bare hand could push you into a vision. I didn't mean to put you through that."

"I'm glad you did," she said around a mouthful of delicious salty spaghetti *Puttanesca*. "Otherwise, you wouldn't have found out about the HeartsBlood Gem. You think you can find it?"

He nodded. "The books in the Roman Coven I tracked down all say it's rumoured to be buried somewhere in Roma, although nobody's been able to figure out where – which is strange given the magical signature it should give off. But now we know Clodia used it in her spell to help hold Sebastio and Lianna and leach their powers, I think I'll be able to recalibrate the magical signature and track it down."

"It could be anywhere in Rome," Violetta said. "It's a longshot to think we'll find it."

"I don't think so," Jules said. They all turned to look at her and she waved her hand. "Given how Clodia used it, the gem would be tied to the area where the spell was cast." They kept staring at her. "Am I the only one here who's read Varagustus's *Treatise on the Properties of Powerful Stones?*"

"I think you're the only one ever to read Varagustus's treatises on anything," Tomaso said dryly. "The man was a positive bore. Not to mention all his treatises are thousands of pages long. And most of them are written in a lost language."

"Not lost," she said. "I understood it."

"What did it say?" Bastien asked her.

She took a sip of water, ordering her thoughts. "Gems like that need a link to someone or something with ties to the Gods. I don't think the link was made to Clodia given her spell backfired."

"Of course," Tomaso said. "The link was made with the place, and to a smaller extent, Lianna and Sebastio." He pointed to the Temple of Vesta. "It must be somewhere here, close to wherever the curse was cast."

"This is fantastic," Bastien said.

"Really?" she asked. "But we'll need to use magic to find it and," she waved her hand at herself, "you can't do that when we're down there looking for the curse-spot."

"We don't have to wait until night to find it," Tomaso said. "I can start to look for it during the day when I can use my magic without it affecting you. I'll find it. I promise."

She nodded, managed a smile. Somehow, despite what he'd done to her, she couldn't help but like and trust him. She supposed it was because Violetta and Bastien did. And he seemed to have so much knowledge about all sorts of things – even if he thought Varagustus boring.

She finished the last mouthful of pasta, drank down another glass of water, then pushed her plate away. "So, what's next?"

Tomaso let out a loud breath. "I want you to look at this map and see if there's anything familiar to you. It might help us to pinpoint where to look if there is."

Jules stared at the yellowing map he placed in front of her.

"It just looks like lines and squares and squiggles."

"I know."

"We're not very good with maps."

"I know."

She stared hard at it, trying to see something. Nothing came. She made a sound of frustration. "I'm sorry. This doesn't look familiar at all."

"It's all right, dearest," Violetta said. "We don't expect you to know much of anything."

"What? Why?" Her gaze jerked to Violetta. Did her grandmama have such little faith in her?

Violetta waved her hand. "The curse, of course. Its purpose is to actively stop you from doing anything that might break it."

"Oh … of course." Her shoulders slumped. "So, I'm virtually useless."

"Not at all," Tomaso and Bastien said together.

"You're the only one who can find the place the curse was cast," Tomaso said. "You're vital to the success of our endeavour."

"What about the pentacle?" Bastien asked, frowning Violetta's way. "Surely that left some magical trace – it was so strong."

Violetta nodded as she and Tomaso shared a look. "From what we saw in your vision, it looked like it was burned up in the final burst of power. Even if it wasn't, the strongest magic would barely register after all these years. You would have to be a super-sensitive to find it."

Jules jerked upright from her slump. "I am." They all turned to stare at her. "What you said about the sensitive thing. I'm that. Maybe not in how you meant, but my allergy to magic makes me super sensitive to it. I might pick something up."

Bastien stilled beside her. "That might be what Esta referred to – about Lianna's soul finding the place. Perhaps she guessed the curse would make Lianna's reincarnations allergic to magic."

"That's a supposition. I don't remember her being certain of anything of the sort," Violetta said carefully.

"But it makes sense." Bastien stood. "We have to get down there and check it out."

"Julianna has only just recovered from her vision. Perhaps we should wait until tomorrow night," Violetta said, her concerned gaze on Jules.

"I want to do this," Jules said, standing. "I might not be able to help track down the HeartsBlood Gem, and I can't help with finding the lover—"

"That's what I tried to tell you before," Tomaso interrupted. "I did an invocation spell when Violetta called to say this was happening. It took a few tries, but I eventually found this Sebastio. I have contacted him and he is excited to be able to meet you … again."

"When is he coming?"

"Not until just before midnight on Valentine's Eve. He can't reveal himself until then because of the curse."

She nodded, relieved Tomaso's knowledge extended to knowing God invocation spells – she'd have to ask him about that one day. But for now … "The only thing I can do is go to the Forum and find where the spell was cast. So let's go."

"We should wait until midnight – it's quietest then." Tomaso looked her up and down. "That will give you time to shower and change. You'll need to dress warmly. It's cold outside."

CHAPTER 9

*B*ells clanged, announcing it was midnight – the seventh passing into the eighth – as they followed Tomaso through a maze of streets that were curiously empty. Their footsteps echoed in the air around them, sounding lonely and a bit lost.

But Tomaso wasn't lost and finally they emerged onto the *Via del Corso*, crossed the *Piazza Venezia* and then made their way down the *Via dei Fori Imperiali*. A few cars and trucks still rattled along the thoroughfare – Rome never truly slept – but it was nowhere near the chaos and cacophony that had deafened – and terrified – her on the crazy taxi ride from the airport to Tomaso's villa three days ago.

They walked silently and quickly down the wide *Via dei Fori Imperiali* towards the Colosseum and the Forum, which lay in ruins beside the behemoth. The Colosseum glowed, dressed in light from the moon and the spotlights on the grounds surrounding it.

"Even in ruins, it is still a colossus."

"It is. And the history in those stones ..."

"It's loud."

"Uh-huh."

She shuddered as something inside her curled into itself. Her skin prickled and crawled uncomfortably, like it did when someone was using magic nearby.

But there was nobody around except for her and her companions and none of them would use magic around her, so it couldn't be that. Still, she had to fight the need to turn and run – far, far away.

"You okay?" Bastien whispered, leaning down so his warm breath brushed her ear.

She took a deep breath, edging closer to him. "I'm fine."

"*Not true.*"

"*It's not not true.*"

"*You know you're not making sense?*"

Tomaso turned. "Come. I've placed a spell to keep the security cameras and guards away for a time. It shouldn't affect you at all because it's not in the air, but more like a virus I placed on the guards and the electronics," he said to Jules, "So don't worry."

She wasn't – she was more worried about what was happening to her right now. She glanced around but still saw nobody near them – and to feel like this, someone would need to be using magic close by.

As they drew closer to the ancient ruins, the prickling increased. As did the shouting of long-dead crowds, the ancient cries of the enslaved and the roars of the animals kept inside for the amusement of the Roman people. The noise surrounded her, pushing at her. Her stomach roiled, her heart beat faster.

They stopped at the edge of the road opposite the Colosseum. The concourse that ran around it stretched in front of her, wavering. Was it moving or was she moving? She wished whatever it was would stop expanding and contracting like that. She was going to be sick.

She had to force herself to keep breathing evenly, to not wrap her fingers tightly around Bastien's arm. He was the only thing that felt real. The only thing keeping her from running away, screaming from the force of history pounding at her from the structure in front of them – because that's what this had to be. She wasn't just sensitive to magic, but to the impact of it through history.

"No point standing here," Violetta said. "Let's go."

They stepped off the curb together and ran across the road.

The moment her foot touched the concourse, history came crashing down on her. She stumbled under its weight, losing her grip on Bastien.

Emotion – terror, elation – vibrated up through her feet. Her heart raced, her skin prickled so it almost hurt. The need to flee was a shout in every nerve.

"Are you all right, dearest? You don't look very well."

"I don't feel very well."

"Jules."

"What's wrong?"

She tried to form words, but pitched forward, landing on her hands and knees, and vomited her dinner all over the stones.

The world span faster. And alongside the spinning, pain began to make itself known. It filled her head alongside the roars and screams.

She couldn't do it. She couldn't go any further. It was too much. Too much.

"Shit," she heard someone say, then arms were around her and she was lifted and carried away.

~

JULES CAME TO SLOWLY, the softness under her head and body telling her she was on a bed. She opened her eyes to be greeted by darkness. She shuddered. Why did it have to be so dark? Her head felt like it was full of wet sand, her eyes equally so. What the hell had happened?

"*You passed out.*"

"*Again?*"

"*Yes. The history in the stones—*"

"*It overwhelmed me. Gods-damned curse.*"

"*You said it.*"

She wondered how long she'd been out. Now her eyes had acclimatised a little, she realised there was a small amount of light in the room but when she turned her head, she saw it came from a night-light. She had no idea if she'd lost more days or not. She needed her phone. It was there on the bedside table – she could see its outline in the glow from the nightlight.

She shifted but couldn't move. A warm weight lay over her waist, warmth aligned along her side – Bastien curled up behind her. He was still fully dressed and dark shadows marked the skin under his eyes. She didn't want to wake him – he'd obviously had very little sleep. But she wanted to know how much time she'd lost. The fact he was still in his human form told her it couldn't be more than a few hours, but still, she needed to check. If there was enough time, she'd like to go back and try again.

She moved carefully, edged forward, enough to grip her phone with her fingertips, then pulled it towards her until she could pick it up.

She pressed her thumb on the home button to light up the screen.

The date lit up with the time:

4:05 am.

10 February.

She jerked upright, clutching her phone.

Beside her, Bastien came to a crouch, hands lifted. "What is it? What's wrong? Who's there?"

"I've lost another *two days*." She turned her phone off then on again, but the date didn't change. They'd gone to the Colosseum at midnight just as it tipped into the eighth and now it was the tenth? "Fuck."

"It's okay." Bastien came down beside her to hug her. "We've got time. And you did so great. You'll do better next time."

She wanted to give in to his comforting warmth, but instead, pushed away to stand and pace. "I did great?" She snorted. "If you call throwing up and passing out for another two days 'great', then I guess I'm the champ at that."

"Don't, Jules. Don't blame yourself," Bastien said softly from behind her. "You're not to blame for how the curse affects you."

"Then who is?"

"Clodia."

"Well, good luck blaming her – she's dead."

"Yeah, and a part of me wishes she wasn't so that I could make her pay for stealing and using Goddess-gifted powers that weren't hers."

"Goddess-gifted powers? How do you know that?" Gasping, she turned to grab his arm. "No. Don't answer that."

His mouth curled into a gentle smile. "It's okay. I can talk about Clodia and my opinions about her. The curse only stops me from talking about Lianna—" He winced.

She brushed trembling fingers over his brow. She hated that he could hurt like this because of her. "Maybe just tell me what you remember of Clodia. Nothing else."

He swallowed hard, nodded, then said carefully, "Clodia was not Vesta's chosen vessel for her most cherished power and she hated that fact. She was sent a vision about who it would be given to, which is how she came to be there to take you from your parents the moment you were born."

"But ... hang on. I didn't think Vestal Virgins were chosen until they were at least six."

"Not usually. But you were an exception because you were Goddess-blessed."

She wished people would stop talking as if she and Lianna were the same person – they weren't, even though Lianna had been with her all these years, a presence in her head, talking to her. So she just said, "My dreams ... visions – they never showed me that. Her parents? They just happily gave her away?"

"I don't know about that. I do know your family always birthed strong witches. Which is how Esta came to be chosen too. She was your – Lianna's – cousin."

She knew Esta was a distant relation of theirs – otherwise, she wouldn't have been reincarnated in Violetta – but she'd never put two and two together and realised that Lianna and Esta must have been related because she and Violetta were related. "She must have been very powerful for Clodia to pull her into the pentacle the way she did."

"She was, but Lianna was more so. Her power frightened Clodia. I think that infuriated her. It also made her insanely jealous. Nobody realised how much until—"

His mouth pulled tight. They were obviously skating close to the edge of what he could and couldn't tell her. She had to move the conversation back to just Clodia. "Tomaso mentioned her spell must have gone wrong. Why? How?"

He frowned. "That's a great question."

"Yes, it is."

"Thank you."

"We always knew she never got your power—"

"Lianna's power," she said. "I don't have any power. Not like her."

Bastien's brow furrowed deeply. "Despite the fact she was a trained witch, she never had access to her full powers either. Clodia channelled them and used them for her purposes as High Priestess from when Lianna was young. If Clodia had gotten full control of them, they would have made her virtually immortal. But she died soon after the casting."

"But something must have gone right," Jules said. "Because her curse has lasted all these years."

"Yes."

She rubbed the ache in her brow that was steadily growing stronger as they spoke. "What I don't understand is where did the power go? If Clodia didn't get it and Lianna didn't get access to it to stop herself from dying – and I certainly don't have it – where is it?"

"I don't know. I've never ..." His frown deepened. "You should discuss this with Tomaso and Violetta in the morning."

"After you recover from your change."

"Yes. After that."

Silence fell between them. There was something she wanted to ask him, but she was afraid it would hurt him.

"Ask me."

"What?" Jules picked at a hangnail.

"You want to ask what power Lianna ... had?" He swallowed hard.

"How did he know?"

"He knows you incredibly well."

"You don't have to tell me. Not if it hurts you—"

"She had the power to light a fire in hearts and hearths," he said quickly but showed no sign of pain.

"It doesn't sound like much, does it?"

She screwed up her nose – she had to agree. "That doesn't seem worth going to this much effort over."

"Are you kidding?" He turned to her, his face alight with an energy she'd not seen in him before, a lightness. "The power to change a man's heart and therefore his thoughts through the power of your very presence. It's influence incarnate. Something that could shape nations. It's the only thing worth this much effort. That and … love." The last word was choked and his hands spasmed on hers.

"Don't." She put her hand over his mouth, his soft, full lips warm against her palm. "Don't hurt yourself. Not for me. Not for this."

He shook his head. "No. I'm fine. I shouldn't have—" He swallowed, paling a little, his eyelid flickering.

"Bastien, stop it." She clasped his face in both hands, her thumbs stroking his cheeks. "You know I hate it when you're hurting."

"So you know how I feel when you hurt."

Her mind skipped sideways in a way that made her feel slightly sick. "Yeah, well … Clodia. Total bitch, right?"

He snort-laughed, his eyes crinkling in that way she liked. "Right. I never—"

His words choked off as he spasmed out of her grasp and flipped off the bed.

"Bastien!" She threw herself down beside him, hardly noting the smart in her knees above the panic rising in her chest, squeezing her breath. "Bastien, stop thinking about it."

"I'm … not," he squeezed out. "Change. Cat."

"What? No." Dawn wasn't for hours given it was still winter. He shouldn't be changing. But he was.

And he'd never make it to his changing booth in his room down the hall.

"Run … away," he said in an agonised whisper.

"No, no," she pleaded. "It's not time."

"Do what he says. Now! It could kill us if we're here when he changes."

"But he's in so much pain."

"We can't help him. Not with this. Not yet. Just go. Run!"

Her stomach turned over and her heart clenched in her chest as the power of his change radiated outwards. She scrambled backwards before the strength of it could touch her, fumbling with the door handle before managing to push it down and open the door. She stumbled out of the room, slamming the door shut before staggering down the hall, trying to get away from the magic that whipped at her, making her bleed, sobbing because of the need to leave her best friend to endure this horrible pain alone.

She made it down the stairs, holding herself upright by sheer force of will and a good grip on the banister, but could go no more than two steps beyond the bottom of the stairs. She leaned against the wall, then slid down it, the cold of the tiles under her bottom a relief to the burning that raced through the rest of her body. She wanted to cry, to sob, to scream and yell, but she couldn't. She had to think. Think.

She'd thought that being bound to a curse because of a love that had never been hers and then losing days because of it was bad enough. But this was a potential disaster because his early change the other night hadn't been a fluke.

"Has he changed earlier on the days you were unconscious?"

"I don't know!"

He'd changed every sunset and sunrise for thousands of years, so what had changed the pattern?

"You."

"What?"

"This started when you found out about the curse."

"Fuck."

CHAPTER 10

Power crackled in the air as Bastien twisted and jerked, his body breaking and reshaping one bone, one ligament at a time. It had taken him completely by surprise and he couldn't hold back the scream that tore out of his mouth. All he could be thankful for was that Jules had managed to get out of the room. He only hoped she'd made it further, because, given he wasn't in the shielding of his changing booth, the magic of the spell would hurt her if she wasn't at least outside.

The door banged open, crashing against the plaster with a loud crack. Then hands were on him – Tamuel. "Where ... Jules," he managed to say.

"Safe." The cupid picked him up and carried him down the hall to his booth, shutting the door. It closed with a woosh and a pop as the magical shield that kept the power of the spell inside the booth, automatically fell into place. Violetta's spellwork was quite ingenious.

"Thank you," he mouthed to his friend as he stood outside the booth, arms crossed, worry deep lines on his face.

Then all thought departed as his lungs, ribs and spine twisted and reshaped and then everything was lost in the agony of the change.

An endless time later, he rolled over and groaned, the sound coming out as a squashed meow. Everything hurt, more than he'd ever remembered it hurting after a change.

It had worsened every night since Jules had found out about the curse. And his time as a human was now down to seven hours.

This was not good.

His stomach groaned and gurgled as the scent of bacon wafted under his nose and he realised just how hungry he was. And thirsty. His tongue felt like a dried leaf stuck to the roof of his mouth.

He pushed upright gingerly, surprised to realise he was on the bed. Jules must have put him here after his change was complete and the shield that protected her had disabled itself. She always saw to his comfort. She'd also placed a bowl of water on the bedside table right next to him.

As he drank his fill, he slowly became aware of the light in the room. Light not from the bulb above him but shining through the window.

Hells. How long had he been out? He needed to find Jules and the others.

He jumped down and padded across to the door, glad it had been left ajar. He slipped out into the hallway, picked up Jules's scent – vanilla and cinnamon – and followed it down the stairs, past the lounge, through the kitchen and out into the private walled courtyard. Her scent angled towards the ivy-covered arches that led to the little garden area.

Typical she'd be out here, even with how cold it was. She loved spending time outdoors, seeking the sun and light whenever she took a break from her work in the library. She and Lianna shared that in common.

He winced at the lash of pain that was punishment for that thought, shook his head, and continued through the archway.

The three of them sat at a small table in an alcove to the left in the only area of the garden that caught the sun in winter. Water trickled down the wall and into a small pond where huge gold and white speckled goldfish swam – he was almost hungry enough to hook his paw in and fish one of them out. But he smelled bacon again. Spotted a plate piled high in the middle of the table. Thank the Gods.

Jules looked up, a smile brightening her face. "Bastien." She patted the table beside her. His stomach rumbled as he leaped up. "You haven't eaten? I left food for you in our room."

"He wanted to know where you were first."

She glanced at Tamuel. "You can hear him?"

"You can't tell her about our cupid-link."

Tamuel shot him a quick look as if to say 'duh' before smiling and saying, "I have a talent for talking to animals. Just call me Doctor Doolittle."

"Oh." She swallowed hard. "I'm glad someone can hear him." She pulled the plate of bacon to sit in front of him and began to cut it into cat-bite-sized pieces. "Eat. Now."

He did. Voraciously.

"Better?" Jules said, stroking her hand down his back with a smile as he finished the plate a few minutes later.

He nodded, even though he was still a little hungry. Not surprising given the change took more out of him and was more vicious than ever before. A shiver chased down his spine. He didn't want to think about what that meant right now.

"You should think about it," Tamuel said.

"It's not important."

"I beg to differ."

Bastien shook his head at the argumentative cupid. *"The only thing we should be worried about is getting Jules through the trials the curse is throwing in her path to stop her from breaking it. What is happening to me is inconsequential."*

"It won't be inconsequential if you can't take your human form on Valentine's Eve."

"What is he saying?" Jules sat forward, hands clasped before her, face drawn and pale, but otherwise seemingly unhurt. She'd got away just in time, or Tamuel had got him into his booth before it was too late.

There were dark circles under her eyes though. Had she slept at all after he changed last night?

Tamuel turned to glare at him. "He doesn't think it matters that he's spending less and less time as a human and the change is sucking power from him."

"Bastien." Jules glowered at him. "Of course it matters. Grandmama and Tomaso are worried that unless you're in the form you were in when the curse was cast, it won't break."

"You're focused on the wrong thing."

Her gaze whipped from Tamuel after he related Bastien's words, and back to him. "Really? The fact you might not be able to hold your human form when the time comes doesn't worry you?"

"Of course it worries me. But only breaking the curse can change it. Worrying is only going to stop you from doing what you must. Besides, I think this is another way the curse has of stopping us from reaching our goal. I think the more you worry on it, the worse it will get because it means it's winning."

"That makes no sense," Jules said as Tamuel finished translating. "Why would the curse suddenly change after all this time? For you and for me? I mean, how does it know we're here and trying to break it? Why is it suddenly upping the ante? I know I'm not an expert on magic, but I didn't think a spell could have sentience unless the witch or wizard who cast it was alive to mould it?"

"Not usually," Violetta said, her eyes shadowed with worry. "But this is not a usual curse. Bastien's right. We must concentrate on the things we can control. You need to focus on how to get into the Forum without passing out. If you can't do that, nothing else matters, does it?"

Jules made a small sound, like a whimper. Bastien put his paw on her hand to comfort her, shooting daggers at Violetta for lumping everything on Jules's shoulders. He knew she valued speaking the truth, but didn't she realise how her blunt speech affected her granddaughter? Especially now. He'd have to have words with her later.

Or maybe Tamuel could say something to her now. He glanced at his friend, saw the glint in his eyes as he looked between Jules and Bastien. *"What is it? What have you thought of?"*

"Jules is right – the curse is acting curiously. Also, it's strange that it is growing more powerful and not less. It makes me wonder what's at the heart of its power source."

Violetta sat forward. "Power source? That would be Clodia wouldn't it – ah." She sat back, expression wondering. "I had never thought of that."

"Never thought of what?" Jules asked.

"The source of power after all this time. Curse lore states that a curse must have a power source – usually that of the witch or wizard who spelled it."

Tamuel nodded. "That's right. But no magical being alone is strong enough to power a curse for this long unless they have progeny to tie into powering their spellwork, and even then, it couldn't be maintained at this level of strength. I've often wondered what kept it going through the ages."

Jules nodded. "Wouldn't the HeartsBlood Gem have something to do with that?"

Tamuel paused, eyebrows screwing up in thought. "Maybe. But only if added to an active power source. And only if it was kept near that power source."

"Well, we think it was kept near the pentacle, don't we?"

"The pentacle lost most of its power in the casting, so no. That wouldn't be it."

"Didn't Esta write in her journal that she thought Clodia channelled into the power of her Goddess to bind the curse?"

"You never mentioned feeling the Goddess Vesta there."

"I didn't."

"What is he saying?"

Tamuel told them what Bastien had said, then followed it with, "But that is pure speculation on the young Vestal Virgin's part because there was no evidence that the Goddess Vesta appeared at all."

"Of course she didn't. Vesta never manifested. She was a Goddess hidden in time and mystery." Jules said. "I've done a lot of research on all the pantheons over the years, and Vesta remained one of the most mysterious and secret. In fact, unlike many other Gods and Goddesses, there was no statue or bust of her in any of her forms. But her lack of manifestation is hardly proof she wasn't there. She could have just reached through her High Priestess to place the curse, thereby ensuring it would be powered for eternity."

"Ah, but," Tamuel raised his finger. "Gods and Goddesses are powered by those who worship them and Vesta no longer has followers. So even if she did help Clodia – which is by no means certain – she would not have enough power now to make the curse stronger and act like it is."

Jules sucked in a breath and chewed on her lip, her brow furrowed in that way she had when she listened to something interesting. Nodding slowly, she said, "That's true, but … isn't she just one face of the ultimate Goddess of the Hearth and Home? The curse would be powered by her connection to that source because we still worship many various faces of that Goddess."

"She has a point."

"True," Tamuel nodded. "But each manifestation could only exist as part of the whole, with worshippers powering them through belief. Without worshippers, there is no power to tether her to the essential power that is the source of all Gods and Goddesses – the Eternal Well." He waved his hands. "And while this discussion is fascinating, we're off track. What I was trying to say is that I'm certain now that the curse is powered by the magic locked inside of you, Jules."

Violetta's eyes widened. "Of course. That's where it went."

"What?" Jules asked her.

"Your power. It never went into Clodia as she designed. It somehow got locked inside you. It has been powering the curse all this time."

"But why does it react so violently against any outward source of power?"

Tamuel shrugged. "Perhaps it's trying to protect her from more tampering?"

"That doesn't make sense. Why would it hurt her?"

"I guess the powers being Goddess-touched has something to do with it. Clodia got away with using them while Lianna was alive because she didn't try to wrest them from their seat – Lianna's soul. Then she tried to use the HeartsBlood Gem to bind Lianna's power and aid in the transference, but it too is Goddess-touched. That power is not meant for anyone but those who have been gifted with it. I guess, the amplification of the two together created a backlash that warped the spell and forced the powers deep inside Lianna's soul. Unfortunately, because the HeartsBlood Gem had been used in part to bind the curse to Lianna and Sebastio, it got tied into the powers now locked inside Lianna. That's why she doesn't have access to her powers – they're caught in a loop of protecting her from possible tampering by external magical forces but also powering the curse."

Bastien stilled, gaze snapping to Jules. She was trembling. He wanted to comfort her, but she looked like she would break at the merest touch. *"Why have we never realised this before?"*

Tamuel shrugged. "You couldn't remember many of the specifics and we didn't have Violetta's memories or Jules's visions to give us the missing pieces of information."

"But what does this mean?"

"It means it's my fault," Jules said as Tamuel finished his translation, topaz eyes wide, face pale. "That I could somehow stop it if I wasn't so weak." She pushed back from the table, her chair clattering to the cobbles.

"No. No, that's not what I'm saying at all," Tamuel said.

"Jules," Bastien cried out, the sound leaving his lips as a strangled meow as she turned and took off.

Bastien raced after her, but she slammed the door and he couldn't get out. By the time Tamuel wrenched the door open, Jules was nowhere to be seen.

Bastien swore, his cat mouth making excellent work of the sounds, but none of it helped. *"I have to find her."*

"We will. But you can't do it like that. Stay here. I'll go."

"Neither of you are going anywhere," Violetta said, joining them at the door. "Jules will be back."

"How can you be so certain?" Tamuel repeated Bastien's question for Violetta.

"I know my granddaughter. No matter how upset she is right now, no matter how much she might want to give up, she won't. She'll be back because she longs to be loved and because she needs to save you." With that, she turned back inside. "Come on, you two. No point standing there gaping at the empty street. We've got a lot of work to do to prepare for tonight. We've only got three more nights to get this right."

CHAPTER 11

*J*ules tore down the cobbled street, through a plaza and into another, weaving in and out of the crowds of sight-seers and locals celebrating Carnevale.

It was too much. All of it – too much.

She was bound to a curse because of a power she had no access to. She was bound to a curse because of a love she'd never felt. She was bound to a curse because an ancient Coven-leader-High-Priestess-bitch-witch had coveted something that wasn't hers.

And because of all of that, her best friend had been dragged into the mess with her. Or he was Lianna's best friend.

She was getting the dregs of Lianna's life – including her lover.

"You want to be loved."

"Not if he doesn't love me for me."

"But he loves Lianna and you are Lianna."

"No, I'm not! You are Lianna and I am … me!" Her shout rang off the walls and cobbled street around her. Birds scattered with a flutter and squawk at the end of the street. A couple of people stopped to stare at her. She stared back before moving on, hands shoved into the pockets of her parka and slouching against the cold.

Thoughts a babble in her mind, she wandered, aimless, past

churches and through piazzas, completely unaware of anything but dodging the people she passed.

Until the grumbling in her stomach became so loud, she couldn't ignore it anymore.

She patted her pocket, relieved to feel her phone – she had a credit card tucked in the back of the case. She glanced around to find a place to eat.

Her gaze stopped and skated up the sixteen granite columns to the domed roof of the building in front of her.

The Pantheon.

"We've been here before."

"No, I haven't. Lianna di—"

Her head swam. She staggered sideways, vision shifting.

"Lianna! Lianna, come away from there!"

A woman stood a few metres away, her white *stola* flowing around her, brows pushed together in displeasure, gesturing impatiently. Four other women dressed just like her stood waiting behind her.

"Lianna. Don't let them touch you."

She pulled her arms in close, but she needn't have bothered. The crowd milled around her, but nobody was closer than two arm-spans. They kept their distance, much like for someone who carried plague.

"Do I have plague?"

"No, we're a Vestal Virgin."

Ah, Goddess. Another vision. *"Not now. Not now."*

"Yes, now."

She tried to push out of it, to grab onto the internal voice and separate herself from it or the memory or something; to reach for clarity where there was fog and ache and confusion.

But it was no use. The tourists that surrounded her in their jeans, warm jackets and beanies, holding their phones up to film and take selfies, dissolved, becoming people in tunics and togas, their heads bowed, hands raised, offering food and floral arrangements, dropping them at her feet as she stopped. Their lips formed words seeking blessings, their need pressed into her. She couldn't catch her breath.

She lifted her hand to rub her aching head, the sleeve of the white gown she wore falling back to show gold armbands twining up her arm like snakes. Bracelets Clodia had put on her only this morning and told her never to take off as they were a gift from the Goddess.

But they were tight and stung her skin and ever since Clodia had put them on her, she'd felt a little strange. As if she wasn't quite herself.

Perhaps she should go inside the temple and pray. She looked up at the Pantheon of Agrippa. It wasn't Vesta's temple, but it would be cool and quiet and she could collect herself in there. And Vesta wouldn't mind if she was prayed to from another temple, even if it was Agrippa's.

"Lianna. Where are you going?"

She didn't answer, just kept moving towards the Pantheon.

"And this brings us to the Pantheon of Agrippa, or Roman Pantheon as it's mostly called." She stumbled to a halt, looking around to see who spoke in that loud, nasal voice. They weren't speaking Latin. They were speaking … English!

English. A language that didn't exist when she was alive. Because she wasn't alive. She was … Jules.

Jules focused in on the voice, the words as the world spun around her.

"Now simply known by most as the Pantheon, it was built in 126 AD during the reign of Hadrian. Its most notable feature is not the sixteen granite columns on its facade. Can anyone guess what it is?"

Someone bumped into her. "Sorry, love. Just trying to hear what our tour guide is saying."

Jules blinked, trying to focus on the woman in front of her – her wide smile, her brassy hair, the outrageously pink coat she wore. "Um … tour guide?"

The woman pointed at a man who was saying, "The Pantheon's most notable feature is the fact that the circular building has the exact same diameter as its height and the dome itself is bigger than the one that graces St Peter's Basilica."

"*Interesting.*"

"*It is.*"

She blinked, the Pantheon rising in front of her. The brassy woman and the tour group were already gone, replaced by another.

What just happened?

"You had a vision."

"Then why aren't I knocked on my arse and out for the count?"

"I have no idea. Perhaps you should figure it out."

"You think?"

A flash went off in front of her, blinding her.

She blinked rapidly, trying to clear the flare of light from her eyes. Then gasped.

It was night.

When had that happened? How long had she been lost in a vision? Hours apparently.

Shit.

She spun around to figure out which direction she needed to go and came to a halt.

Bastien stood there, Tomaso and Violetta at his side.

Oh Goddess. What must he think? She swallowed hard. "I—"

"Are you okay?"

She snapped her mouth closed and breathed in sharply. He was worried about *her*? "I'm fine. I'm sorry I ran off like that. I just needed to think."

"You don't have to apologise. There's a lot to take in."

"There is."

He erased the distance between them in a few steps and took her hand in his.

Calm flowed through her. His touch. It was like home – friendly, familiar, warm. Even staring into his white eyes was a balm.

Soon to be gone forever.

She forced herself to smile past the threatening tears even though he couldn't see it and answer him. "Shall we go?" She took his arm and headed down the nearest street.

"Are you okay to try again? It's okay if you're not up to it—"

"No. I want to. I need to." For you.

"Then why do you sound so sad?"

She bit her lip and looked down at the cobbled street they walked down. She shrugged, not wanting to mention him leaving her again.

"Jules." He touched her cheek briefly, his mouth curling into a sad little smile. "You know you can tell me anything."

"I know. But it doesn't matter. All that matters is freeing you—"

"Us."

She nodded. "From this curse."

"You don't look so good, Jules," Tomaso said as he came up beside them, Violetta on his other side.

"I'm okay. I just had another vision."

"You did?"

"Are you okay?"

She bit her lip. "Yes. Obviously."

"But … you're not unconscious or sick?"

She told them about what had just happened.

"That's amazing. Do you know how you did it?"

"I don't."

"Tell me exactly what happened and what you were doing."

She glanced at Tomaso. "Can we get something to eat first? I'm starving."

"Of course. We've got time."

"Even if we didn't, we'd get her something to eat," Bastien growled.

"Of course we would," Violetta said. "Come on, there's a pizza place on the corner there that looks a little less busy than the rest. We should be able to get something there and make it down to the Forum by midnight."

"Pizza okay?" Bastien asked her.

"Sounds perfect."

As they walked towards the hole in the wall serving pizza, she couldn't help but grimace at the thought of going down to the Forum again. A part of her didn't want to go. She didn't want to find where the curse had been created, didn't want to break the curse in three nights and see this lover of Lianna's look at her and realise she wasn't the same. Wasn't enough.

What about Bastien?

Bastien. She glanced up at him. Yes. She had to do it for Bastien. He needed to be freed so he could finally live his own life. And then she could get on with her life too – possibly more loveless and lonelier than before, but that was a price she was willing to pay for him.

"But you'll have your magic. And Sebasti—"

She winced as the voice that was Lianna mentioned her lover's name. *"Yeah."*

Violetta ordered as they found a seat at a little wobbly table, wolfing down four slices and a big bottle of water. When she was done, still having time to kill, they wandered through the slowly emptying streets. The cool night air caressed the heated skin of her face as they came out next to the Tyber. She wanted to stop, to stay, just stare down at the lights twinkling in its black surface.

"Do you feel like talking about what happened at the Pantheon now?" Bastien asked softly.

She nodded and started to relate how she'd found herself in front of the Pantheon and how the vision had slowly crept in. "I think I was young – I was being escorted by other Vestal Virgins. But I didn't feel well. The gold armbands Clodia had put on me that morning hurt and I just wanted to go into the cool of the Pantheon and pray to Vesta in peace and quiet."

"Gold armbands. Lianna always wore them. She couldn't take them off—" He stumbled.

"Bastien." She pulled him upright.

"Is he okay?" Violetta asked, turning to face them.

"I'm fine." He waved them on.

Jules frowned at him, but he pulled her on, asking, "Do you think it could have been the tour guide? What he said? You love learning new things."

"It could have been because you got shoved. Or the flashes."

"No. They came after. He's right. It was the information."

She leaned up and kissed his cheek. "You're a genius."

"Why is he a genius?" Tomaso asked.

She told him.

"That is genius. Should we give it a little trial?"

"How?"

"As we get to the concourse where it hit you hardest last time, I'll tell you something I know about the Colosseum, and we'll see what happens."

"Okay." She couldn't think of a better way to see if this information would help.

Shouts and cries started pressing into her mind as they drew closer, prickles chasing over her skin. By the time she'd stepped onto the concourse, images wavered through her mind: crowds of people rushed around her, their excitement about today's upcoming spectacle in the Flavian Amphitheatre made nausea roll in her stomach.

"Do you know how the Colosseum got its name?" Tomaso asked. She shook her head. "There was a monstrous statue the Emperor Nero commissioned of himself to show the Roman people how great he was."

She nodded. She could see the ghostly silhouette of the statue, the men who had stopped to lean on its base. Guards moved the men on, but not before she heard them agree to meet at the feet of the *Colosseo* same time next week.

"So, people started to call the monstrous statue *Colosseo*." Tomaso's voice filtered through to her. "The statue of Nero was eventually knocked down but the nickname *Colosseo* had, by that time, transferred to the amphitheatre."

"That's funny. I always hated that statue."

"It's an eyesore."

The vision faded enough for her to see three curious faces staring at her.

"It worked." Kind of. Ghost-like people rushed towards a *Colosseo* lit up by sunlight but also curiously draped in night, with lights colouring its exterior.

Bastien's ghost-like eyes glowed as he looked down at her. "I knew you'd find a way."

Always such trust. She cleared her throat. "Thanks."

"Jules? Are you okay?"

"Can we just move back? I need to catch my breath."

They bustled her back across the road, far enough away that the press of history wasn't so bad.

Tomaso clapped his hands together as she leaned against a wall, taking in deep breaths. "This is wonderful. It seems, my friends, we have a plan. Let's head home and look up interesting facts."

"Go home? But why don't we just try now?"

"That little fact only got us a few feet onto the concourse."

"But you must know more."

"I do, but not nearly enough to get you all the way to the Vestal Temple and beyond."

"But … I don't want to lose another night."

"Better that we're fully prepared than run out of facts and lose you to a vision for another two days."

"He's right, Jules."

Her excitement fizzled out, her shoulders sagged, exhaustion making itself fully known. "I feel like I've just put another barrier in our way."

Tomaso touched her shoulder. "On the contrary. You've just found us the way through the maze. Violetta, how about you and I head back and start searching up information? We'll meet you back at the villa."

With that, he and Violetta hurried across the road and when they were far enough away, disappeared, their magic taking them back to Tomaso's home.

Even at this distance, the magic shoved at Jules, making her stumble.

Bastien caught her, held her to him. "You okay?"

"Yep. Fine. Just disappointed."

"Don't be. This is good news. Just concentrate on that."

"He's right."

As they began to walk away from the Colosseum, the press of the past faded almost immediately. As they passed the *Area Sacra di Largo Argentina* with its community of cats, Jules had a sudden memory from her vision and stopped.

"Jules? What is it?"

"Clodia said something about an army of cats when she started her spell." She frowned over the memory. "Do you think that was a punishment she meted out to those who displeased her, like you did? Maybe some of these cats are actually the ancestors of people she cursed."

He shook his head, mouth cocked a little on one side. "No. I think that punishment is unique to me."

"Maybe I should come back and check these are all actually cats after I get my powers back."

"Yes, *we* should." He turned, reaching out to cup her face, a deep frown furrowing his brows. "What you said before, about me leaving you. You don't have to worry about that. I promise."

She wrapped her cold fingers around his warm wrists, trying to steady herself, blink away the tears. "Don't make promises you might not want to keep."

"It might be you who doesn't want me with you."

She chuckled, a hoarse, broken sound. "Never going to happen." She expected the voice to say something, but it stayed curiously silent.

Their breaths mingled visibly in the air between them for long moments, then he leaned down and pressed his lips to her forehead, their warmth lingering as he pulled away.

She sucked in a breath and closed her eyes, his scent all around her. Oh Gods. It hurt too much to think of him going away, but despite what he said, she wouldn't hold him to her. He deserved his freedom.

He smiled as he tucked her arm in his again. "Tell me more about the Rome you see."

Her voice was hoarse by the time they made it back to the villa. Once inside, Violetta insisted she go upstairs to rest and leave them to search out the reams of information they'd need for their try tomorrow night.

"But don't you need my help?"

"It's best if we tell you things you might not have heard."

"Bas can stay," Tomaso said. "He and Violetta will know best what you'll find interesting."

Bastien made a sorry face, but before he went to join Tomaso said, "I'll be up before I change."

"Okay."

She headed upstairs, frustratingly aware she only had two more nights to get everything right. The thought of breaking their curse and freeing Bastien should make her happy – instead, she struggled not to break into tears.

CHAPTER 12

"*A*re you ready?" Bastien asked.

"Sure."

"You don't sound very confident."

"Shut up."

The clocks struck twelve in the city around them, signifying the change from the eleventh to the twelfth. She came to a stop opposite the Colosseum, clutched Bastien's arm even though he was still recovering from his change just over an hour ago – so much later than the day before.

Screams and the vibration of pain from the ruins opposite thrummed through her.

Tomaso lifted the folder he carried. "Shall I read this out to you? Or do you want Violetta to do it?"

She wished Bastien could do it. But she couldn't ask him – even if he wasn't blind – because he was too weak still. "You do it," she said to Tomaso.

"Everyone okay with that?"

"Absolutely," Bastien said, his voice husky and threaded with pain.

"Let's do this," Violetta said. "Before the security guards come back this way."

Jules nodded. She swallowed hard then whispered to Bastien, "Don't let go, okay?"

"I won't." His hand slipped down to hers, squeezed.

Together they stepped off the curb.

At least if she succeeded, she'd be happy to set Bastien free to pursue his own life. And she'd have the second-hand love of her lover to—

She winced as the curse stabbed her in the chest.

"Jules?"

"Fine," she said, straightening up, rubbing her knuckles against her chest surreptitiously. "I just thought something I obviously shouldn't."

"Yeah, I'm having problems with that too." His voice was strained. He looked worse than he had when he'd come downstairs after his change.

"Do you need to sit down?"

"No. I just need to stop thinking about what we're here for."

He leaned on her more heavily as they walked forward. She held on tight, struggling to keep herself upright in the face of what the curse threw at her.

"I think we need to start now," Bastien said as they drew even with the others at the edge of the concourse.

"You okay?"

Bastien nodded stiffly. "Just the curse making itself known."

"And what about you?" Tomaso asked Jules.

She rubbed the side of her head. "It's loud in here and my vision is starting to fog. I can see ghostly people over there."

"Right then, let's get started before it gets too bad. Try to empty your mind and open it up only to the flow of information I read."

She nodded and took a step forward as Tomaso began to speak about the Colosseum and surrounds.

Shouts. Screams. Jeers. Cheers. They rose to greet her, louder and louder with every step. Pressing in.

"Concentrate on what Tomaso is saying," Bastien whispered – or maybe he shouted. It was hard to know over the noise wrapping around her.

"On our left, you will see the remains of the ancient fountain the gladiators used to wash in after a match. Unfortunately, there is little left of this remarkable piece of Roman ingenuity due to the fact Mussolini drove over it in a tank because it was in the way of his parade!"

"A tank. Wish we'd seen that."

"It would have been awful. How could he destroy something with so many stories?"

She could see the fountain, ghostly gladiators washing themselves in the late afternoon sun, slapping each other's backs. A woman ran up and gave one of them a hug.

"Aww."

"He's all sweaty."

"You're just jealous because you've never hugged a man like that."

She *was* jealous. It had been so long since anyone had touched her with kindness or affection, except Esta – and her cousin didn't count.

Lianna longed to be touched. Ached for it.

Wait. What? No. You're Jules. Not Lianna. Don't give in to it. Listen to Tomaso. Listen to ...

A sharp pain in her shoulder. "Ouch." She reached up to rub it, turning to see who had thrown whatever it was, ready to give them a serve. The words died as her gaze met the most beautiful peridot-coloured eyes. No, they were white eyes. Now peridot. Strange. But not strange.

The owner of the eyes strode closer until he stood so close he could touch her. Then he smiled down at her, his fingers brushing over the sting on her shoulder. It disappeared. *"Scuzi, bella,"* he murmured. "This was not meant for you."

Oh. His voice. It was like a caress. As she looked up at him, the world spun.

"Lianna." She blinked. Looked down at the young girl before her, dressed all in white. "I didn't think we were supposed to talk to strange men. Won't Clodia be angry?"

"Not if we don't tell her," she whispered, touching little Esta's nose through the veil, delighting in the smile that lit the young girl's face.

She let her young companion drag her away, but she couldn't help turning to look back at the man, his broad shoulders and tapered-in waist limned by the sun. He glowed.

He watched her with his unusual eyes, which oscillated from peridot to white. His features were strangely unclear, but she knew he was handsome, with a devilish smile. And the aura of power emanating from him – she'd never come across anything like it. Who was he? She longed to find out. Maybe she would. It couldn't hurt to discover his name. She held up her hand, indicating she wanted him to wait there – that she'd be back in one hour. Would he understand?

He nodded.

Excitement tingled through every pore as she followed Esta through the crowds to the temple. One hour. Then she would return to the fountain and assuage her curiosity …

"Jules. Jules? Can you hear me? She's coming around, I think."

Jules opened her eyes and looked up to see three faces looking down at her. Their expressions were hidden in the night's shadows, their heads haloed by the lights of the Colosseum behind them. "Shit." She forced herself to sit and clutched her head, groaning. "I passed out, didn't I?"

"Yes."

She rubbed the heels of her hands into her aching head as she stared at the hulk of the Colosseum opposite them. "How far did I get?"

"Further than before," Violetta said, a strange smile pulling at her lips. It wasn't very reassuring.

"How far?"

"Almost to the entrance of the Forum."

She groaned. Still not close enough. "What time is it?" Bastien was still in human form, so at least there was that. She really didn't think she was going to be able to do this without the feel of his hand in hers.

"It's twelve-thirty."

Bastien changed at two last night, so given the regression, he had until one, maybe one-thirty. "Okay. Let's go again."

The world swayed as she went to stand. She sat down with a plop.

"Take it easy," Violetta muttered.

"I can't take it easy. We don't have time."

"You won't be able to try again if you can't even stand without falling over."

"She's right."

"I don't have time to baby myself. Look at Bastien."

"He looks terrible."

The curse was really punishing him tonight – or was he nearing his change?

"It's time to be his hero. I need to put on my Wonder-Woman-big-girl-pants."

"Did we pack any of those?"

She huffed out a laugh.

"Jules?"

"I'm good." She took a few steadying breaths then pushed to her knees. The world swayed a little, but not as bad as before. After a few more deep breaths, she made it to her feet.

"You good?" Bastien said.

She took his outstretched hand. "I'm good. Let's go again." She glanced over at Tomaso. "Could you stand closer and talk louder? I could barely hear you over the ghosts in my head."

"I didn't want to be too loud in case there are guards around. My spell on the equipment and some of the surrounds won't cover the noise we make."

"I'll take care of any guards if they come running," Violetta said.

"But Jules won't be able to take the magic you use."

"I'll move as far away as I can without losing sight of you. That should help mitigate the problem."

"Do it." Jules was happy to put up with more pain if it kept everyone else safe from being caught.

They let Violetta go ahead then moved off. Voices and screams rushed at her, but Tomaso stood right beside her this time, talking loudly. She still had to concentrate on his words – the noise of the past was louder this time – but she heard enough to keep the visions at bay.

As they drew closer to the Forum, the visions pressed in on her, closer, louder. The buzz chasing over her skin turned into a prickling pain. The urge to stop, to turn around and run back the way she'd come, or submit to the darkness creeping at the edges of her vision, increased with every step, every harsh breath, but she couldn't give in. Couldn't give up. This was something she had to do if she wanted Bastien to go free. If anyone deserved more than her best effort, it was her best friend.

"That's it, Jules," Bastien said, his breath hot on her ear, his voice barely audible above the noise around her. She clung to his hand as the bits of history Tomaso related conjured up images of what it must have been like in ancient times – visions she remained in control of. The further they went, though, the harder it got. Her head was full, so full, it felt too heavy on her neck. So heavy it might just fall off.

"Off with his head."

"They didn't do that here. That's more a French Revolution thing."

"Or a Queen of Hearts thing. Off with his head. Off with hishhead. Offwishhishead!"

She giggled.

"Why is she giggling?"

"I don't know."

"Jules! Concentrate."

She took in a deep breath and shook her head. "I'm good. More. Louder."

Tomaso started shouting information, his lips almost up against her ear. The words helped to build a wall against the visions.

"Ahead is the rostra where speeches were made to the Roman people."

Her vision shimmered and she blinked rapidly to clear it. It was difficult to see what she knew was before her – the ruins. All she could see was a man standing on a rostra, temples and other marble buildings shining in the sun behind him. "Many a senator stood on the rostra here to talk to the people of Roma, but you could also find any man with a voice and a thought and the will to speak having their say. It's thought that Julius Caesar himself ..."

His voice disappeared into the angry shouts of the crowd throwing things at the man on the rostra, his gestures and expression impassioned, pleading with them to listen.

"Lianna. Where have you got to? I need you in the temple now."

Clodia, her white gown flowing around her, her anger evident even with the veil shrouding her face, moved through the crowd nearby, obviously searching for her but not seeing her. The golden bands on Lianna's arms tightened, but she held out against their insistence – she'd already done her service for today and was wrung out. She needed more time—

A hand gripped her arm and pulled her around a corner, out of sight of her High Priestess. She looked up. His face was hidden in shadow, but she knew him, his touch, the tall, muscled strength of him glowing with power, his beautiful eyes. "Sebastio."

"Meet me at ten at our usual place."

She nodded, breathless as he lifted her veil to kiss her, lips lingering, hands cupping her face in that way she adored. "I love you," he said, before letting go and disappearing into the crowd.

She hadn't returned his words of love. She would make certain he heard them tonight.

Tonight.

She pulled her veil over her face to hide her smile and moved out quickly into the crowd towards Clodia. Thankfully, the High Priestess hadn't seen her meeting with Sebastio. Lianna hated the need to keep their love a secret, but she would not be free for another few months, so she had no choice.

She had no idea how she would keep the secret for that long, but she would. It was imperative. She couldn't give him up, so hiding and secrecy was the only option.

"Jules. Listen to Tomaso. Don't let anything else get between you and his voice."

She gasped for breath as the voice she knew so well echoed through her mind.

Bastien.

"He's talking to you. Not me."

"I can't feel him."

"Hold more tightly. He's there."

"It would be easier if you kept your memories out of my head."

"I can't. They're your memories too."

She didn't have the energy to argue, so gripped Bastien's arm more tightly, leaning into him. He stumbled, too weak to hold his own weight, let alone hers. She loosened her grip. She could see Violetta standing on some stones at the end of the path, something about her stance suggesting worry and fury. She had to get this done. "How far?"

"Not far," he said. He stumbled again. Goddess, what was this doing to him? She let go of him.

Ghostly figures crowded around her. Darkness edged her vision, Tomaso's voice a bare whisper in the distance despite feeling his breath flutter her hair as he spoke right next to her ear. Her head rang with the cries of the ancient crowd surrounding her in the midday sun. Except, it wasn't day. It was the middle of the night. And the buildings around her were no longer shining monoliths to Rome's glory, but rubble and dust.

She gasped, trying to catch her breath. Her heart pounded and her knees trembled. She stumbled, caught herself, kept going.

"Jules? Jules, are you okay?"

She nodded.

"I'm so sorry. I can't touch you to help you. Even holding back my power I could still send you spiralling into a vision or hurt you if I did. Can you keep going?"

"More … info."

Her head swam as they made their way down into the ruins, the pain increasing. Her companions were mere shadows around her, their presence, their words, helping, but every step was a nightmare as her vision schismed between the past and the present. But she had to do this. Had to.

They passed the Temple of the Priestesses of Vesta.

"Home. Where I'm keeper of the holy flame."

"No. That was me. You're Jules Stevens, Coven librarian."

"Failed witch."

"Don't call yourself that."

The repartee with the Lianna-presence gave her something else to cling to. Breath sawed in and out of her chest, the pain intensifying with every step she took.

Something warm slung around her shoulders, squeezed. "Jules. You're doing it."

Bas.

One step. Another.

And another.

For Bastien.

Her lungs squeezed. Tears streamed from her eyes and she could barely see – not the ruins, not the images of ancient temples and buildings she knew so well.

Oh Goddess. It wasn't going to be enough. She was fading, falling, neither here nor there. Not Jules or Julianna or Lianna. She was nothing but pain and a screaming rage that filled her ears and took everything from her.

"The magic of the pentacle. Look, there it is! She's found it."

"I knew she would."

"Tomaso, help me get Jules up. She can't touch it any longer. She's already bleeding."

"My power."

"Pull it right back and touch nothing but her jacket. The combination of your jacket and hers should act as enough of a shield to protect her from anything you can't keep from slipping out."

She was lifted, relief shuddering through her as the pain lessened, but the world still spun around her, nausea a sickening roil in her stomach. She was put down to lean against a large stone. Bastien's arm went around her again, his lips near her ear. "You did it. You did it."

"By Eros's grace. It's glowing faintly. Can you see it? How could we have not seen this before, Violetta?"

Jules barely had a moment to register the joy of her success before Bastien's cry of pain lit the night. His entire body tensed then jerked violently, the arm around her shoulders a crushing weight, bearing them both to the ground.

"Bastien!"

"Jules, run. Get away."

But she couldn't. Couldn't let go of him. The magic of his change, the darkness and pain, sucked her into their madness and everything was gone.

CHAPTER 13

*J*ules didn't wake until the day was almost over. It had been an agony just to sit there and will her to wake in time, but it was even more of an agony to watch her once she finally did.

She barely touched the meal Violetta brought her, instead sitting on the window seat to stare out the window at the gathering shadows of night, flinching at every strike of the city's bells as the hours passed. The slump of her shoulders and the stiff line of her back told him all he needed to know about how she felt. Tension sang from her, almost as loud as the Carnevale celebrations lifting from the streets and plaza below.

Bastien wished he could tell her everything was going to be okay, that despite her thinking she was weak, she was the strongest person he knew, but he couldn't say any of it. He was still a cat. All he could do was sit on the bed and watch her.

Damn his changes. It was bad enough it took so much out of him, but that it had almost taken down Jules ... Even though Tamuel had grabbed him and magicked him away, it hadn't been fast enough – or far enough away. There hadn't been time. The magic of his change had already begun to cut into Jules – there had been so much blood –

so rather than pull Bastien away, Tamuel had just grabbed him and gone.

The scream that had followed them – hells. He thought he'd killed her. Somehow though, she hadn't been too badly hurt. Lots of bruises and shallow cuts, the worse one on her forehead from when Tamuel's translocation magic had hit her that hadn't even needed stitches. All that magic so close had drained her though, far too much. She looked almost as bad as he felt.

She turned back now to smile at him, face drawn, the bandage on her brow just under her hairline only a little paler than her face.

She touched it. "Please, Bastien. Don't blame yourself. It's not your fault."

He wished he could tell her it wasn't her fault either. It would have to wait until he changed tonight.

But his change, when it came just before eleven, was brutal.

Afterwards, he needed Tamuel's help to shower and change and get downstairs, helping him to sit in the chair at the little table outside opposite Jules. Her aura was slow and a little muddy, but not as bad as it was when she woke. Still, she wasn't herself.

As he ate, Tamuel announced they wouldn't try for the Forum again tonight. "We have discovered what works to get you into place, Jules, but need to find more information to grab your attention and help keep you in the now."

"I think it's good idea," Violetta said before either he or Jules could protest. "Besides, I think it best if you both preserve your energy. You're going to need it tomorrow night."

"I'm fine. If Jules wants to go down and try again, I'll be ready." He had to be.

"No, you're not. You look like shit."

"Stop trying to baby me," he snapped to Tamuel with mind-speech. *"I won't let this curse stop me from helping Jules break it."*

Tamuel placed his hand on Bastien's shoulder, the buzz of power giving Bastien a little boost of energy. *"Of course not. But while I can help you with a little boost of power, I cannot do so for Jules. She's exhausted. She must rest. Surely you can see that in her aura? But she will go down there again if you say you're okay. We can't let her do that. Not if we want her to be as strong as possible tomorrow night. Given what's been happening to you, losing so many hours in your human form, this might be our last chance."*

Bastien fell silent, then said, "Actually, I do feel terrible. Resting up tonight and researching more information sounds good." He picked up a chop and tore into it.

Jules slipped onto the bench beside him. "Is it really that bad?"

"This is helping," he said, waving the chop bone.

She cleared her throat but said nothing.

"Eat up, Bastien," Violetta said briskly. "Then Jules best head upstairs and get a good night's rest. Bastien, you can do some research for a few hours, but then you need to rest too."

"That's my cue to go then," Tamuel said, standing and grabbing his coat.

"Go where?"

Tamuel's aura twinkled. "Our success last night helped me pin down where the HeartsBlood Gem is. And it's probably better I get it tonight than risk waiting until tomorrow. I'd also like to do some prep on the area to make certain everything is as ready as it can be for tomorrow night. Rest up, Bastien. You too, Jules. I'll see you all tomorrow."

Jules, at Violetta's urging, left Bastien to finish his three plates of food in silence and think over everything that had happened so far. Violetta disappeared as well after saying she was off to the Roman Coven to find some more information that covered the magical history of the area around the Forum.

Bastien finished eating and then spent an hour doing research and writing down some notes for Tamuel. But after an hour, he struggled to focus, his gaze returning more often to the stairs. He still had two hours as a human. He didn't want to spend it alone researching or sleeping. He wanted to talk to Jules now. Needed to talk to her, to touch her one more time as a human before whatever happened tomorrow night.

He made his way upstairs to her room and halted outside.

There was no sound. He pushed the door open.

Soft sounds of her sleeping reached him – she really was exhausted. Even though he ached to talk to her, to hold her one more time before everything changed, he backed out of the room, closing the door quietly behind him.

~

JULES AWOKE MID-MORNING, feeling far more refreshed than she had in days. She blinked into the bright sunlight streaming into the room, then sat upright with a gasp.

She'd missed talking to Bastien last night before he changed back into a cat.

She spun. He was on his bed, curled up and fast asleep – he must have come in after his change. She ran her hand over his soft head and down his body – so thin – but he didn't wake, so she left him alone and went downstairs to prepare food for him.

When he finally padded into the kitchen, she turned with a bright smile on her face. "You're awake. I've made you all your favourites." She gestured to the table. He gave a grateful meow, leaped up and began to eat.

She continued to cut up more ham. She'd never felt the need to fill the silence with him, but now, suddenly, she couldn't stand it. "So, Valentine's Eve tonight. Big one, hey? Maybe by Valentine's Day, we'll both get our happy ever afters." Her face crumpled.

Oh Goddess. What did I say that for?

She tried to pull it together, but it didn't work. Already, she felt the loss of her best friend in all the world – the one person who wasn't family who liked her for her. Maybe even loved her for her.

Pain spiked through her head at the thought, but she hid her wince, spinning away from Bastien's curious gaze. "I need to clean my teeth," she said and rushed out, sprinting up the stairs and into their room. She went into the bathroom and only then realised she still had the big knife in her hand she'd used to cut the ham. She put it down with a shaky hand and tried to breathe, tried not to vomit, tried to just keep her shit together. But it was so hard.

"Don't you want to help him?"

"Of course I do. But I'm going to miss him." She rubbed her chest. *"I just wish Bastien could be my forever love, my soulmate— Agh!"*

She pushed the base of her palm into her eye where pain stabbed. "Bloody, stupid, idiot, bastard, fuckity-shit curse," she said, smacking her other fist against the bathroom counter, the sting on her knuckles bright and an almost welcome relief against the throb in her head and the heavy sensation of claustrophobia squeezing around her heart.

"If Clodia wasn't already dead—"

She looked down at the knife she'd picked up.

"I've long wanted to stab that ancient bitch-witch in her cold dead heart."

Wow, she never realised she had such violent urges. Or were they Lianna's urges? It was hard to know. How could she trust how she felt about her lo— No. She wasn't going to think about him.

"Meow?"

She swung around to see Bastien sitting in the doorway, eyes full of her pain. "Don't," she said to him, rushing past to stare out the window. She couldn't face him now – not with this raw, empty hole in her heart. It was like he'd already left her and she was left with … nothing but memories.

But of course, Bastien being Bastien leaped up on the windowsill, rearing up to put his paws on her shoulders and look in her eyes.

"Bastien," she said, unable to stop from meeting his unblinking gaze. Such beautiful peridot eyes.

Peridot eyes like Seba—!

Pain exploded behind her eyes, her vision fracturing, split between Bastien's peridot-coloured cat-eyes and a pair of long-lashed almond-shaped eyes, the flashes of gold and emerald in the depths sparking with heat and an eternal passion she dreamed of every night since … since … he'd been taken from her by Clodia and cursed.

"Bastien," she whispered. "Bas … tien. Bas … Bas." Darkness flew towards her and she was falling, falling…

So lonely. She knew there was only a month to go, but she needed Bas now.

Power flared around her and he appeared as if he'd heard her need.

He always came when she needed him.

"Bas." She held her arms out.

"Lianna," he said, his deep voice a caress. "My love."

"I need you."

"Come." He wrapped his muscled arms around her, holding her close to his warmth, then transported them away. They landed softly in the bed he'd made for them in a little cottage in the forest. Their clothes were already gone – all except her golden armbands that never came off. His magic tingled against her skin, caressing, making her gasp.

He rolled over her, bare skin sliding against bare skin as his lips took hers. Passion that had simmered for the days she'd been without him flared to vibrant, all-consuming life. Their tongues tangled, his breath becoming hers. His taste – oranges and spice – filled her mouth. She moaned deep in her throat. It was her favourite flavour, essence of Bas. As was his scent – spicy and citrus with a bit of something deeper, like fresh-cut wood.

Her hands dug into the silkiness of his thick black hair as his mouth left hers to explore her neck and shoulders. "I love you," he said between nips and licks and suckles.

"I love you too," she gasped.

His hands were on her breasts, then his lips were there. She cried out as he sucked a nipple into his mouth, his free hand diving into the curls at the juncture of her thighs, stroking in time to his licks and sucks in that way that drove all thought out of her head and lit lightning sparks behind her eyelids.

"Look at me, Lianna. Look at me."

She opened her eyes and met his gaze. Such fire in the beautiful green-gold depths. It made her gasp and shiver as he drove a finger inside her, then another, his thumb playing her pleasure like a finely tuned harp. He kept his gaze locked on hers as he pushed her into orgasm then over the edge once, twice, three times, ignoring her begs and pleas to come inside her.

But then finally – finally – he was there, the thickness of his erection pushing into the slick heat of her, filling her in one quick glide. She moaned, her fingers digging into his hip and back as he seated himself deep inside her and began to move. Slow – oh so torturously slow. He loved to tease her with his control. But she knew some tricks herself.

She ground herself against him, fingers moving over his bottom, up his back and into his hair. She pulled his head down for a long, gloriously wet kiss before kissing a path down his strong neck to the glory of his shoulders. Then she bit down on the place between neck and shoulder where his pulse beat fast and strong.

"Witch," he groaned, then pumped faster, deeper, harder, just as she needed him to.

"God," she shouted as her muscles clenched, riding his rhythm.

"Demi-god," he said, full lips quirked in that bewitching smile she so loved.

"*My* demi-god," she said, before capturing his mouth for another long, lingering kiss.

He reared back. Gazes clashed, held as their hands gripped. Stars sparked as the wave broke over her, through her, their cries of shared passion joining in the night, a magical note of joy.

CHAPTER 14

*L*ianna came to, wrapped in his arms, legs tangled, her face pressed against the warm strength of his chest, his breath brushing over her crown. She looked up. Their gazes met. He smiled and pressed a kiss to her forehead, then one to her lips.

She settled back against him and revelled in the sensation of being here with him.

Home. Love. Fulfilment. She'd never thought to have any of these things and yet Bas gave them to her every time they were together and promised a lifetime more when she was finally free.

There was a little slither of guilt that she'd broken her vows – but there had been no stopping this once they'd met. One look and they were lost in each other. It didn't even have anything to do with the cupid's arrow he'd loosed at the woman behind her but had accidentally hit her instead. She'd never needed Bas' assurances that he hadn't 'done an Eros and Psyche', as he called it. That bolt meant for another had never worked on her. All it had done was made her turn and see him. The fact they were soulmates had taken care of the rest.

Still, it made her a little nervous. The timing was terrible – she had only a few months left of her service. She should have held back, but

221

she couldn't. Neither of them could. And now there was one month to go until she could be with Bas openly and honestly.

One month more to be in Clodia's control. One month until she could remove these horrid golden armbands that ceded her powers to Clodia while she was in the service of Vesta. She touched one now, cold where it should be warm.

Clodia said their Goddess had given Lianna the powers of a High Priestess by mistake, that she was too weak-hearted and not intelligent enough to hold her own among the cut-throat Senate and High Priesthood of Roma. "I'm doing you a favour," she'd told Lianna time and time again as she'd sapped her of her power to use in the Goddess's name, to increase the hold she held over the Senate and the people in her machinations to make the Coven of the Temple Vesta a true power. To stay in power herself. She should have stepped down years ago, but Lianna's power enabled her to keep her youth and position – and if Lianna had to put up with a bit of pain and Clodia's temper tantrums about power being given to the undeserving, she was happy to do it if it meant she never had to become like Clodia.

Power corrupted. She almost wished at times she could get rid of hers. If she had, then she wouldn't be in this position now. She would never have been a Vestal Virgin and would have been able to be with Bas free and clear right from the moment they met.

"Not long now," he murmured, speaking her thoughts out loud as he often did.

"I just hope she doesn't turn her eye to Esta."

He nuzzled her neck, his erection brushing against her side. "She won't. Esta isn't powerful enough to tempt her. She'll be looking for another Goddess-touched witch like you to use. Esta will be safe. And you will soon be free and have full control over your powers. I can't wait to teach you a thing or two."

"Really," she said, rolling over him and taking him inside her again. "Perhaps you could teach me now."

"Perhaps I could."

After their passion was spent for a second time, she snuggled down, cuddling Bas's head to her chest, rubbing her cheek against him.

He yawned. His hand brushed over her stomach, then froze. "Lianna." He bolted upright, lines of confusion furrowing his brow. He moved his hand over her stomach again as his eyes met hers. "Lianna. There is life growing in your womb."

"What? No. That's impossible." She sat up, shaking her head. "I've spelled precautions. I should not be able to fall pregnant until I release them." The dregs of power she had access to were strong enough for that.

He ran his hand over her again. "I'm not wrong. I can feel him. Our son. Growing even now."

She grasped at her stomach. "Impossible." But it wasn't. She felt what he felt. The spark of life inside her growing where it shouldn't be able to grow. How was this possible? She closed her eyes and checked her binding spell.

It had a break in it. A black thread of Clodia's control had snaked out from the armband and sliced through the binding. She was no longer protected against the seed of a demi-god.

"No. No." This was proof she'd broken her vow.

"It will be okay. It is just taken. You will be free before anyone knows."

"But the babe … it will grow faster than usual because of who you are. I will show in a few weeks."

"I'll help to keep the babe hidden. It will be okay. Soon you will be free and then we will be together in full – you me and our son."

She wanted to cling to his words, to hold onto them and never let go, but realisation hit her, making her feel sick. "You don't understand. She won't let me go. She never intended to. She did this on purpose. She'll use this to bind my power to her forever."

"I won't let that happen.

"How? She'll sense your interference. And she's too clever not to have thought of every single plan we might make to get out of this. Oh Goddess. If she accuses me of treason and I am buried alive, she'll be able to syphon off my power and I won't be able to stop her. She made certain of that." She touched one of the gold bands on her arms then clutched her stomach. "This is the proof she needs to do it. To take my powers for her own. I knew she seemed too accepting about my time under her power coming to an end. She meant for this to happen." Her gaze slammed into his. "Oh, Bas. Is she the reason we fell in love? Your bolts never miss their target – so why did you hit me?"

He grasped her hands. "I don't know. But it didn't work, so even if she was involved, it has no bearing on this. You are my soulmate."

"That is just a lucky coincidence. I know she did this. She meant for that bolt to hit me so I would fall in love with the first man I saw – you. She didn't need for us to be soulmates." Her stomach rolled and she swallowed down bile, trying not to show how truly frightened and panicked she was. "I know she did this. She made it so I would break my vows and now she's going to use it for her own gain." Goddess – if she could do this to one of her own Coven, then what would she do to anyone else who got in her way? Tears streaming down her face, she pushed away from him. "You have to go. Save yourself."

"I will never leave you and our child."

"But you must." She shoved at him, trying to get him to leave their bed. "It is our only chance. I fear she will soon discover this pregnancy through whatever magic she has spelled these armbands with. She will strike quickly. I need you to be safe from her machinations. I need you to make sure our child is safe."

"I'm a demi-god. What can she do to me?"

"This."

Lianna swung around at the sound of Clodia's voice behind her. The High Priestess stood in the doorway, eyes gleaming in the red glow of the gem she wore around her neck. "No!"

Bas made a choking sound. She turned to see him frozen in place, mouth open, eyes popping like he was choking.

"Stop. Stop! What are you doing?" She scrambled off the bed, legs tangling in the sheets, and landed at Clodia's feet to look up into eyes of madness. "Please. Please stop this. I'll do anything you want. Just don't hurt him. Don't hurt our child."

Clodia cackled. "I have you now." She gripped Lianna's arm, fingers pinching, and hauled her to her feet. "You thought you could leave me and have it all – a man, a child, a happy life and the power that was meant to be mine too?" She leaned in, her spittle sizzling on Lianna's cheeks as she spoke. "You will never have your true love and perfect life. They, like your powers, belong to me now." She put her hand over Lianna's stomach. "He's already quickening." Lianna looked down to see her stomach expand, the child inside her growing ten times faster than a human babe because of the powers that lived in his cells. "The child of a demi-god and a Goddess-touched witch. The power will make him even more valuable to me than you and he'll be in my grasp so very soon."

"No!" She cried, trying to engage her powers, to save herself, Sebastio, their child, but Clodia lifted the glowing red gem, its red-heart pulsing with a sickening throb, and she was falling, falling …

… "Wake up. Wake up, you silly bitch."

Her cheek stung as a slap sounded in the air. She blinked, pulling herself up and out of the vision.

"Wake up. Faster." Another slap.

Head ringing, she raised her arms in protection, peering through them to see who was hitting her. "Grandmama?" Violetta had slapped her?

"I am not your grandmama. By the Goddess, are you too stupid to see?" She lifted her hands as if to showcase herself. Her perfect bob was a crackling halo around her head, and her features kept flickering between her own and someone else's.

"Clodia."

"Are you sure?"

"Yes."

"Clodia?"

The ancient witch wearing Violetta's face smiled viciously. "Yes. Your grandmama came snooping around my temple the night she arrived in Roma. So eager was she to help break my curse, to try to gain back more of Esta's memories, that she stupidly came to the temple ruins at the witching hour and called on the spirits. The moment she did, she opened herself to me and I slipped in. I've been with her, controlling her, since before you arrived."

Jules pushed herself upright from where she'd slumped on the floor. The room swayed around her as she gasped, "How were you still there?"

Clodia chuckled, low and raspy. "I've been haunting the place, knowing you'd be back one day to break my curse. And here you are."

"But why take Violetta?"

She sniffed. "She was easy pickings. I've been pretty convincing, don't you think?" She patted her hair. "Even the cupid didn't know it was me." Her smirk made icy fingers crawl up Jules's spine.

"What cupid?"

Clodia snorted out a laugh. "Your son, of course. Tamuel. Sorry, I mean Tomaso." She chuckled. "Clever cupid escaped me all those years ago somehow even though he was but a new-born; and he almost escaped me now. I would never have guessed who he was if he hadn't used his magic to whisk Sebastio away from the Forum two nights ago. He didn't even think to mask his magical scent. So like his father."

"His father?"

"Your lover, of course. Sebastio. Bas. Bastien." She pointed at him – he stood frozen on the bed, back arched, fur ruffled, mid-hiss. "He's not the servant you thought he was. There was never any servant – that was just a false memory planted to make it so you never remembered who he was. Although, given all the visions you've been having, I thought maybe you had guessed. I guess my curse is not as weakened as I thought."

"Weakened?" Was she crazy? "It's stronger than ever."

Clodia snorted. "You're stupider than Lianna ever was. And more gullible. The curse hasn't been getting stronger. If it had, you would never have seen the things you've seen in your dreams and visions and you wouldn't have been able to speak to Bastien, let alone be friends with him. Violetta had started to suspect how weak the curse was becoming, but thankfully I got to her before she could mention anything. And then it was a simple matter to make you all think it was strengthening with the help of all this lovely magic she has access to. Do you know how delicious it's been, using your beloved grandmama's magic against you?" Her smile was horrible – Violetta's face moving in a way it never had before. "It was so much fun to make things harder for you. You always had it too easy."

"You won't win. I'm going to break the curse."

"Goodie." She clapped her hands, cackling. "Oh, the look on your face. You think I was trying to stop you from breaking the curse? On the contrary, I've been waiting here since my death, unable to take my rightful power or place among the Gods." She leaned closer, the ghostly eyes behind Violetta's manic. "I will break the curse at midnight on this Valentine Eve so that I can slowly drain you of power as I meant to do 2,000 years ago, and you will be unable to stop it. Finally, I will get my due."

"Tomaso will stop you."

Clodia's shriek of laughter rang around the room, making Jules' head throb more. "Tamuel has already been bound into the pentacle."

"What? But he went to get the HeartsBlood Gem."

"And he never came back."

"Yes. You were right about where it was. After your power failed to come to me, powering my curse in a way I never intended when it buried itself deep inside you, I couldn't make the HeartsBlood Gem move from your burial place. I had to leave it there, in its own grave at the heart of the pentacle. Tamuel was so thrilled to find it, he didn't even question why I was there as he freed it – something he could do only because he is your son despite the fact it is magic only meant for women of power to use. But once he'd freed it, it was easy enough to take it and use it, as I did against Sebastio, binding him to the pentacle as I did the night of his birth."

"You're a monster."

"No. I'm a Goddess in the making. Now, for your instructions for tonight's events."

Jules struggled up from the floor, limbs heavy and uncooperative. "You can't make me do anything – if you could, you already would have."

"True. Like that night centuries ago, you had to agree to be there of your own free will. And like that night, I will use your love against you. When I threatened to abort your unborn babe, you agreed so easily." She flung out her hands. There was a pop of noise and a rush of wind and suddenly Bastien lay in her arms.

'No!' Jules took a stumbling step forward.

Clodia gripped his neck, squeezing. "If you do not come, your lover will never be human again. And I will make sure Violetta and Tamuel pay too. I'm very good at curses, as you know. And I have the HeartsBlood Gem to help bind them."

"No. You can't." The ground pitched under her; her head still hazy from her vision.

"I can and I will, if you don't do as I say."

"How … how do I know you will free him – free all of them – if I come like you ask? You broke your word last time. You cursed all of us."

"I was wrong. You aren't as stupid as Lianna." Clodia's slow smile made her shiver. "I vow on the life and power of our Goddess that I will not harm them if you come of your own free will. But if you do not come, all will die." She glanced at the clock. "You have an hour to decide." Then with another pop and displacement of air that pushed Jules against the wall, Clodia disappeared.

Jules scrabbled over the bed, grabbed her phone and stared at the date and time.

11:00 pm.

13 February.

Despair flooded her, stealing her breath.

She'd lost the day to her vision of Lianna and Sebastio.

"Why did you show me now?"

"You had to know. To know who Bastien is to us."

But she had known. Had always known. He was her best friend, her constant companion and the one she loved as she loved no one else.

And he loved her. Her. Not because she was Lianna. He'd shown it in so many ways over the years and she'd never seen it. Never been able to see it because of the curse. And her own self-doubt. But none of that mattered now – she loved him. She had to do anything to save him.

"Hang on. Wait a minute. Why is there no pain?"

"Oh!"

Her power. It hadn't punished her via the curse. Had it all been Clodia? No. She'd felt pain before coming here. Something else had changed – what? Did it even matter if it gave her an edge now?

She prodded at the power that had been locked inside her entire life. It flared under her touch – but not painfully so. Bright and strong, it leaped to life, making itself available for her command as if it had only been waiting for her to welcome it, to make herself open to it.

"Goddess. I can feel our power!"

"Can you use it?"

"Can you?"

"I have no idea. I know the theory but I never got to use any of it myself."

"Well, you better figure out how, because it's the only thing we've got going for us."

"Not the only thing. You are so smart. I know you'll think of something."

Lianna was right. She might not know how to wrangle her power, but she'd spent most of her life reading about how others used their power. She could … no, she would work something out. And if this was the last time she would ever have to use her power, she was going to make it count. She could feel it now, coursing inside her, a spark quickly turning into a fire, a blaze. One she could not allow Clodia to have control over.

But how could she make certain of that and save Bastien, Tomaso and Violetta?

She had no time to figure it out. She just had to hope it would come to her. Disaster would reign if she didn't.

CHAPTER 15

*J*ules slowed as she approached the Colosseum, waiting for the barrage of visions to take her over, but nothing happened.

Clodia. It *had* all been Clodia's doing using Violetta's magic. How had none of them realised?

There had been little things that should have told her something was wrong with Violetta – little comments that stabbed at her confidence, a look she'd misinterpreted. Easy to not think it was something more nefarious given they were all under such stress – none of them had been behaving normally.

Clodia was so clever. So practiced with using magics. How could Jules ever think to beat her?

"No. No time for second guessing yourself now. I did that and look where it led me!"

She swallowed hard. *"You're right."* Stopping now wasn't an option even though she still didn't have a clue how to save her loved ones.

Her footsteps echoed against the ancient stone as she walked across the concourse and into the Forum. She'd never seen it like this, her mind too full of visions of the past. The ruins shone pale in the moonlight, the shadows shimmering with darkness. It should have been eerie, but it wasn't. It was just crumbling and sad – proof that even the strongest could falter and fall.

She straightened her shoulders as she picked her way across the ruins of the Temple of Vesta, to what had once been a lush private garden, and was now dirt and ruins and weeds. She came to a stop.

Clodia stood at the head of the pentacle Jules had unearthed two nights ago. Tomaso – Tamuel – stood at the point he'd been placed in as a babe all those centuries ago, eyes and mouth open in horror, his body unmoving.

Where was Bastien?

There, on the ground, naked and glistening with sweat, body twitching from the magics of the change that had obviously just taken place.

"Bastien," she cried, racing towards him. His breath was shallow and his ribs showed clearly through his skin. He moaned as she touched him. "Shh, shh, I'm here."

His eyes flickered open, glowing in the night, the white giving way to stunning peridot – another sign the curse was weakening. But not gone. It still needed to be broken.

"Julianna." He reached up, hand trembling, to touch her face. "So beautiful."

"You can see me?"

"Yes."

She cupped his face, thumbs stroking across too sharp cheekbones.

He swallowed hard, eyes closing. "I'm so sorry. I couldn't stop her then and I can't stop her now. The gem is too strong."

"It's not your fault." She kissed his brow. "None of us could have known it was her. Here, I've brought you something to eat." She leaned back and pulled a chocolate bar from her jacket that she'd taken from the kitchen before she left. He reached for it, but his hands shook so badly, so she unwrapped it and held it to his lips, encouraging him to bite. It wouldn't be enough, but it was all she'd had time to get, hoping she would find him transformed by the time she got here.

He swallowed the first bite. "Thank you," he said on a grateful sigh.

"Enough." Clodia's voice snapped through the air. "It is almost time. Take your position."

"No," Bastien said, grabbing at her arm as she went to get to her feet. His grip was pathetically weak, but she stilled anyway as he whispered harshly, "Don't let her take your power. Save yourself."

She bent down and kissed him, lips lingering. "I will never leave you. Not again. Besides, I have to save Grandmama – and our son."

"Our son?"

"Tamuel."

He gasped, gaze flickering to where Tamuel stood, trapped just like he was. "Of course – I should have seen it. There was something so familiar about him. I thought it was because he was a cupid, but it is because he looks a bit like his mother." His gaze returned to her. "If only I had some of my power. He and I could open a tear into the Heavenly plane and shove her where she should have gone long ag—" He jerked and cried out, face screwing up in pain, chocolate squishing in his fist.

"Bastien!"

"Leave him or I will increase his pain."

"Please, stop. I'll do as you ask." She scrambled to her feet.

Clodia smiled slowly, then lowered her hand. Bastien stopped writhing, but even though his muscles still twitched and he was covered in sweat, he looked up at her and whispered, "Don't do it."

"I love you," she whispered, then moved away to stand where Clodia told her to, where she remembered Lianna had given birth to their son. She looked across the pentacle at Tamuel. "I love you too," she said.

"I know, mother. I remember. I remember it all now. Do you?"

His voice – a youthful voice, not Tomaso's older one – rang in her head, his question capturing her mind.

Something clicked inside her. A rush of power surged, bringing with it knowledge, Lianna's and hers – learned but never used. She and Lianna might be the same, but they were also very different. And they'd learned different things about how to use magic. Where her knowledge faltered, Lianna's filled the gap. Just as where Lianna didn't know how to use what had not been practiced, Jules wasn't so constrained. She'd always known the strength of knowledge and how to use it.

And she knew exactly what to do with her powers to save those she loved.

That love, aided by the HeartsBlood Gem, had partially protected her in the past, stopping Clodia from reaching her goals. Love had chipped away at the bonds of the curse all these years; enough so that she was able to build a friendship with Bastien – loving him; enough that she loved and was loved by her grandmama and her parents; enough that she felt the connection with Tamuel even though she'd not understood it. It was enough to make her different from all those who'd come before.

Enough to give her the ability to use her unused power now because she finally understood its true strength.

And that love was even stronger now. It would be the thing that sent Clodia to hell.

She took her place in the pentacle. Clodia lifted her hands, the HeartsBlood Gem glowing on her chest. Jules almost laughed – Clodia had no idea what she was wearing. It was a part of Vesta. The essence of her power still lived inside it as it still lived inside Jules – that of home and hearth and fecundity and love – and it could never be used by someone who did not understand. It was a power that would never properly bend to Clodia's will.

It would destroy her.

"Are you sure about this?"

"Hell yeah. If Clodia wants our power, she can have it. All of it."

"Jules, no!"

Bastien pushed himself to his knees, arm stretched out towards her, the light of life in him horribly dimmed. The darkness of Clodia's power twined around him already – she would never keep her word. She was going to sap him and Tamuel and Violetta of power to do this thing.

Jules wouldn't let her. "Trust me?"

"You can't give her your power. Not to save me."

"Or me," Tamuel said in her head.

"Trust me," she said to both of them.

They both nodded wildly. "I do. Always."

"As do I." The words echoed doubly in her mind, Tamuel's voice combined with Lianna's.

It was all she needed. She turned back to Clodia. The ancient witch had finished her spell, ready to release it. She sucked power from Bastien and Tamuel and from the fifth, empty point – a link to the Eternal Well? Even better. The Gods and Goddesses would not like what Clodia was doing. "I'm ready," she said, her voice calm.

"Open yourself to me, girl, so I can break the curse and begin the transfer," Clodia shouted. "Let me have what should have been mine. Now."

Clodia's dark power darted towards her. An intense pressure then a breaking pop in her head as the curse broke. She had no time to breathe in relief as more dark power was sent her way, this time intent on draining Jules's power slowly, painfully.

Jules had other ideas. She lifted her hands. Power shot through her, sparking out of her fingers, lighting the night, arrowing to Clodia in an almighty burst.

The night lit up with the brightness of the sun as the power hit the HeartsBlood Gem then shot into Clodia, amplified.

The witch screamed. "No, no, it's too much. Slow down. I can't take it all at once."

"You wanted it all," Jules said, grinning. "You can have it." She concentrated harder, sending more power through the conduit Clodia had unwisely opened, allowing Jules access to the naked, dark heart of her. That heart was strong. Weakened, but not destroyed yet.

She'd have to use all her power.

She shoved power and more power at the bitch-witch. Clodia screamed, the sound a shrieking echo of rage and terror.

"Jules, not all of it." Tamuel's shout reached her – she'd freed him and Bastien with her action – and they had raced across the pentacle to her side.

"It has to be all," she whispered, then pushed every last ounce of what was inside her out and into Clodia. "It is the only way to be truly rid of her."

The blast of power had the effect she wanted – it shoved the spirit out of Violetta. Her grandmama collapsed onto the earth, unconscious – but it wasn't quite enough. Clodia was diminished but still there, her ghostly figure hanging above Violetta's body, trying desperately to reach her again – the only way she could now survive was in a living body.

"A tear. We need to shove her where she'll never bother us again," Jules gasped.

Bastien and Tamuel put their hands on her shoulders and opened themselves to her. Such love. Such trust.

She took their power and bound it with her own love and trust for them. "I forgive you, Clodia," she said. "But I don't think the Gods will. They don't like it when people have the hubris to steal their power. Tamuel, now."

He shoved power into her – such incredible power – and she tore open a fissure into the realms of the Gods, and with more of her power, bolstered by Bastien's, Jules shoved Clodia through the tear.

Clodia's scream disappeared into the shimmering grey beyond the tear, but it didn't close. It pulsed then she felt something tug at her. Gods! The void wanted more – it wanted all the power that had torn a hole in it. It tugged at her again, pulling her across the pentacle. "Fight it!" Bastien, Tamuel and Lianna all yelled.

But she couldn't. She saw the fingers of darkness from within – the remnants of Clodia's dark powers or something else? – reaching out, seeking, heading towards her love and her son. "No!" she cried, shoving what remained of her power at the tear so that it caught at the darkness then flew into the Void. The tear shimmered, warped then closed with a whoosh.

Wind whipped up, wiping away the last embers of the pentacle.

Silence fell.

Her knees buckled.

Her lover and her son caught her and carried her over to sit on a flat stone. Despite the chill in the air, the stone was warmed from the magic that had burned the air only moments ago.

Magic powered by a love that had lasted through the ages.

Bastien came down before her, clothing himself as he did, his gaze full of love and yet tinged by sadness. "Jules. Your power. You sent all your power into the void with her. Why did you do that?"

"It was the only way," she said, wishing he'd stop talking and just kiss her. "Didn't you feel it? There was something coming out of the Void – Clodia or something. I had to close the tear before she/it could take a hold. It wanted my power so I gave all of it. It was the only way to save us all."

"My love." He stroked her face, his eyes full of loss. "I'm so sorry."

"It's okay. I'm okay."

"How did you know to do that?"

She looked up at Tamuel. "I read about it."

He gaped at her. Bastien chuckled. "Of course you did."

"And Bastien – do I call you Bastien? Or would you prefer Sebastio?"

"I'm Bastien for you."

Her smile felt like it took up her entire face. "Bastien gave me the idea about sending her through to the Gods-plane." She smiled at Bastien, staring into his peridot eyes. "So beautiful. I'm so glad I finally get to see these and not just dream about them."

He took her hand and kissed her knuckles. "I would give up my sight if it meant you could have your magic back."

"I wouldn't." She cupped his cheek, making him meet her gaze. "Why do I need it? I have my work. I have you. And now I also have a son." She reached out her free hand to Tamuel. He took her hand in hers, holding it to his chest. She smiled up at him then back at Bastien. "It's all I've ever wanted. All I've ever wished for." She looked back at her hand wrapped in Tamuel's. "And I can touch you without worrying how it will affect me. That is magic enough."

"So wise," Tamuel said, then shimmered, his suave older man form changing into that of a young man, with twinkling peridot eyes and hair as darkly auburn and curling as hers. He squeezed her hand, his smile blazing brightly enough to light the night. "You may not be the mother that birthed me, but you're the mother of my heart."

"My son. Tell him I love him."

She did just that, brushing away the tears that leaked from the corners of his eyes.

Bastien put his hand on Tamuel's shoulder. "Son. Why did you never tell me who you were?"

"It was forbidden. To keep me from being swept into Clodia's curse, Eros took me from the pentacle in the confusion after Clodia's spell went awry. He wanted to take you too, but you were bound in ways I wasn't. So, he hid me and gave me to Persephone until it was time for me to become one of his cupids. She told me of you and what had happened and helped me look for ways to break the curse's hold on you both. She followed Esta, thinking she was a key and rescued her journal from the house fire all those years ago, but she didn't give it to me until just recently when it became clear that now was the time to use it. That you," he turned his gaze to Jules, "were the one who could break the spell."

"So in a way, my father did help me."

"I suppose he did given he gave me to the one goddess who might help. I'm so sorry though."

"For what?"

"That it took so long to be able to help you. Until a century ago, I was forbidden to contact you."

Bastien cupped Tamuel's cheek. "That is not your fault, son. The Gods and Goddesses do things for their own purposes. You were bound as much as Jules and I."

"But I almost blew it tonight. Persephone mentioned that Clodia's spirit might still be hanging around the place of her greatest defeat, but I didn't remember the warning until it was too late. I let her take the HeartsBlood Gem from me because I was too prideful, too stupid."

"No. You trusted," Jules said. "Don't ever feel sorry for that."

"Mother," he said, tears in his eyes. "I am sorry. So sorry the ultimate sacrifice was your magic."

Jules touched his cheek. "I'm just glad the sacrifice wasn't this." She cupped his cheek with one hand, Bastien's with the other. "Clodia thought my magic the most valuable thing, but it wasn't. This is. So don't be sad. Not when we've finally found each other."

A moan from the other side of the cleared area had her pushing to her feet. "Oh Goddess! Grandmama," Jules cried, rushing over to where Violetta had fallen. She couldn't believe she'd forgotten her grandmama was still there.

Violetta looked up at her, her eyes shadowed as Jules reached her. "You did it, my girl."

"I did."

"Your magic?"

"Gone. I had to use it all to defeat Clodia and close the rip into the Void."

Violetta sighed and nodded. "I am sorry."

"I'm not."

Violetta nodded, her gaze skating over Jules's smile. "Bastien and Tomaso – I mean, Tamuel?"

"Here," they both said, then helped her up.

She trembled, her form thinner than it had been before – Clodia had pulled a lot out of her in the possession and final spell. She pulled the HeartsBlood Gem from around her neck. "Here, this is yours." She held it out to Jules.

"No, I—"

"As a reminder of the strength you showed tonight and of what truly matters."

Jules took the gem and hung it around her neck. It pulsed warmly there, feeling like it belonged. "Let's go home."

"Let me," Bastien said. "I haven't been able to use my powers for 2000 years." He waved his hand. The air shimmered around them and then they were in the villa's kitchen.

Jules held still, waiting for the nausea and pain, but it didn't come.

She was finally free.

She hugged Bastien to her as Tamuel helped Violetta to a seat, put the kettle on and began to raid the fridge.

Bastien hugged her back, his smile warming her like the sun.

"Jules. You know I will never leave you. You have no need to doubt that."

"I know. I understand now. You're *my* love. Forever."

"Forever together, *my* love." His lips met hers and everything faded as she lost herself in Bastien's touch, in his kiss, and it was better than anything she could ever have wished. Love cursed no more. She was love blessed.

IN THE DISTANCE, church bells tolled one am. Tamuel glanced over at his mother and father, then, mouth quirking in happiness, put a plate of meat, cheese and bread in front of Violetta. "It's Valentine's Day," he said.

"Yes." She glanced over at Jules and Bastien, lost to everything else in the joy of their kiss. "It seems fitting."

"I'm going to find some way to get her power back to her."

Violetta's smile grew wide as she picked up a piece of cheese. "That would be nice. Although, I don't think she needs it to make her happy. Not now she finally knows the man of her dreams."

"The man of her reality," Tamuel countered.

Violetta winked at him. "May we all be blessed with such a reality."

Tamuel nodded but didn't say anything further.

Nobody could know he planned to bargain anything – even his greatest power – for his mother's magic. The power of a cupid. It was one of the most sought-after powers among the Gods because what was stronger than love? Look at what it had done here tonight.

Jules deserved to be the witch she was born to be. Not just to have magic, but to have true immortality. His mother and father deserved to be together forever.

And he was the cupid who was going to make it happen. He vowed it.

A rumble in the distance signalled acceptance of his vow.

He smiled.

THE END ... OR IS IT?

IF YOU ENJOYED Jules and Bastien's story, then continue the adventure with Tamuel and Korinna's story in:

Soul Cursed

IF YOU'VE GOT A MOMENT, I would love it if you could leave a review for _Love Cursed_. Reviews can help readers find books, and also help tell me where I'm going right and where I'm going wrong. I am grateful for all honest reviews. Thank you in advance for taking the time to let others know what you've read, and what you thought – you can leave your review at Goodreads, BookBub or the ebook retailer where you bought your copy. You can find links to the ebook retailers at:

https://www.leislleighton.com/paranormal-romance-novels/

LOVE A FREE BOOK?

YOUR FREE BOOK IS WAITING

One Fate, one mate, a bond too strong to deny ...

Paul Collins, duty-bound Pack Warlock and seer, must marry a strong witch for the good of Pack McVale. But his hidden feelings for his best-friend's sister, maternal wolf Ivy McVale, make this a more difficult pill to swallow every day. Especially when they begin to mate.

Then Paul has a vision: If they mate, Ivy will die. Desperate, Paul uses his powers to change destiny and make Ivy think she's always hated him. He can deal with any punishment the Fates make him pay for tampering with destiny, as long as Ivy lives.

After recovering from a bewildering month-long illness, Ivy notices her nemesis, Paul, is tormented by something. And strangely, she is the only one who can feel it. Unable to endure such unhappiness—even if he does call her Poison Ivy—she is determined to help him, no matter the cost. Because Pack McVale cannot survive without him, and curiously, neither can she ...

Simply sign up to my newsletter and I will email your free copy of Witch Bound to you. You will also receive the latest on upcoming books, sales, giveaways and relevant bookish news.

Get My Free Copy of Witch Bound here:
https://www.subscribepage.com/w2g6b9

ALSO BY LEISL LEIGHTON

Climbing Fear: Book 1

Blazing Fear: Book 2

ECHO SPRINGS SERIES

Dangerous Echoes: Book 1

Books 2-4 in this series, (written by Daniel deLorne, TJ Hamilton and Shannon Curtis) are also available now at all ebook retailers.

ABOUT LEISL

Leisl Leighton is a tall red head with an overly large imagination. As a child, she identified strongly with Anne of Green Gables, and like Anne, is a voracious reader and born performer. It came as no surprise when she went on to a career as a performer, script writer, script doctor, stage manager and musical director for cabaret and theatre restaurants.

After starting a family, Leisl stopped performing and began writing the stories plaguing her dreams. She now writes emotional stories mixed with mystery and a little bit of what goes bump in the night. Her novels have won and placed in writing contests here and over-seas. She is a passionate advocate for the romance genre, was President of Romance Writers of Australia from 2014-2017 and when she's not writing romantic stories of redemption, she is helping other authors reach their dreams with her Author Services.

You can contact Leisl through her website :

www.leislleighton.com

or sign up to her newsletter and be the first to find out about new releases, appearances, special deals and exclusive giveaways. You can find the sign-up page here:

https://www.subscribepage.com/w2g6b9

And if you want to get to know the Perfectly Paranormal Anthology authors a bit more, get sneak peeks of what's coming up for the APP Anthologies, as well as giveaways, special offers and just some PNR fun, then join our Perfectly Paranormal Paramours Facebook Group.

Find us here:

https://www.facebook.com/groups/251663560162131

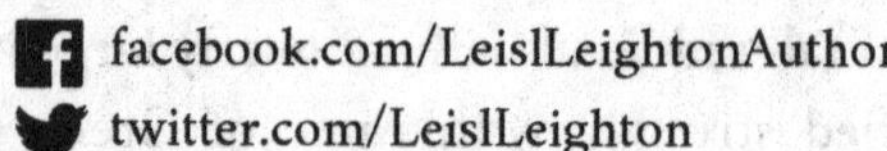

facebook.com/LeislLeightonAuthor
twitter.com/LeislLeighton
instagram.com/leislleightonauthor

ACKNOWLEDGMENTS

Thanks go to all the usual people: my hubby, my boys, my mum and dad, my writing group friends—Anita, Marnie, Chris, Laura, Frana—for all their love and support through the good and bad in this very terrible year.

Thanks will always go to Helen and Liz—your counsel and amazing friendships will always be missed.

Thanks to my agent, Alex Adsett, for encouraging me to go off and pursue getting these stories out there myself.

Thanks to my editor, Marnie St Clair—working with you is always a joy.

Thanks to Samantha Marshall for your amazing cover. It's always such a pleasure to work with you.

And a big thanks to my fellow A Perfectly Paranormal writers – without you, this tale would probably never have seen the light of day. I'll be eternally grateful that you thought of me when coming up with the idea for the anthology. May there be many more.

Finally, thanks to all the readers. You are a big part of why I do this crazy thing. I hope you enjoy my stories as much as I enjoyed writing them.

BAD BATCH

MARNIE ST CLAIR

BAD BATCH

An Owlscroft Coven Novella
Book 1

~

Marnie St Clair

ABOUT BAD BATCH

Avery Lloyd does not like being a witch – it's all rules, bureaucracy and hard work. And heaven forbid a witch should use her ability to help herself out. Avery also hates dogs – as in, really hates dogs. So when her boss – too-good-to-be-true Alec Hewittson – insists she attend the Lost Dogs Home for their annual Valentine's Day charity event, Avery is not happy. The temptation to cast an unlawful spell to get out of it is too great.

But something's not quite right about this batch of magic, and before she knows it, Avery has ruined Alec's life. Unless she can fix her mistakes by Valentine's Day, the consequences will be permanent and she'll never be able to make right what she has done.

To my New Year's Valentine – thank you for all the support.

CHAPTER 1

"All in favour of the Lost Dogs Home?"

Across the HewTech conference room, a sea of hands rises. Mine is not one of them.

My stomach tightens; bile fills my mouth. I will not be going to a dog shelter. No way.

"Great. Settled. And that's a wrap. Avery, can you stay a minute?" Alec directs the last bit at me.

I notice, not for the first time, that his eyes are the exact colour of the aqua glass accents the interior designer insisted on including in here. To increase creativity, she told Alec. I think she was probably more than a little smitten by the hottest young thing on the Australian start-up scene.

It's a very pretty colour. Undeniably.

Still seated, I watch while my colleagues – traitors – file out. They send me looks as they pass; a mix of sympathy and guilt – I'd argued hard for Bongrace Soup Kitchen – but it's too late. They cast their votes and the damage has been done.

I'm left with Alec Hewittson, founder and CEO of HewTech. He's the one who's really to blame for this entire situation. A Valentine's Day corporate love-in, with the lucky winning charity voted on by staff. This fourteenth of February, we (minus me) will be doling out pats, throwing sticks, and mucking out pens. Doing good while building stronger workplace bonds, all on the company's dime.

It's so Alec. Blech.

He leaves his position at the front of the room and comes to sit on the table near me. He's going for casual, cool boss, but he uncharacteristically misjudges, and somehow, mid-hoist, his suit-covered knee hovers right near my mouth.

I jerk back in my seat. Alec launches to his feet. Which means he's looming over me, looking down from this weird, intense angle.

I propel up out of my chair. For a moment, we're absurdly close, mere centimetres apart. I take a step back. Another. Alec does the same.

We eye each other warily across the now absurdly large distance between us.

I notice his breathing is uneven. Then realise mine is too.

Alec is so good-looking he's just outright beautiful. It's hard to say if that's part of why I find him irritating. I like to think I'm not that shallow, but who's to say.

What's worse, he's also nice. I don't have anything against that particular trait. Lots of people are nice and it doesn't get to me at all. It's just the exact manner of Alec's niceness that jars. Extra special, like him. Like last year, when Eleanor's mother died suddenly of a heart condition no one knew she had, Alec somehow knew her mother's favourite flowers were pink tulips and sent her a massive bunch. Who knows their graphic designer's mother's favourite flower?! Down to the colour!

Point is, Alec is too good to be true, and it's just too much.

Right now, however, he looks less than poised. Almost dishevelled.

He pushes a hand through burnished gold hair – I watch in fascination as it re-falls into its usual perfect formation – then brings his hand down on a nearby chair. "Sorry Bongrace didn't get up."

His words remind me of lost dogs and I shudder. Most people think dogs are cute. I am not one of them. I don't like dogs at all.

Most witches don't, because we're all half cat.

Ha – kidding. We're not half cat – none of us are any part cat as far as I know – but the canine animosity? It's a thing.

Dogs can smell the witch on us, and they don't like it.

The feeling is mutual.

Some of my distaste must be on my face, because he frowns. It makes him look pensive, sulky and desirable. "We'll save your idea for next year."

"What makes you think I'll be here next year?"

He goes very still, gaze locked with mine. It steals the breath from my lungs. Just a little. "Are you looking for something else?"

I'm not. We all have to have some kind of average day job, to help us blend in better. I'm pretty good with numbers – not as good as my twin Amelia, who's powering her way through postgraduate statistics, but not too shabby nonetheless – so I studied accounting.

I had this idea that accounting hours would be regular and the job itself not too demanding, so I could phone it in and focus on my coven commitments. But it appears I can't do anything by halves. Which means I'm effectively working two full-time jobs – and trying to excel at both.

Juggling everything is touch and go at times, but if I have to have a day job, this one is okay. "No," I say grudgingly.

My genuine regret at having to admit that seems to come through and the corners of his mouth tip up. "Good. I can't lose my BDO."

I was brought on almost two years ago as bookkeeper, but at my last performance review, I pushed for the new job title of Business Development Officer. Alec likes to call himself a transformational leader, so that kind of self-directed promotion is right up his alley. Not that I didn't deserve it. Frankly, I do more than work on cash flow. Including all the pain-in-the-arse jobs no one else wants. I don't know much about the tech side of things – HewTech designs virtual reality software for live e-commerce – but I've done a lot to improve profitability. While I was an adequate bookkeeper, I'm an excellent BDO. I've asked for more and contributed more at every opportunity.

"You asked me to stay behind?" I prompt.

He regains his focus. I see the moment he remembers why he

asked me to stay back because the skin around his eyes and mouth tightens. "Where were you this morning?"

This is one of those touch and go times. "Something came up. Family situation." Coven situation. A group of nuns on their way to a church convention, about to die in a fiery car crash. Dealing with that took precedence over turning up to work on time. "I was a little late in. Sorry."

"It's quarter-past two. You arrived 45 minutes ago."

He's clocking my hours now? Chalice. "Okay, quite late. Did I miss anything?"

"Did you miss anything." He gives me this assessing look, like I might be pulling his leg. I'm not. "You forgot about the meeting with Blanc?"

With all the drama, I did. But honestly, even if I had remembered … Am I supposed to let a carful of nuns go up in a fireball?

But it does explain how intensoid Alec is being. His older sister made some prestigious list of Australia's top 30 entrepreneurs under 30 years old just after I joined HewTech, and Alec is running out of time to match her. He said landing Blanc would get him there, and he was kind of joking, but also not. "It was an emergency."

"Seems to be a lot of those in your family."

"Un-huh," I offer vaguely. "Isn't it the same for all families?"

"Not mine. We don't do drama."

Okay then. Too-perfect Alec and his too-perfect family rise to the fore again. "So what happened with Blanc?"

"We had to reschedule. I needed you there. Blanc had questions about your numbers."

Heat flushes over me. I know I had no choice, but I still feel bad. "I'll phone them now. Apologise. And make sure I have exactly what they want for … When did you reschedule to?"

"Wednesday. Afternoon."

I nod and turn.

"Avery."

I turn back.

"I need to know I can rely on you. I'm starting to feel like I can't."

That stabs at me. "When have I ever let you down?"

He gets that look on his face. "This morning. Last Wednesday when you disappeared at three and the tax office called. Need I go on?"

"I sorted things out with the tax office. Everything's fine. And now I'm going to go call Blanc and sort that out." I wait for him to agree that he's overreacting and I am in fact solid despite the at-times chaotic timetable, but he doesn't. "I always come through," I insist. "I do."

He breathes out. Slowly. "So far – somehow – you do." He pushes a hand through his hair again. "I need you there at the Lost Dogs Home."

"Of course." I feel guilty because there is actually no way I will be there. I'll have to call in sick. The idea ties my stomach in knots, because even though my whole life is based on deception, I don't like lying to him. It's too much like losing the high ground.

His head tilts. He's studying me. I meet his piercing gaze with a guileless one of my own, but it doesn't work. "You're thinking about not turning up."

"I'm not." I'm not *thinking* about it; there's nothing to *think* about. But I won't be there.

"You weren't at the last team-building exercise. And you skipped the Christmas party."

More coven emergencies. There is nothing I can say in my defence.

"It hasn't gone unnoticed, Avery. Some of the junior staff are starting to think these things are optional. That it's alright to not turn up, to turn up late, to leave early. It's not. We can't build the workplace we want if we're not leading by example."

Twist that knife. "I know. It's just …" I trail off. *It's just the dogs*, I was going to say. I should just tell him about my difficult relationship with canines, but he would have SO MANY QUESTIONS. I know Alec. He can't leave anything alone. He'd want to get to the bottom of it, fix it. He can't. "What if I'm sick on Valentine's?"

"You're never sick."

It's true. It's an offshoot of working with magic. I'm disturbed that he's noticed. Alec notices a lot. Like, everything. And that's one of the reasons – apart from the fact that he's annoyingly perfect – that nothing could ever happen between us. Those pretty blue-green eyes see all.

And what they see now is that I'm not coming.

His gaze narrows. "Let me make this more compelling. You don't show, there's no Hawaii."

My jaw drops. That's so unfair. Alec came across the prestigious 'Women in Business' leadership conference and put me forward for it. I didn't even know I was interested in something like that, but now I desperately want it. "You're the one who said I should go!"

"I did. But since then, you've been far from leadership material."

Because things at coven have been crazy busy. But he doesn't know about that, and it's not his, or HewTech's, problem.

"You need to get your head back in the game. Start committing. Or it won't just be Hawaii you lose."

For a moment, my heart stops. Then races ahead like Pharlap out of the blocks.

But he's joking. Exaggerating. He won't sack me.

"I'm serious, Avery. This can't go on."

"You just said you can't lose your BDO!"

"So don't force my hand."

I'm having trouble breathing.

There's colour high on Alec's well-defined cheekbones and his eyes have a heavy look to them. I can feel the heat from his body.

Chalice! I haven't noticed when it happened, but somehow, we're close again.

I look down. His hand is gripping that same chair. Which means it's me who's moved.

I look back up, lock gazes with him again. Big mistake. His bright eyes hit me with force, suck all the breath from my lungs. My mouth goes dry, my pulse races.

I can't step back; it would be too obvious. Which means I'm stuck here, within range of his body heat and expensive-soap-and-sunshine smell.

It's been a moment since either of us has spoken. We're just standing, well into each other's space, staring. I don't know if I want to move closer or back away, but staying still is proving challenging. I itch with my need to do something.

"I don't want to have to discipline you."

His voice has a rasp to it that sends my stomach into freefall and a thrill exploding up my spine.

"And I certainly don't want to have to fire you. You have brilliant, out-of-the-box ideas that have made a real difference to this company. And, despite the erratic movements, you do always find a way to deliver. I can accept a certain amount of ... unconventional behaviour. But when it starts impacting the company culture—"

"I get it," I say in a rush. I don't know what to do about it, and I don't appreciate the dressing down, but I get it.

His gazes rakes over my face. "Is there something going on I don't know about?"

There's a lot of things going on that Alec will never know about.

"That family situation you mentioned. If you need someone to talk to ..."

I get another rush of feeling. One that urges me to confide. Part of me would love to tell him everything. But I can't. If I need someone to talk to, it won't – it can't – be Alec. "I'll sort it out." My voice has a tightness to it.

"If you need me, I'm here."

My gaze drops to his lips. His well-cut, perfect lips ... And this time, I'm not just looking but actively imagining how they'd feel pressed against mine. The strength of the feeling has me swaying closer, face lifted.

I'm not the only one drawing closer. There's a hair's breadth between his mouth and mine. He breathes out slowly. Apart from that, he is totally still. It is me; I am almost kissing him.

I look up. His eyes, heavy, dark and bright, pierce right through me. For a moment, I feel totally exposed. "I feel like you're breaching me," I blurt.

Something in his gaze flares. "This is not me breaching you," he says slowly.

I exhale sharply and step back. Then give myself a firm mental shake. Alec and his stupidly pretty face and his best-soap-in-the-world smell have confounded me, and I've said the wrong thing. "I mean, you're breaching my workplace rights. You can't hold Hawaii hostage like that."

He was, wasn't he? Breaching my workplace rights?

I am not even convincing myself this time.

His mouth quirks. "Be there, Avery."

I won't be. I can't be. I'm going to have to think of something.

CHAPTER 2

oday is Monday. Monday means one thing: all-coven. Not that it's the only time during the week I head to the coven-stead – every witch is expected to turn up at least twice, and I usually go for extra sessions – but all-coven is strictly non-optional.

You probably think being a witch is fun. It's not. It's rules, bureaucracy and a lot of hard work. I can't speak for every coven in the world, but at Owlscroft, we're at it constantly – monitoring quantity and quality of batches of magic, scanning for anything nasty on the horizon, and taking pre-emptive action.

And, of course, we practice, practice, practice.

Think of making a cake. You can use the same ingredients, in the same quantities, in the same order, and follow the same timing for everything, and you can end up with a perfect sponge or a perfect flop. Some batches of magic are nicer to work with than others. Sometimes the intent is clearer in the witch's head, sometimes in her words. It all affects the final result. We practice constantly, aiming for consistency and control.

It's a major commitment. It's our whole lives.

At least, that's how it is for me.

Meels texts me just as I arrive home to say that she and Mum are driving to Owlscroft if I want to join, but it's a gorgeous summer evening and I have to do something with all the pent-up energy from my encounter with Alec, so I decide to take my bike.

It doesn't take me long to ride from the dilapidated but lovely Victorian terrace I share with Meels in Carlton North through inner-north traffic to the Yarra, and then I wind my way along the bike path next to the river. At the end of a hot day, the air is heavy with the dry, bright scent of eucalypts. Overhead, ibises glide gracefully to their nests. It's a beautiful and surprisingly still evening. The paths along the river can be full, but tonight, there's only the occasional jogger.

As much as I sometimes whinge about being a witch, I love Owlscroft – a Queen Anne mansion in a quiet street of Hawthorn. It's a towering two stories, set on a rise, all red bricks and turrets. The gardens are huge and the ten-foot red brick fence with its looming conifers behind just adds to the 'leave-well-enough-alone' effect. And that's before you take the deterring protective spells into account.

I stop a moment to let the spell on the ornate but imposing iron gate recognise me, then walk my bike quickly through the colourful late-summer garden up the long winding path to the house that's felt like home since I joined the coven as a neophyte. The day Meels and I turned eighteen.

I rest my bike against the veranda, then push through the heavy black front door into the cool, dark foyer. Empty, of course – everyone's already in the ballroom.

If you were generous, you could call the covenstead decor shabby chic, but if you were also honest, you'd have to admit the emphasis is on the shabby. There are large rooms and medium-sized rooms and small rooms, all assembled in random rabbit-warren formation. The ceilings are sky-high, and a grand dark-wood staircase, complete with fairytale-themed stained glass in the alcoves above, sweeps to the upper floor. There are also cracks in the plaster and the paint is peeling in more than one spot. It's freezing in winter, and no less freezing in summer. Water damage and a general air of must and dust complete the overall picture.

You'd think, given that we're magic, we could fix it up a little. We could, but it's not the kind of thing we're allowed to do. No spelling yourself up a new dress. No curing a big night out's hangover. No making any inconvenient someone disappear.

Magic is highly unpredictable and dangerous, and it can all too easily go wrong. To counter, we choose what we focus on and use a set stock of spells, developed over a long history of trial and error. Everything has to be aimed at the common good, as defined by the Coven Council. Missing kid? We'll locate her and slip a tip to the police. Drought? We'll cast a chance spell to increase the probability of rain. Accidentally inhabited by a demon? We push back constantly against the dark forces.

We can't fix everything, but we try to take the edges off.

As much as the world sucks at times, let me assure you, it would be worse if it weren't for us.

I head into the ground-floor ballroom we use for all-covens. We seem to have had a bit of a growth spurt over the past year or two – we're almost one-hundred now – and the room is packed. Not that the extra witch-power means we're any less busy. Quite the contrary somehow. It's a constant scramble.

As a member of the Council, my mum – looking all glam academia with her wavy blonde bob, pearls and tweed-ish blazer – is sitting up the front. I give her a discreet wave, then scan for Meels and make my way to the seat she's saved me.

We're not identical, but we're close to it. We have the same thick brown hair, wide-set green eyes and pale skin with a smattering of freckles. There is an unmistakable feline cast to our faces. Despite our similarity, Amelia somehow manages to look like the world's most adorable kitten, while I fall more on the feral side of the spectrum.

"Hey," I say as I slip in next to her.

"Hey." She raises a brow. "Take it nuns went okay?"

"Yep." I told her about it on my way out the door this morning.

When I should have been heading to work.

I glance around and catch my cousin Everly's gaze. We grin at each other, then her sister Harlow's head tilts into view. I wave and Harlow smiles back but there are dark shadows under her eyes. At least she made it tonight.

The general chatter dies down and all gazes turn to the front as Aunt Bernie, our Head Witch, stands to signal the start of the meeting. Everyone calls her Aunt Bernie, but she's our actual aunt – my mum's oldest sister. Of the seven leadership roles on the Council, my family accounts for three. We're a pretty big part of the magical history of Melbourne.

It's a lot to live up to.

Given our lineage, there were high expectations for the four of us. Which the other three met effortlessly. Meels is brilliant with chance spells. She's the only witch in Owlscroft history to achieve a perfect score on the chance test, a simple coin toss done a 100-times over. Badass that she is, Meels managed to produce 100 tails in a row. Harlow's our demon hunter – she's out evicting demons every night – and Everly is a rare and powerful future witch. I'm moderately-to-very good at most things, but I don't truly excel at anything. I compensate by providing an exceptional level of commitment.

I sit up straighter as Aunt Bernie, tall, lean and severe looking, runs quickly through the agenda for the evening. She throws to Aunt Nettie, who oversees batch scanning and reports an unusual glut of magic hanging around. To be honest, I'm not sure Aunt Nettie likes me. She thinks I'm a bad influence on Everly. Which is funny because, believe me, Everly doesn't need any help on that front. Mum says Aunt Nettie's always been a worrywart, but if Harlow and Everly were my daughters, I'd be anxious too.

One by one, the Council Members give their updates. It's the usual story. Problems that require our attention, news from other covens with problems of their own, calls for volunteers to work on a never-ending list of tasks.

I consider where I'll be of most use, wondering which of the competing priorities I could or should take on. The more I consider, the more the pressure builds. My hands are gripping the underside of my chair, my shoulders are scrunched high. There's always so much to do. This alone could be my full-time job.

And then there's Alec, breathing down my neck to turn up on time and be more reliable.

And the thing is, the coven's problems are the same ones I've been hearing for years. It boils down to too few witches, too little, or poor-quality, magic, and outdated spells.

Our approach is just so inefficient. It's frustrating. There must be a better way.

If we had better spells, we could do more with less. We use the same spells, with minor adaptations, from 500 years ago. We haven't developed any genuinely new forms in ages. Not while I've been a part of the coven, and as far as I know, not for a long time before that.

But the world is not the same.

We need to have a close look at our spells. We need to—

I launch to my feet, thrumming with adrenaline.

Aunt Bernie stops talking; a peeved but resigned look crosses her face.

This is not the first time I've had an unscheduled contribution to make.

"Avery?" she prompts.

I beam a smile around the room. "Good evening. I would like to put forward an idea. While I am proud of what we do here at Owlscroft, I think we could do better. We've been working with the same set of spells forever and it's limiting us. I would like to propose a new unit dedicated to spell innovation."

Mum's eyebrows arch high, Aunt Nettie's mouth drops open.

Aunt Bernie is covering well but I can see I've thrown her too. "A new unit is a significant endeavour," she manages.

"Yes, but we need it. It would represent a significant investment, but one that could vastly improve our efficiency. I'd be happy to work up a cost–benefit analysis, if anyone was interested." I look around the room at blank faces, and realise I'm drawing a little heavily on my business background. It's not the way decisions are made in the witch world. I change tacks. "I think we can all admit things have been crazy lately. We need to do something. It will take a little while to set up the new unit and produce results, but it would be a way for us to do more with less."

"Who would be in charge of this *new unit?*" Aunt Nettie says dourly. "You, Avery?"

"Not necessarily." But actually, it's a role I would love.

"Avery does enough around here," Mum protests. Mum is broadly supportive of anything I do, but she also thinks I spend way too much time at coven, and is always encouraging me to have more of a life outside.

"Well, it's not like anyone else has the time, Nicolette," Aunt Nettie snaps back.

"I have to agree," Aunt Bernie says. "The idea has merit, Avery, but given everything we have on our plates at the moment, your proposed new unit can't be regarded as a priority at this time."

"Maybe next year," Mum adds in a bid to sound supportive. "When things have calmed down."

I should have anticipated this. Somehow I let my own excitement convince me it would go differently. "There's never going to be a perfect time," I argue.

"Perhaps not. But we can't spare anyone right now," Aunt Bernie responds sternly.

My frustration builds. "That's my point. We can't spare anyone ever. That's why this is so necessary. If we don't develop new spells, we're always going to be stretched." There's only so many of us, and even changing the world a little bit takes work. We can't do everything we'd like to. We have to pick and choose. But if we actually invested time and effort into improving our spells, that might change. "This is actually a solution for our over-allocated resources."

"I think it's a great idea." Across the room, Everly has jumped to her feet. "I personally would like to see the limits on how far we can look into the future extended."

I suppress a groan. No doubt Everly is trying to help, but she's just introduced some major scope-creep and muddied the waters big time.

Aunt Nettie's head snaps to Everly, and then she glares at me, like

Everly's words are somehow my fault. She moves fast to shut Everly down. "That's far too risky."

I actually agree with Aunt Nettie. The future – time – is not something to mess around with. "If we could focus on the new unit—"

Aunt Nettie turns back to me. "And that goes for *spell innovation* too. Have you considered the risks?"

I manage not to roll my eyes. I get the need for caution. It's been drummed into me my entire life that being able to change the world is a lot of responsibility. "That's why I propose setting up a dedicated unit and doing it properly. We'd go slowly. Proceed with care. Of course there's some degree of risk in developing new spells, but it would be minor relative to the benefits. Especially if we manage it well. With protocols and monitoring and evaluation and everything."

I look around but every face I see is some combination of sceptical, confused and bored. "I really think it's the right step going forward."

"I think it would be a disaster," Aunt Nettie snipes.

"Nettie!" Mum chastises, but she doesn't actually say she backs my idea.

There's a lull for a moment or two. Hope flutters in me. I look along the row of faces of the Council witches and then those all around me. I imagine them moving past their initial reluctance to seeing the logic.

Then another member of the Council says, "I don't see that there's anything wrong with our existing spells."

"Really! I think we do well enough as we are," another witch in the audience sniffs.

"What's wrong with the way we've always done things?" someone from my right chimes in.

A rumble – a discontented kind of rumble – builds. I look at Amelia, screw my mouth sideways. She smiles back, but there's a tinge of pity there.

Aunt Bernie raises a hand. Everyone quiets. "While I appreciate your enthusiasm, Avery, and the idea is not without merit, it's a major undertaking. More than we can commit to at the moment. We'll revisit when we don't have so many other things to attend to." Aunt

Bernie's tone signals the discussion is over. "And next time, you might like to approach me first before raising something of this magnitude at all-coven."

Mum mouths a sorry at me. I make a not-your-fault face because I don't blame her for how tonight went. I should have anticipated better. I love Aunt Bernie but she's so conservative – they all are – and it's so frustrating. We're overwhelmed and stagnating and no one is willing to do anything about it.

I sit with a plop.

"It's a great idea," Amelia whispers. "They're just dinosaurs. Don't worry. We'll try again. They'll see the light."

I shoot her a wry smile, but I'm not sure they will.

The meeting continues but I don't take any of it in. I fume and fume some more and only realise it's over when everyone stands.

"Can you tell everyone I had to take off? I don't want to ride in the dark."

It's an excuse. I'd usually stay and help wherever I'm needed, but I'm in no mood tonight. I've been knocked back twice in one day – first Bongrace and the whole 'Don't make me sack you' thing with Alec and now this. All I want is to go home and sulk.

I look towards the front of the room to wave goodbye to Mum. She's huddled with my aunts and they're all looking at me. No doubt discussing what a problem child I am.

So not in the mood.

I set off before I'm trapped in further discussion of why a new spell innovation unit is not appropriate right now and really lose my cool.

CHAPTER 3

lec spots me on his way past my office door. A second later, he returns to fill the space. "What are you still doing here?"

I'm not usually here late; I mostly go to coven. But not tonight. I'm still fuming.

I open my hands to display my laden desk. "I would have thought that was obvious."

He rests one shoulder against the frame. "I don't expect you to work late."

"You shouldn't overload me with work and threaten to sack me then." It comes out snipey; I'm still bitter about the general turn of events this week.

Alec frowns his disapproval. "Is it Blanc? Are you worried about the meeting?"

Now I feel guilty, because although I was working on the numbers for Blanc before, for the past hour I've been scouring various OH&S guides to see if there is anything about animals being prohibited from the work environment. I haven't been able to find anything useful, no matter how creative the interpretation, but I can't let that stop me. "No. But actually, I'm glad you're still here. There's something we need to discuss."

He cocks his head. His eyes turn warm, radiating a marine-like glow. "Agreed."

"I don't think a visit to Lost Dogs really meets our corporate vision of global citizenship. Bongrace better aligns with our core value of …" Chalice. I've forgotten the term. I shuffle through the papers on my desk, trying to find the relevant glossy brochure. When I look up, Alec's gaze has lost some of its glow. I change tack. "Let's face it. Most people love dogs. I bet they don't struggle for volunteers at the shelter. But homeless dudes, they don't always get the support they need."

He folds his arms. "I admire your passion. You clearly feel strongly about supporting the homeless."

I incline my head in demure acknowledgement, but actually, I am ashamed to admit, I am more driven by my need to avoid everything canine.

"However," Alec continues. "We voted. The overwhelming majority wanted the dog shelter."

"My point exactly."

He is starting to get exasperated, the skin around his eyes and mouth tightening. He looks at his watch. "It's late. My blood sugar is running low, and I'm going to assume it's the same for you. I should feed you."

I stare at him for a second before I realise what he's saying. I stand. Then regret it immediately – I don't want him to think I'm ready to walk somewhere with him. "I'm not hungry. I've got somewhere I need to be."

His expression is almost a wince. Probably one of those excuses would have sufficed. "We agreed we need to talk. You won't have dinner with me?"

He's put me on the spot and I have no choice but to answer directly. "No."

He pushes off the doorframe. "Can I ask why not?"

"Apart from the fact that you're my boss?"

He winces for real this time. "Apart from that."

Because you're too smart and too attractive and that's a killer combination for a witch who can't let a guy like you get close.

I can't say that. I say the first other thing that comes to mind. "I don't date men whose names start with A."

"You … sorry?"

His eyes are wide. I've shocked him. It's unbecoming to admit, but it's so satisfying. "I've been one-half of an A-name duo my whole life, and I have absolutely no intention of signing up for a second round."

He raises a brow at me.

"I have a twin. Amelia."

He takes a moment to absorb, then murmurs, "How did I not know that?"

I shrug noncommittally. I know the answer – I take great pains not to divulge much of anything personal. Especially to Alec, who puts two and two together way too quickly.

"Would it help if I told you my name is actually Hubert?"

Now he's shocked me. "Is it?"

"Yes."

"Hubert?"

"It's a family name. My mother's side."

"Hubert Hewittson."

He winces for a third time. "I go by Alec."

I can see why.

I know I'm not one to talk, but Alec's family sounds intense. His mum is a thoracic surgeon, his father's a QC, and his older sister, Pippa, who he's been competition with since before he could walk and talk, made her first million by sixteen. The Hubert should not have surprised me.

But does it make a difference to dating him? I pretend to consider the impact for a weighty pause, then peer at him with what I hope is nonchalant superiority. "No. No difference."

Alec just smiles and leans against the doorframe. "In that case, it's not a date. It's an overdue discussion about a path forward, with food."

There is no path forward for Alec and I. "I need to get back to Blanc," I hedge. "You'll have to find someone else to feed."

He stares at me hard. His head drops, then rises again. "Just so we're clear … I broke up with my last girlfriend a few months after I hired you."

"Oh. Okay. Um, noted." I am trying for prosaic but my heart races at his words.

He looks at me for another long moment. "We're not going to talk about what happened yesterday?"

My belly rolls over. My gaze drops involuntarily to his mouth. "Nothing happened."

"Avery." It's a rebuke.

"I have no idea what you're talking about." It's a lie. I know exactly what he's talking about. I almost kissed him. He almost kissed me. Him wanting to talk about it is not unreasonable, but … there's nothing to discuss.

His gaze has turned unimpressed.

I look down and almost weep in relief when I spot the brochure I was looking for earlier. "Empathetic altruism!"

No wonder I couldn't remember it.

His gaze narrows. "We're back to this again?"

"Yes." We sure are. "Bongrace aligns better with our core value of empathetic altruism. You have to admit it."

"Do I? How would you define empathetic altruism, Avery?"

Stuffed if I know. "You know that's a ridiculous way to phrase it and the rest of the world would just say compassion?"

Alec's jaw sets in a tight line. "Lost Dogs fits empathetic altruism just fine. That's what we're doing, and you will be there."

"Are you going to threaten me with Hawaii again?" Just the thought renews my seething. It was Alec's idea but I'm invested now. I want that leadership course.

"Do I need to? Do I need to threaten you to get you to turn up for charity?" He pushes a hand through his hair. His eyes are dark and somehow blazing. "Avery, Valentine's Day is an important part of our company culture. You may not see it as a priority, but you're on the executive leadership team and people take their cues from you. I expect you to be on board. And be there."

I'm crankier now than I was before we started this conversation. I don't deserve that criticism. Minus the dogs, I agree with everything he said. But I can't even defend myself, so I just return to glowering.

Alec looks like he's doing some good seething of his own. "Don't work much longer. We have standards here."

He stalks away. Off to pursue some balanced life activity no doubt. Rock climbing. Hot yoga. Shamanic drumming. I wouldn't put anything past him.

I collapse back into my seat, irritation and frustration thrumming through me. I battle an urge to swipe everything from my desk.

The unfairness of it!

Despite what Alec thinks, I actually spend most of my time and energy making the world a better place. I might not be gifted like Amelia, Harlow or Everly, but I do try to do my bit. And fair enough, I can't tell Alec how and why this happens, but I hate having to stand there like a gormless mute while he questions my motives. The assumption that I'm some kind of miserly misanthropic princess is grating.

I cannot go to the dog shelter.

I couldn't anyway, but I know what Alec will be like. He'll make it impossible. He'll be pushing me to the front, trying to get pictures of me with the dogs for the staff newsletter. I just … can't.

If I could cast a spell, I could make the whole stupid situation go away.

But I can't.

I mean, I could, but I can't.

Can I?

God forbid I should do something to make my own life just a little better. Something to compensate for the hours and hours I devote to making life better for those in need. Something that wouldn't affect anything material, and in fact, may even benefit the world.

Yes. Benefit the world.

Alec can't see it – he's stuck on democratic process – but my argument is sound. People love dogs. Soup kitchens struggle for volunteers.

It's not like I'm planning anything radical. It's a small change. Low risk.

And didn't Aunt Nettie report a surplus of magic at the moment? I'm not stealing it from any more worthy cause.

If I'm busted, I think I could talk my way out of it. It's dogs, after all. Every other witch will get my desire to avoid the shelter. And I could say I was worried my colleagues would wonder why the otherwise-cute pooches seemed hellbent on eating me for dinner. We all have some kind of duty of care to maintain our cover. Seen this way, the reason I'm casting an unlawful spell is to protect Owlscroft.

I'd have to be very unlucky to get caught. We don't have the resources to do much monitoring of our own members; we rely on general compliance. And despite the fact that I'm regarded as some-what of a troublemaker, I've followed the rules my whole life.

But look at what following the rules has got me – nothing and nowhere.

I've had enough.

I'm going to do it.

As soon as I've decided, an overwhelming sense of relief floods me. I slump back into my chair, exhaling a huge breath and looking at the ceiling. I've been carrying this horrid canine dread for days, and it's finally dissipated.

I just have to decide on an approach. I sit forward, mull it over a little and decide to focus on the dog shelter end. An outbreak of dog flu? Even given my feelings about dogs, I am not really suggesting unleashing disease on them. Just the impression would be enough. A false positive.

But it would be disruptive. The shelter might really have to shut down and people would follow up on it.

There's an easier way. Simple admin error. Happens all the time.

The bookings manager will look at the upcoming schedule and see a double-booking for Valentine's Day. That's all that's required.

Now the spell.

A spell doesn't have to be pretty. It doesn't have to rhyme. It just has to be serviceable. Clear and specific are the main things. Magic can't be given too much wriggle room.

Once I've got something I'm happy with, I reach out. Open up my awareness and send it skywards, searching for the current batch of magic hovering in the vicinity.

It comes rushing towards me like a long-lost friend.

It's so astounding, I almost fall backwards.

A casting starts by tethering a batch of magic. The problem is, magic doesn't particularly want to be tethered. And I get it. Imagine you're magic. You're just kind of floating, chilling, feeling the sun and the breeze. Then some witch grabs at you and starts binding you to a spell. She binds you real tight, weaving and knotting you around the words, so you've got no choice but to do what the spell says. What would you do? Rebel, right?

Magic that's eager is an anomaly. But this batch is golden with enthusiasm, leaping about like it can't wait to get started.

Well. That makes two of us.

I take a deep breath and focus.

Just as I'm about to start, I have a moment's misgiving. Though I'm constantly pushing the boundaries at coven, I've never actually totally disregarded the rules before.

But Alec has left me with no choice. He's boxed me in. I cannot go to Lost Dogs. It would be an unequivocal disaster. At the same time, he's made it clear he's not going to let any absence slide either. I can't have him pushing more on this. It's dangerous and it's … just too close to the bone.

This has to happen.

As an added boost to intention, I visualise another of the concrete outcomes of the spell. Hawaii. I see golden beaches. Fresh-cut tropical fruit. Palm trees against a blue, blue sky.

I start.

Two sets on Valentine's
Mistakes happen all the time
Simple, simple

The solution is simple
First in, best dressed
Double-booking, no drama
First in, best dressed
Cancel that second booking

I repeat the spell, three times, binding tightly. The words must be precise, but so must the intent in the witch. You have to concentrate, keep your goal clear.

I visualise the dogs' shelter logo. I visualise the double-booking on the screen, the checking of who got in first. I visualise the cast of eyes towards the phone.

This batch is a dream to work with. When I conclude, I know it's going to work, and I feel better than I have in days. With a new level of jauntiness, I shut down my computer and sling my backpack over my shoulder. I am just about to set out when my phone buzzes.

It's Meels. "Where are you? You weren't at coven and you're not at home."

She sounds worried and I twinge in guilt. I should have let her know I wasn't going to coven tonight. "Still at work. Lots on." In case she asks what, I divert. "How was it?"

"Aunt Bernie was asking after you."

"That's nice." It comes out a little sarcastic and I soften my tone. "I'll catch her tomorrow."

"Oh. No. Actually, coven's been cancelled until further notice."

I tense. Did someone catch me? But it can't be related to the spell I just cast. That was only moments ago; coven would've been over by then. "Why? What's going on?"

"Drama with an incoming batch. It's behaving oddly in testing apparently."

Batches come and go, and every batch is put through a standard set of tests before we risk general use. Issues with testing are common enough, but cancelling coven is a little extreme.

"All non-essential activities have been cancelled until the Council gets to the bottom of it," she continues.

I consider then exhale. This has nothing to do with my recent activity, and in fact, the timing couldn't be better. I still feel unappreciated and undervalued and I am not ready to return.

"When will you be home? I've made lasagne."

It's my favourite. She's made it because she knows how upset I was about last night. I smile. "Thanks, Meels. Give me fifteen."

CHAPTER 4

$\mathcal{M}$elbourne in February can be like an oven, but today is perfect. Clouds like marshmallows, the sky that perfect summer blue. Walking to HewTech's Collingwood offices, it feels like it's going to be a good day.

I want to go see Alec immediately, but I know I need to give it a little longer. Who knows what time the admin staff at Lost Dogs start? So instead I go to my office. I call Bongrace and make sure they can still take us for Valentine's Day later this week. A subtle signal to the universe that I'm expecting this to work. Then I settle to work on Blanc.

As soon as the clock hits ten, I figure it's reasonable to check on progress.

Alec's door is open. His chair is pushed back from his desk, his hands are laced behind his head, and he's staring up at the ceiling. I try, unsuccessfully, not to notice the way his pale blue shirt stretches across his chest.

I knock and beam. "Good morning, future prime minister!"

His mug is front and centre on his desk, declaring Alec's political ambitions to the world. It's a present from his mother – some sort of family joke, apparently, but he still uses it. I can never resist taking a dig, but to be honest, I'm genuinely triggered by it. My first serious boyfriend – the only guy I've ever told about being a witch – had exactly the same one. Not that Alec knows that.

He straightens slowly, gives me an assessing look. Which is fair enough given how we left things last night. "You're in a good mood."

I'm also on tenterhooks. I need to know if my spell has worked. "You're not?"

"Surviving, Avery, not thriving." His gaze is brooding and distinctly un-Alec.

I come into the room, stand behind the chair opposite his. "What's going on?"

"Busy morning. Something to make your heart sing. I've had a call from the dog shelter. Some kind of mess up at their end, and they've double-booked. They've had to allocate the spot to the group who got in first. Understandable, but it means they can't take us for Valentine's."

I suppress my urge to fist pump. "That's a shame." I try to inject a note of exasperation into my voice – other people and their mix ups! – and add a little worry – what will we do for Valentine's now? But I'm not fooling anyone. I shrug. "I know everyone else really wanted it. But we can always go with Bongrace. They're still free."

His head tilts. "Now, how would you know that?"

Because I spoke to them not long ago. "I've been in contact with them a bit over the week. I think maybe they're still holding a place for us? What I meant was, I'll check if they're still free."

I am about to hurry back to make the booking, but he stands. "Actually, I want to talk to you about last night."

"Last night?"

"I was thinking about what you said. About not dating people you work with."

"Actually I said I don't date people whose names start with A."

He gives me his be serious look.

I look behind me, then lean forward and whisper. "The door's open."

"I can see that." He looks irritated. It strikes me that he's looked that way a lot lately. He never used to. "It's not a state secret."

Only Alec would insist on open communication around an office fling. Should I add it as a dot point to the next executive team meeting agenda?

"I know it's potentially messy," he continues.

"Yes," I agree quickly. "I mean, HR 1-0-1, right? Messy. Very messy."

He nods, slowly. "The problem is, I really enjoy working with you."

This is getting too close to some kind of real conversation and my anxiety spikes. "If you sack me, I won't be dating you. Just so that's clear."

His eyes do that blazing thing. "You really think I'd do that?"

"You literally said you were going to sack me two days ago."

"That was different. That was deserved." He rakes a hand through his hair. "What I meant was, I wouldn't want anything that happened between us to interfere with work."

"Me neither. Good. Glad that's settled. I'll go and phone Bongrace."

I'm deliberately misinterpreting and he knows it. He gives me a stony stare, then stalks to the window. His hands are in his pockets as he looks out at the green of the park across the street. I try not to notice – again unsuccessfully – how it pulls the fabric tight across his butt.

I've said the wrong thing. Alec had been trying to start some kind of dialogue, and I've shut it down.

I know he's attracted to me and I know I'm giving off mixed signals. I haven't indicated a lack of interest because I actually am attracted to him. I can admit it to myself, if not to him. Despite what I tell myself and anyone else who'll listen, Alec is not annoying, even though he is too damn perfect. He's smart and thoughtful and smoking.

But honestly, it doesn't do either of us any good. Apart from the fact that it would be messy workwise, I'm not free to date. Not someone like him. There are plenty of guys I could start something with who wouldn't care if I had 'French lessons' or some other bogus commitment several times a week. Some I could even tell I was a witch, and they would just assume I meant I collect crystals and burn sage. Indulgent smiles all round. Alec is not that guy. If I dated him, I would have to come clean, and that's a big step for a witch.

"I like working with you too," I say. It's not what he's hoping for, but I'm trying. From the set of his shoulders, it's not helping much. "I'll go phone Bongrace."

He turns, leans back against the window frame, arms across his impressive chest, one ankle over the other. "That won't be necessary."

"What do you mean?"

"I've made alternative plans."

This is unexpected – I've assumed that if it wasn't Lost Dogs, it would be Bongrace – and an adrenaline response pings inside me. "What alternative?"

"We've all been working really hard over the past few months. Too hard. What HewTech needs is a holiday."

"Like a day off?" That doesn't sound too bad.

"A week. A corporate retreat. I've booked us into a resort in Hawaii."

I try to quell the flare of alarm. "I don't understand. When you say 'us'?"

"HewTech. Each and every one of us." He shrugs, like it's nothing.

My little accountant's heart almost goes into cardiac arrest. The scale of it! "But the schedules. The budget."

"Will work themselves out once everyone is back on the same page. One week. No schedules, no budgets. Just good clean fun. A chance to reset."

Alec is a bold leader. He sometimes takes risks, goes out on a limb, but this idea is Elon Musk bizarre, and I don't even know where to start. "Not everyone can afford that."

He shrugs again. "The company's paying. Flights. Accommodation. Activities. It's all covered."

Chalice! Over my dead body. "People can't just up and leave their families for a week with no notice."

"They can bring them along. I've booked everyone a family suite."

So, we're talking double the already huge sum. My hands go to my hips. I attempt to keep my tone calm. "Just so I'm across this ... You're planning on putting up the entire HewTech staff, and their families, including flights, in a resort in Hawaii for a week."

"Not planning. It's booked."

I cringe. "Do I even want to know how many stars this resort has?"

"I left it to Taylor. But there's no point doing it if people aren't comfortable."

Taylor, our travel agent, won't hold back. Top of the line then. All the stars. "I don't think I want to know, but as your BDO, I feel compelled to ask. What's the damage?"

He has the grace to look a little embarrassed. "We'll take it out of the capital fund."

That is not what I set the capital fund up for.

I do some quick calculations, but I can't see how this trip would total less than a couple of hundred grand. Maybe even half a mill. Not enough to send us broke, but not too far off. What is he thinking? "We can't afford that. We have to cancel."

"I don't want to cancel. I'm confident this is the correct course of action. It came to me last night. One of those flashes of inspiration that comes straight from the higher self."

My general feeling that something is off condenses into a cold ball of dread deep in my belly. I stick a hand out to steady myself on the chair in front of me. "It just came to you?"

"Last night. Not long after I left you working too hard. I decided to head down to St Kilda. Clear my head a little. I saw the outline of palm trees against the sky, and there was just this moment. You know those moments? And I thought it's really ... It's so simple. Simple."

The palm trees, the sky.

Simple. Simple.

Sudden stark knowledge floors me. It's a repeat of the spell. My hand is gripping the chair in front of me so tight, my knuckles are white. "What did you say?"

"It really can be simple, Avery."

There is a compelling earnestness in his clear blue-green gaze, but

I have no time for it. That spell was intended for the dog shelter. It reached them, but somehow, it reached Alec too. And it was going to cost him. Big time.

"When the email came in this morning … It felt like serendipity."

It wasn't serendipity. It was me.

I'm a rush of sensation, mostly bad, and I need to get somewhere dark and quiet and think this through.

"Avery—"

"I have to go. I'm not feeling well." The words sound strange and forced, as if I'm in pain.

I am.

Back in my office, I shut the door and lean against it. Then fold forward over my legs and expel a huge shaky breath. Despite what Alec thinks, this is not some perfect moment of clarity and insight gifted to him from his higher self. It's my spell.

My fault.

I stand, hands on hips. Physically, I am still unsteady, but my brain is crystal clear on what I have to do. Fix it.

It's too big a hit. If Alec had decided to shout everyone a nice meal, I'd feel bad but I'd let it go. Hawaii is just too much. Yes, Alec is wealthy, and yes, HewTech has had an amazing year, but I'm not going to let him wipe out the entire capital fund.

No one's come to bust my arse about the spell I cast last night. I can only assume that the monitors, already limited in number and scope, are concentrating on the new batch and the spell slipped through unnoticed. I'll have to risk it again. If I get caught, I'll just have to cop it.

I'll be more careful this time. This batch is turbulent, but my binding skills are not too shabby, if I do say so myself. I can work with tricky magic. I know I can do this.

But I can't do it here. I need to focus, really focus, and I can't do that with the threat of someone knocking on my door about some new tax regulation or whether we've got budget to bring on another developer.

I head downstairs to the park opposite. Despite everything, the day is still perfect. It's that weird time – well clear of breakfast, but nowhere near lunch – and the park is pretty much empty. There's a grotto area that abuts the small lake in the middle, and that's where I'm heading.

Inside, the grotto is all greenery and rocks. It's quiet and dark and I have it to myself. Perfect. I take a few moments to breathe and calm myself.

This will be okay. I'll fix it. But first, I need to figure out what went wrong.

That batch had no business seeking out Alec. There was nothing in the spell about him, so I don't rightly know how it happened. But then I recall how, just as I reached for it, I had second thoughts. I was griping about how Alec had cornered me and reminding myself of the trip to Hawaii.

The batch must have somehow latched onto that as a component of the spell even though I hadn't started to bind with it yet. I'd felt that it was eager, but it hadn't occurred that it would start without me. Usually, you have to drag magic kicking and screaming to the spell, so to speak.

And somewhat comfortingly, the spell did work. It got Lost Dogs cancelled and me to Hawaii to boot. Well, all of us to Hawaii.

What did Alec mean by needing a reset?

Did the spell plant that idea in his mind, or does it go deeper?

I recall his earlier words. *Surviving, not thriving.* Those kind of sentiments are very un-Alec – he's a manifest your own destiny, self-actualising type who's all about working hard and playing hard and living your best life. He's a thriver alright.

I know we've got some unresolved issues and I know I'm dodging them and just generally handling everything badly. I didn't want this thing between us to come to a head. I've enjoyed my attraction to Alec, and his to me, in its totally unconsummated way, because that's about as much as I can hope for. I've tried a real relationship and it didn't end well. I suppose I've resigned myself to the status quo, seeing as there is no real choice for anything else.

But it's not the most Alec can hope for, and he doesn't have to resign himself to the status quo.

He can't begin to guess where I'm coming from, and I can't explain it. But that means the whole situation is not fair to him. I'd been teasing the other day, but maybe I *should* find something else. Let him move on and get on with his life.

Things would be a lot easier for Alec if I wasn't his BDO.

It's a painful thought and I close my eyes for a moment.

First things first. I need to get Hawaii cancelled and I've got a bad batch of magic to contend with. So long as I maintain focus, everything should be fine.

I formulate a spell to reverse the Hawaii situation. I had no problems with actualising a cancelled booking last time and I am going to follow the same process.

I clear my mind. Really clear my mind, till there's nothing but dark and quiet. Then reach for the new batch.

It's excited to have a new spell to work with. I can feel it ducking and weaving around me, through me, looking for the spell I haven't started to cant yet. It's unnerving, but I have to forge ahead.

Trip to Hawaii
No way, no way

I falter when I realise I'm rushing to keep up with it. It's not satisfied with the words. It's looking for more, though I'm not sure what. There's definitely something off, but at this stage it's more dangerous to stop than to keep going. So I cant the whole spell, three times over, doing my best to inject moderation, precision and clarity.

Trip to Hawaii
No way, no way
Simple, simple
The solution is simple
Cancel everything
It's the only way

Refund the cost
It's the only way

I visualise Taylor looking at the many, many bookings she's in the process of making. I visualise her realising there's a bug in the system – flights and accommodation she thought were available have been cancelled. I visualise her bringing up Alec's email, ready to type an apology and offer a full refund.

The batch seems to bind so easily, it's so compliant in its rush to be used, but I can't help but feel it's got its own end-game.

Unlike last night, when I finish, I have no confidence that this will work.

CHAPTER 5

I'm edgy and restless all afternoon. Overheated and unbearably stuffy one second, shivering the next. Totally unable to focus. Waiting for something to break. Needing to know. Terrified to know.

I've recast the spell a thousand times in my mind, turning it over, checking for weak spots. Reassuring myself that it will work. Then struggling for breath moments later when I can't convince myself everything will be fine.

I'm a woman of action. I hate feeling powerless, having nothing to do but wait.

It's a relief when Alec arrives in my doorframe. "Hey."

"Hey." I watch his face closely, trying to read if there's been anything from my spell yet. I don't even know whether to hope it's worked or not.

"You okay?"

It takes me a moment to realise he's referring to the way I rushed out of his office earlier. "Yes. Just … low blood sugar," I say, borrowing his excuse from last night.

He nods like that is totally reasonable. "You good to go?"

"Go where?"

His gaze narrows. "Blanc."

Our rescheduled meeting! In all the chaos, I'd forgotten about it. "Yes. Of course."

Something like concern crosses his face.

"I actually am prepared," I say.

He doesn't look convinced, but we make our way out of the building and head towards Blanc's CBD HQ, talking through our strategy – despite us being convinced we are a perfect fit, Blanc remains to be convinced.

We take a shortcut through one of the city's quaint Victorian arcades. There are ornate mosaic tiles underneath, high-arched ceilings with glass panels to let light in, and chic boutiques every step of the way.

Alec stops and pulls the phone from his pocket. "It's Blanc," he says, then answers. "Alec Hewittson."

There's a brief interchange, which ends with Alec saying, "No problem. Same time tomorrow."

"Meeting's rescheduled again?"

"Yes." He looks pensive and intense.

"Is that a problem?" I ask.

"Not if they end up signing." His phone buzzes again. He takes a look at the screen and takes the call. "Taylor," he prompts.

The travel agent. Adrenaline pings through me. This is it.

I watch his face carefully, aiming to pick up on the whole conversation from his murmured series of "I see".

I am so tense about the outcome, I am starting to feel queasy.

Alec finishes the call with a "We'll let you know" and lowers his phone.

"What did Taylor—"

I break off as repulsion hits in a nauseating wave, freezing me in place with its power. There is something monstrous right behind me.

Alec's gaze shifts past me. He grins.

I don't turn around – I'm not sure I could even if I wanted to given my paralysis – but I don't need to. I know exactly what's behind me. Partly because I can hear the moist heavy panting, and partly because there's a sensation of spiders crawling all over me and violent sickness rising in my gut.

I was so focused on Alec and the call that my usually impeccably functioning dog radar failed.

Alec, oblivious, walks past, still grinning. "What's his name?" he says from behind me.

The panting turns into that mewling sound dogs make when someone they like is giving them attention.

"Angus. Gussie." A woman's voice. She sounds totally self-satisfied, totally confident she's spreading delight at every turn.

I'm not delighted. The dog stench is turning my stomach. If I take so much as a single breath, I'll spew.

"Come and meet Gussie, Avery."

I tell myself to say something, so he knows. But I can't. I can't do anything.

"Avery?"

I make a superhuman effort and rotate my turned-to-stone body. Alec rises from his crouch. He takes in my shoulders, bunched up somewhere near my ears, and my tightly clenched fists, in balls against my sides, and the smile falls from his face.

The woman is looking at Gussie, not me, and she leads him forward. Towards me. Horrified, my gaze drops to a golden lab almost every person on this planet would find adorable. Eyes fixed on me, he sniffs the air and starts to growl. Which rapidly evolves into a series of short, sharp barks, followed by a baring of teeth over another growl.

The woman's expression shifts from indulgent to accusing, as if I'm the problem here.

Without taking his gaze off me, Alec says quietly but firmly, "Nice to meet you, Gussie. We'll let you continue on your way."

With a final accusing stare and a firm tug on the lead, the woman manages to drag Gussie away. A few shops along, the barks stop and Gussie's tail starts to wag again.

I am still frozen to the spot.

Alec approaches slowly, eyes on mine, and cups my shoulders. It feels good. Warm and firm and Alec.

"Avery, sweetheart, breathe."

"I can't," I manage eventually. Trying to say something makes me realise my teeth are chattering.

"You can."

No, I can't. All I can do is look into his stunningly clear eyes.

"Breathe, Avery."

I suck in air, exhale in a rush, and draw in another breath, suddenly frantic to replace oxygen.

Then I throw myself into Alec's solid warmth, wrapping my arms around him.

I know his schedule, so I know there's a lot of cross-fit in there, but it hasn't prepared me for the impact. He's a firm wall of chest and it's lovely.

His arms come up slowly around me, hugging me tight into him, and it makes it even better. My legs are still jelly, but I feel warm and safe. This feels righter than anything ever has. Nuzzled against him, I fancy I can hear his heart beat, strong and steady.

"I'm sorry," he says quietly against my ear. "I didn't know."

Through my still-heavy draws in and out, I make a non-verbal sound meant to represent 'how could you?'

"This is why you didn't want the dog shelter."

"Yes." I am feeling marginally better but am still clinging to him. I should step back, but I don't want to. Not yet.

"Why didn't you just tell me? I would have taken it out of the running."

"We had a vote. Everyone wanted it. And besides, it's ridiculous."

He makes a sound of disapproval. "It's not ridiculous. It's a phobia."

He doesn't know the half of it.

"Have you talked to someone about it?"

"Not really," I murmur. Actually, we witches bitch and moan about it all the time.

"Maybe a psychologist could help. If there was a triggering traumatic event, they could help you identify it. Or perhaps there's some kind of treatment protocol."

I almost laugh; there's no solution short of not being a witch. "I'm actually … not that comfortable talking about it."

He gives me a gentle squeeze. "Fair enough. But I wish you'd just told me why you were so against visiting the shelter."

I sigh. "You were angry with me. I thought you'd think I was making it up. And I didn't think you'd change it just for me."

He makes another sound. "Of course I would have changed it. I wasn't kidding when I said you're important to HewTech." His grip on me tightens and he exhales, sending warm air over my neck. "To me."

I tilt my head up. It brings my lips to just below his jaw. "You know, you're pretty hard to hate."

He stills. "You hate me?"

"Not even a little bit."

He squeezes me tighter. "Good."

I sigh. "It's not good. It's a problem."

He chuckles quietly. "It's not a problem."

But it is.

For another few moments, we stay as we are. With Gussie gone and Alec close, I am recovering. I still feel good against him, but it's rapidly turning into a different kind of good. Less one of comfort, more one of building awareness. I'm starting to feel taut and tingly. I can tell from minute changes in Alec that he's noticed the change in the vibe too. Not that he makes a move to back away.

Which means I have to. With an internal sigh, I release him and step back. I'm surprised by just how hard it is, how much I miss the press of his body against mine. It's almost painful.

"Are you sure you're okay?" he asks.

Not yet, not totally, but it was just a dog. I'll live. "Yes," I breathe out.

His gaze wanders over my face. I've never seen his face look quite like this. His eyes have a heavy look to them, his colouring is high. He looks dishevelled. Undone.

It occurs to me that this is probably what he looks like in bed.

I press a hand to my cheek and attempt to divert my thoughts. Where were we?

Taylor had called. Thank Chalice. One thing going right at least. "What did Taylor have to say?"

He shrugs. "Our flights have been cancelled. She's not sure why; she's trying to find out. Before you ask, since the problem's at their end, we'll get a full refund."

Is that it? It can't be. "And?"

"And what?"

"You tell me."

Alec's gaze narrows. I know I'm making no sense. With this bad batch, I'm just so primed for something to be wrong.

I try to relax. Maybe I got lucky. The Hawaii trip is off – maybe there's no more to it. No nasty side effects. If I can just get Alec to agree to hold off on any further ideas until the bad batch has passed, everything will be fine. "Can we please just not do anything for Valentine's? I know it's an important part of our culture, and I genuinely do support HewTech's values, even empathetic altruism, but can we just leave it? Maybe do something later in the year?"

He rubs a hand over his jaw. "At this point, I'm thinking that's a good idea."

"Great." I am so relieved that he's agreed, I almost collapse. Instead I smile.

He smiles back. It spreads slowly across his face. I watch, mesmerised, as it transforms him from handsome to irresistible. I'm a little dazed.

And then something starts to shift. A new energy, a new brightness. His head goes down and both hands come to his hips. He starts pacing, back and forward, slowly at first but building speed, the same track over and over.

I know Alec. I know what this means. An idea has struck.

"What?" I ask.

He pauses, crosses his hands behind his head. "I'm just thinking."

"I know," I say. "But what are you thinking?"

He doesn't reply and I get this bad feeling. A prickling sensation along my spine. This is not going to be good. "Alec—"

"I'm going to sell."

A fresh wave of prickles hits. "You're what?"

"I'm going to sell HewTech. To Feenex."

"We hate Feenex." Feenex is one of our main competitors. They've tried to acquire us many times. We always turn them down.

His mouth quirks. "We don't hate Feenex. I've just never been inclined to sell before. But things are changing. Evolving." He shrugs. "I'm not happy with the way things are. And I don't have to settle for the status quo."

I know he's not happy. *Surviving, not thriving.* And it was only this morning in the grotto that I was thinking how he doesn't have to settle for the stat—

My stomach goes wobbly.

No. No. No.

It's the spell. I knew there had to be more to it. For some reason, it's making him want to sell. It must be. First I was going to cost him millions; now I'm going to cost him his whole company. Tickets to Hawaii pale into insignificance.

I try to quash down my desire to panic. "You can't do that," I say sharply.

He just looks at me. A look that says it's his company; he *can* do that.

"I mean, you don't want to do that. Think about it, Alec. You don't want to sell."

He rubs a hand over his jaw. "That's what I thought for a long time."

"Yes. Exactly."

"But I'm ready to move on."

"You're not."

A look of confusion crosses his face. Followed by something more knowing. "It's not what you think."

It's not what I think? It's not what *he* thinks! But how can I get him to see that without touching on my magical nature?

"We better get back to the office," he says.

Reluctantly, I turn and we walk in silence. He's busy with his thoughts; I'm busy with mine. I can't let this happen. But I can't fix it with the current batch. It's way too unpredictable. I need some regular magic to work with. Sooner or later, we'll get a decent batch again. But I know Alec; once he's decided, he moves fast. "So, you probably want to think about this more, right? We should at least wrap-up our current projects."

That would buy me a couple of months.

He shrugs. "Why wait? In fact, I'll call Feenex as soon as we're back."

I squeeze out a smile. "Promise me one thing."

He raises a brow.

"Don't sign anything without telling me first."

I have to do something; unfortunately, I have no idea what.

*M*eels hasn't returned any of my texts asking when she'll be home. Which means she's sitting at a desk in a library, lost in a thousand-page tome on probability theory, completely unaware that her phone is sitting uncharged at the bottom of her bag. I wish I could give her a telepathic zap but, unfortunately, we don't have that kind of freaky twin power.

At a loss, I've cleaned every inch of our little house. Partly because I've got a lot of energy to burn through and nothing else to do, and partly to butter Amelia up. She's somewhat of a neat freak, and I'm … not. But I've spent hours dusting and scrubbing, and now there's nothing more to do. I'm pacing the hallway like a mad woman.

I need to do something, so I decide to phone Mum.

Coven is cancelled, but that might not apply to neophyte training, which Mum is responsible for. I suppose it could have been awkward when Meels and I joined the coven having Mum as our teacher, but we had a blast. She's a great teacher; she teaches Elizabethan history at Melbourne University and she's always winning best lecturer awards. If neophyte training is still on, she may have news about the bad batch. I'll have to be careful though – under that veneer of academic absentmindedness, she's extremely perceptive.

"Hello, darling," she greets warmly.

"Hi. Busy?"

"No, but I do have to dash to a tutorial in a moment."

Good. That means she'll have less time to realise the state I'm in. "I won't keep you. Any updates from Owlscroft?"

"Coven's cancelled."

"I know. But I thought neophytes might be excluded."

"Bernadette thought it safest to cancel everything."

"Oh. Have you spoken to Aunt Bernie or Aunt Nettie?"

"To be honest, I've been enjoying the break."

Mum does her part, and does it well, but she has a full outside life. Unlike Aunt Bernie. And unlike me. "Do we have any more test results on how that new batch is behaving?"

"Not that I'm aware of, darling. I think the plan is to wait it out."

"When that will be? Are we talking days or weeks?" Please, let it be days.

"No one knows yet." A pause as Mum processes my intensity. "Was there something you needed to tell me, Avery?"

"No," I respond with no doubt telling quickness. That's what I mean about deceptively perceptive.

"No?"

For a moment, I lean in to my desire to tell her everything, but it wouldn't be fair. She's on the Council and it would put her in a difficult position. She'd probably feel like she had to tell Aunt Bernie what I'd done, and although I'm increasingly resigned to the fact that that's going to happen, I'm not there yet. "I just wanted to keep up-to-date. See if there was anything I could help with."

I can almost hear her frown. I know she thinks I spend too much time at the covenstead or mulling over coven business.

"You're right about it being good to have a break though," I add quickly, before she can start the usual gentle chiding. "It's leaving me with more time to …" I look around. "Clean." I grimace. That's the wrong thing to say to my mum, who always wants me to go out with friends and 'have fun'. I don't really have friends outside of the coven or work. I don't have time. "Have you heard from Meels? I can't get in contact."

Another pause. "Should I have?"

"No. I just need … I mean, I just want to talk to her."

"Darling. You sound very much at a loose end."

I laugh a little maniacally. If only that was my problem. "I know. Outside hobbies and all that. I'm going to start working on it."

"Good. And if you're interested in what's happening at Owlscroft, Bernadette would always welcome a call or a visit. Sorry, darling, I have to run. Ciao," Mum says and ends the call.

I wouldn't mind her input, but there is no way I can call Aunt Bernie.

I look for something else to tidy until Meels gets home.

When I hear the front door open, I rush to intercept her in the narrow hall. I am in a fever to confess, so we can get to the part where she helps me. "Don't get mad at me."

Amelia tosses me an amused glance and deposits her brown leather satchel and sunhat on the sideboard. "I knew it. I knew something was up." And then she clocks the impeccable state of our house. "Wow. It must be bad."

It is, and I don't like to admit how my impulsive actions have caused things to yet again go wrong for me – even to my twin – but if I want her help, I have to. I lead the way along the hall to the small lounge area. Arms across my chest, I turn. "I cast an unlawful spell."

"You what?"

"Two."

She's gone very still; her eyes are moon wide. This is not the minor misdemeanour she was expecting, but something that could land me in a lot of trouble.

I bite my lower lip. "I know. I shouldn't have."

"Chalice, Avery." Amelia is a big believer in rules. A dotter of i's and crosser of t's. Calm, organised, precise, logical, analytical. It's amazing we're related at all, let alone twins.

"I know. It gets worse. That new batch, it's made everything spiral out of control." I turn again. "I want to fix it, but I'm scared to try another spell. I need your help."

Amelia sits carefully on the couch, then looks at me askance. "I don't know what you think I'm going to be able to do."

I hover, not ready to sit yet. "Chance magic?"

"Un-uh. No way. I'm not joining you on the dark side."

"Come on, Meels, it's just a chance spell."

"Just a chance spell?" she says dryly.

"You know what I mean."

We cast a lot of chance spells. They can be surprisingly effective. Take a bushfire – happens a lot in Australia and it's the kind of thing we try to help with. Of course, as witches, we could work directly with the elements, but given the size and the heat, it wouldn't be terribly effective. Better to cast a chance spell to increase the probability of rain. It's not a particularly direct route, and outcomes vary, but negative side effects seem to be lower too.

"I think you better tell me exactly what happened."

She's right. I'm a little panicked and I haven't even told her. "It's Alec's fault." My mouth twists; it's not really. "It involves dogs," I settle on instead.

She scrunches up her nose delicately.

"Alec was trying to force me to go to a dog shelter for Valentine's, a charity thing, and of course that's not happening, so I cast a spell to change it."

"Avery."

"I know. But it was before I knew about the bad batch. And I was so cranky at Alec. And Aunt Bernie. And I just thought, what's the harm?"

"Mmm," she murmurs.

"Anyway, it worked but then the bad batch made Alec book a trip to Hawaii for everyone – like, literally everyone at HewTech – and of course, I couldn't let that happen. So I cast another spell, and Hawaii's off but now Alec wants to sell his company. And I know him, he moves fast – if I don't do something, those papers will be signed before the week's out. I can't let that happen, but given what's happened with my last two attempts … All I can think is to try a chance spell instead."

"Do you have any reason to think the bad batch will play nicer with a chance spell?"

She's going to say no. I know she is.

I feel my eyes filling and I turn before she can see. "No."

I know Meels is right. She shouldn't use magic right now any more than I should. I just don't want Alec to lose HewTech. I pace to the window and look out onto the narrow side passage that runs along the house.

"Avery?" Her voice has an uncertain sound to it. I'm generally not an emotional person.

"It's his whole life, Meels. He's worked so hard to build HewTech, and we have really big plans for the future. And now, he's going to lose it and it's my fault. It's not right." I rub my chest against the sudden tight ache.

"I will help you," Amelia says, tone full of the comfort and support I need. "Of course I will. I just don't think that more spells are what we need right now. We need a different approach. Come and sit down, and we'll work something out."

I nod, shoving any hint of tears back in where they belong and go to take a seat. I start from the beginning and go through everything in detail.

Amelia listens carefully. When I finish, her head tilts and her lips are pursed. "So how tight was the binding?"

"It felt firm, I suppose? I don't know. It's so hard to tell, Meels. This new batch, it just leaps right in there and the binding's done before you know it."

"Can you chip away at it, get it to loosen a little? Not with magic, just by talking to him? Like you said, who knows with this batch. Maybe it's not that tight. Maybe he'll change his mind."

Could that work? Can I talk him out of it, remind him of the plans he has for HewTech? Loosen or dislodge the spell? "I can try."

"Try. As soon as you can. Maybe the bad batch doesn't stick so good. And if that doesn't work, we'll think of something else."

"Okay. Thanks, Meels."

I don't feel one-hundred per cent confident, but I feel better than I did before we talked. Although I don't know how things turned out like this, if I talk to Alec and discover more about what he's thinking and why he wants to sell, maybe I can counter.

Meels is looking at me searchingly. "I'm surprised you care this much."

"Of course I care! I don't want to be responsible for stuffing up someone's life."

"That's not what I meant. You seem upset on a personal level … A really personal level. I thought you hated Alec."

"I never hated him," I mumble, looking down at my hands. Though the way I'd carried on, even to my sister, I'm not surprised everyone has formed that impression. It's a little embarrassing, to be honest.

She's still studying me. I can feel it even though I'm looking resolutely at my fingernails. The silence lasts long moments, then I hear a puff of breath.

"Oh my God," she says. "You like him."

"I do not!" I look at her in outrage.

She just smiles. "You're allowed to, you know."

Witches are allowed to date, of course. I used to, when I was at university. It's easy to keep things casual when you're twenty. Guys aren't exactly complaining if you can't account for large chunks of time. But as you get older, things get more serious. A relationship might lead to living together, and then your partner might wonder where the hell you are all the time. And you have to make the decision on whether to disclose the whole witch thing.

"It wouldn't do me any good anyway," I say.

"Why do you say that?" I don't answer straight away, and her gaze turns sympathetic. "Because of Evan, right? You can't let one bad experience turn you off forever."

I got together with Evan towards the end of my degree. I don't dive into relationships, I don't share easily, and I didn't tell him about being a witch for a long time. But he was considering various post-grad options and I was tossing up potential starts to my career and we were trying to work out what to do about our relationship. He decided on the Kellogg School of Management at Northwestern in America and asked me if I'd consider applying for jobs in Chicago. I thought things were serious if we were moving overseas together; I thought he was the one. So I told him.

I don't know if he believed me or not. We didn't even get that far. I was expecting him to ask questions – all kinds of questions – but he didn't. He ghosted me. Totally and utterly. A few horrible weeks later, I found out he'd discovered a sudden urge to backpack around Europe before starting his program and had left without even saying goodbye. It was just too weird, too much for him.

I don't like being vulnerable. I'm tough and I'm pragmatic, but when I hurt, I really hurt. It took me a long time to get over him. I've had a couple of casual flings since then. I'm not looking for anything more than that.

"It's not just what happened with Evan. It's Alec. He just wouldn't get it. It wouldn't work."

"You don't think he'd accept it?"

"No." There's no way. He downplays it, but he's ambitious. That 30 under 30 list, even the stupid prime minister mug … It's a joke, but it's not really. He's going places. And so am I, but we're not going to the same place. I picture his ideal partner – someone poised and proper, who'll say and do the right thing all the time, who'll turn up to fundraising balls and charm foreign dignitaries with tales of the children's equestrian medals … I just don't see how a witch, especially one like me, could fit in with all that.

"Maybe just don't tell him? At least for a while."

"That wouldn't work either." Any relationship with Alec is not going to be casual. He's not going to buy my having an intense schedule of French lessons. He'll probably turn out to speak French himself, and quiz me, and then where will I be? "Besides," I say, "it's not just the witch thing. I just don't know if we'd really mesh. I'm too chaotic and impulsive. I always seem to get into trouble." I sigh. "Put it this way, Meels, he has a mug that says 'Future Prime Minister of Australia.'"

She screws up her nose again. "Eww. He sounds like Evan."

Apparently I have a type – golden boys who'll never love me and my crazy back. "Evan had that exact same mug."

"No way."

I scrunch my nose to match hers.

"By the way, you're not as chaotic as you seem and you're only a little bit impulsive. You're loyal, you're hardworking, you're creative, and you've got a lot of heart."

I frown. "What about the getting into trouble part?"

"Makes life interesting. You're awesome, Avery. If he doesn't accept you for who you are and love you back, he doesn't deserve you."

I can't help but smile. Everyone should have a Meels in their corner. "I'm going to go see him."

Amelia said 'as soon as possible', and I've decided she's right.

CHAPTER 7

*A*lec lives in a high-end boutique apartment in Collingwood. I know this not because I've been there but because it's a company asset and I was involved in the paperwork. It's only a fifteen minute walk or so, so I decide to hoof it. I've turned up with no notice and one goal in mind. To talk him out of selling.

I enter through the automatic door at the front and head for the 24/7 concierge on my left. He takes my name, makes a call and says I can go up. When I step out of the elevator on Alec's floor, he's standing in the doorway to his apartment, waiting for me. And the expression on his face – the intensity, the expectation …

Heat flushes all over me; I have a moment where I have to stop.

"Sorry about just turning up," I say when I can think again. How can it be that he's not wearing shoes, but his hair still forms a perfect golden wave? He's wearing low-slung track pants and a soft, worn grey t-shirt and his feet are bare. HewTech doesn't require formal office attire for the most part, but I haven't seen him like this before, and it's a very good look for him.

"Everything okay?"

"Yes," I say, although the reason I'm here is because everything is very much not okay. "We just … need to talk."

His gaze narrows and he waves me into his apartment. It's as gorgeous as I suspected, set out in an airy open plan. Minimal and luxe and so well-appointed I want to cry. There is floor-to-ceiling glass in front of me and to one side, with views over city lights starting to twinkle in the dusk, and a seating area with the kind of couches that feature in architecture magazines and a couple of quartz-topped coffee tables. I hover, waiting for Alec to close the door and join me.

"Take a seat," he says. "Can I get you something? A drink?"

I sink into one of his heavenly white couches. "Better not. Thank you." We need to keep this professional, and that's going to be challenging enough without booze.

He settles back gracefully on an adjacent couch, and I have to admit, he doesn't look troubled by the upcoming sale. In fact, he looks more relaxed than I've seen him in ages. A lightness that's been quashed by the responsibilities of running a rapidly growing tech juggernaut. Part of me wishes I could leave him like this. I'd be happy for him if he wasn't about to make a terrible mistake.

Now that I'm here, I don't quite know how to start. I look around and spot a distraction on the side table nearest me. "That's a great photo," I say, leaning closer. It's a young Alec with a couple of guys with huge white grins in some kind of tropical setting. "Where is it?"

He smiles. "Ghana. I spent a couple of months volunteering there one summer, refurbing old and broken laptops from the UK for a primary school."

Something tightens in my belly. Evan did a similar thing, but it was Laos, not Ghana, and it had something to do with microfinance. "That's … amazing," I manage to get out.

"It was my mother's idea. For my CV, to help with postgrad scholarship applications. But … they were good times."

He looks happy in the photo, I'll give him that. But I didn't really need the additional reminder of everything that went wrong with Evan and how he and Alec are weirdly twinning through life. I steer the conversation away. "Look. The reason I'm here. This thing with Feenex … " I let my voice trail off, hoping he'll fill the gap. If I'm going to talk him out of it, I need to know where he's at with it, what he's thinking. *I* know it's the spell, but *he* doesn't – how could he? No doubt he thinks he has his reasons. If I knew what they were, I'd have a better shot at talking him out of it.

He shifts forward, forearms coming to his thighs, expression not as expectant as before. Probably this is not what he'd been hoping for when he got that call from the concierge.

When he doesn't say anything, I'm forced to continue. "Selling HewTech seems to have come out of nowhere."

"I wouldn't say that."

Well, I would. Selling a company is a big deal. If he's been thinking about it, why hasn't he shared it with his BDO? "Last time it came up, you were hellbent on refusing any offer from Feenex."

"I changed my mind." There's a certain cool edge to his tone.

"It's not even three months since we came up with our new five-year strategic plan." I'm perched on the edge of my seat, almost trembling with my need to make this right.

He stares at me with that level, unblinking focus he has. "The strategy applies to HewTech. It'll go with it to Feenex, if they want it."

I suppose. I frown. "But a sale wasn't on the cards then. We have goals for HewTech, Alec. Goals we're excited about. You always said you wouldn't sell until you'd taken the company as far as you could on your own. We've done well, but we're just getting started." Out his window, the lights of the city flicker. It's a gorgeous view – one I might appreciate more if my mind weren't so occupied with the impending disaster. "We've made so many inroads over the past year. We've managed to land our first major client outside of Australia. Our developers are ahead of schedule with the improvements to the sensory immersion. If we land Blanc, you have every chance of making 30 under 30."

He gives a small nod of acknowledgement. "We've done well. We're doing well."

"So? Why are you selling?"

"Good progress. Wrong goals."

"They're not the wrong goals; they're part of our strategic plan."

"Right goals for HewTech. Wrong goals for me."

Since when? "How long have you been thinking like this?"

He shrugs, as if that's irrelevant.

"It was just today, wasn't it?" I press.

The look in his eyes is scorching. But I know it's a yes. If I needed any more proof that this whole 'I want to sell' thing was driven by the spell, that's it. Right there.

He leans back. "I've been in denial. Today, for the first time, I saw my situation, my life, with total clarity. I can't ignore it any longer."

He can and should ignore it. It's just a bad batch of magic. "Maybe it's just a passing thought. A phase. You've always said HewTech is your first love."

He looks at me, a muscle in his jaw ticking. "I'm giving it up for something more meaningful."

"What, exactly?"

He just looks at me. "Is this the only reason you came tonight?"

He's not going to tell me. To be honest, if the 'something more meaningful' is the two of us, it's not something I want to talk about either. I can't help but think it's my feelings for Alec that have got us to this point. And maybe also his feelings for me. "I'm your BDO. Don't you owe me at least a little hint?"

"When I'm ready, you'll be the first to know." His brows are drawn down and there is a steely note in his voice that serves as a warning not to press.

I back up a little. "It's just all happening so fast. Don't you think you should take more time to make sure it's what you really want?"

He gives me a forced, out-of-patience half-smile. "I appreciate your concern, Avery, but I'm sure."

He appears unshakably – suspiciously – confident that he's doing the right thing, and it's not giving me much to work with. I renew my attack from a different angle. "Did you think about how the rest of us might feel about you selling?"

His mouth twists down.

Sensing weakness, I launch a full assault. "What about all that stuff about building a culture? How important that is to you. You've always led everyone to believe that this is more than just a job, that HewTech is more than just a company. It's community, values, mission. But now you're selling us. Just like that."

His face has a stony cast. "I'll ensure the deal is favourable to current HewTech staff. Feenex have wanted to acquire us for ages. I'm in a strong position; I should be able to get concessions. And they're not a bad outfit; they look after their staff. I wouldn't sell to them if I had any concerns on that front. You know that."

I do know that. I'm just vexed at my lack of progress. "Can't you just … not sell? Step away from HewTech on a day-to-day basis if you need to, but not sell it?"

He shakes his head. "I'm going to need the capital."

I hate admitting defeat but I feel like I've hit a wall. If I can't talk him out of it, I at least need to know what I'm dealing with. "So what are the plans?"

"I'll be in meetings with Feenex over the next couple of days. We're aiming to sign off on the sale by COB on the fourteenth."

My heart almost stops. "Valentine's." The word signals impending doom.

"Valentine's," he agrees.

That's two days away. Worse than I thought. It sends a fresh wave of panic through me. I might have to delve into some emotional honesty. Blech.

I take a moment, staring at my fingernails and working up the courage. "I have to be honest, Alec. You're doing this for the wrong reason."

If he's doing it so we don't work together anymore, so we can pursue some kind of relationship … It's not going to make any difference. The biggest reason we can't be together is not that he's my boss; I'm a hot mess of a witch who's always saying and doing the wrong thing, and he's Hubert Alec Hewittson – future prime minister.

When I meet his gaze, he says, "I know what I'm doing and why."

"You don't!"

His brows go up.

I need to stay calm, convince him there's no future for us. "Alec, I think you think that if you sell HewTech … certain things that can't happen at the moment might suddenly happen. But it's probably not going to turn out that way. In fact, it's definitely not going to turn out that way." Chalice! I'm making a hash of it but I'm beyond uncomfortable.

Something like amusement crosses his face. "I'll take that chance."

"It's not a chance. There's no chance."

"We'll see."

"There's really no chance."

He smiles. "Okay."

But I know he doesn't believe me. I almost scream in frustration.

I'm not one to linger when it's time to go. I need to regroup and relaunch. I stand. "You're making a mistake."

He stands too. "We're going to have to agree to disagree."

I can't do that.

It's depressing, to be honest. If Alec loses HewTech, I'll never forgive myself. "I don't want you to sell." The words are lame and inadequate, but I just don't know what else to say or do.

"I got that," he says. He comes to stand in front of me. His hands come to my shoulders, skim down my arms. "This will be okay, Avery."

I do a bad job of suppressing a huff. Of course he'd think that. He doesn't know what's happening. You're about to lose your company, I feel like shouting.

I squeeze out a smile, but I'm devastated and it must show. "I'm going to go now."

"I'll drop you home."

"It's not far. I can walk."

"I'll drop you."

I look out at the now-dark sky and nod. We take the lift down to the basement carpark. Alec has a Tesla. Of course. It's so him. If I wasn't in such a mood, I'd probably tease him about it.

I direct him through the quiet evening streets, but otherwise we don't talk. I've got nothing more to say. Short of explaining about the spell itself, I can't think of anything else I can throw at this.

"This is me," I say, when we reach my little Victorian terrace. Amelia has left the porch light on and it radiates a warm glow, enough to see the roses in the pocket-sized front garden and the picket fence with a crossing pattern of wire across the top.

Alec pulls in, kills the engine and has a good look at it. It's nowhere near the level of glamour of his place, but whatever he sees has him smiling.

I unbuckle my strap but I don't get out. I look at the moon out my window for a moment or two. I have to do something. I turn. "Alec—" I start, but the way he's looking at me stops me short.

"Why are you so convinced we don't have a future?"

I realise I'm staring at his mouth. I look at the moon again, praying for strength. "We've been through this. We work together."

"Not for long."

He might be right, unless I can figure out how to stop it from happening.

"You have to know how I feel about you."

His words are a dainty little knife, twisting in my heart. Because unfortunately, I do know. I'm also aware of how I feel about him. Fat lot of good it does either of us. I happen to be attracted to exactly the kind of guy it would never work with.

"I'm just … not the right girl for you. We wouldn't work."

"We do work."

I huff out a breath. "Can you honestly see us together?"

"Yes." His response is immediate and sure.

I should hate that, but I don't. I love hearing it, but it also makes me sad, because it's not going to happen. I bite my lip. "There's things you don't know about me. If you did, you wouldn't be interested."

"I don't believe that."

"It's true. And it's a dealbreaker." It was for Evan.

"Why don't you let me be the judge of that?"

I look away. I can't tell him.

"Talk to me, Avery. Please."

I turn in my seat to face him. His gaze rakes over my face,

searching for answers, but I've got nothing for him. "I can't." It comes out husky and choked.

He's got that calculating expression that says he's thinking through the possibilities. I almost tell him not to bother. He's not going to be able to guess the truth.

"You don't already have a …" He pushes a hand through his hair. "You're not already seeing someone?"

"No." It occurs to me too late that making someone up would have been the quickest and easiest way out of this, but I won't lie to him. Not about something like that.

This conversation isn't going to end unless I make it end. Unless I give him something, some reason he can work with. "The truth is, it's hard for me to date. It's … my family."

He grimaces. "The family again."

"Yes." He probably thinks I'm in the mafia. "I have commitments."

"Commitments."

"I'm not really at liberty to … But it's full on and it's …" I scramble to find a way to describe the work we do in any way that would make sense to him. "Important."

He leans further towards me. "Okay. You've got commitments. But there has to be space for you to have a life too, right?" He says the words fiercely.

No witch in my coven would dispute that. Not even Aunt Bernie. But it's up to all of us how we get there. I answer with a shrug.

"I understand what you're saying. I have my own things to manage. Whatever it is you've got going on … I wouldn't expect you to give any of it up."

He's making this hard. Really hard.

"I don't know what to say," I admit eventually. It's true.

He reaches out, touches a strand my hair. "Tell me this. If we leave aside work and we leave aside your commitments, if we leave out everything that isn't just you and me, do you feel something for me?"

I should lie but I can't. I can't drag my gaze away from him. I feel my eyes, my face soften as the whole truth of it hits me. "Yes, Alec. I feel something for you."

"Good." He moves closer, and I'm flooded with the smell of soap and man. "That's all I need to know."

A hand around my waist holds me. He looks into my eyes, then down to my mouth. I bite my lower lip in some kind of weird involuntary reaction. He looks back up and his other hand comes to cup the back of my neck. And then it's happening. He lowers his mouth to mine.

At the first press, exhilaration surges through me, making me feel like I'm flying. As the pressure firms, heat blossoms and an electrical current courses through me. It's dazzling.

I'm done for. I'm so done for. I kiss him back with wild hunger. My heartbeat is ringing in my ears. I'm no longer aware of the street, of the night, not even my name. I'm not aware of anything but him. I don't want it to end. Ever.

When he draws back, I follow but he holds me steady until I open my eyes.

His eyes are dark like I've never seen. His chest is rising and falling rapidly, his breath heavy, uneven. The hand on my nape comes around to cup my jaw. "This will be okay. Trust me. Just give me until Valentine's."

I don't reply. I'm not yet capable of coherent thought.

Then his words hit me.

Valentine's! I scramble for the handle and out of the car. Then stand on the side of the road, arms wrapped around my chest.

What did I just do?

The car glides off silently. My heart is still pounding as I watch it round the corner.

I was trying to convince him we can never be together.

Why did I let him kiss me?

Why did I kiss him back?

No wonder he doesn't believe me! I don't even believe me.

That's all I need to know.

I have to agree. That kiss has eroded any doubts I've been desperately clinging to about how into Alec I am.

I'm *very* into Alec.

CHAPTER 8

$\mathcal{A}$lec has been in negotiations with Feenex all day, but we've agreed to meet at the Blanc offices at four to make our pitch.

When I see him in the foyer, a rush of feeling sweeps over me, leaving me light-headed. Even knowing it was a mistake, all I want is to feel his lips on mine again.

"Hi," I say.

"Hello." Only the heat in his eyes betrays anything of what happened last night. "Ready?"

"You know it." This at least I can get right.

We get in the lift and head up. I don't ask how the discussions with Feenex are going – I can only assume he's on track to sign off on the sale. There's nothing more I can say that I haven't already tried, so I resist the urge to hassle. I've got a new tactic now – one last shot to *show* him how much he's got at stake, how much he doesn't want to sell.

We're lead to a conference room where the Blanc family are waiting. Two brothers and a sister – average age 80 – and a couple of lawyers and other hangers on – spring chickens at 65.

Alec goes first, and introduces HewTech and the broader context of VR and e-commerce. Then I stand to talk my way through the

316

numbers. I worked really hard on putting together the business case and it's strong – HewTech can do great things for Blanc. But the more I scan the room, the more I see that it's not the numbers they don't like.

It's the whole idea.

They don't want to change. They were probably told they should take this meeting, find out what all the fuss about e-commerce is about, but they've gone in with a strong bias to dismiss. They don't understand this new way of making sales. They don't understand the tech or what it can do. More than that, they don't understand that if they don't embrace change, they'll go out of business.

I need to make them see. I switch tacks. "So that's the numbers. But as good as they are, this can only happen if you want it to happen. And I know you're probably thinking that the way you've always done things works, so why the need to change? Especially in what probably seems like a radical direction." I imagine a whole room of Aunt Bernies. And heaven knows I've never been particularly good at convincing her of anything, but I need to stick the landing this time. "But the thing is, the world is changing, and if you don't change with it, you'll find yourself irrelevant. Out of business." I pause for full effect. "Adapt or perish."

The collective flinch lets me know that hit home.

"Change is hard. It's a risk. I get that. Another organisation I work for—" Alec's head lifts to mine. "Worked for," I amend quickly, "found itself in much the same position. Not in the retail sector. In … another industry." I shoot a glance at Alec, who's looking back at me, gaze narrowed, but it's too late to stop now. I turn back to the Blanc siblings. "They're constantly scrambling to keep up with the increasing demands of the world. They're so stretched, they think they don't have the time or the resources to invest in new ways of doing things. But I've been telling them, it's because they're so stretched, because everything is always evolving and ramping up, that they need to do exactly that."

Evelyn Blanc leans forward. "Are they listening?"

"I'm still working on it. But I'm hopeful." I look around and say it once more, with impact. "Adapt or perish. Not an if, a when." I pause, and then continue. "But it doesn't have to be that way. You can choose to adapt. And if you're considering a tech partner, choose HewTech. We're not the biggest, but we're the best. We have the best technology, but more than that, we have the best people. From Alec and myself down to every developer and every member of the support staff. And the reason for that is this man sitting right here." I tilt my head at Alec. "Right from day one, he's put everything into building our company culture. I can't tell you how much weight he puts on our values, our mission. We're not a dump and run company. We won't saddle you with tech you can't get to work. Your success is our success. We want to be your partner; we'll be there with you every step of the way."

Earnest Blanc leans forward. "So, what you're saying is, we should trust you."

"You can, and should, trust Avery," Alec says. His tone is warm, and so is his gaze on me. "She always comes through."

Oscar Blanc stands. "You've given us a lot to think about, but I think I speak for all of us when I say," he looks at his brother and sister for confirmation before turning to us again, "we'll be in contact."

We wrap up the meeting and head out. I am thrumming with excitement, sure that Blanc are not only thinking they have to invest in VR e-commerce, but that they're going to choose us. Outside, the atmosphere on the street is as lively as my mood.

I turn to Alec, grinning. "That went really we—"

But the remainder of my thoughts are muffled as I'm drawn into a warm, enveloping embrace.

"I don't know how, but you're pulled through again," he murmurs against my ear.

I could get used to this—the smell of him, the strength of his arms.

He releases me, but there is still heat in his eyes. "I better get back to Feenex."

He turns and starts off in a southerly direction. I race to catch up with him. We got Blanc, but that's the start of this conversation, not the end.

He glances at me. "Where are you headed?"

"Work," I say.

"Ahh," he says. "Your other job. The one that accounts for at least half of your time, explaining why you're never at HewTech when you should be."

My heart almost stops. I realise with some alarm that we are headed in roughly the direction of Owlscroft. Then I realise he's joking, referring to what I said to Blanc. I let forth a bright peal of laughter to cover my shock.

"Something you made up on the fly?"

It's totally the wrong reaction but I'm offended. I frown. "I wouldn't lie to get Blanc's business."

"I know that. You're the most honest person I know."

I'm not. There's so much I can't, and won't ever, tell him. My mouth quirks, but I straighten it before he can see.

"No, but seriously. I can't remember seeing anything like that on your CV."

Goddamn Alec and his inability to let anything go. "You've got my CV memorised, stalker?" But he's going to keep pressing. I shrug and say as casually as I can manage, "Just some people – family – I worked for a while back. I still … um, consult to them on occasion."

"The mysterious family strikes again."

I divert. "Anyway. We did it. We got Blanc." I stop walking, grab his arm. "No need to sell."

He looks down at my hand on his arm, then back up. The smile drops from his face. "Avery … I'm still selling."

"But you said you needed capital. Blanc will give you capital."

"It's not just the capital." Those fine stress lines are bracketing his mouth again.

"Well, 30 under 30 then. You said you'd make the list if we got Blanc."

He shakes his head. "I don't care about that anymore."

"So why did we even bother pitching to Blanc if you're going to sell?" My tone is bitter.

A hand comes to my elbow. "You did great in there. And now I can take Blanc to Feenex and drive an even harder bargain."

"We asked them to trust us, to come with us."

"I asked them to trust you, and you'll still be there. Besides, Blanc will be a key client for Feenex just as much as they would have been for HewTech – Feenex will take very, very good care of them."

He's right but chalice! I was sure that this would dislodge the spell, remind Alec of everything he's spent so long building, all the goals HewTech has yet to meet. But I've made it easier for him to sell, not harder. "I can't believe this."

He shoves a hand through his hair. "I'm sorry if you were under the impression that securing Blanc would change my plans."

It was the only thing I could see that might work. "I wish you would just believe me when I tell you you're making a mistake."

He shakes his head, frustrated. "Why can't you let this go?"

"Because I can't sit back and let you sell your company for me!"

He looks a little taken aback. "I didn't say I was selling it for you."

"Are you really trying to tell me this has nothing to do with me?"

He looks at me hard, then looks away. I can see him tossing up various responses, but he's not a liar either, and he can't say that it doesn't. His hands come to his hips. "You know when I was happiest?" He pauses but it's rhetorical. "Those months I spent in Ghana."

"Are you saying you want to go back to Africa?"

He gives a quiet low chuckle. "I'm saying that I'm not happy like that at HewTech. That I haven't felt good like that since then."

"You were nineteen," I say. "You were volunteering overseas; there was no pressure."

"It's not just that. I was helping people. It meant something."

He looks at me like I need to understand something. "This constant battle to be the best. To win all the time. Even against your own sister ... It's the way I was raised; it's all I know. Bigger, better, faster, stronger. And it's addictive. But I'm starting to realise it's a trap. When was I truly happy? When I wasn't living with that pressure. Those expectations." He looks at me. "Maybe I'm not explaining it well."

He's explaining it perfectly. "You think I don't get family expectations? Believe me, I get it," I say with intensity. "The only difference between us is, you meet your expectations, whereas I … fall short."

"That can't be right," he replies immediately.

I shake my head. "It's true." I mean, I try hard but I don't live up to my lineage and there's nothing I can do about it. But what hasn't occurred to me before is that maybe meeting expectations is not a guaranteed path to happiness. That maybe Meels and the other two have struggles of their own. Maybe, in some ways, it's worse. "But listening to you talk … Maybe I should be grateful I'm not exceptional."

He gives me a hard assessing look, then laughs. "Are you serious?"

"What? I'm not." It's true, and I have proof – I've been tested and everything. "I'm mediocre."

He lets out something like a soft chuckle. "Avery, there's nothing mediocre about you."

His words melt me. I can see he believes it. His gaze is deep and warm, and it makes my insides all soft and squishy. I want this to be real.

If only this could be real.

My phone buzzes. I retrieve it from my bag. I turn a little for privacy and read the text from Mum. All-coven's been called.

Relief swoops through me. Hopefully the bad batch has moved on. "I've got to go."

"Family commitments?" he asks.

"Family commitments."

He leans forward, hand on my jaw and kisses me. My eyes close automatically. It's quick but everything inside me still lights up.

"This will be resolved tomorrow."

He turns and continues south towards Feenex.

He's right. One way or another, this all comes to a head tomorrow.

~

I RIDE IN AGAIN, arriving early, then sit alone in the Owlscroft ballroom, hoping devoutly for a breakthrough that solves all my problems. I'm running out of time. Tomorrow is Valentine's. Unless there's good news tonight, when Alec realises what's happened, what I've done, how he no longer has HewTech, he's going to hate me.

Witches stream in around me, chatting excitedly. Everyone seems pumped to be back. Everly and Harlow wave and take their regular seats. Amelia slips in beside me. She raises her brows, checking if I've made any headway since we last spoke. Meels has been a trooper since I told her – a real fount of support.

I shake my head sadly.

"Don't worry," she says. "Let's see what comes out of tonight."

If the batch has passed, I'll use magic to stop him. I don't care about breaking the rules or getting caught anymore.

"Witches, seats please!" Aunt Bernie's authoritative voice rings through the room. She gives everyone a moment or two to settle, then continues. "We've got a lot to cover tonight. I know everyone is keen to learn what has been happening with the new batch. Let's get started."

I grip the base of my chair as a series of witches stand and provide updates. The bad batch is still with us and there is no end in sight; no one has been able to discover anything about the batch's provenance or why it is behaving the way that it is; none of the other covens we're in contact with are experiencing anything similar, nor have they; the batch is still not passing the basic tests, and therefore, non-essential magic is being deferred for another week.

None of it, not a single bit, is of use to me. My shoulders slump and my chest feels tight. It's crushing. It's been almost a week, and we've made no progress. I don't have time to defer magic for another week. I need it resolved. Now.

I stand.

Aunt Bernie looks resigned rather than enthused but she calls on me anyway. "Avery?"

I hadn't planned this. I don't know what I want to say, but I start with what I have. "Don't you think we should take a more proactive approach?"

Next to her, Aunt Nettie's mouth makes a moue of disapproval. "Believe it or not, Avery, we've been very busy trying to get to the bottom of this. Just because you haven't—"

Aunt Bernie's hand goes up. Aunt Nettie looks outraged but stops.

"What did you have in mind, Avery?"

Good question. "I'm sorry, Aunt Nettie," I make sure to start with. "I know you've been working hard on the problem and I didn't mean to imply otherwise. But I can't help but think things like this are going to keep happening. We can't just sit back and wait till the coast is clear. This is not exactly the same as the new spells innovation unit, but it kind of is. Too much of the time, all we're doing is reacting." I'm warming to my theme, my thoughts coalescing into what I want to say. "Why do we just have to accept whatever batch has decided to grace us with its presence? Can't we find a way to make it go away, bring a different batch in? Or find some way to process all new batches as they come in, make them more uniform, more predictable."

"Like pasteurising milk?" Aunt Bernie offers dourly.

I huff. Why will no one at this coven take me seriously? Especially Aunt Bernie. "We're just such victims and I hate it."

"Avery!" That's Mum, with a very rare reprimand. She manages to look both furious and disappointed.

Aunt Bernie doesn't look angry – she looks offended, hurt. Regret at my words stabs at me. I didn't mean to hurt her. I don't want rifts within Owlscroft. I generally think Aunt Bernie does an excellent job wrangling all her various responsibilities.

And what I'm talking about – changing our whole approach to how we source and process our raw material, so to speak – is something that would take months, if not years, to work through. I might have a point – I like to think I have a point – but it's not going to help my current situation with Alec. And going on the attack at all-coven when everyone is already a little frayed around the edges is definitely not the time and place.

It's my frustration with my own situation, which I caused all by myself.

I'm about to apologise to Aunt Bernie – not for the overall idea, which I realise has been mulling around in my head for ages – but for the poor choice of delivery, and hurting her, but Everly stands before I can get the words out. I think she's about to add something 'helpful' again, but one look at her almost-translucent eyes and blank expression, and I give Aunt Bernie what I hope is an apologetic look and sit.

With her blonde hair and doll-like features, Everly looks positively angelic. Looks can be deceiving and they certainly are in Everly's case. I love my cousin and she's the sweetest, but future magic is freaky. It's like separating a part of yourself – I don't like to bandy the word soul around lightly – but it's separating and sending a part of yourself into the future.

Most witches don't like future magic, and it's considered something of a specialist skill. Everly delights in it. "The rollercoaster at Luna Park is going to come off the tracks at twelve past eleven tomorrow. Thirteen children between the ages of eight and fourteen will die." She's not totally back yet and she says all that with a smile on her face.

"Thank you, Everly," says Aunt Bernie crisply. "As I'm sure you all agree, current batch notwithstanding, we need to stop that from happening. I'll cast the spell myself. All-coven is over for tonight. We'll meet again next week."

Everyone around me stands. Some of them give me disapproving looks.

I understand where they're coming from, but this is exactly what I'm talking about. Right now, we're trapped between a bad batch and multiple fatalities. Always just trying to deal with what the world throws at us.

We need to take control.

CHAPTER 9

I wait for Alec outside his apartment building. It's not much after seven in the morning but he's an early riser. He'll be along soon.

My mind keeps going back to Luna Park. I don't disagree with Aunt Bernie's conclusion that we have to prevent the accident, but something will surely go wrong. I want to worry more about it – after all, I've had two spells backfire on me, so I have more insight than most – but I'm not likely to do any better than Aunt Bernie and I've got my own pressing problems.

And then I see Alec, striding towards me in corporate warrior mode. When he sees me, he slows and his expression softens.

"Can we talk?" I ask as he approaches. "Let's walk."

I don't wait for an answer. I power off and hope he catches me.

He falls into step beside me. "Happy Valentine's, by the way."

I give him a quick tight smile. "Happy Valentine's." We're walking along Johnston Street and there's a stream of people to navigate. It's not the best location for a serious conversation.

He casts a sideways glance at me. "Let me guess. This is about the sale to Feenex."

"Yes."

He swivels to give someone room to pass. "It really doesn't concern you."

"Yes, it does! Because I'm involved! I've made you think the wrong thing. About selling. About me."

"I'm a big boy, Avery. I make my own decisions."

But did he really?

I grab his arm. We come to an abrupt halt, irritating hordes of randoms trying to make their way. "Look, I know you probably don't get exactly what I'm trying to say, but it's not the right choice for you to sell. You never wanted to. Remember? You've had offers from Feenex before and you've always said no because HewTech is your life."

"I don't want to go through this again."

"I know you said things have changed, but have you stopped to think about what's changed? And why?"

"I know what. And why." He swivels to the side again, then spots a side alley and drags me in there. It's covered in Melbourne-style graffiti and it's a little smelly, but at least we're not dodging all and sundry anymore.

I disentangle from his grip. "You *think* you know. But whatever you think, whatever reasons are going through your head, they're not right. It's … me. I'm to blame. I know you don't understand exactly what I'm trying to say, but just … believe me anyway."

"Despite what you seem to think, Avery, you're not that hard to follow. You don't think we have a future."

"No," I agree sadly.

"You know what? I wasn't the only one in that kiss."

He's right. He's so right. "I shouldn't have done that. I shouldn't have kissed you."

It's hard to describe the look in his eyes. A little hurt, a lot of frustration. I've said the wrong thing. As usual. I try to pedal it back. "I told you, it's hard for me to date."

I know he thinks that's a lame non-excuse. The look he gives me is scorching.

I'm trying my best to communicate but it's not working. I steel myself and try again. "I want to be really clear. You cannot sell HewTech."

"You know, I usually like your persistence," he says, voice deep and soft. "But I've made my decision. It's happening at midday."

Midday? Chalice! "You say you make your own decisions. Tell me this sale has nothing to do with me."

I see him wrestling with it. He wants to be able to say that it doesn't, but he can't, and in the end, he just shakes his head.

That's what I thought.

I know what I have to do. I don't want to do it. I have a strong feeling it's going to be a disaster, but I don't see how I have a choice. "Alec, there's something pretty big you don't know about me. I'm not sure how you're going to feel about it. I'm not even sure if you're going to believe me."

He makes a sound that's close to a scoff.

My cheeks are hot, but everything else feels cold. A ball of dread is pitted in my stomach, my palms are sweaty. This is the hardest thing I've ever done. "I'm a witch."

I feel silly saying it. Not because being a witch is silly, but because I know what people think: pointy hats, black cats, broomsticks.

His face is blank. I've never seen it so blank.

I can't tell you how disgustingly vulnerable this whole thing is making me feel. I want to disappear into some void. But I can't go anywhere. I need him to understand.

"I'm a witch." It doesn't feel so bad the second time. I pause, draw strength from the word, and say it again. "I'm a witch, and the reason you want to sell your company is that I cast a spell. Not to make you sell! But I was working with a bad batch of magic and it backfired. It's my fault. Completely my fault. Please don't sell."

He's watching me intently. Probably waiting for me to admit this is all some kind of strange joke. But it isn't and I don't. His expression slowly changes from blank to stony, and I know he doesn't believe me. "The only reason you're saying you're a witch is because you don't want me to sell."

"Yes," I admit. I would never have told him otherwise. And then I get what he means. "No." I grit my teeth and clarify. "Yes, the only reason I told you was to get you to see what's going on. No, I'm not making it up."

His expression is pure scepticism. I warned him he wouldn't believe me and he scoffed. But I had it right. Painful thoughts ricochet around my brain. He doesn't believe me and he never will. He thinks I'm a liar or I'm crazy or anything and everything in between. Things are never going to be the same between us; I've lost him for good.

The hurt that took months to work through with Evan has reared its head; it's about to topple me again. I squash it down as best I can. I haven't got the time. I need to keep trying. "That commitment I was talking about that makes it hard to date? It's being a witch. That second job that you were joking about yesterday? It's not a joke – with the hours I devote to it, it is like a second job. All those evenings when I run off in a hurry? I'm on my way to coven."

That prompts a response. "Coven."

"Coven," I agree.

"Ominous."

He's not taking me seriously.

"It's not. We're good witches." I'm just going to persevere. I'm going to ignore the look on his face – confusion, disappointment, scepticism, and my personal favourite, scathing abhorrence – and continue. I let Evan walk away too easily, and I'm not making the same mistake again. Not with Alec. "I actually only know good witches. I've heard there are some of the not-so-nice variety, but I've never met one. The witches in my coven—it's called Owlscroft, by the way—"

"Avery."

I stop, breath catching in my throat.

"If you don't want to be with me, just say so."

I don't know what to say to that. It's not that I don't want to be with him. I'm pretty sure I'm in love with him and have been for heaven knows how long. I try to put that whole bag aside. I need to focus on the here and now.

"I am a witch." I say it firmly. It's becoming easier and easier to say, but his refusal to believe is getting harder and harder to take. "I cast a spell and it backfired and made you want to sell HewTech."

We stare at each other for another minute before he pushes a hand through his hair. "You cast spells?" he asks eventually.

I nod.

"Can you cast one now?"

Yes! Proof. I should have gone straight there. "Got a coin?"

I'm not Amelia, but I can change the number of heads that come up enough to be convincing.

But then I falter.

Alec must be able to guess what's coming because a funny expression comes onto his face.

"I can't at the moment." I shift from one foot to the other. "That bad batch I mentioned? We're not supposed to do any magic till it passes."

"Convenient."

"You don't believe me."

"Did you think I would?"

My eyes sting at that. I blink furiously till they clear. Given that I have assumed for years that no one would believe me if I told them, I am taking Alec's lack of faith surprisingly hard. While my conscious mind has been hyper-aware of the stupidity and danger of disclosure, some inner part of me – the buried-deep romantic – must have been holding out hope that it would go differently this time. "We've known each other for almost two years. We've talked pretty much every day over that time, and you've trusted me with some pretty big things. I've never lied to you. Why would I make this up?"

"Believe me, Avery, I have no idea."

"I wouldn't!" I cross my arms, close my eyes, turn my face to the sky. Then keep trying. "You think you like me enough to sell your company for. You stand in front of me when I tell you we can't date, and you kiss me and make me fall for you, even harder than I already had!"

The muscle in his jaw is working.

"I tell you there's no chance for us, but you say it'll all work out and to trust you. So I trust you. I tell you this thing about me, this thing that …" I have to take a moment. "This thing that's hard to share, actually. And I tell you I'm not lying but you don't believe me. You asked if I saw a future for us? This is why we don't have one."

Alec's expression is dark. Like he's angry with me for throwing this curve ball. Maybe I should be sympathetic because I suppose it can't be an easy to just accept when someone tells you she's a witch. Especially when it's someone you think you're already invested in. Maybe I'll find it in myself to be sympathetic later. Right now, I feel as dark as he looks. And not just at him. For the first time in my life, I really hate being a witch. I love him and I want to be with him, and the whole witch thing has got in the way again. This is how my life goes.

"I'm sorry I've caused you to sell HewTech. I know you're going to wake up in five years and wonder why the hell you did. And probably hate me. But if you're not going to believe me, and I can't use magic, I don't know what else I can do."

I turn and stalk away, hands in fists at my side, heartbroken over something I never truly had.

CHAPTER 10

I walk … and walk … and walk.

As tempting as it is to leave Alec to his 'big boy' choices, I can't do it.

I've had no success with not-magic. I need magic. I had the idea right last night. I need to take back control. Figure out what the hell is up with the current batch and how to work with it.

After all, magic isn't sentient. It doesn't have a will of its own.

It's energy.

Maybe.

Okay, even though I'm a witch, I don't know exactly what magic is, but the point is, if I understand what's going on with this batch, I may be able to use it.

It strikes me that, although he's not magic, if anyone can shed light on this, it's Dad.

Some part of me must have known this because I've just arrived at Melbourne University. I stride through the mostly empty grounds, all green lawns and sandstone buildings. It's nice here. I always like coming.

It's still early – not even nine. Too early for the few students who are on campus before the start of the academic year. But Dad will be there – he and Mum walk in together from their Princes Hill home every morning at eight. Which is ridiculously cute, but that's my parents. Dad has random grad students pop in for lengthy discussions, but mostly, he's alone in his office. I'm hoping that's the case today.

"Come in," he says when I knock.

I open the door. He looks up and smiles. Dad's in his late sixties – almost fifteen years older than Mum – and he has unruly grey hair that curls in all sorts of unexpected directions, hazel eyes that are always bright and interested, and a mild manner.

"Avery," he says in apparent delight. Although we're not particularly alike, we've always had an easy, close relationship. He waves me in.

"Hi, Dad." Being around him in this room, with its familiar smell of wood and dust, has already made me calmer. "I have a question."

He puts down his lead pencil – mathematicians always use lead, apparently – and inclines his head in interest.

"What makes things change?" I ask.

He picks his pencil up again; his gaze turns sharp. "You're referring to Aristotle?"

Talking to Dad is always interesting but often exasperatingly obscure. I've learned the best thing to do is to go with it – though the path is murky, you almost always end up with something useful. "Sure," I agree.

"Well, there are the four causes."

Four sounds good. Like there's a lot of options, and surely one will apply.

"Material, formal, efficient and final."

I can tell by the speed at which he delivers that list that it's one he's rattled off many times. I try to absorb, but it's not immediately obvious what the words mean. "I might need you to break that down for me."

"Well, first, to discuss change, we should start with a continuum – the subject, the actualised potential, so to speak, and an opposite."

There's a reason I studied accounting. Unlike the rest of my family,

I do not care for overly abstract nonsensical thought experiments. I am concrete and practical, and happily so.

Dad knows me well. He takes in my expression and tries again. "What's changed?"

I don't know how much to tell him. I mean, he knows he's married to a witch of course, and he knows his daughters are witches, but it's not something we discuss over dinner. Coven business is coven business, and Dad deserves to live his life without being subjected to it every day. I keep my description of the bad batch vague. "Like if something was always difficult – a total pain in the arse – and now it's enthusiastic, eager. Leaping right in there to get straight to work."

"So, from unhelpful to helpful?"

I think about this characterisation. The results have *not* been helpful, not at all, but … is the bad batch trying to help? I'm so used to thinking of it as the bad batch, it takes a moment to come to terms with the fact that it might be trying to be helpful. I nod, though I'm a little unsure.

"Well, then, helpful. What is helpful made of, what are its materials? What is the form of it? In what way is it helpful? Who made it helpful, and to what end?"

Excitement rises in me. Dad's nailed it. The more I think about it, the more obvious it seems. Someone's changed our magic; someone's tried to make it 'helpful'.

"I suppose the key point Aristotle makes is that any discussion of the state of affairs must feature what or who is responsible."

Indeed. "Thank you, Father. This has been most enlightening."

"Good. Glad to help."

I should go. I have something urgent to take care of, but I hover. "Dad?"

"Avery."

"What was it like when Mum told you? About being a witch?"

He smiles fondly. "It was … a process. That's the only way I can describe it."

"Really? But you're so together." My parents are always so in sync, it's hard to imagine a time when they weren't.

"As we were then, all the way through it. But you can't expect to tell someone something like that in one hit and that's the end of it. It requires a major adjustment to conventional thinking about the way the world works."

I suppose so. It's just when I told Evan, he wasn't interested in sticking around long enough to make that adjustment. "Did you think she was lying when she first told you?" Heat beats against my cheeks; my last encounter with Alec is still raw. "Or crazy?"

"I would never think either of those things about your mother. But I was … confused by what she was saying. And I didn't really know what it meant, of course. You can't just tell someone you're a witch and expect them to know what that means."

"No." He's right. There's a lot to it that normal people don't know anything about.

"I would describe it as an episode of significant cognitive dissonance. I didn't believe in witches or magic, but I did believe in Nicolette. It took a while for my mind to integrate the two."

"What's it like being married to a witch?" Why have I never thought to ask these questions before? I suppose what you grow up with is your normal; you don't think to question it until you hit the same things in your own life.

"It's wonderful." He beams.

I grin. My parents are the sweetest. "But all those times when Mum's called in to coven unexpectedly, when she skips out on friends' birthday lunches or conference dinners … It must get to you."

"Nicolette's very good with boundaries; she finds a way to manage it. And if she has to cancel a prior engagement … I trust she has her reasons."

I'm not good with boundaries. I give my everything to coven. Alec's words from the other night come back to me: *There must be space for you to have a life too.*

Am I willing to make space?

That's if Alec can get past the witch thing …

I stand. "Thanks, Dad. I better get back to work."

"Lunch on Sunday?"

"Absolutely."

I leave him and power back through the university grounds, feeling much more hopeful. Maybe there's still a shot for Alec and I.

But first, I have to stop him selling.

What I'm now sure of, thanks to Dad, is that someone, or something, has been mucking around with our magic.

It's unbelievably cheeky. We witches use magic to cast spells and change the world, but we don't cast spells *on* magic. That is something else entirely. Even what I was saying last night about trying to exert more control over the batch we have to work with – I wasn't thinking of actually casting a spell on it. How would you even do that? Could a batch be used to cast a spell on itself?

But someone has done just that.

Knowing the specifics would help, but even if I don't have all the answers, I now have ideas to try. The best place to experiment is Owlscroft, because the whole site is covered in a protective shell. It's where we train neophytes – believe me, you wouldn't want some of those castings let loose on the world.

I head to Melbourne Central and train it to Hawthorn. Fifteen minutes later, I'm there.

The front gate is surprised – it wasn't expecting to see me – and it takes a little longer than usual to clear. When it opens to admit me, I don't go up to the house. Instead, I wander around to the back and find a quiet, secluded spot in the garden.

I sit in a shady spot and think.

When I cast the spell to cancel Lost Dogs, I was thinking about my trip to Hawaii. And that's what the spell delivered. When I cast the spell to cancel Hawaii, I was blaming myself for making Alec's life difficult and wondering whether I should resign. And what happens but that Alec comes up with a plan that means we won't be working together anymore.

The batch *is* trying to be helpful. It's trying to make us happy. It's just a little wayward. It's overreaching, looking beyond the spell, to what's in the heart of the witch, but it's getting confused by the difference between what we want in our heart of hearts and what we want in real life. It's sweet, in a way. It's not helpful, but it's trying to be.

It's not a bad batch. Not at all. It's trying really hard to do the right thing.

If it's determined to be helpful, I need to let it know we witches are happy with limited but predictable results. I need to let it know to just stick to the actual spell.

It's worth a shot.

I look around, then pick a stem of white yarrow.

I reach for the batch, and now Dad's said it, I can feel it. That rushing – it's practically vibrating with its desire to make my life better. To deliver me what my heart desires.

"Hello," I say quietly, unsure if it can hear me. I've never spoken to magic before. I'm usually too busy trying to hold it still so I can bind it. There's no need to hold this batch at all – it's right at hand, hovering at the ready. "Listen, first, I want to say thanks. For trying, that is. But also, to stop." I think I sense a little vibration of outrage at that. "I appreciate what you're trying to do. I do. But what I really need is for you to do exactly what I ask. Just exactly what's in the spell."

It seems to slow a little, as if it's sad.

"I know it's not as fun, but it's what I really need. Let's give it a go."

I'm going to go for a simple colour change spell. Though there's not much use for it in real life, it's something I've done a million times because it's part of our training – the first spell we learn, actually. It also should have instantaneous results. I close my eyes and focus.

White to yellow
White to yellow
Change these flowers
From white to yellow

The magic is ducking and weaving and I can sense it searching for more. For the meaning behind the simple intent of this simple spell.

When I open my eyes, the yarrow is the most beautiful aqua – a colour I've only seen in one other place. My heart squeezes. He didn't believe me, and it hurts.

"I know what you're trying to do, and you're right. I do want him. But it's complicated, and some things you just have to work out on your own. So as much as you want to help, if I give you a colour, you just have to stick to the words I say."

I don't get much back from the batch. Am I getting through to it at all? I have no idea. "Let's try again."

I close my eyes.

Aqua to yellow
Aqua to yellow
Change these flowers
From aqua to yellow

It takes longer to join in this time. Maybe I've offended it by not appreciating the beautiful colour it gave me last time. And I get it, but I really need it to start listening. By the time I've repeated it three times, it's going with the flow, and I'm quite hopeful.

I open my eyes.

Rose red.

I sigh.

"I imagine you're thinking Valentine's Day. They're beautiful. But unfortunately, the only way I get any joy this Valentine's is if we can make these flowers yellow. You have to trust me when I say yellow. I know there doesn't seem to be any genuine desire for it in my heart, but hearts are weird and sometimes they don't know what's good for them. I hate having to constrain your better impulses, but as boring as it may sound, if you want to help, I just need yellow. Let's try one more time."

I close my eyes.

Red to yellow
Red to yellow
Change these flowers

From red to yellow

I open my eyes and beam when I see the sunshine shade. "Thank you. Perfect."

I am thinking about whether I need to run other experiments or whether we now have a good enough understanding – the batch and I – that I can reliably try something outside of the confines of Owlscroft when my phone buzzes.

It's a text from Aunt Bernie and it's an emergency.

CHAPTER 11

I enter the lobby to find Aunt Bernie pacing, hands behind her back. She comes to a halt when she sees me. "Avery. That was quick."

"I was in the area."

It's a weak excuse – I should have dallied longer – but Aunt Bernie is too distracted to notice. She is all but wringing her hands. It's strange to see unflappable Aunt Bernie like this.

"What's the emergency?"

Her eyes hold mine for a few moments, then she says slowly, almost reluctantly, "It's … Luna Park."

My stomach drops. The thirteen children. I'm already seeing a horrific visual. "The spell didn't work?"

"It worked." I feel some measure of relief, but Aunt Bernie resumes her pacing, hands clasped in front of her. "That at least I can be happy about," she says.

And then I get it. The bad batch strikes again. "But?"

"But. Indeed."

I try not to let my familiarity with how the new batch works show. "There's been some kind of unintended consequence?"

She looks at me, lips pursed. I sense part of her doesn't want to share, even though she needs help, and I totally understand that. "Well." She pauses, runs a hand over her already neat hair. "It's …" She stops, whirls in the opposite direction. "Why don't I show you?"

It's then I notice she has a phone in her hands. That's what she's been gripping for dear life. I close the gap between us and she brings up some kind of livestream video on the screen. It's footage of five men, some buff, some not so buff, all with big smiles on their faces but no clothing whatsoever. It looks to be the St Kilda foreshore. They're merrily handing out hugs to anyone who'll take one, singing and dancing their way along the path and generally carousing.

"It's the Luna Park maintenance crew," she says. "The ride was fixed and the children will be fine, but I've somehow made them … do that."

I look at the footage again and can't help but smile. I mean, it's not the world's biggest deal. They seem very happy. And very naked – bodies of all shapes and sizes and skin of all hues gleaming in the sun. Like a mixed group of happy little cherubs. I look up, meeting Aunt Bernie's grey-green gaze, looking for some hint of amusement. "What on earth were you thinking when you—"

Aunt Bernie's cheeks are pink.

I break off abruptly. It's pretty obvious what must have been in Aunt Bernie's mind when she cast the spell. Valentine's Day and hot tradies.

I look back at the screen.

One of the maintenance cupids peers straight into the camera and shouts that they're on their way to Hawthorn.

Aunt Bernie's concern finally reaches me. Sure, they're footloose and fancy free at the moment but where will it end, and how will they feel about themselves when it does? Fines for indecent exposure? Divorce?

"I can fix this," I say.

The hope in Aunt Bernie's eyes is a powerful thing. I can see her desire to believe that this whole thing could go away before anyone else, at the coven at least, sees these naked men and connects the dots.

But then it abruptly dies. "Thank you for the offer, but we should wait for the rest of the Council. We need to work out how to handle this."

I need to tell her about my experience with the bad batch. This could get dicey. "The thing is, Aunt Bernie ... I'm actually pretty confident I can handle it. As in, I know I can."

Suspicion flares in her eyes, but I keep going.

"As in, the reason I was here so quickly is that I came to Owlscroft to practice with this batch. I understand how it works now. I guarantee I can fix this."

Her expression has turned a little sour. "You came here to practice? Even though we cancelled all non-essential magic? Why?"

It's going to take a while to explain and I'm going to be in a fair amount of trouble when I do. "Let's get some clothes back on those guys and then I'll explain."

She nods, terse.

I invite the batch down and remind it firmly about the importance of following instructions. Then I start.

> *Party's over*
> *Day's done now*
> *Back to Luna*
> *Clothes on now*

I can tell the batch is not happy about undoing its efforts to spread love and joy and make Aunt Bernie's Valentine's wishes come true, but I hold firm. Then Aunt Bernie and I sit on the overstuffed lobby couch, phone extended in front of us, watching while we wait for the spell to take effect.

"Aunt Bernie?"

"Yes, Avery."

"I'm sorry about last night. I didn't mean it."

"I think you did mean it," she rebuts swiftly, glancing my way.

She's right. "I didn't mean it to come out the way it did. I was angry. With myself mostly. I think you're an awesome Head Witch."

She smiles but it's a little sad. "Thank you, dear. You're right, by the way."

"About what?"

"We do need to change. Everything you said was right. It's just … not easy."

A warm glow spreads through me at her unexpected words. "I know. But we don't have to rush it. In fact, we shouldn't rush it. We should think the whole thing through carefully and set everything up properly. Monitor and evaluate every step of the way—" I break off to stare at the screen.

The new spell is taking effect; the fog is lifting. It's not that the maintenance crew don't know or can't remember what they've been doing, but more like they can't remember why it seemed like a good idea. The make-merry vibe disappears. Heads down, furtive glances all around, they turn and sidle back towards the theme park.

"That was very effective," Aunt Bernie says, leaning back against the couch.

She looks tired. I realise with some alarm that she is not young anymore. That perhaps the Head Witch role is taking its toll.

But then she bucks up, her expression changes, and I know she hasn't for a moment forgotten about my part in this. "I think it's time for you to tell me what's been going on."

It's almost a relief to come clean. "I made a mistake. I cast a spell, two spells, and I've got my own naked cupid situation happening. I know it was wrong. I've well and truly learned my lesson. I've tried to fix it without magic but I haven't been able to, so I came here today to experiment. To figure out how to deal with the bad batch."

I tell Auntie Bernie all about the spells I cast and the things that happened. I don't include kissing Alec but I disclose everything else. She looks surprisingly sympathetic, especially when I mention the dogs.

"I know there's going to be repercussions. Maybe I'll even be expelled. I'll accept anything you hand down. I deserve it. But I'm begging you, Aunt Bernie, you have to let me fix it first. I know I can reverse whatever is making Alec want to sell."

She looks across the lobby, thinking. "It's interesting, isn't it? I've never seen anything like this batch. It sounds like you think it's been made this way deliberately?"

I tilt my head. "Well, I'm not sure. I don't have any proof. It was just something Dad said, about thinking about the causes of change. No batch has ever been like this. It's such a dramatic change. When I started to think about it, I couldn't see how it couldn't be deliberate. I wouldn't be surprised if someone has cast a spell on actual magic."

"Ah." Aunt Bernie says the word short and sharp. "Ah," she says again, then stands with the force of some new thought. "Avery, I think we have a visitor in town. Magic. Male."

I feel my eyes go round. A wizard.

We don't know a lot about our male counterparts. Because, strictly speaking, they're not our counterparts. Witchery is a matrilineal thing; wizardry is a patrilineal thing. As far as we know. I mean, we can't exactly front up for DNA testing. After the events of 500 years ago, you'll excuse us for being nervous about taking our existence public.

But what we do know is that witches almost always have baby girls, and the rare boys just aren't magic at all. Based on our very limited number of observations, we've come to the conclusion that wizards have wizard fathers.

They don't do things the same way we do. There aren't that many witches, but there are even fewer wizards. Unlike us and our covens, they're less likely to form a troupe, much more likely to be lone wolves. They have their own way of using magic.

I've never met a wizard before, but now, it seems there might be one in Melbourne. And for some reason, he's jinxed the current batch.

Then I start. He hasn't jinxed it; not in a negative sense. The bad batch tries to give us what we really want. It doesn't work, but it's trying. "It's a present," I say. "The bad batch – it's a present. The wizard, whoever he is – he's trying to make friends."

"Yes," Aunt Bernie agrees slowly. "I think you may be right." She smooths her skirt. "He must want something. We can't have him running around our city without knowing what he's up to. We'll have to find a way to locate him and make contact. Can I send you to deal with him? Take Harlow with you."

"Yes. Of course," I say. Then I look at her sharply. "I'm not expelled?"

"Of course not. We need you far too much."

I look at her blankly. "You do? But I don't have any specialty. I'm only moderately-to-very good at most things."

"Well. So am I."

I sit upright. She's right. There's no one particular thing Aunt Bernie excels at.

But this coven wouldn't function without her.

"Not that you are in any way deficient in your use of magic, but you've got other talents, Avery. Seeing the big picture, bringing in fresh ideas, getting things done. Despite your constant questioning of the way we work, you're devoted to this coven. You're sensible, insightful, effective and not afraid to stand up for yourself or others. You're a natural leader. Sarah-Kate is moving to Singapore in July. I want you to take her spot on the Council. And you'll take over from me, of course, in due course. I've had you in mind for years."

"Oh!" Head Witch. Me. I had not seen this prior to Aunt Bernie saying it, but she's right – it's a job I was born for. "I would love that." Head Witch is one of the few full-time coven jobs—it comes with a generous stipend and use of Owlscroft to live in, if required. I wouldn't be torn between two jobs. If I took the position, when it eventually becomes free, I could bring all my business development experience to the job. I could— "But ..." I hesitate.

"Yes?"

"If you don't mind me asking, why did you never marry, Aunt Bernie?"

She looks away. I hope I haven't raised a topic that causes her pain. Maybe she had someone; maybe it didn't work out. "This coven, the work we do ... It's so important, and it's easy to let it take up your whole life, if you let it." She looks at me, eyes serious and bright. "Don't let it, Avery. Don't make the same mistakes I did. Even a Head Witch does not have to spend her life without love."

I nod. It's not just up to me, but I can try.

"Consider this whole bad batch episode forgotten. Go. Make him believe you. And give him a chance to love you."

CHAPTER 12

*I*t's after eleven, and Alec is planning to sign at noon. I race to the station, train it back to the city and intercept him as he's about to enter the Feenex building.

"Are you still selling?" I ask.

He slides me a cold, level look. "Are you still a witch?"

"Unlike your decision to sell, that's not something I can change."

The muscle in his jaw ticks in response to that.

"Give me five minutes. That's all I'm asking. I'm about to give you the proof that's so important to you."

He doesn't by any means look convinced by my offer, but he glances at his watch, then back at me. "Five minutes."

I reach for the batch and I keep my focus on Alec the whole time, so it understands exactly where I'm coming from. I say the words quietly, not particularly wanting to draw the attention of every person on the street, but Alec can hear me.

Heart's desire
Hard to know
Clear the path
Clear the path

The expression on his face can only be described as incredulity, but I don't flinch. The batch and I, we're so in sync we're almost vibrating with it. I finish three rounds and look at him, waiting.

"Is that it?" he asks.

"Yep. Are you still selling?"

"Are you still sticking to the witch story?"

"It's not a story."

He shrugs. Waits a beat. Shrugs again. "Is it supposed to have worked by now?"

"It depends," I hedge, but something that simple? Maybe.

"Nothing's changed. No offence, but you don't seem to be a very good witch."

He's unwittingly hit me right where it hurts, except I'm not feeling so vulnerable in that spot anymore. I draw up. "I may not be exceptional, but I can hold my own."

He looks at his watch. "Three and a half minutes."

"Plenty of time."

But my worry builds as the seconds drag on. I can only hope that the spell is taking its sweet time to come into effect. I must admit, it's cutting it pretty fine. For the first time, I seriously consider that nothing I do might change Alec's mind. That I've ruined his life for good. I bite my lip.

"You could just believe me," I blurt. "I know it's a lot to take in, but you could just trust that I'm not lying to you."

His eyes rake over my face. "You know, Avery, I'm trying to understand what's behind all this but it's well and truly eluding me. I don't understand where this is coming from. It's not you."

"It *is* me," I point out. "It is exactly me."

"Maybe I just don't know you as well as I thought."

My mouth twists at this new wound. "There's a lot I haven't been able to tell you. Partly because I knew this is how you'd act."

His jaw ticks again.

"Still selling?" I check a moment later.

"Of course."

He does know me. He just didn't know this one thing. "Why would I make something like this up? What could it possibly gain me?"

"That's what I'm trying to work out."

"And what have you come up with?" I pause for a meaningful beat. "You can't think of anything, can you?"

He looks down at his watch again. "Two and a half."

I've got two minutes and I'm going to use them. "It was hard for me to tell you about being a witch. I knew there was a good chance I'd lose you because of it. That you'd think I was a freak—"

He exhales hard. "I don't think you're a freak."

"Well, what do you think then?"

"I don't know what to think. I really don't."

That's probably reasonable but it's not something I can work with. "Like I was saying, it was hard for me to tell you. But that you don't believe me? That's even harder." My voice almost breaks.

Alec's gaze is intense. I can tell he knows I mean it. But then he shakes his head and checks his watch again.

"Still selling?"

"Still selling."

Why isn't it working? I go over the spell in my head again. I check in with the batch. As far as I can tell, it seems to think it's done the right thing. What is going on?

I sigh, shake my head.

Alec watches me. "Why is it so important to you that I don't sell?"

"Because I don't want to ruin your life! The only reason you want to sell is because a spell of mine backfired."

"I've told you many times. I know why I want to do this."

"I know you think you do, but the timing, Alec … I cast a spell with a misbehaving batch of magic; on the very same day, this totally new thought pops into your head to sell. Can't you see that it's not a coincidence?"

He shrugs. "It didn't just pop into my head. I have my reasons."

"I know you think you do—"

"What do you think I'm thinking?"

I look away. "I mean … it was probably mostly me, wanting to be with you … but maybe also you, wanting to be with me … and the bad batch, the one I've been telling you about, is always trying to make the witch happy … It thought we couldn't be together because we work together, so it found a way to make it so we don't work together."

"But according to you, we can't be together even if I did sell."

"Because of the whole witch thing." I raise a palm skyward to make my point. "I couldn't tell you I was a witch. I knew you wouldn't believe or accept."

"But you did tell me."

"Yes."

"So that's not a barrier anymore."

"No," I answer automatically, but his words don't quite compute. I stare at him for a few moments. "Look, Alec … I'm never going to be that perfectly poised, woman-behind-the-man, Jackie O type."

His mouth twists. "What are you on about?"

"Your political ambitions. Your future prime minister mug. I suck at interior decorating and diplomatic small talk."

His gaze narrows. "I told you that was a present from my pushy mother."

"But still."

"I don't have any political ambitions. It's not going to happen." His hands come to rest low on his hips. "And even if I did … You think I would base my choice of partner on that? And somehow that means it wouldn't be you?"

I shrug. "Not deliberately maybe. But I'm never going to fit into your perfect life. I'm always going to have my coven commitments. And I'm always going to be … me."

"I hope so."

My heart swells. I want desperately to believe him, to believe this could actually happen, but I just can't. "I always say the wrong thing."

"You don't. You just don't say what people expect to hear. You're genuine, and you say what you think. It's one of the things I love about you."

I can find no words. I'm about to melt on the spot, like another famous witch.

"And as for working together … That's your call. I like working with you and you have a flair for business development. We're highly complementary. But if you want to join me at my new venture, you'd have to come in as my partner – I'm not doing a boss–employee thing with you again. We've outgrown that."

I blink at him. "You want me to come with you?"

"Of course I do." He looks at me like I'm the crazy one. "Feenex wants you to stay with HewTech, of course – you're a valuable asset and it's been a major bone of contention during the negotiations – but thanks to you, I had Blanc as a bargaining chip. They'll make their offer to you and I'll make mine. The choice is yours."

I want to say something but I can't land on anything, so I'm silent like I rarely am.

"And if you want to join me as business partner, but not partner in any other capacity … Just be honest with me. I don't want to be the guy who doesn't hear no as no, and I don't want to limit your opportunities because you don't like me back. If you want in as business partner only, I'll deal with my feelings. It won't be an issue."

A rush of feeling threatens to overwhelm me. "You want to be my partner in some other capacity?"

"Avery, you must know how I feel by now. I'm crazy about you."

Warmth floods through me. Elation that lights me up inside. "But I'm a witch. And you don't even believe me."

"I don't know what I believe. You've never lied to me and I can't work out why you would now. And either way, it doesn't change how I feel about you."

"It's a lot to take in," I acknowledge.

He gives me a you-can-say-that-again look.

"Major cognitive dissonance."

He huffs out a laugh. "Is that what they call it when your head almost explodes?"

"Yes," I grin. "Dad told me that's what happened to him when Mum told him she was a witch all those years ago."

His mouth slants up in a half-smile. "You being a witch would actually explain a lot. Like how for the past two years, you've simultaneously been both my worst and my best employee." He shakes his head, then his whole body. "I don't know what I think anymore. You'll have to give me time."

"I can give you time." I can't believe this might be real. "And I *can* prove it to you, if that'll help."

His head cocks. "Isn't that what you're trying to do right now?"

Oh yeah. With all this talk, I'd forgotten about the spell. "Are you still selling?"

He nods.

What on earth is happening? Why is it not working? A new idea strikes me. A sense of wonderment dawns. It's not working because … "You genuinely want to sell."

"Yes," he says with emphasis.

I can't believe it. Giddy amazement floods me. Alec wanting to sell has nothing to do with me. Or at least, nothing to do with my bad batch spell. I try to clear my head. "This new business venture … What is it?"

"I'll be developing some new tech. Starting from scratch."

"What kind of new tech?"

He hesitates. I know how he feels about sharing ideas before they're ready.

"Come on, Alec," I say. "If I'm going to join you, I need to know what we're doing."

The tips of his mouth curl up. "I want to help people, not just sell to them. I'm going to focus on developing VR software to help overcome phobias. Next-level, less-scary exposure therapy."

My heart squeezes. Helping people overcome phobias? This is because of what happened with Gussie. When he saw my reaction to dogs, that's when he got the idea. "That's why you couldn't say selling HewTech didn't have something to do with me."

He nods.

It did have something to do with me, just not in the way I thought it did.

"You're so confident, so capable, but you were pulling yourself in all kinds of directions trying to get out of going to Lost Dogs. And your face when Gussie came near you … I'll never forget it. When I saw how it affected you, all I wanted was to do something to make it better. And then I realised I could."

It's beautiful. "You know the reason I have issues with dogs is because I'm a witch?"

He runs a hand over his face. "Of course it is." He looks down at his watch. "That's time," he says.

"You can sign. I don't have any issue with you selling if that's what you really want. But can you give me one more minute?"

I trust the not-so-bad batch. I'll let it loose, see what it comes up with.

Let him see
The real me
For the first time
Show him the real me

This is the most exciting spell I've cast for it yet and the batch is almost manic with its fervour to get started and deliver me my heart's desire. It's got almost total free rein. I whisper the words, eager to see what it comes up with.

When I'm done, Alec is looking at me with heat in his eyes. I'm not sure if he believes me yet, but he likes me enough to want to know more.

And that's what I'm going to give him.

From around the corner, a slightly smaller, slightly translucent version of Gussie comes trotting out. I don't feel even a flicker of panic. The new and, in my opinion, improved Gussie seems to feel the same way – there is no pulling back of the lip, no snarling.

The blank look is back on Alec's face. He double-takes at the transparency. "I don't understand," he says.

"It's proof." I pat the fake Gussie, and he pants out fake breaths. No smell, no humidity. "To help with the cognitive dissonance."

Alec comes closer, but seems leery of touching. Which is only natural. It's his first up-close-and-personal encounter with an illusion. "Is this some kind of joke?"

"No."

"How did you get the VR tech up and running so quickly?"

I roll my eyes. "Can I remind you that you're not wearing any kind of headset?"

"Hologram?"

"Magic," I insist.

He comes closer, passes a hand over Gussie. He's investigating thoroughly, trying to work out exactly what's in front of him. "If it's mechanical, it's very sophisticated. I've never seen anything robotic this real-looking."

"It's not a robot," I confirm.

"It's not real either," he rebuts swiftly.

"No," I confirm patiently. "It's the spell I just cast."

He stands. He doesn't say anything, but he's looking at me with a lot less certainty than before. When I don't say anything, he crouches again, looks into fake Gussie's eyes and resumes his investigation. I leave him to it. He can take all the time he needs.

After another assessment, he stands.

"Do you need to look more or is that enough?" I ask.

"That's enough." His gaze on me, then Gussie, is speculative. He is intensely curious, and his disbelief is fading by the second.

"Bye, Gussie."

Gussie gives one short, sharp bark goodbye, then disappears.

Alec's eyes narrow. His hands are on his hips. "So, you're a witch," he says.

There's something open about his face, some genuine curiosity in his tone that tells me the scepticism has shifted.

A tendril of hope unfurls in me. As I look at him, at the way he looks right back at me, it gathers pace, evolving into an exquisite flourish of elation coursing through my veins. Alec might not totally believe yet, but he's not turning away. Telling him might not have been a disaster; it might have ben the best thing ever. "Yes."

"You cast spells, and things actually happen as a result."

"Yes."

He runs a hand over his jaw. "It's still a lot to take in," he says eventually.

I imagine it is. "I'm not really supposed to go around casting spells willy-nilly – we're pretty careful about how and why we use magic, but … Do you want more proof?"

Aunt Bernie said I could fix it. I'll cast another spell if I have to.

"I think I'm good." He is looking more comfortable by the moment. "I'm going to have questions. A lot of questions."

Trust Alec to adjust to a new reality at lightning speed. I told you – he's too perfect and it's just too much. I grin. "Alec?"

"Yes."

"I'm crazy about you too."

He smiles. That gorgeous break-of-day smile that floors me every time.

And I can't resist. This might be the last time I ever cast such a flippant spell, but I can't resist. I reach but there's no immediate 'bad batch' response. It's a shock after the eagerness of my partner in crime; the bad batch has moved on and I'm going to miss it.

I have to tether and work hard to get a bind with some run-of-the-mill new batch. I reach behind my back and bring out a red rose. "It's Valentine's, after all," I say.

Instead of taking it, he moves in, wraps his arms around my waist and brings me close. "Avery?"

"Yes," I breathe.

"I told you this would all be okay." And he kisses me.

~

I HOPE you enjoyed Avery's story! Of course, the other Owlscroft Coven witches need stories of their own. Harlow's story *Good Riddance* is now available in *A Perfectly Paranormal Halloween*, while Everly's story *Sweet Hereafter* is available in *A Perfectly Paranormal Easter*. Amelia's story *Long Shot* will follow some time later in 2022!

. . .

Reviews can help readers find books, and I am grateful for all honest reviews. Thank you for taking the time to let others know what you've read, and what you thought.

ALSO BY MARNIE ST CLAIR

If you enjoyed this story, you may enjoy my other works:

No Place Like You

A sweet but sizzling rural romance

Blue Steal

A witty and suspenseful romantic mystery

ABOUT MARNIE

After years of forecasting the price of tea in China, Marnie St Clair finally shut down the spreadsheets and got serious about her passion for romance, especially the kind that blends charm, humour and a dollop of magic and mystery.

A country girl at heart, Marnie now lives in Melbourne, Australia, with two surprisingly civil teens and a weatherman husband. She likes prosecco, cottage gardens, driving at night, sandalwood-scented anything and a really strong cup of coffee. Or preferably two.

You can contact Marnie through her website www.marniestclair.com, where you can also sign up to her newsletter to be the first to find out about new releases, special deals and exclusive giveaways.

And if you want to get to know the Perfectly Paranormal Anthology authors a bit more, get sneak peeks of what's coming up for the APP Anthologies, as well as giveaways, special offers and just some PNR fun, then join our Perfectly Paranormal Paramours Facebook Group.

Find us here:

https://www.facebook.com/groups/251663560162131

facebook.com/Marnie-St-Clair-1424659434526822

instagram.com/marnie_st_clair

ACKNOWLEDGMENTS

A big heartfelt thanks to the *A Perfectly Paranormal Anthology* contributors – Hellucy Howe, Leisl Leighton and Samantha Marshall – and former contributor Georgia Tingley for inviting me to be part of the group. *A Perfectly Paranormal* has been a blast to be part of and I look forward to future instalments.

Thanks as always to lovely Mady (no sister like you) and my writing group pals Leisl and Frana for the continued support and friendship.

A million kisses to my biggest support and own personal weatherman.

CATNIP

SAMANTHA MARSHALL

CATNIP

A Merged Worlds
Novella

~

Samantha Marshall

❋ Created with Vellum

ABOUT CATNIP

When vampire spy Luxor Dragomir responds to a plea from the gods, the last thing he expects is to seek shelter in a run-down cottage in the middle of nowhere. To make matters worse, the place he thought abandoned is home to a real, live dragon whose wit is as sharp as her teeth.

For reclusive dragon Oaklyn Airecross, spending Valentine's Day with a stack of book boyfriends and chocolate mousse sounds like heaven - until an uninvited guest picks a fight with her least favourite bean bag, and she's thrust into a mess of runaway cats, vampire intrigue and frypans.

Lux's mission is of the utmost importance - not to mention top secret - and with his only ally injured, the prickly vamp is forced to accept that he cannot manage his sacred task alone. Having a dragon as a secret weapon seems like a dream come true, but he can't shake the feeling that by the time this is over, Oaklyn might steal more than his only remaining beanie.

Fascinated by Lux in spite of herself, Oaklyn sets aside her large TBR pile to help him on his quest. After all, a dragon must do her duty to the gods... and the woman intends to find out exactly what that bulge might be when it twitches inside of his pants.

For those who've always wondered where they fit.
For those who've struggled to find their place.
For those who dream too big, and for those who love too hard.
Most of all, for those who believe in the magic of dragons.

I see you.

1

QUIET, I'M READING

OAKLYN SNAPPED HER BOOK SHUT with a growl and tossed it across the room. The offensive paperback thumped into the far wall with pages akimbo, where it stuck to the rough brickwork for a fraction of a second before bouncing off a standing lamp and dropping behind an oversized beanbag.

"Serves you right!" she shouted at it, banging a clenched fist on the floor. "I've never seen a more pathetic excuse for a dragon romance in my *life!*"

Great gods of the sky, would it kill these humans to do a little bit of research every now and then? The state of paranormal dragon romance was enough to make an *actual* dragon lose hope for the future of the world. At the rate Oaklyn was going, the only way she was going to get a remotely believable draconic book boyfriend was if she wrote him herself.

"Ridiculous," Oaklyn muttered, rolling onto her back to stare up at the ceiling. "I mean, that bit about the two tails. Please." She snorted, and a gentle cloud of mist shot into the air. "No dragon has *two tails.* And if his dick is big enough to masquerade as a tail, then run away! I don't want that thing anywhere near me, and neither should you."

Something thumped onto the floorboards upstairs, cutting short the tirade she was settling in to enjoy. Oaklyn frowned as the creaking announced whoever-it-was walking from the fireplace towards the kitchen. Considering she lived alone, unless the visitor was Santa Claus testing out the idea of Christmas in February, creaky floorboards meant an intruder. Narrowing her eyes to slits, Oaklyn rolled right side up and pushed her least favourite beanbag into the corner of the room. Three steps … two steps … one …

There was a click, and a yelp, and then the trapdoor dropped open and Oaklyn's uninvited guest tumbled face first into the beanbag.

Male, she decided, staring at a lean butt clad in skinny black jeans. The muffled cursing emerging from the depths of the beanbag backed up her theory, as did the pheromones edging his vetiver and myrrh scent. Anything else was impossible to decipher, because in the Great Battle of Man vs Beanbag, his royal intruderness appeared to be losing.

Badly.

Oaklyn watched curiously as he struggled to free an arm, only to lose both legs to the worn corduroy. This did succeed in tipping the guy on his side, but apart from a glimpse of olive green knit, the rest of him was lost to a flurry of combat-induced frenzy. Another arm popped free, quickly followed by a squeak as the beanbag exerted dominance by tipping Robberpants McGee onto his ass and then jumping on top of him, leaving only a pair of ragged brown canvas shoes sticking out the bottom.

Did it count as murder if he lost a battle to the beanbag?

Would she have to eat him to get rid of the evidence?

Oaklyn made a face. She had chocolate mousse setting in the fridge; having to eat a home invader would completely ruin her appetite. Sighing in resignation, she hooked a claw in the man-eating beanbag and tugged, tossing it over one shoulder. Freddie Felon slapped both hands to the floor in a move that would have seen him flipping upright, but however fast he was, Oaklyn was faster. She set her now beanbagless foreclaw in the middle of his chest and leant on it ever so gently.

Wouldn't do to crush his ribs, after all.

Home Invader Harry subsided with a grunt, his eyes rolling around in his head while he struggled to regain the wind she'd so emphatically stolen. Oaklyn took advantage of the situation to drink him in – lean to the point of being skinny, with gentle copper skin and almond-shaped eyes of a pale, yellowish green. Sharp cheekbones, an angular jaw and a face just shy of too long. Soft grey and black hair poked out from beneath the hem of a tattered slouch beanie which, despite having gone several losing rounds with a beanbag, was miraculously still in place. In spite of the grey in his hair, Robbie Robberson didn't look old, nor did his slender body have the frailty of age. In fact, his pheromones hinted at virility, and the smooth texture of his copper skin agreed.

Barry Burglar chose that precise moment to blink rapidly, showcasing a set of lashes that made Oaklyn instantly jealous, and focus his pale eyes on her face.

"Hi," she said.

He screamed.

A high-pitched, loin-girding, testicles-in-his-throat scream that had Oaklyn jerking her head back as far as it would go. He screamed until he ran out of breath and then drew a lungful for round two, which she aborted via the simple expedient of shoving the corner of a wadded up blanket in his mouth.

"Stop that," she snapped. Invader Ian lay perfectly still, his heart a jackhammer beneath her palm and his lovely copper skin blanched sickly white. When she was mostly sure he wasn't going to have a heart attack, she tapped a claw against his sternum. "If I take that blanket away, are you going to behave? Because I crocheted it myself and I'm not sure what your spit will do to the yarn."

After a tense silence, he nodded, and Oaklyn tugged the blanket free. They regarded each other for a long moment before he said, "Dragon?"

"Well, your eyes work, Bob, so I guess that's a start."

"Bob?" His voice was after-scream husky but otherwise lovely, with the hint of an accent she couldn't quite place. "Who's Bob?"

"You," Oaklyn growled, and watched him pale all over again as she bared her teeth. "Robberpants McGee. Freddie Felon. Home Invader Harry. Robbie Robberson. Barry Burglar. Invader Ian. B'n'E Bob. Get the idea?"

He let out a long, slow breath and dropped his head against the carpeted floor with a thunk. "Right. Of all the places I had to pick to hide, the ramshackle ranch house turns out to have a dragon's lair in the basement. Did I threaten your hoard, or something? Of course I did. Gods *dammit.*"

"Dragons don't have hoards," Oaklyn snapped.

"What?" He gave her an incredulous look. "Of course they do. They're dragons; they breathe fire, guard hoards, steal fair maidens and eat sheep."

"Listen here, bucko," Oaklyn growled, curling her claws in his jumper and dragging him up to her face, "I *am* a dragon, and I can categorically tell you that in the same way not all humans eat salad or enjoy cricket, not all dragons breathe fire. In fact, unless you're a fire dragon, none do. And the hoard thing? Have you never met a human with a house piled high with junk? Why does every dragon need a case of OCD before we're classified as normal? Some of us have hoards, sure. Most don't. As for the fair maidens, the actions of a single megalomaniac should not the entirety of draconic mythology dictate." She gave him a shake, tendrils of mist curling from her nostrils. "Just like male dragon pubic plates don't iris open like the portal on a freaking spaceship so their genitalia can explode forth like a conquering alien parasite. Honestly, where do people come up with this trash?"

"Er …"

Oaklyn tossed him back on the floor, barely noticing the way he landed in a neat crouch rather than on his ass, like he should have. "Is it really so hard to spend a few hours alone in the basement with a good book? *Is it?*"

"No?"

"Wrong, Carson Criminal! So wrong." Oaklyn jabbed a finger at the pile of rejected books on the other side of the room. "There is not a single dragon romance I've read yet that has been right. Not *one*. I mean, that doesn't mean they're not out there, but how's a girl supposed to fall for a dragon hero when he's so completely unrealistic?" As abruptly as her temper had fired, it sagged, and Oaklyn with it. "I'm running out of time."

Her self-invited houseguest paused in his less-than-obvious attempt to scooch along the wall towards the door, and tilted his head up at her. "Running out of time for what?"

"To find my perfect book boyfriends, of course," Oaklyn snapped, rolling her shoulders in irritation. "Valentine's Day is only a few days away, and I'm setting up the perfect date for myself. I was hoping to include a dragon amongst my selection, but it's not looking good." She sighed. "I might have to go back to the vampire romances. At least they never fail to be Tall, Dark, Handsome and Broody."

"Right." He nodded, a subtle tension firming his face. "Gotta love those vamps. Super trustworthy, know how to show a girl a proper good time and all that."

Oaklyn watched him sidle another few steps to the left. "You read a lot of paranormal romance?"

"Not really."

"Then why agree with me?"

Another step. Another. Then he flashed her a brilliant smile, the fear edge dropping from his vetiver and myrrh scent. "Because you're insane, and I didn't want to provoke you into ripping my arms off." His fingers closed around the brass doorknob. "Also, I'm a vampire, and we're pretty awesome, if I do say so myself. Bye."

He yanked open the door, leapt through, and slammed it shut behind him.

2

OUT OF THE FRYING PAN

HE MOMENT LUX TURNED from the door to race up the stairs to freedom, he knew he was doomed – because there weren't stairs at all, or even so much as a hint of freedom. Setting his shoulders against the flimsy, not-at-all-dragonproof wood, he slid to the floor and buried his face in his hands.

Good job, Lux. Taunt the crazy dragon, then lock yourself in its bathroom. You've really outdone yourself this time.

When the dragon didn't immediately smash the door down to reclaim him, Lux lifted his head and took a second look at the bathroom that had become his prison. Tiled in white, with the same rough brick walls that characterised the room he'd just escaped, it was both spacious and modern. A luxuriant, claw-footed bathtub lounged against the far wall, easily big enough for three people – but not a dragon. Likewise, the toilet would comfortably accommodate a human backside, but not a reptilian one the scale of which he'd seen moments ago. Well, technically he hadn't looked past the beast's enormous head, but Lux was assuming the rear end was in proportion – and if it was, the dragon would be more likely to lose the toilet somewhere unmentionable than sit on it.

375

So. Person-sized bath. Person-sized shitter. Person-sized towels, sink, soap, shampoo and toothbrush. Ergo, a person must live in the house ... somewhere. Unless the dragon already ate them, of course.

"Naughty Ned? You all right in there?"

Fighting the insane urge to giggle, Lux thumped the back of his head on the door. "No."

"You ... need anything?" There was a pause. "What do vampire criminals need, anyway? Untraceable blood or something?"

Deciding it couldn't make the last few minutes of his life any worse, Lux ignored the dragon in favour of padding to the sink and throwing water on his face. When the cool shock didn't dispel the illusion of his current predicament, he stuck his mouth under the faucet and took a few steady gulps. It wasn't as good as blood or hard liquor, but it'd do in a pinch.

That done, Lux searched the bathroom for anything that might come in handy as a weapon against a dragon – if there even was such a thing. After a couple of fruitless laps, he dropped onto the closed lid of the toilet with a sigh. There wasn't even a towel rail to bend out of shape; the linens were all neatly stacked in a built-in alcove by the essential oils and the lavender-scented body wash.

Maybe he could squirt soap in the behemoth's eye?

"Raiding Roy?"

Oh, for the love of—

Before he could question his own stupidity, he was across the room and yanking the door open. "It's Lux."

"What's Lux?"

"My name."

"Your name is *Lux?*" The dragon took a step back in shock, and for the first time since his terror-stricken arrival, Lux got a good look at it. Huge, obviously. Covered in what might have been scales, or might have been hide – no way was he getting close enough to check – the creature's body was a shimmering baby blue, which darkened to mauve towards the spine and lightened almost to white at the tips of the extremities. The dragon stood on all fours, with sweeping feathered wings folded along its back in a soft, aqua-edged white that matched the ruff of fur starting in the centre of the creature's forehead and extending down to the feather duster-style tip of the tail. Two pale blue antlers extruded from the top of its head, gnarled like a young deer's and faceted as though made from crystal. It stared down at him from a pair of cornflower blue eyes that were as fathomless as they were breathtaking and said, "Lux as in … Deluxe?"

He sighed. "No. Lux is short for Luxor."

"Egypt." The dragon blinked, and drew its lips wide to display an array of enormous, sparkling white teeth. "I see the elegance of it in your bone structure."

"My mother is Egyptian." Lux gestured behind him to the bathroom, trying to look as non-threatening as possible. "Do you have people here I can talk to, or did you eat them all?"

The dragon blinked again, then narrowed its eyes. "Always with the draconic misconceptions."

Lux opened his mouth with the intent of removing his foot, but before he could utter so much as a word, the dragon snorted out a plume of smoke. *No, not smoke,* he thought as it curled around his ankles, *fog.*

The fog thickened until the dragon was hidden from view, and Lux stepped back into the relative safety of the bathroom, ready to slam the door if the giant creature barrelled out of the indistinct whiteness – not, he reflected, that it would do any good. His fingers bit into the thin wood of the door and he stared so intently at the fog that his eyes were watering by the time it cleared.

Where the dragon had once stood was a beautiful woman wearing a blanket like a toga. Tall – perhaps an inch under his six feet – and willowy, though not delicate. Her skin was smooth and tanned, her tumbled hair a shining, snowy white that fell almost to her hips. It was only when he stared into her cornflower eyes that he realised who he was looking at.

"You're a person?" Lux demanded, propping his fists on his hips in a futile effort to hide his astonishment. "A person who turns into a *dragon?*"

"No," she snapped – and it was the dragon's voice, melodic and husky, though an octave lighter. How had he not picked her as female from the start? "I'm a dragon who can turn into a person."

"Isn't that the same thing?"

"Not in the least. There's no such thing as a person who can turn into a dragon; any dragon will tell you so."

Lux raised an eyebrow, his tension easing away in the face of this far less threatening creature. "I've never met a dragon before. I thought they only appeared in stories."

"No. Dragons are everywhere … and nowhere." Sadness flashed across her features, and she tugged the crocheted blanket – the corner of which had been in Lux's mouth not so long ago – tighter around her torso. It hung to her knees and disguised the naked body underneath, but a look at her face and lower legs was all Lux needed to know she wasn't old; perhaps not even as old as he.

Fuelled by a sudden spurt of courage, he stepped out of the bathroom and offered a hand. "Luxor Dragomir, vampire, at your service."

"A burglar who introduces himself?" She tilted her head, the faintest hint of a smile teasing lush, full lips. "Oaklyn Airecross, sky dragon."

"Sky dragon," he repeated, turning the idea over in his mind. It fit; the feathers, the fog, the delicate shades of blue and white. "I've never heard of a sky dragon before."

She glared at a scrappy jumble of books in the far corner. "People fixate on the fire dragons, for the most part."

Shoving both hands in his pockets, Lux rolled onto the balls of his feet and tried not to look like he'd been fixating on fire dragons, or reveal how relieved he was that she couldn't, in fact, burn his vampire ass to a crisp.

Small mercies.

"So …" Lux cleared his throat. "Now that the formalities are out of the way, I guess I'll just be heading off. I'm in something of a hurry, I'm afraid."

Oaklyn immediately snapped to attention, a frown marring her elegant features. "Oh, no, you don't. Not until you tell me why you dropped down my chimney without so much as an out of season Christmas gift."

"Um."

"Yes?"

"I was hungry?" Lux offered what he hoped like all the gods was a disarming smile. "Like you said."

The dragon's lovely face softened, the corners of her lips kicking in response. "Oh, well, in that case I— Wait. You said you were a vampire, but I heard you going through my kitchen. Why look in the fridge?"

Oh, shit.

Oaklyn took a step closer and sniffed. "You don't *smell* like a vampire."

Oh, double shit.

Lux tried to back into the bathroom but before he'd so much as lowered his weight to his heels, Oaklyn had one hand fisted in his jumper and her face buried in his neck, breathing nice and deep.

"Vetiver and myrrh and not the least bit vampirish," she confirmed, her lips soft and satiny against his throat.

Was triple shit a thing? Could he call triple shit? Lux tried to swallow past the heady sensation of physical contact, his heart pounding so hard it was a wonder his entire frame didn't rattle.

"Vampire," he croaked. "I swear it."

Oaklyn leant back far enough to catch his gaze with piercing cornflower eyes. "Show me your fangs."

He pressed his lips together.

Lifting Lux off the floor like he was a bag of feathers rather than flesh and blood, she gave him a stern shake. "Look, buddy, if you don't—"

She broke off, and once Lux's eyes stopped rolling in his head, he realised his beanie had slipped during the draconic shakedown and Oaklyn was now staring at his left ear. Or, rather, where his left ear would be, if he were a regular old vampire.

How many shits was he up to? Four?

Lux reached up with desperate hands but, again, Oaklyn was faster. She snatched his beanie off his head and tossed it over one shoulder, where it hit the far wall and stuck against the rough bricks. Her eyes locked onto the top of his head, and her jaw dropped.

Fuck.

3

KITTY LITTER

OAKLYN KNEW SHE WAS STARING. She also knew staring was rude. Regardless, she couldn't quite help the way her jaw dropped and her eyes widened at the sight of Luxor Dragomir without his beanie on.

His hair was a mix of black and smoke grey, and flopped softly over his face in a silky wave that invited touch. It was long enough to partially obscure his eyes, tickle the edge of his jaw and brush the back of his neck – and poking up from that gently tousled mop of incredible hair were a pair of matching grey and black cat's ears.

"Holy shit." Oaklyn took a step back, shook her head, stared again. "You're a … a tabby?"

"No." Lux lunged at his beanie, but she snatched it from the wall and danced out of reach.

"You are," she insisted, watching in fascination as his ears – his *cat ears* – flickered back and forth. "Oh, my gosh, you're a kitty burglar!"

"I'm a vampire," he insisted, snatching again at the beanie and missing.

Oaklyn stuck out an arm and he cannoned into it. "I don't believe you."

Lux hissed, curling his lip to display a set of fangs that were, whilst undeniably fangish, only about half the size of a regular vampire's. She blinked. "Awwwwwww, they're adorable!"

"They're fangs," he shouted, waving both hands over his head. "I'm a *vampire!*"

"A tabby vampire." Oaklyn took fresh stock of his lean body and the pale green eyes that were, now she thought on it, perfectly tabby-cat coloured. "Or … a cat vampire." She frowned. "Isn't that a band? Cat Vampire? Are you a musician?"

"No, no, and no," he snarled, shoving free of her arm to pace across the room with – yeah, she was going to say it – feline grace. "Forget it, okay? Sheesh, next you'll be asking to see my bloody tail!"

"You have a *tail?*"

Lux slapped both hands across his ass and spun to face her with his adorable kitty eyes adorably kitty wide. "No."

"Oh. My. Mother. Goddess." Something flippity flopped in Oaklyn's chest and she grinned. "You have a tail! Show me."

"No!"

"Pleeeeeeease?"

"I've known you less than half an hour," he pointed out, backing up against the nearby bookshelf. "There is no way in this world I'm taking my pants off for you, no matter how gorgeous you are."

Oaklyn stopped stalking him like a juicy sheep and blinked. "You think I'm gorgeous?"

"No."

She narrowed her eyes and adjusted the crochet blanket before she accidentally popped a nipple through one of the holes. "Do you know any other words aside from no, kitty burglar?"

"I'm not a kitty burglar!" He shouted, rolling his eyes to the ceiling and banging his head against the bookshelf. "I'm. A. Vampire. Dammit!"

"Prove it."

Lux froze. "What?"

"You say you're a vampire, but you don't smell like one. Or look like one."

"Oh?" Lux propped his fists on his hips. "And what are we supposed to look like? Aside from the ears."

Oaklyn plucked one of her favourite books from a nearby side table and brandished the cover at him. "Tall. Dark. Broody. Super fangy. Muscle bound. So sexily masculine you could cut cheese with the blade of your virility."

"And my nipples, apparently," Lux muttered, glaring at the naked male chest on the book cover. "Did someone steal his shirt?"

"Vampire," Oaklyn insisted, shaking the book for emphasis.

Lux raised a dark eyebrow. "Just like all dragons have retractable loin plates, hoards of jewels and the ability to breathe fire?"

"No, that's—" She cut herself off, drew a deep breath, and waved the book again. "Look, I've met some vampires and they're all really like this."

"There are as many different types of vampire as there are flavours of chocolate," he snapped, pale eyes flashing. "You might've met a couple, but that's like saying you've patted a dog and are now familiar with every breed of canine under the sun."

"That still doesn't mean you are one, *kitty*."

Lux blew out a long, slow breath. "Why am I even bothering to argue this with you? It's not like I'm hanging around."

Oaklyn huffed and whacked him over the head with her novel. "Excuse me? You can't just break into someone's house, claim to be a vampire with cat ears, refuse to provide proof and then leave. At the very least, I need to check my possessions before you go."

"I haven't stolen anything, I swear. I just needed a place to lay low until daybreak, and I thought your house was empty." Lux rubbed the back of his head and glared at her. "How was I supposed to know there was a bloody dragon in the basement?"

He wasn't; that's why she'd been so careful with the house she'd chosen, and had dug out the basement herself. Oaklyn sighed. "Fine. If you're not going to prove your vampiracy—"

"I'm not."

"—or show me your tail—"

"Definitely not!"

"—do you want some hot chocolate?"

"What?"

"Hot chocolate. You know, milk, chocolate, saucepan? Heat it up, pour it in a mug? Oh, wait. I forgot. You're a 'vampire', aren't you?" Oaklyn hooked her fingers around the word. "You're on a high-iron diet."

"I'm a daywalking half-breed," Lux muttered, his greenish eyes slanting to the side. "I can drink liquids other than blood."

Oaklyn snorted. "So, a vampire who's half cat and claims Daywalker blood? At this rate, you're going to have to bite me before I believe you – and no, fluffybutt, that wasn't an invitation. Now, do you want some hot chocolate or not?"

When he didn't immediately answer, Oaklyn crossed the room to one of her many bookcases and slid it aside to reveal the hidden doorway to her bedroom. With a final warning look at her uninvited houseguest, she slid the shelf back into place and hunted out a bra and some underwear, followed by comfortable jeans and an off-the-shoulder t-shirt in soft aqua with a rainbow on the front and the saying 'unicorns are real'.

She half expected Luxor to be gone when she walked back out to the den, but instead he was standing by her pile of discarded books, inspecting some of the covers while he resettled his slouch beanie over his cat ears. He turned as she crossed the room and his gorgeous green-yellow eyes went wide, travelling slowly down to her ankles and back up to her face.

"To your satisfaction?" Oaklyn drawled, leaning against the bookshelf.

Bronze cheeks darkened with a blush. "Um. I … I don't have a right to comment. I … you're very beautiful."

"I meant the books." She winked. "But thanks, pretty kitty, you're not too bad yourself."

"Oh." He cleared his throat, his cheeks darkening further. "I was just … wondering why these were all in a heap when the others are neatly stacked on the shelves."

Oaklyn twisted a lock of hair in her fingers, reliving her disappointment all over again. "They're the rejects. I'm looking for my favourite book boyfriends, to make a shortlist for Valentine's Day."

"A shortlist of ... book boyfriends?"

"Yeah." She waved a hand at the small stack of books on her coffee table. "I'm tired of Valentine's Day always being a letdown, so this year I decided to spend it with the best book boyfriends I could find. I imagined a roof-high stack of sexy men, true love and good adventures, alongside a hefty dose of chocolate mousse and ice cream. Problem is, I'm having trouble finalising my selection."

Lux blinked rapidly, his face shifting through a range of expressions that might have been comical if the situation weren't so dire.

"So what's wrong with these?" He asked at last, nudging the discard pile with his foot.

"Depends on the book." Oaklyn sighed, twirling her hair until it was a corkscrew around one finger. "This might sound crazy, but it's incredibly difficult to find a man who appeals to me, even in fiction. I've looked, and looked, and *looked,* but none of them are quite right. Not the broody ones, not the playful ones. Not the unrequited best friends, not the cowboys, not the hockey players, not the wolf shifters. Definitely not the ones who tie their love interest up and keep them in the basement – I mean, each to their own and all, but no thanks." She waved a hand at the discarded books. "I don't want to be the damsel in distress who gets rescued; I want to save myself. Are strong, intelligent women undesirable?"

"Of course not," Lux protested. "You deserve to be loved just as you are."

Oaklyn thumbed herself in the chest. "I'm a *dragon*. Ain't no way I'm getting into any of those books."

"None of them are about dragons?"

"Not real ones – and most of the dragons are men."

Lux tilted his head to one side. "You feel underrepresented. No, it's more than that; you feel like you're not good enough."

Gods of the sky, he'd hit it on the head twice in a row. In her youth, she'd been the naïve girl who'd believed in love, who'd sought a place for herself in the world. Only, she didn't quite fit, the force of her personality either scaring prospective lovers away or the weight of her draconic power inspiring covetous greed in those she should have been able to trust. Time and a good many repeated mistakes had demonstrated that she wasn't so much a person as a curiosity, a magical being whose purpose was not to enjoy love the way others did, but to protect those others from the vast and various dangers life presented. On Earth, dragonkind were little more than myth and legend, just like every other species that originated in the magical land of Mu. Now that the mystical barrier separating the two realities had collapsed, allowing Mu and Earth to merge, creatures were freely crossing the veil between one plane and another. Cultures intermingled, magic flowed and life went on – but the few rare dragons stayed hidden, only interfering where absolutely necessary and keeping the painful loneliness of their existence to themselves.

Oaklyn turned away from the books and the adorable burglar studying them. She'd feel better with a drink in her hand, and making the hot chocolate would take her mind off not only the emptiness of her life, but the entire dismal business of Valentine's Day. Positioning herself beneath the open trap door, Oaklyn bent her knees and jumped, landing neatly in a crouch on her hardwood kitchen floor. She flipped the light on as she straightened, taking a moment to check that nothing was out of place in the kitchen. Satisfied, she crossed to the stove and began pulling things out of cupboards.

Saucepan; check. Chocolate; check. Milk, spatula; check and check. Marshmallows? Oaklyn paused in the pantry doorway, then shook her head and reached for the chocolate biscuits instead. If she was going to snack at 4 am, she may as well go all out.

She turned to find Luxor hauling himself up through the hole in the floor, eyes wide as he looked around her retro-styled kitchen. His peculiar hair and sharp features drew her, his lean body gracefully strong. When that pale gaze flicked to hers, goosebumps broke out over her skin and she struggled against the urge to press her thighs together. If she didn't compose herself – and quickly – her vampiric guest was going to notice either the quickening of her blood or the inevitable change in her scent as her addled brain wondered what Luxor Dragomir might look like naked.

"You never did answer me about the hot chocolate, pretty kitty." She forced herself back to the stove to dump an entire block of milk chocolate in the saucepan, followed by a whole litre of milk. "So I'm going to make you some anyways, since you said you can stomach liquids."

"Um." Lux scratched at his jaw. "Why are you being so nice to me? I broke into your house."

Oaklyn shrugged, stirring the mixture in her saucepan to make sure the chocolate melted evenly. "You didn't steal anything; I checked. You also said you needed a place to lay low until dawn."

"I do."

"Well, then, consider yourself my guest. And if you're here until dawn, the least I can do is make you something warm to drink." Oaklyn lifted two mugs down from the hooks overhead and set them on the bench. "I do have a price for my hospitality, however."

Lux edged closer, tugging on the hem of his tattered khaki knit as though to make it sit better. "Oh?"

"Sure." Oaklyn checked the heat on the milk. "I want to know what such a pretty kitty is running from."

"That's not a good idea." Lux curled his fingers over the back of one of her vintage chairs as though to pull it out, then sighed and stepped away. "I really should be going. It'd be better for both of us."

It would, and yet she wanted him to stay, wanted to explore the curious, tingling heat that formed when he looked at her. Oaklyn watched him slouch towards the back door and check over the yard, imprinting his silhouette in her memory. She frowned. His shoulders were prominent beneath the raggedy jumper and the skinny jeans that should've been tight were alarmingly saggy. "When was the last time you drank a proper meal?"

"I'm fine," Lux muttered, twisting the key to unlock the door and cracking it just enough to peer outside. "Thanks anyway." He glanced back, his green-yellow eyes catching the moonlight so they seemed to glow. "Good luck finding your book boyfriends. You deserve a happy Valentine's Day."

The door clicked shut. Oaklyn told herself it was for the best as Lux made his way across her moonlit yard, shoulders hunched as though the silvery light was painful. Turning off the heat on the stove, she picked up the cast iron frypan beside the sink and made to put it away as a soft, gentle thump sounded on the roof overhead.

Three ...

The scrape of fabric over tile.

Two ...

Hesitation, as of someone teetering on an edge.

One ...

A dark shadow sailed through the air and hit Lux square in the shoulders, flattening him in the middle of her herb garden.

With a sigh for the vagaries of fate, Oaklyn tugged open the door and went to rescue her kitty.

4

HOT CHOCOLATE AND
SURRENDER

*L*UX CHOKED ON RAW HERBS – was that *catnip?* – and tried in vain to draw a breath as his attacker's knee pressed hard into his spine.

"Stay down," hissed a low voice.

Instead, Lux drew his elbows in close, braced his knees and wrenched to the side, rolling his opponent into the garden and managing to end up on top. The newcomer was crushingly strong, his skin cool enough that it seemed likely he was a Nightstalker; a breed of nocturnal vampires who enjoyed the bulk of their power at night and were all but helpless during the day. As a Daywalker, the night – and most especially the moon, which was almost full overhead – sucked Lux's strength to such an extent that he should've been less capable than the average human. Baring his teeth, Lux took a better grip on his opponent's coat and thumped him hard against the earth, earning a grunt of pain. Satisfaction coursed through his veins. The vampire half of him might be useless, but the feline part was more than happy to stand up and be counted.

"Lux, *stop*," growled the enemy, his voice so suddenly familiar that Lux hesitated. He was instantly slammed into the ground and a heavy weight settled over his chest, long, dark hair hiding his opponent's face. "Listen to me for a second, will you?"

"Danger?" Lux's nostrils dilated, the fight going out of him in an instant. "What're you doing here? Why do I smell blood?"

His friend grunted. "They caught me sneaking out. I know we were supposed to meet up tomorrow night but I'm not going to be any use to you now. I need to heal, and you need to know – I lost the talisman."

"You *lost* it?"

"I got staked, stabbed and shot," Danger growled. "I barely made it out of Chraxis' castle still breathing and yeah, somewhere along the way, I lost the talisman. So you're going to have to find another way to cross back to Mu, and you're going to have to do it without me."

Lux opened his mouth to deliver a pithy reply, but stopped when the silhouette of a woman wielding a frypan blotted out the moon. A sound much like the ringing of a gong echoed through the night, and Danger slumped on top of Lux in a boneless heap.

"Excuse me," Oaklyn snapped, fisting her hand in the collar of Danger's duster coat and giving a solid yank. "Those are my herbs you're destroying."

"Careful!" Lux winced as Danger's body quivered like spaghetti. "He's injured."

Oaklyn regarded her prisoner's unconscious body for a long moment, then carefully laid him out on the lawn. "You know him?"

"Yeah, he's my brother from another mother. I was supposed to meet him tomo— Never mind. It doesn't matter now."

"Hmm." She stashed her frying pan under one arm and held out a hand. "Here."

He eyed her wiggling fingers for a moment, then sighed and slid his hand into hers. Lux already knew Oaklyn's strength was far greater than it appeared, but he still staggered as he regained his feet, grabbing her wrist with his other hand to keep his balance. She was warm and soft, her skin like silk. "Sorry. I mean, thanks. I mean, sorry about your herbs."

Good gods above, what was wrong with his tongue? Oaklyn didn't seem to mind; in fact, she smiled. It was a breathtaking smile, lighting up a face silvered by the moon, her hair glowing white. They were almost eye to eye, her figure all tight muscle and wicked curves, Lux maintaining an edge in shoulder breadth only to lose it in the swell of her hips.

"I heard your friend mention Chraxis," she said, her voice carrying a natural breathiness and the faintest edge of a lyrical accent that made his gut tighten. "I presume you mean the one and only Lord Chraxis, ruler of the Nightstalkers here on Earth and custodian of the North Castle. What in the world did you do to piss him off, pretty kitty?"

He should *not* want to purr when she called him that. Gently tugging his hand free from Oaklyn's grasp, Lux made a show of dusting himself off and straightening his beanie.

"If I tell you, they'll hunt you." He stepped out of the herb garden with a groan. "Dammit, I'm going to have bruises."

"Probably." Oaklyn tilted her head to the side, checking him over the way one might a prime cut of beef. "I hate to break it to you, gorgeous, but I'm not afraid of vampires. Aside from that, I'm already involved. Captain Fangface found you in *my* yard. He tracked you here, and he probably left a bloody trail a mile wide while he was doing it. I know you were trying to protect me by leaving, but exiting the house only saved your friend the trouble of facing the same beanbag that bested you earlier."

"It didn't best me," Lux grumbled, stomping over to the collapsed vampire. "It's inanimate." Guilt ate away at him, and his shoulders slumped. He and Danger had been a team for centuries, and while there was always the inevitable hiccup now and then, never before had his friend been so wounded he couldn't complete a mission. Not only that, but the gorgeous, wild creature who'd done nothing more than relax in her basement with a book of questionable quality was now well and truly embroiled in his shit show, whether she wanted to be or not. "I'm sorry. I should have stayed away."

"Eh, I was due for a reading break anyway. So, considering you're safer with me than you are on your own, you may as well tell me who this guy is."

Lux sighed and gave in to the inevitable. "His name is Danger."

"*Danger?*" Oaklyn screwed up her face. "What sort of a name is Danger?"

"His real name is D'Angelo. His mother used to call him Angel, but he hated it so much he changed it to Danger instead."

Oaklyn raised an eyebrow, moving closer to the unconscious man on the lawn. Her breath caught and Lux's heart sank. There was a reason Danger had once been nicknamed Angel; perfect dark brown hair, deep brown eyes, sweeping cheekbones and a sculpted jaw. At six five, with massive shoulders, washboard abs and thighs strong enough to bench a truck, he could've stepped right off the cover of one of Oaklyn's vampire romance novels. Well, if he was shirtless. As it was, with his hair dishevelled and the moonlight painting his pale skin silver, Danger was a walking advertisement for dark, wicked, soul-shattering sex.

"You weren't joking when you said Monsieur Toothington is someone you love like a brother, then."

"Nope; we even have matching tattoos." Lux's eyes narrowed. "And no. I am not showing you."

Oaklyn looked faintly disappointed as she ran her gaze down the length of his body. "No injuries on you, pretty kitty?"

He swallowed around a sudden lump in his throat and offered what he hoped was a charming smile. "I'm fine."

"Good." Oaklyn tugged Danger's leather duster open to run her hands over the sculpted chest beneath. "There's a lot of blood here, but the wounds are already starting to close. Your friend will live, if he has somewhere safe to rest."

Jealousy spiked in Lux's gut as he watched her explore, and that only served to piss him off. An hour ago, he was fearful of being eaten. Now, what? He was jealous of an unconscious body?

Oaklyn's hands hesitated near the hem of Danger's t-shirt and she chewed on her lip. "You said you have matching tattoos?"

She was going to look, and suddenly it was more than he could bear. Lux smacked his hand over hers. "Don't."

"Yeah, it seems weird, doesn't it? It's okay, I won't peek." Oaklyn offered a smile. "I've got somewhere safe we can stash him while he heals, if you like."

Lux studied her face, those enormous cornflower eyes luring him ever closer. Her skin was a soft, pale brown, and he'd seen enough of it while she was wrapped in her afghan to know it was her true colouring rather than a result of too little sunscreen. He wanted to stroke it. He wanted to stroke *her*.

The force of his desire had Lux jerking backwards so fast that he fell on his ass. His beanie, normally a faithful companion no matter the odds, decided to ditch him for the lawn and he clapped both hands to his head, leaning down between his spread knees as he searched for his traitorous hat. Naturally, by the time he found it, the soft beanie was dangling from Oaklyn's fingers. She crouched in front of him, jeans hugging her curves and her wide necked t-shirt sliding down one shoulder to reveal a raspberry pink bra strap. Lux didn't bother wondering how she'd moved so fast. Dragons, it seemed, were special in a variety of ways – and damn if that wasn't the hottest thought he'd had in days. Scratch that – years. Decades.

Fuck, he was in trouble.

"Hey," she murmured, the gentle timbre of her voice hitting him hard in the chest. "You don't need to hide from me. I've seen it already."

Lux glared. At this point, it was the only defence he had – opening his mouth would just lead to him saying something stupid, like *you're beautiful* or *kiss me*. Why, why, why was this happening to him? Now, of all times, when he was vulnerable, tired, hungry—

He blinked.

Of course. His stomach was trying to convince him to take what he needed most, by any means possible. Drawing a deep breath, Lux lowered his hands and sat up straighter. He wouldn't do it. He wasn't an animal, dammit, he was a man. A man with a moral compass, and enough fucking standards that he wasn't going to try and seduce this gorgeous, incredible creature just so he wouldn't starve.

Right.

No seducing.

At all.

Lux shot a glance at Danger and snorted. Who was he kidding? Even if he tried, he didn't stand a chance with Tall, Dark and Perfect in the same vicinity.

"Habit," he forced himself to croak. "Saves the weird looks."

"I get that, but I'm weirder than you, so feel free to be yourself." Sliding a knuckle under his chin, she tipped his face up until he had no choice but to meet her gaze. She was smiling, and it stole his breath. "You're perfect just as you are, pretty kitty."

Lux tugged free of her touch and, when she tucked his beanie into the waistband of her jeans with a look that dared him to come and get it, shook his head to settle his hair more comfortably.

"I'm not perfect, or pretty," he muttered, turning back to Danger and zipping up the Nightstalker's leather duster. "That's Danger's job." Oaklyn didn't say anything, and there was no way he was turning back to see the confirmation of his statement in her eyes. Instead, Lux eyed the giant lump of meat his friend had become and said, "Where do you want to stash him? He's heavy, and there's not long until dawn."

She blew out through her nose, puffing fog in his direction, then pushed to her feet. Before Lux could protest, Oaklyn had slung Danger's massive body over one shoulder and sauntered off across the moonlit lawn.

"Or, you know, you could just carry him," Lux muttered, shoving upright. By the time he dusted himself off and jogged after her, Oaklyn was in the process of unlocking the door to her garden shed. "You really don't need to do this, you know."

"So tense, pretty kitty. Is it really so hard to believe a random stranger might decide to help you out?" She gave him a once over, then raised a white eyebrow. "Apparently so. Take a breath and relax, gorgeous."

Relax. With his friend injured and the talisman lost. Yeah, sure.

Lux waited until she cracked the door, then slithered sideways through the opening. The interior of the shed was … well, like the interior of a shed, he supposed. It held a basic concrete floor covered with heavy-duty felt carpet that didn't quite stretch to the sturdy timber walls, and a long bench under a slatted window through which moonlight filtered, covered with an array of gardening tools, dirt and discarded plant pots. Rickety shelving lined the opposite wall, and the small clear space by the door held a pegboard with the empty outlines of tools traced upon it. In the far corner, a grimy lawn mower stood guard over a haphazard stack of rough wooden crates and a couple of bulging hessian sacks that stank of horse shit.

"You're going to hide Danger in here?" Lux gestured at the uncovered window. "As soon as the sun comes up, he'll fry."

"Patience, grasshopper," Oaklyn muttered, lowering Danger into a sitting position against the wooden shelving. "Keep an eye out in case he stirs. We don't want him making those injuries any worse."

Lux took up a reluctant guard position by Danger's side while she pushed the lawn mower in front of the door and piled the bags of horse crap on top. Someone had drawn a smiley face on the topmost bag, putting Lux face to hessian with an oddly compelling, if odious, snowman rip-off. The dragging of wood garnered his attention and he goggled at Oaklyn's ass as she bent in front of him, pulling wooden crates aside without bothering to dismantle the stacks first. Gods above, he wanted to grab her hips and—

Stop it. Just, stop.

"What are you doing?" he asked, hoping his voice didn't come out as strangled as it felt.

Oaklyn waved a lazy hand over one shoulder, stretching even further – gods, if she didn't learn to bend her knees he was going to die – to curl her fingers around the edge of the felt carpeting. She peeled it back to reveal the concrete floor beneath, into which a square shape had been cut. Bracing her palms flat on the concrete – fuck, how flexible *was* this woman? – she looked back at him and winked.

"Ready?"

Gods above. Her throaty voice, her pose, her freaking lavender and spring rain scent that was so strong in his nostrils it even managed to drown out the horseshit snowman. Who, by the looks of him, was as happy with the show as Lux was. How was he supposed to deal with her looking at him like that? His heart began to race in his chest, his breath coming short and sharp. Pressing his lips together, Lux managed a nod.

As soon as Oaklyn turned away, he slid a hand into his jeans, tucking his hard-on up against his body and securing it in place with the waistband of his underwear. It was neither a comfortable nor foolproof solution, but at the very least, it made the bulge less noticeable. Slipping his hand back out, Lux tugged his baggy knit down until it was mid-thigh and tried to look innocent. When Oaklyn curled her fingers down the side of the cut concrete and heaved to reveal a trap door in the floor, his jaw dropped and his dick throbbed.

One, she was *so* strong. Gods, but it was hot.

Two, what the fuck?

"You have a trap door under your shed?" Lux's voice came out all squeaky, so he cleared his throat, gave his hips an adjusting wiggle, and tried again. "Why do you have a trap door under your shed?"

Oaklyn dusted her hands together and crossed the shed to scoop Danger up in her arms like a baby. "You'll see. Come on."

Lux shared a resigned look with horse poo man, then followed her down a narrow set of metal stairs. Artificial lights flickered to life as they descended, and fifteen steps later, Lux found himself in a square, windowless room that looked like it could double as a bomb shelter in a pinch. Glass-fronted bookshelves lined the walls and on second glance, he realised they were atmospherically controlled, like those in a museum. Books were stacked neatly inside; some leather-bound, some pieces of yellow parchment held together by string, even some that were scrolls.

"Wow." Lux turned a quick circle. "Not a hoarder, huh?"

Oaklyn huffed an irritated breath as she laid Danger out on the floor. "No, and this is not a hoard."

"So … it's … a not-at-all-hoard-like collection?"

A low, bestial growl echoed through the room and Lux found himself grinning as she stalked over to poke him in the chest. "Not. A. Hoard."

"All right, all right." He held up his hands in surrender. "I'm sorry."

Cornflower eyes slitted, and a tick formed in her jaw. After a moment, Oaklyn sighed and stepped back. "I like to read, okay? Over the years, I've found it difficult to part with my favourites – and these are getting pretty delicate, so they couldn't stay in my normal shelves anymore. The underground factor negates sun damage. I keep it hidden not because of their material worth, but their sentimental value." Her eye twitched. "In a non-hoarding way."

He could have kept teasing her, but instead, Lux simply nodded. "I get it. I've kept things for a long time that are important to me, too. Doesn't make you a hoarding dragon – just the regular kind."

Oaklyn's expression eased and she offered a tentative smile. "Thanks." The moment drew out, and her cheeks tinted pink as she cleared her throat. "Danger will be safe here. I'll engage the lock to keep him protected, but I'll leave the code so that he can get out when he wakes." She jogged to a small desk with a notepad and pen on top, and began to write. "Fangpants can read, right?"

"Of course he can read."

"Hey, don't be like that." She shot him a sharp glance. "It took me several hundred years to get the hang of reading – I've learnt the hard way not to assume."

Lux blinked, his eyes shooting to the shelves full of books as her words settled into his bones. Earlier, he'd assumed she was far younger than he, but now … "How old are you?"

"How old are *you*?" Oaklyn grumbled, slapping the pen down and stomping back to the narrow stairs. She prodded at an electronic lock, muttering under her breath. When she clattered up the steps, Lux hurried after her in case she decided to shut him in for his impertinence.

He stood back as she lowered the concrete trap door into place, listening to it hiss and clunk as the locks sprang into position. Rather than cover it with carpet or crates as it had been earlier, Oaklyn stacked the shed so that the corner was hidden from casual view but Danger, when he was released, would be able to exit without having mountains of stuff drop on his head.

"Eight hundred," Lux said as she straightened, dusting her hands on her thighs. Oaklyn froze, and cornflower eyes examined him from beneath pale lashes. He shuffled his feet and took a deep breath. "Eight hundred and thirty-one, to be exact."

She huffed out a breath, blowing hair away from her face. Tension rode every line of her body, their gazes locked in an electric moment Lux didn't understand.

"Two thousand, four hundred and eleven," Oaklyn announced, then walked out of the shed and slammed the door behind her.

BETTER THAN FICTION

TWO THOUSAND, FOUR HUNDRED *and eleven.*

Why had she thought it was a good idea to go and blurt that out? Oaklyn stopped in the middle of her yard and drew deep, steady lungfuls of dew-laden air until her equilibrium returned.

"There's something special about the dawn, isn't there?"

She turned, her heart fluttering to find Lux close enough to touch. His voice blended smoothly with the stirring of the world and he held an easy masculinity that made him approachable rather than intimidating. Oaklyn's fingers itched to stroke the soft velvet of his ears, to tunnel into the silky weight of his hair – but from the way he'd reacted earlier, she was almost certain he wouldn't welcome the caress.

"Yes," she murmured, drawing another breath – this one laced with the smooth vetiver and myrrh of his scent. "A new day brings new possibilities. I imagine for you, as a Daywalker, it also brings energy."

"You believe me now, huh?" His lips twisted, then he shrugged. "Sorry if I upset you with the age thing."

"It's fine. You weren't to know it'd strike a nerve." Oaklyn smoothed her hand over the slouch beanie still tucked in her waistband, watching the way the breeze shifted Lux's hair until it flopped over his eyes. The yard around them was a symphony of shadows and greys, highlighting the hollows in his cheeks and the way his collarbones jutted a little too much beneath the sagging neckline of his knit.

"Come back inside," she invited. "Have some hot chocolate. Rest for a little while."

Green-yellow eyes flicked to her face, then away. "I should go."

"Because you want to stay?"

To his credit and her delight, Lux nodded. "I put you in danger just by being here. I broke into your house, for the gods' sakes. I shouldn't want to stay."

"Once the sun rises, the Nightstalkers can't chase you." Oaklyn tangled her fingers in the sleeve of his khaki knit and pitched her voice low. "I'll keep you safe, Luxor Dragomir. I swear it."

Those incredible lashes, a fascinating mix of black and grey, lowered to fan his cheeks. He shivered. Slumped. "Two hours."

"Three," Oaklyn whispered, sliding her fingers down his arm and twining them with his. Bony wrists, palms wider than hers, long, elegant digits. "Trust me."

Lux's lips pressed into a thin line and his nostrils flared, but he made no move to pull free. When she tugged him forward, he followed her into the house and dropped into one of the retro chairs at her kitchen table. Oaklyn busied herself with mugs and a plate of biscuits, using the distraction of the hot saucepan to mask her smile. How long had it been since she'd felt so alive? How long had it been since she'd had a ... whatever Lux was at her kitchen table?

"Here you go, pretty kitty." Oaklyn set a mug in front of Lux and watched the sharp line of his cheekbones flag with colour. Then he blinked down at the mug, and his jaw dropped open.

"What is *that*?"

"Hot chocolate, of course." Oaklyn retrieved her own mug and slid into the chair opposite, taking a sip. "I like my cups big, so I can use them no matter what shape I'm in."

"I guess that makes sense." Lux took a tentative sip of his drink, then another, more confident swallow. The movement highlighted the contours of his throat, and Oaklyn frowned.

"When was the last time you had a proper meal?"

He waved a dismissive hand and Oaklyn clicked her tongue against the roof of her mouth. So many of the vampire romances she read had options for fake blood, but in reality, it wasn't that simple. There was some mystical quality in blood while it was circulating a living body that disappeared once bottled or synthesised. Such measures worked perfectly well for medical transfusions, but vampires didn't get the sustenance they required unless their meal came directly from a living host. Half-breed or no, Lux would slowly starve without ingesting blood on a regular basis.

"I've been busy," he grumbled, running a slender finger around the rim of his mug. "It's not so easy to get blood in a soup bowl with a handle."

"So snarky." Oaklyn snatched a chocolate biscuit from the plate, bit off two opposing corners, and set one of the bitten ends into her drink. While her guest watched, she fit her lips over the other bitten corner and sucked her hot chocolate up through the biscuit as though it were a straw. "If you don't like it, don't drink it."

Lux swallowed, his eyes glued to the melting biscuit in her fingers. There was something intense about his expression, something that sent a warm, tickling shiver down Oaklyn's spine. Lowering her lashes to half mast, she put the biscuit back in her mouth and sucked again. The hot chocolate was working as intended and she got a mouthful of near-scalding milk and gooey, chocolatey goodness – but the true revelation was not the decadence in her mouth, but the way Lux's hands clenched to fists on the tabletop as he watched the show.

Was it possible … was he attracted to her?

With a thrill of anticipation, Oaklyn slipped her finger between her lips and sucked the chocolate off. Those green-yellow eyes flashed with heat and she fought the urge to squeeze her thighs together all over again. He *was* interested. Curling her lips into a smile, she nudged the plate of biscuits in his direction. "Want to try?"

"Gods, yes," he rasped, then cleared his throat and blinked. "I mean, sure, but I can't. Liquid diet, remember?" As though to prove his point, Lux wrapped trembling hands around the mug that was almost as large as his head and drank deeply. When he at last lowered his arms, his expression had shifted from heated interest to weariness, and he slouched further in the chair. "You might be surprised to find I stole something."

"Oh?" Though she burned to tease him a little further out of his shell, Oaklyn swallowed the urge and allowed the change of subject. "So you're Robberpants McGee after all?"

He closed his eyes and nodded. "Have you heard of Ra?"

Oaklyn paused, her fingers tightening on her mug as all thoughts of play fled from her mind. Meeting Lux might have been serendipitous, but now that he'd mentioned Ra, Oaklyn knew she couldn't let him leave – not only because he was exhausted and in need of protection, but because she had duties of her own, draconic duties she'd sworn to carry out long ago, no matter the cost.

"I'm over two thousand years old, kitty. Yes, I've heard of the Egyptian sun god." She pursed her lips and affected a nonchalant tone. "A very, *very* long time ago, before either of us were so much as specks in the starry sky, Ra fell in love with Lilith – a Sumerian goddess, a queen, and the first vampire. They have a daughter, Solaris."

"Yes." Lux's eyes slitted open a fraction, revealing a slash of greenish gold. "I'm surprised you know that; it's not in the history books."

"I'm a dragon." Oaklyn waved a vague hand, as though the words were explanation enough on their own. "I've spent my fair share of time in Mu and I know that the currently accepted versions of both history and mythology are a garbled reproduction of tales told by an ancient wanderer in order to keep the truth – and the people who lived that truth – safe. What's touted in books and schools these days is almost entirely bullshit."

"Indeed it is." Lux's mottled grey and black lashes settled on his cheeks once again, his voice taking on a dreamy quality. "Not long ago, Solaris turned down a marriage proposal from Lord Chraxis, one of the Nightstalkers responsible for policing Lilith's people here on Earth. Shortly afterwards, she collapsed into a cursed sleep."

"Chraxis doesn't take rejection well," Oaklyn muttered. "Let me guess – he offered terms that were unacceptable to Lilith, so you and Danger were sent to break the curse?"

"Pretty much." Lux braced his elbows on the base of the chair, now so slumped in his seat that his lower half was completely hidden beneath the table. "My mother is one of the healing priestesses of Bast … hence the ears." He gestured at his head with a self-deprecating twist of lips. "She recognised the spell Chraxis used and as a hybrid, I was able to as well. Long story short, if we reunite Solaris with the item that was used to curse her, she'll wake. My ability to sense the magic meant I could also sense the focus item, so Danger and I volunteered to sneak into Chraxis' castle and steal it."

"I'll bet Chraxis loved that."

"About as much as a stake in the heart, yeah. Danger and I decided to create as much confusion as possible, then meet up tomorrow – tonight, now – and cross back to Mu, but the talisman Ra gave us to allow passage through the veil was lost in the fight." Lux patted at his chest and made a face. "Now I've got the means to set Solaris free, but no way to reach her."

Oaklyn chewed the inside of her cheek, but instead of asking more questions or potentially saying something monumentally stupid, she took his empty mug and put their dirty dishes in the sink. "As urgent as the situation is, you're no good to anyone if you're exhausted. You need to rest."

Lux ran a hand over his face, then nodded. "Yeah, you're right."

She ushered him into the basement, then strode to her bookshelf and slid it aside to reveal her bedroom. "You can sleep here. I only changed the sheets yesterday, and clearly didn't sleep last night, so everything's clean."

"Are you sure?"

"Of course I'm sure. This is the safest place in the house. Oh, wait." Oaklyn blew out a cloud of fog. As soon as it obscured her from view, she stripped off her clothes and returned to her dragon form. After a quick stretch and a resettling of her wings, she blew the fog away with a stiff breeze. "There. Guarding you, as promised." Wrapping a claw around his waist, Oaklyn stuck her foreleg through the bedroom doorway and tossed Lux bodily onto the bed. "I'll be right here the whole time – got a bunch of book boyfriends to find, remember?"

Lux stared pale-faced from the middle of her deep aubergine quilt, then slowly nodded. "Okay."

"Good." Oaklyn slid the bookshelf closed and curled up with her back to it. "Sleep tight, pretty kitty."

At first, silence. Then, the thud of shoes hitting the floor and the rustle of bedcovers. A harrumph. A sigh. Muttering … quiet. A gentle, purring snore.

Oaklyn noted the time, then snatched the next book off her pile and settled in to read. Try as she might, she couldn't focus on the characters or the plot, her thoughts circling back incessantly to the hybrid vampire sleeping in her bed, and the tempting conundrum he presented. Their conversation over hot chocolate had her believing in his honour, but … telling him everything would require breaking a promise older than Lux himself. Something she couldn't do, no matter that when he found out the truth, he'd likely be pissed as hell.

Ugh.

Best not to think on it for now. Whether she liked it or not, her hands were well and truly tied, and she wasn't the sort to mope over something that couldn't be changed. Shifting her weight into a more comfortable position, Oaklyn refocussed on the book in front of her, determined to finish at least one chapter. The plot was solid enough and as dragon romances went, it wasn't bad; certainly not the worst she'd come across.

Or is it your disposition that's different?

With a huff at her inner voice, Oaklyn closed the book and checked the clock again. Nearly time to wake Lux, which meant she'd spent more time mooning over his gorgeousness than attempting to solve her Valentine's Day problem. Oaklyn drummed her claws on the novel's cover, then pushed it aside and shifted back to human form, hunting out her clothes and dragging them on. A gentle push had the bookshelf sliding sideways on well-oiled hinges, revealing her bedroom, softly lit by a bedside lamp. Lux lay beneath the covers fully clothed, apart from the ragged shoes he'd kicked halfway across the room. His face was turned away from the light, highlighting the weary lines of his body.

Sitting on the bed beside him, Oaklyn flattened her hands over his quilt-covered chest and gave a gentle shake. "Lux."

Nothing.

"Lux?" Bracing herself on one palm, she slid her other hand up the smooth skin of his throat and over the stubble of his jaw, patting gently at one cheek. "Come on, pretty kitty. Time to wake up."

He mumbled something incoherent and rolled into her touch. As his lips brushed the skin of her forearm, Lux's eyes flew open, pupils dilating. His chest inflated in a rush, and Oaklyn caught a glimpse of something dark in his expression before he shoved her so hard she tumbled backwards off the end of the bed.

"Don't touch me!" He cried, slapping both hands over his mouth.

Wrapping both fists in the bedclothes, Oaklyn dragged herself to her knees and glared at him over the expanse of the mattress. Lux's hair stuck off his head as though charged with electricity, cat ears flat with displeasure. His chest rose and fell in a ragged rhythm, and he'd squeezed those gorgeous eyes shut as though fighting desperately for control.

"You're hungry," Oaklyn realised, sitting back on her heels. Lux shuddered, but didn't answer. "When was the last time you had blood?"

He mumbled something behind his hands and shook his head.

"Don't be a fool." She stormed to the side of the bed and yanked the quilt down. Lux sensed her intent and tried to sit up; Oaklyn grabbed his shoulders and thumped him back into the mattress. "How long, dammit?"

Green-yellow eyes glittered up at her, the fight going out of him as quickly as it arrived. "A few days."

"A *few days?*" Oaklyn's fingers clenched tight enough to bruise. "Have you lost your mind? How bad are the cravings right now?"

Lux turned his face away, jaw clenched. "I'm a hybrid, remember? I can manage longer than a pure vampire, and I'm not a beast to fall prey to bloodlust. Sure, I'm hungry – but I'm not about to take anything that's not freely given."

"You stubborn, stubborn man," she hissed, pressing the inside of her wrist to his lips. "Here. Freely given."

He froze beneath her, lips hot and intimate against her skin. When his voice came out, it was nothing but a whisper. "Don't do this to me, Oaklyn."

"I'm doing nothing but offering strength." Her heartbeat pounded out the lie, her voice growing breathier with every moment. "You can't complete your mission half starved – you'll be caught, and then what? Danger has to take news of your death back to your mother, and comfort her while she mourns your loss?"

"Oh, yeah, poor Danger," Lux snarled, wrenching away from her wrist to glare. "Poor, unfortunate Danger, safe in your underground library, sleeping the day away. I mean, I'm up here arguing with an angry dragon while facing a journey that's borderline suicidal, but yeah, let's take a moment to consider *Danger's* feelings. Maybe you'd like to discuss his killer abs, while we're at it? He is Tall, Dark and Fangy, after all. Perfect for you."

Oaklyn blinked. Grinned. "You're jealous."

"No!"

"Your pants are on fire, fibber-kitty." Oaklyn dropped her full weight on his chest, feeling a twinge of satisfaction when he grunted. Twisting her free hand into his hair, she angled his head until they were nose to nose. "Am I playing stacks-on with Danger right now? Am I offering Danger my blood right now?"

They stared for a charged moment, then Lux muttered a curse and bared his teeth. "Fine. Maybe I *am* a little jealous. Danger's a big, strong, heroic type while I'm a scrawny, half-cat hybrid. There; are you happy now?"

"No." Oaklyn grazed her teeth down the sharp line of his jaw, unable to stop touching now that she'd started. "What if I told you I knew another way into Mu? That I could get you there without the need to search out a new talisman?"

"What?" Lux drew a breath, held, let it out in a gust. "Wow. Okay."

"I'll cut you a deal." She shifted back just far enough to slide her arm between them, brushing the inside of her wrist against his mouth and revelling in the contact all over again. "Drink, and I'll explain."

The silence took on weight and substance, the air filling with charge. Lux's hand slid over the back of her forearm, slender fingers pushing her wrist against his mouth with new purpose. Oaklyn's nerve endings ignited, the rest of the room fading until all she was, all she knew, was the glittering anticipation of this one perfect moment.

With his eyes firmly locked to hers, Lux sealed his lips over her vein and bit down hard.

6

THREE SHEETS TO THE WIND

*L*UX HAD NEVER TASTED anything better than Oaklyn's blood in all his long life. Thick like honey, it oozed into his mouth rather than spurted, inciting him to lock his fingers tighter around her slender wrist and take deep, rhythmic pulls that had them both groaning.

He tried to tell himself it was because he was starving.

That he was so dedicated to his purpose he'd take any hope offered, even one so vague as the promise of a virtual stranger.

The more he drank, the more he knew them for the lies they were; Oaklyn just flat-out tasted like paradise, and nothing else he put in his mouth from this point on would ever stack up.

Gods above, he was so *hungry*.

"Lux," Oaklyn panted. Her soft curves fit against his hard edges like they were made for it, and Lux spread his free hand over her lower back in a gesture so blatantly wanting he'd never dare it if he weren't already drunk on the sheer, unrelenting power in her blood.

Oaklyn whimpered and shifted against him, pressing her hips into the hard ridge of his erection with a rolling motion that made him gasp. With a final swallow of the ambrosia in her veins, Lux swept his tongue over her punctured wrist and yanked it aside. Her mouth crashed into his, their kiss open-mouthed and desperate. She cupped his face and he twisted a hand in her hair, their tongues curling together in a heady mix of passion and euphoria. Energy burned in Lux's veins, dulled senses roaring to life with the fury of a dragon as his body absorbed Oaklyn's blood with the sort of enthusiasm that only true hunger cultivated. When they broke the kiss to gulp in air, his thoughts were a shattered kaleidoscope of dizzying power and depthless need.

"Holy shit."

She laughed, the sound breathy with desire – and he knew in that moment that if he asked, she'd strip them both naked and take Lux on the most glorious ride of his life. It hung in the air between them, a sensual, velvety promise that lured him like a siren.

Yet staring into her passion-drenched gaze, Lux couldn't bring himself to take that one wild ride, knowing that if he did, if *they* did, it would crush the tiny, blossoming connection that hovered unseen between them. And no matter how stupid, he wanted everything. Woman, dragon, blood, freedom, weird book fetish, hot chocolate from a bowl ... everything. Every night, every day, for eternity.

"What did you do to me?" Oaklyn whispered, voicing Lux's own thoughts.

He managed the tiniest shake of his head. "I'm sorry. I didn't know that was going to happen."

"Me either." Her cheeks coloured, cornflower gaze shifting away. "I've never done that before."

Lux sorted through the various ways he could translate that sentence and wasn't sure if he should be pleased or not. "Over two thousand years old, and you've never shared blood with a vampire?"

"I ..." She cleared her throat. "It's not something dragons tend to do, as a rule. I made an exception in your case because you were desperate."

"Sorry."

"That's twice you've apologised." Hurt flashed across her face. "You didn't like it?"

"Gods, no." Lux caught her as she flinched away, tightening his grip in her hair. "Your blood is incredible, Oaklyn. I've never tasted anything like it."

"Dragon blood is life," she muttered, still not looking at him. "Magic incarnate."

Though he'd never felt so strong, Lux was dead certain she could break free if she wanted, so he let his words tumble out before it was too late. "The kiss was even better. I apologised because I didn't mean to kiss you uninvited, but I'm not sorry it happened. It was the hottest damn kiss of my life."

At long last, she met his gaze. "Mine, too. Will that happen every time?"

His cock hardened further at the thought of feeding from her again, and Lux had to force air into his lungs so that his voice didn't sound strained. "I don't know."

"Hmmm." Oaklyn shifted against him, negating any hope that she didn't notice his reaction. "Right now, I'm not complaining. You're smuggling a proper package down there, gorgeous."

Lux snorted out a giggle, the sound causing them both to freeze. After a moment's embarrassment – and a bit of choking as he tried desperately to keep another giggle inside where it belonged – he managed, "I feel like I'm drunk."

"You are." Her wicked smile was better than watching the dawn. "Poor kitty, three sheets to the wind on dragon blood. Don't worry, I'm not going to take advantage of you while your brain is turned to fairy floss."

"Oh." Simultaneously relieved and disappointed, Lux blinked up at her like an idiot. "So … what now?"

"We made a deal, remember? You drink my blood, and I'll talk about crossing the veil between Earth and the magical, wondrous realm of Mu. Ready, kitty?"

No. "Yes."

"Good." Shifting her pelvis so they weren't pressed quite so intimately together, Oaklyn set her lips against Lux's ear. "There's an Old Road not far from here that we can use to cross into Mu."

Just like that, the fog in his brain cleared. "There is?"

"Yup." She leant back with a wink. "Better yet, I can get you there quick-smart."

"I'll still need a talisman to cross over."

"No." Oaklyn laid a finger across his lips. "You weren't paying attention before, were you? Dragons are magic incarnate. Dragon blood is life. *I* am a talisman."

He stared.

She grinned.

"You ..." Lux cleared his throat to banish the squeakiness in his voice. "Surely that's a dragon secret."

"Yeah, a pretty tightly kept one. Still, I trust you." Oaklyn gave him a once over that made Lux shiver. "Are you going to spill my secret, pretty kitty?"

"No!" The thought of what could happen to her, how badly she'd be hunted if anyone knew ... Lux twisted his hands in her t-shirt as though that alone would keep her safe. "Never."

"Good." She smiled and rolled them over, sitting up in a smooth movement that put Lux on his feet. After a moment to adjust her rumpled clothes, Oaklyn stood and brushed a gentle kiss to his cheek. "Now, I think a shower to help get your head screwed on straight might be a good idea, don't you?"

Lux pushed a hand into his hair. "Do we have time?"

"Of course we do, gorgeous – unless you're going to waste that time by arguing with every suggestion I make. Go on, now." She pushed him towards the open door with a gentle pat on the butt, and Lux jumped forward like he'd been bitten.

"Stop looking for my tail," he groused, and stomped off to the sound of her laughter.

Lux slammed into the bathroom and wrenched his jumper off over his head. His jeans followed, crumpling against the tile floor. On his way to the gleaming glass and silver shower, he caught sight of himself in the mirror and paused. His face was pale, his hair a wild, tumbled mess. The cat ears that had haunted him most of his life – and that Oaklyn, unaccountably, seemed to adore – trembled as though in a breeze. His cheeks were slapped with colour, eyes wide and pupils dilated. When he looked down at his hands, they were shaking. Drunk, indeed.

With a grimace for his dirt-smudged reflection, Lux got in the shower and made quick but thorough work of washing his hair and scrubbing his body so clean it stung. By the time he got out, dizzy euphoria had subsided into crystal clarity, his hands steady and his mood light. So much so that when he towelled himself off and discovered his clothes had been replaced with a soft pair of black track pants, a dark grey t-shirt and a navy fleece hoodie, he didn't even blink.

The clothes smelt of Oaklyn, the pants loose on his hips and the t-shirt a little baggy. It had a skull and crossbones on the front, the print faded to look vintage. With the hoodie clenched in his fist, Lux ran a hand through his hair and made his way to the kitchen, where he found Oaklyn head-first in the fridge. His fingers itched to smooth over the bronze expanse of flesh visible between the waistband of her low-riding jeans and the hem of her aqua top. Instead, he crossed his arms and leant against the stove.

"Having mousse for breakfast?"

"No." Oaklyn straightened to face him with a stick of preserved meat in hand. Her eyes travelled the length of his body and back up again. "Clothes fit, I see."

"More or less." Lux plucked at the t-shirt covering his chest. "Looks like we're about the same size."

Oaklyn nodded. "I ran your other clothes through a quick wash. As soon as the washing machine pings, I'll dry them and we can go."

Lux watched her demolish her wrinkled sausage, then turn back to the fridge for a covered dish. She lifted the lid, sniffed, then fished a spoon from the drawer beside him and tucked in. Catching his gaze, she lifted the spoon his way. "Soup?"

"Thanks, but I'm pretty full right now," he replied, trying not to notice the way her lips wrapped around the spoon as she went back to eating. "Did I weaken you?"

"No." The corner of her lip twitched. "You probably feel like you gorged, but you didn't take much. I'm just trying to keep my energy up for next time."

Lux turned away from the intensity in her expression, drifting over to the large window by the table and staring out at the garden shed in her yard. Crockery and silverware clattered as Oaklyn dumped her finished meal in the sink, and her footsteps receded. Lux continued to examine the weathered shed until she returned, dropping something on the table beside him with a wet, slapping sound. When he turned around, it was to find her with a hip cocked and a frown on her beautiful face.

"What is it?"

"I don't know, kitty. I still feel like you're doubting me, and to be honest, it's making me a little pissy."

Lux ran a hand over his face. "My head's still spinning. Not from your blood, but from the rapid shift in events over the last few hours."

"Think of it this way. You – and by extension, the gods – need help, and this is something that's well within my power to give. I'd be a real shitty person if I let you walk out that door on your own." Oaklyn tipped her head to the side. "Am I a shitty person, Luxor Dragomir?"

"No," Lux muttered. "I might've only known you a few hours, but I can say that with certainty."

"So, relax." She drifted closer, reaching up to tickle one of his ears. "The Old Road opens when the moon is full at noon, which is tomorrow. We'll spend, what? A day in Mu? Unless you want me to just drop you off, of course."

"I don't know yet. What about your plans for Valentine's Day?"

Oaklyn snorted, her breath a soft puff against his throat. "I spend Valentine's Day the way I spend every other day; by myself. We should have plenty of time, but if I'm late back, it'll only be the book boyfriends who pout – and even that's just my imagination. They're not interested in me, you realise. Apart from being fictional, they've already found true love."

Lux couldn't stop his lips from twitching, even as he ached at the thought of her being lonely. "Fair point."

Oaklyn gave his jaw a playful flick, then picked up his wet jeans and shook. Water splattered all over her hardwood floor, but she simply inhaled, paused, and then exhaled in a steady stream. The black denim flapped as though in a gale force wind, and when she laid them over the back of a dining chair, they were dry. Lux's jaw dropped as she repeated the process with his tattered khaki jumper.

"Air dragon," Oaklyn said, giving him a smug grin. "You want to change, or take these with us?"

"I …" Lux cleared his throat. "The lighter we travel, the easier it'll be, right?"

"Yeah, but it won't hurt to take a couple of things." She waved at a sleek black backpack sitting on one of the other chairs. "Extra clothes are fine. It won't be too heavy."

"I'll stay as I am, then."

She nodded, folded his clothes with neat efficiency and packed them into the bag. "I noted you didn't have a t-shirt or underwear – and I can't help with the underwear, but I did chuck in an extra tee. Consider them both yours."

Gods, she was going to kill him with her generosity. Moving his fingers to the lumpy pendants beneath the t-shirt that was now his own, Lux curled his fingers around the familiar weight and forced out a breath. "Thank you."

"Oh, look at you, pretty kitty." She winked. "Progress."

Lux propped both fists on his hips and stuck his tongue out. Oaklyn's laughter was deep and pure, the simple joy making his meagre attempt at play entirely worth it.

"I'll give you progress," he muttered.

Oaklyn was still chuckling as she did a final check of the backpack, then zipped it up and slung it over one shoulder. "All right, pretty kitty. Let's go wake the sleeping princess, eh?"

ONWARD AND MOST DEFINITELY UPWARD

OAKLYN BADE LUX WAIT on the back porch, dropped the bag at her feet and snorted a giant cloud of mist. As soon as it cloaked her body from view, she stripped off her clothes and returned to her natural form. The feeling of freedom incurred by the simple stretching of wings and settling of her weight was impossible to articulate, a kind of *being* that was only possible for another dragon to understand.

When the fog cleared to reveal Lux staring at her, however, Oaklyn wondered if he might not have an inkling of some kind. The glint in his eye as he looked her over, the way he lifted a hand to his exposed ears – recognition of what it took to be unique, the incredible wonder and dreadful loneliness of it. The shock of connection when their gazes locked was so visceral Oaklyn had to physically shake it off.

"Can you handle the backpack, or shall I?" Oaklyn folded her human clothing and carefully hooked the tip of a claw through the backpack's zipper toggle, drawing it open so she could drop her things inside. The task was awkward with her claws so much larger than the bag, and after a moment, Lux took over, fingers lingering on his slouch beanie before he shoved it deeper into the backpack and zipped it closed.

"I'll carry it." Lux cleared the raspiness from his throat and gripped the bag by both shoulder straps. "I … uh … how does this work?"

"You have two options. One, I carry you in my claws like a stolen sheep. Two, you sit on my back and hold on tight, like I'm a giant air horse."

He snorted. "Pretty sure that's called a Pegasus, babe."

"You did *not* just 'babe' me."

Lux raised a challenging brow and grinned, all dimples and mischief. "Oh, I see. You're allowed to call me pretty kitty, but I'm not allowed to call you something in return?"

Delighted by his play, she bumped him in the chest with her snout. Lux stumbled backwards but instead of falling on his rump, he clung to the ridged edges of her nostrils, feet scrabbling for purchase – and then leaving the ground entirely as she lifted her head, balancing his length across the end of her nose.

"You can drop me a pet name," Oaklyn purred, "but it needs to be more inventive than babe."

More meaningful, too.

Lux stared down the length of her snout, green-yellow eyes wide. When it became apparent she wasn't intending to move, he hauled his body up until he knelt in the space between her nostrils. "You have scales."

His voice was full of wonder, his expression soft as he brushed a hand over the shimmering iridescence of her snout. When the caress didn't garner an objection, he shot her a look from beneath full lashes and did it again, a firmer, more exploratory touch.

"That tickles."

"Sorry." Lux crawled further up her snout, then abruptly stopped and laughed. "You've gone cross-eyed."

"How else am I supposed to look at you? Now, option one or two, pretty kitty?"

"Um. Two?" He slid to a sitting position, legs draped over her nose as though astride a horse. "Except I dropped the bag when you bumped me. If you want to put—"

Lux cut off with a squeak as Oaklyn reached up to grab him around the waist and deposited him in the space between her wings and shoulder blades. As he wrapped his hands convulsively in the thick white fur of her ruff, she scooped up the backpack and waited while he gathered the courage to let go long enough to slide it onto his shoulders.

"Lie flat against my neck," Oaklyn ordered, stifling a groan as he did exactly that. Lux might be only a fraction of her size, but his warmth was a beacon that appealed to every female cell in her body – and having him pressed up against her back returned memories of their kiss. The way he gripped her fur for balance reminded her of his hand in her hair, and the legs he spread to better grip her neck rubbed the crotch of his jeans against her spine. She longed to shift back to human form and test whether his earlier response had been real or a side effect of the blood sharing, but the sun was already inching into midmorning.

"I think I'm ready," Lux said at last, his breath puffing over her scales and causing a shiver.

"Okay. Hold tight, now."

"How tight?"

"As tight as you need – you won't hurt me. And, in the unlikely event that you fall, I'll catch you."

Lux whimpered, and Oaklyn decided to put him out of his misery. Bellying flat on the ground, she bunched her muscles and leapt skyward. Her wings beat hard, great, booming sweeps that caught the air more efficiently than any bird and sent them rocketing into the ether. Lux's whimper became a scream, and then abruptly cut off as he buried his face in her fur and held tight.

His courage warmed her heart. Riding a dragon wasn't as simple as books and movies liked to make out; it was jerky and wriggly and wild, and took a level of skill that hovered somewhere between brave and suicidal. It also required a *willing* dragon – anyone stupid enough to leap aboard without permission would swiftly find themselves dead in a variety of fascinatingly gruesome ways.

Despite Lux's healthy fear, his body moved in complete synchronicity with Oaklyn's. He was as boneless as a cat, instinctively understanding that to stay mounted, he needed to surrender rather than stiffen up. The further they rose into the air, the more he felt like an extension of her body until by the time Oaklyn flattened out, she knew nothing short of a direct blow would knock him free.

"You okay back there?"

"Yeah." His answer was almost snatched away by the wind and the thump of her wings.

"Opened your eyes yet?"

"Are you fucking kidding me right now?"

Oaklyn laughed, settling her wings into a gliding position. "Go on. I'll keep us steady."

A heartbeat passed. Two.

"Holy fucking shiiiiiiit!" Lux's legs clamped impossibly tighter and his face returned to her fur. "How fucking high are we right fucking now?"

Oaklyn rumbled another laugh. "I don't know. Not quite cloud high, otherwise it'd be impossible to navigate."

"Faaaarrrrrrrk." He pressed harder into her spine. "How can I even breathe up here?"

"My draconic aura steadies air pressure in my immediate vicinity, making it easier to breathe and hear each other speak – but your vampire kitty fabulousness helps, too. Sensitive ears and all that."

Lux's voice cut in and out, a disjointed series of what Oaklyn assumed were muttered curses. She grinned to herself, concentrating on keeping her wingbeats slow and deep in an effort to give him time to acclimate.

Towns, rivers, forests and cities passed by below and the sun was well into the afternoon when Lux finally asked, "Why isn't anyone running around screaming 'dragon' or trying to shoot us with missiles?"

"Active camouflage."

"I'm serious, Oaklyn."

"So am I." She banked slightly to the left, pleased that his grip no longer tightened convulsively with the movement. "In case you didn't notice, I'm a blend of blues, mauves and whites. My scales have a shimmer that changes depending on the lighting and the time of day, but basically, I blend into the sky so well I'm practically invisible. No more than a scudding cloud, or a lens flare, or whatever other optical illusion you prefer."

He rubbed his cheek against her scales. "What about me, then?"

"You're not only small but on my back. For the most part, those on the ground can't see you – and even if I tilt so they do, you're a speck, kitty."

"Liable to be mistaken for a bird?"

"Or dirty glasses."

Lux snorted. "That's me, all right. A smudge on someone's glasses."

"Better than a bug on the windscreen, right?"

His snort turned into a laugh. "Right."

Clouds began to gather, and Oaklyn dipped lower to pass beneath them. The leading edge carried a misty chill and Lux gasped appreciatively when the tips of her wings carved trails in the curling cumulus. She longed to play with him in the air but knew it'd shatter the fragile confidence he'd grown, so settled instead for the elegance of cruising.

"I've thought of one," Lux said at last, his body shifting against hers. "A pet name, I mean."

"Oh?"

"Yeah."

"Well, don't keep me in suspense, gorgeous."

A warm hand smoothed over her scales, then regripped her fur. "You might not like it."

"As long as it's not Heifer, I think you'll be fine."

"Damn, that was my first choice. How about Chompy, then?"

"Funny."

"Tarragon?"

"The dragon herb? Bonus points for the ode to my crushed garden."

"Fluffy?"

"Kitty, do you want me to roll over and tip you off?"

He laughed, the sound vibrating through Oaklyn's body and drawing her lips into a grin. "Okay, okay. Flappy."

"*Lux.*"

Oaklyn stretched her wings into a glide, beginning a slow, downwards spiral while her kitty howled with laughter at his own bad jokes. She backwinged in to land in a field of late summer flowers and waving grasses, tucking her wings close to slip into the forest beyond. Ducking beneath low-hanging branches and winding between the widely spaced trunks, she came at last upon a little log cabin built on the banks of a happily babbling brook. Locating a nice sandy spot just back from the water, Oaklyn dropped to her belly and stretched a wing towards the ground.

Taking the tacit invitation, Lux slid down her wing to the water's edge. Instead of standing, he flopped back against her feathers and groaned. "I can't feel my legs."

"Gripping too hard." She used her wing like a scoop and a moment later the recalcitrant, mildly floppy vampire was cradled in her cupped foreclaws. When she lowered her face in mock threat, he opened his arms as though for an embrace and before Oaklyn knew it, her nose was in his lap – or at least, part of her nose, being that she was far too big for the entire thing to fit.

Lux pressed a kiss to her scales. "I hereby anoint you cream puff."

Oaklyn rumbled a laugh, even as her hearts lurched in his direction. That was the trouble, being a dragon – two hearts, too much love to give. So easy to feel *everything*, with a speed and intensity that tended to chase others away rather than entice them closer. Lux had already questioned how suddenly and completely she'd devoted herself to his cause – what would he think if he knew the rest?

He won't stay, and you'll be alone all over again.

Neither of her hearts were inclined to listen and without their co-operation, it was only a matter of time before she'd be attempting to patch herself back together with chocolate mousse, fluffy blankets and a mountain of books. There was something about Lux that wrapped around Oaklyn's most primal, draconic core, urging her to give protection, loyalty, trust … love.

Damn.

Pushing her nose at Lux's chest, she rumbled gently in appreciation and said, "I love it, pretty kitty. I love it."

8

LOOGIE CABIN

CCORDING TO OAKLYN, the little log cabin was a way-house that belonged to nobody and everybody. The ambiguous sentiment had Lux frowning until he laid his hand on the porch railing and felt the thrumming song of a spell – old, and very, very powerful.

"You have mage friends?"

"I don't know if I'd call them friends, per se." She winked. "Just a couple of acquaintances who owe me a favour or seven."

Lux blew out a sharp breath between his teeth. "Friends or not, if you don't know the password for these wards, there's no way we're getting through the door." He stroked the banister again, feeling out the magic, and shivered. "This place is a bristling fortress."

In answer, Oaklyn lowered herself to ground level and spat on the front door, a giant, sloppy mess of mucus that landed with a wet *splat* before it soaked into the rough-looking wood and disappeared entirely. Lux felt the immense, threatening presence of the magic waver … then the lock clicked, the door handle turned, and just like that, they were welcomed inside.

"You're meant to use blood," Oaklyn said in response to his astonished expression, "but I'm too big to fit on the porch. Spit carries the same qualities, as far as the magic goes."

Then she patted him on the head, muttered something about dinner and took off in a massive sweep of aqua and white-feathered wings, leaving Lux alone with their backpack on the steps of Loogie Cabin.

Inside, the space was all one big room, with a couple of elegantly carved support pillars – mage sigils for strength and protection, if he was translating correctly – tattered but comfortable-looking furniture, a basic kitchen and an even more basic shower nook. A fold-down set of stairs led up to a loft containing a mattress so big Lux fancied it would fit six people without issue. He stared at the comforter for a while, his throat dry as he imagined sharing it with Oaklyn, then realised he'd worked up a boner of such strength that the front of his borrowed sweatpants were gaping at the waist. Tucking his erection up against his stomach, Lux retied the draw-string to keep the damned thing in place, ditched the backpack by the bed and retreated downstairs.

The cabin's floor-to-ceiling windows provided an excellent view of the surrounding forest. Thick with evergreens and no doubt teeming with wildlife, it was the perfect setting for a peaceful weekend retreat – and for a moment, Lux pictured himself and Oaklyn spread out on the generous couch in front of the fire, sipping from each other's lips as they watched the sun set. He sighed. The spark between them was real enough, but what did he have to offer a dragon? Danger was the perfect warrior with killer hair, the one whose smile buckled knees and incin-erated underpants. Lux, was … well, himself. A little short, skinny in spite of the muscles clinging tenaciously to his frame, and with a pair of fucking cat ears that spent most of their time hidden under a grotty old beanie. While Danger was flexing his guns and waggling his eyebrows, Lux was hissing into his beer and trying to fade into the background in case someone gawped at him. Yeah, he was a regular Romeo, all right.

"You need a distraction," he said aloud, jumping at the sound of his voice in the echoing room. Wiping his palms on his thighs, Lux straightened his spine and cleared his throat. "Chores. Chores will work."

With one eye on the enormous windows, he set about exploring the cabin in greater depth. By the time Oaklyn backwinged into the clearing outside, Lux had fetched water from the stream and boiled it pure, ratted through the cupboards for potential dinner ingredients and completed a thorough investigation of the small, slightly overgrown garden at the back of the property. His cock, which had decided to behave itself rather than risk strangulation by drawstring, twitched in rebellious glee when Oaklyn puffed out the signature thick cloud of mist that preceded a shift.

Should he offer her a blanket from the bed upstairs?

Look the other way so she could pass through to the loft?

Stare and drool like an imbecile?

Before he had time to decide, the door to the cabin slammed open and Oaklyn strode through. Though her human form was compact in comparison to the dragon, her sheer presence was more than enough to fill the room, wrapping Lux in the scent of lavender and spring rain. Mist curled around her body like a fine cloak, protecting her modesty even as it flashed hints of delicate, pale brown skin so perfect it couldn't possibly be real.

"I was going to hunt something bigger, but then I realised you're not going to be eating." She dumped a dead rabbit into the sink and offered a smile. "This poor little hopper just wasn't fast enough to get away."

"Oh?" He shot her a look from the corner of his eye. "Maybe it didn't want to escape. Gods know I wouldn't."

She blinked. "Pretty kitty, if I didn't know any better, I'd say you were flirting with me."

Lux's heart gave a wrenching thump. "Would that be a bad thing?"

Oaklyn opened her mouth to answer, but no words came out. Instead, her eyes unfocussed and her brows beetled as she swung to face the door.

"Do you hear that?"

"Hear what?" Lux pricked up his ears. The cabin, powered entirely by magic, was silent. Beyond that, there was only the trickling of the creek, the soughing of leaves in the mild breeze, the chirp of evening insects, and … "Oh, shit. Is that a darkhound?"

The sound came again, a thready, bloodcurdling cry that raised the hairs on the back of Lux's neck. His claws shot out, digging hard into the benchtop, the primitive drive to *run* pumping hard in his veins.

"Yes," Oaklyn murmured. "That's exactly what it is – and darkhounds never travel alone."

Lux swallowed, one hand creeping up to the lumpy pendant that bumped against his breastbone. "Chraxis. It has to be."

"That'd be my guess, too." Oaklyn's eyes were slitted, nostrils dilating as she sampled the air. "This guy wants you bad, pretty kitty."

"Of course. I'm the means to breaking Solaris' curse, and that curse is the only thing standing between Chraxis and a grisly death at the hands of his goddess. Lilith is many things, but forgiving is not one of them." Lux glanced at the sigils painted and carved all over the cabin. "If we bunker down—"

"No." Oaklyn shook her head with enough force to send her long white hair flying about her face.

"Why not? The cabin's spells look strong enough to keep us safe."

"Oh, they are, but when the hounds return to Chraxis at dawn, they'll be able to tell him exactly where you are – and I'm willing to bet my feathers that the force he sends next will be far, far worse than a gaggle of ghostly canines. No, we have to take them out." Oaklyn paused, sucking her lower lip between her teeth. "Ever fought darkhounds before, kitty?"

"Once." He grimaced, squashing memories of desperate flight and hectic combat. "It's not something I ever intended to repeat."

"Smart." She turned to face him then, expression softening as she ran a light fingertip over one of his long, wicked claws. "As though you hadn't already done me in with the ears and the tail. Now you have these, too."

"And I know how to use them," Lux croaked. Blood surged for entirely the wrong reason as her fingers trailed up his arm to grip his jaw. "What are we doing, Oaklyn?"

"Besides leaving the relative safety of this cozy room to take on a pack of darkhounds? Hell if I know, gorgeous." She kissed his cheek, filling his senses with lavender, spring rain and warmth. "Come on, now. Bring that perfect ass outside and let's make a mess, hmm?"

She released him to walk away, Lux's heart keeping beat with the rhythm of her steps. Time fractured, a perfect moment that would see Oaklyn forever silhouetted in the cabin doorway, mist clinging to the lean lines of her body and the moonlight shimmering on her pale hair. When the corner of her lip quirked in a smile, there was nothing Lux could do but follow, the very sight of her a siren song he was powerless to ignore.

They walked in silence to the creek, and though part of Lux strained to catch the ethereal cries of the darkhounds on the ghostly breeze, a far larger part of him was captivated by the woman who crouched to dip her fingers in the icy water.

"What's your idea of the perfect Valentine's Day?" She asked, her voice a velvet thrum in the dark.

"Huh?" Lux blinked. "You're asking me that *now*?"

"Now is as good a time as any, isn't it?" Oaklyn cocked her head, no doubt cataloguing the time between calls and answers as their enemies drew slowly closer. "Valentine's Day is a relatively new celebration, as far as human history goes. There are a couple of theories about how it began, but my favourite was always a guy in Ancient Rome named Valentine. He was in prison, and fell in love with his jailor's daughter. They passed each other love notes through the bars and his were signed 'from your Valentine'. That's why, on Valentine's Day, people pass notes."

"I've never really celebrated the day, if I'm honest." Lux slipped his hands into the pockets of his borrowed sweats, curling his claws into his palms until they pricked at his skin. "It's become awfully commercialised the last couple of centuries – and besides, why do I need a special day to express my love to someone, when I can do it whenever I please?"

"I've heard that sentiment before, but I've never really understood it." Oaklyn lifted damp fingers to her nose and sniffed. "It's like saying you don't need a birthday to give someone a birthday present … and yet, you don't go around singing at them over cake on some other random day, do you?"

"I guess not." Lux shrugged, his eyes on the treeline, where he was certain the first of the hounds would appear any minute. "My perfect Valentine's Day would probably involve a soft rug in front of an open fire. A glass of … wine. Intimacy."

"Corny."

"You asked, cream puff." His chuckle was dry. "Besides, I already know yours. Sexy books, chocolate mousse and solitude."

Oaklyn stood and shook the water from her fingers, her expression shuttered. "That's not the ideal situation, kitty. Just the reality of someone who learnt her lessons the hard way."

"So what would you prefer, then? If you had the choice?"

Howls echoed all around, and the scent of sulphur began to creep into the clearing. Oaklyn drew close enough to Lux that the mist enveloping her body curled against his skin, cool and slightly damp.

"A soft rug in front of an open fire," she whispered, moonlight refracting in her eyes. "A glass of wine. Intimacy."

The moment hung between them and Lux vibrated with the need to close the distance and kiss her, but the bushes on the opposite side of the creek parted with a soft rustle and creatures of smoke and nightmare padded into view.

About the size of a lion, the darkhounds had thick, black fur that stood on end and gave off an indistinct, shadowy aura. Lux got the impression of glowing red eyes and scythe-like teeth but was unable to make out any individual features that might identify one hound from the next. It was how they were built; half in, half out of the phys-ical world, capable of travelling long distances very quickly and, once they were set upon their prey, impossible to stop.

There were five in total – a standard pack. They growled and whined as they spread along the banks of the creek, their voices echoing in a space somewhere behind Lux's inner ear. Five perfect clouds of death crouched at the water's edge – but before they could pounce, there was a flurry of mist, and quite suddenly, a large sky dragon crouched in the open space before the cabin. Oaklyn curled her tail around Lux and lowered her head, rumbling out a deep, rolling sound that couldn't be mistaken as anything other than a warning.

As one, the hounds hesitated. Legendary creatures supposedly afraid of nothing and no one, they exchanged decidedly nervous looks. After a long moment, one of the hounds edged forward. The creature's shadowy aura thinned enough for Lux to glimpse a squashed snout and powerful jaws. With deep crimson eyes locked on Oaklyn, it whined, a complex sound that carried the cadence of speech without ever quite forming words.

"They're operating under a geas," Oaklyn said quietly. "Chraxis commands them against their will."

Lux felt a flash of pity for the monstrously powerful creatures. "The Lord of the North Castle never dirties his own hands if he can use someone else's."

"A coward, in other words." Oaklyn rumbled at the lead hound and it gave a tense, all-over shake, followed by another whine. "Their instructions are binding. You either give them that which they've been sent for, or they try to kill us."

Sheer bloody-mindedness was all that kept Lux from reaching for the pendants hidden safely beneath his clothing. "I guess that means we fight."

The lead hound inclined his head and his pack leapt the creek, sliding through the air with liquid ease. Oaklyn unwound herself with the speed of a whip, her enormous tail swatting one of the beasts out of the air. Ducking beneath her, Lux raked his claws along the flank of a second hound, whose jaws had been aimed at the dragon's hindquarters.

The beast hissed in pain as it landed. Lux jumped on its back, digging one clawed hand into the creature's ruff while the other slashed towards the shadowy throat. The darkhound turned insubstantial before the blow connected and his hand passed right through – followed quickly by the rest of him as he thumped face first into the dirt. Hot breath tickled the back of his neck and Lux reached blindly overhead, digging in with his claws. Blood flowed and the hound howled, a sound that cut off when Lux twisted and rolled them both, straddling the creature's midsection as he dug his claws into the monster's throat and tore it out.

Black blood spurted over his hands and the smell of sulphur intensified, followed quickly by the hiss of burning flesh. Gritting his teeth through the pain, Lux rolled free of the hound's corpse and began wiping his hands on the grass, removing the caustic blood before it could burn him beyond repair.

He'd barely finished when agony bit deep into his shoulder, a second large body bearing him to the ground. A roar split the night and the weight abruptly disappeared, a startled yelp lingering in the space where it had been. Lux scrambled to his feet, clutching his injured shoulder as he staggered for the relative shelter of a broad-limbed tree.

Oaklyn spun and snarled in the middle of the clearing, the darkhound that had bitten him clinging tenaciously to the white-furred tuft on the end of her tail. Another of the creatures danced away from her snapping jaws and swiping claws, whilst a third sunk through the shadows towards Lux. Twin black smears on the grass were all that remained of their companions, the creatures having dissolved upon death in order to transfer their energy to those that still lived. If even a single member of the pack survived, the hounds could be resurrected to fight again another day – and in the meantime, the lost souls resided inside their living brethren, a deadly cocktail of magic and menace.

The darkhound feinted left then lunged. Lux leapt up and back, ignoring the flare of agony in his shoulder to dig the claws of both hands into the tree trunk behind him, bracing his weight with one foot while delivering a thundering kick to the darkhound's face with the other. Using the creature's head as a springboard, Lux launched higher into the canopy, curling his good arm around a branch and flipping into a crouch atop it.

Snarling and snapping, the darkhound surged upright, dug thick claws into the trunk and began to climb. Lux swiped with his claws as the creature came within range, raking deep gashes from shoulder to jaw. The hound grunted but kept coming, taking slash after slash until it was dragging itself onto the branch as well, eyes glittering and fur smoking from an excess of sulphuric blood.

With nowhere left to go, Lux curled his lips back to expose his fangs and hissed. Taking the taunt for exactly what it was, the dark-hound launched at him with a hair-raising howl. Lux met the hound head on, hot breath scalding his cheek as he avoided snapping jaws by a hair's breadth. He let the creature's weight carry them out into space, fisting one hand in thick fur while he used the other to slice the hound open from groin to throat. Blood and worse spilled over him, scalding his skin and splashing into his eyes. With a shout of agonised effort, Lux wrestled the dying beast underneath him and sprang free.

Something large and warm snatched him out of mid-air, the impact enough to drive the breath from his lungs. Lux had the barest moment to register Oaklyn's lavender and spring rain scent before he was dumped unceremoniously into the creek, rushing water closing over his head with an icy shock. His eyes swept open, claws digging into the creekbed to hold himself under as the shallow water sluiced the corrosive darkhound blood from his skin. When Lux could take no more, he surfaced with a choking gasp, his vision a blurred ruin. For a moment he panicked that he wouldn't find the shore but then Oaklyn's claw closed around his waist, far more gently this time, and he was laid out on the grass.

"Oh, kitty," she murmured, her deeper dragon's voice thick with concern. "What did you do?"

I'm fine, he tried to say, but what came out was a gurgling groan.

Cool mist kissed his bare skin and a moment later, Oaklyn's human hands patted at his cheeks. "Kitty, no. Don't you pass out on me now."

Lux opened his mouth and promptly choked as something warm and soft was pressed against his lips. It was only when hot blood began to rush down his throat that he realised Oaklyn had slashed her wrist.

"Come on," she growled. "Drink it, Lux."

The sound of his name on her lips was so alien that he stirred, rousing enough to sink his fangs into her already mangled flesh. When his hand flopped about, she caught his fingers and guided them to the back of her arm, so he could press – or pretend to – her wrist into a better position.

Swallow. Breathe. Swallow. Breathe.

It went on interminably, strength rushing through Lux's cells only to drain a moment later as his body laboured to heal the damage he'd taken. Twice he tried to draw away, but Oaklyn growled and pressed her wrist harder against his fangs, widening the punctures so that the flow of her blood increased. Finally she pulled back and he blinked, vision now clear enough that Lux could see her worried face.

"Okay?" he managed.

Some of her concern faded, the corner of her lip quirking. "A couple scrapes, nothing major. You scared me, kitty."

"Sorry." Lux grimaced. "Hate darkhounds."

"Me, too, but don't worry – they're all dead, which means they're free of the geas and Chraxis knows diddly squat about our location." Strong arms slid beneath his knees and shoulders and the stars wheeled overhead as Oaklyn lifted him against her chest. "Rest now, gorgeous. I've got you."

Yeah, you do, he thought, but his voice had failed again, his body burning with the healing power of a dragon. With a sigh of surrender, Lux turned his face into the soft skin of her neck and let the darkness take him under.

9

JUICE BREAK

OAKLYN PATROLLED THE FOREST until midnight, then curled up for an hour or so of sleep in the cradling embrace of some thick tree roots. She dreamt of darkhounds, wild magic and a creature who was half dragon, half woman, her hair a mane of fiery curls, her skin patched with sunset-coloured hide and the unmistakable, bat-like wings of a fire dragon arching high overhead. Though the woman spoke, the language was foreign and Oaklyn found it impossible to determine what was said. Every time she tried to get closer, the dragon-creature dissolved into a cloud of thick, dark smoke so completely opposite from Oaklyn's own curling mists that she broke into fits of violent coughing.

When her internal senses informed her it was nigh on three in the morning, Oaklyn startled awake in relief. She took a long few moments to search for the mysterious dream dragon, but though she swore smoke lingered in the back of her nostrils, there was nobody else in sight. Not sure whether to be reassured or disappointed, Oaklyn stretched and slunk over to the cabin, pressing her nose to the skylight above the loft.

Lux sprawled in the enormous bed, grey and black hair adorably mussed and sweet tabby ears relaxed. Lashes fanned exquisitely over

432

pale copper cheeks, sharp bone structure making him more ethereal than when he was awake and in motion. The fear she'd felt seeing him so badly wounded haunted her, a very real ache in her throat that, should she have been brave enough to return to human form, might have come out as a sob. As it was, neither of her hearts had been able to find a comfortable rhythm since she'd tucked him into bed to sleep off the last of his injuries – and her own meagre sleep had been plagued by those terrifying moments when his breathing had turned sluggish and he could barely raise enough energy to swallow her blood.

Oaklyn tapped a claw on the thick glass, wincing when Lux startled awake. With careful talons, she unlatched the skylight and levered it open. "Sorry to wake you, kitty, but it's time to go."

"Already?" He rubbed a hand over his face and frowned at the undisturbed side of the bed. "Didn't you sleep?"

"I mostly kept guard, but I slept a little – outside, in case any more of Chraxis' friends decided to drop by." She watched him throw back the covers, revealing the damp, tattered clothing he'd worn earlier. "Are you well enough to travel?"

"I'm tired and a little stiff in the joints, but otherwise, yes. Have I got time to shower and change?"

"Sure." Oaklyn smiled, her heart fluttering when he didn't so much as flinch at the sight of her draconic teeth. "Meet me down by the creek in ten."

Lux appeared precisely eight minutes later, smelling faintly of toothpaste and wearing his worn black jeans and the second t-shirt she'd packed for him. This one was a faded green two shades darker than his eyes, with a splattering of black ink and a feathered quill curling across the front. It clung to his shoulders, hugging his chest before draping around his narrow hips, leaving one seriously spectacular butt on perfect display.

Lux caught her staring and narrowed his eyes. "What?"

"What, what?"

"Your face is all screwed up. Are you going to sneeze?" He took a large step sideways, out of the direct path of any draconic splatter.

Thank the mother goddess he didn't know how to interpret draconic facial expressions; then she didn't have to explain she'd been thinking about kissing him. Oaklyn gave herself a shake and snuffled her snout against her foreleg. "Pre-dawn allergies, you know? I haven't spent the night outside in a while."

"Fair enough." Lux shouldered their backpack and shook his arms out. "Okay. I'm ready."

Once again, she lifted him to her back, waiting patiently as he settled against her scales. This time, when she launched skyward, he didn't scream or hide – didn't react at all, save for a tensing of his legs that soon relaxed. Mindful that he'd been seriously injured only hours earlier, Oaklyn flew as gently as she could, heading east. The rising sun peeked around the edge of a low mountain range and beside it rose the moon, wide and heavy in the sky.

By midmorning, the mountains loomed before them. Oaklyn's destination glittered in the sun; a small valley cradled partway up the cliff containing a shallow lake, a flower-dotted stretch of grass just big enough for her to land and a couple of late-blooming fruit trees.

"Hold on," she said to Lux. The moment his body melted more firmly into hers, she tucked her wings close and dove.

This time, he did scream, the sound muffled by her fur and the whistling sound of their descent. Oaklyn flared her wings at the last minute, executing two large, determined backsweeps before her hind feet touched down, followed closely by the rest of her.

"We're here," she announced. When Lux didn't reply, she twisted her head at an uncomfortable angle to try and get a glimpse of him. "You with me, gorgeous?"

"No. I'm dead."

Oaklyn snorted and plucked him from her spine. "If you peed on me, pretty kitty, we're going to have *words*."

"Excuse me?" Lux's cheeks flagged with colour. "I did not pee on you!"

She made a show of inspecting him from head to toe, then nodded and placed him gently on the ground. Lux promptly stomped off in the opposite direction, muttering curses under his breath. Oaklyn left him to regain his equilibrium by sauntering to the edge of the lake, where she lowered her head to lap at the water. Thirst quenched, she curled on her belly, rested her chin on her foreclaws and closed her eyes.

There was a thump and a rustle behind her as Lux shucked the backpack, then the swish of branches and a grunt. His soft footsteps drew closer, punctuated by the unmistakable sound of teeth digging into the flesh of an apple.

"Thought you were on a liquid-only diet, pretty kitty." She chanced lifting one eyelid and found him standing by her hindquarters, staring out across the mirrored surface of the lake.

"Joof," he said.

Oaklyn watched his throat work in fascination. "You can vamp the juice from an apple?"

"Mmm-hmmm." The apple shrank and shrivelled until it looked like a green prune, at which point Lux extricated his adorable kitty fangs and gave her a self-conscious smile. "It helps settle the cravings."

"Cravings?" Her eyes narrowed as she took his meaning. "You need blood."

One of his shoulders lifted in a graceful shrug, and he tossed the apple with a smooth over-arm motion. "Eventually. My body's healed, but the process takes a lot of energy. I'm going to burn through blood until my immune system resets itself."

"Why didn't you just tell me?"

"And what? Snack on you while we were flying?" He raised a brow. "I'd likely break a fang."

Oaklyn grunted. "Possibly."

"So … what now?" Lux waved a hand at the sun and the moon, chilling side by side in the azure sky. "We've got a few hours to kill before noon."

"I didn't realise we were finished with the blood subject," Oaklyn replied, brows furrowing. When he didn't answer, she twitched her tail in irritation. "What is it?"

"You gave me a lot of blood less than six hours ago. I don't want to run you dry."

"Yeah, well, while you were snoozing last night, I turned that rabbit into a bolognese and ate the hell out of it." Oaklyn stretched her wings, then folded them tight against her back, letting the warm sun tempt her eyelids closed. "I also wasn't injured fighting those hounds, so I'm more than up to the task."

"I don't like treating you as a meal on legs."

"Better than tits on legs."

"*What?*"

"What, what? I'm a big girl, kitty. I know my body. Make a popsicle out of me if you want – I don't care."

"Oh, for the love of—" Lux made a frustrated noise in the back of his throat, and a second later something bounced off the end of her nose.

"Did you just throw a *shoe* at me?" Oaklyn's eyes snapped back open, her head lifting from her claws. She flinched as a second missile bounced off her forehead. "You did!"

"It seemed the only damned way to get your attention!" He growled, peeling off his socks and balling them up before they bounced harmlessly off the side of her face. "If you stop blowing hot air for one second, you'll see I'm worried about you. More than that, I'm so damned attracted to you I can barely think – and if I sink my fangs into you in this mood, I'll be tempted to do something you might not want me to do!"

"Huh?" Oaklyn's jaw dropped, but he wasn't finished. Lux dragged his t-shirt off over his head with one hand, mashed it between his fists and threw that at her, too. She caught a glimpse of bronze skin and black ink before warm cotton tangled on her antlers and flopped over her eyes.

"I want you," Lux said, his voice carrying the guttural edge of a growl. "I wanted you two days ago, in your house, but I was worried our kiss might've been a reaction to taking your blood. I wanted you yesterday, while we were flying. I wanted you last night, when you came in the door with that fucking rabbit wearing nothing but mist and wilderness. I want you so damned much it's choking me, but I'm too scared to go through with it in case the hypnotic qualities of my vampire bite are inventing feelings that aren't reciprocated!"

Lifting a claw, Oaklyn removed his t-shirt from her face and set it aside. He hadn't moved from his earlier position, but his body quivered with pent-up emotion, hands clenched to fists so tight the knuckles were white. Without a shirt, the chain he wore around his neck was revealed, supporting two pendants that shifted against his breastbone with each breath. One, a gold and silver cartouche with jade hieroglyphs, and the other, a wire-wrapped crystal point in deep, dark red. She shifted her gaze to take in every line, dip and hollow of his torso, masculine perfection wrapped in the gentle copper silk of his skin. Lux's tattoo curled over the left side of his ribs and chest; a bat-winged tabby cat in an Egyptian collar with heavy eye makeup and gold rings piercing the delicately pointed ears. Above the cat's head, between the spread wings, was the symbol of the triple moon, with an ankh in gold suspended in the centre. Curling beneath the cat's running paws were a curious blend of hieroglyphs and both Daywalker and Nightstalker vampiric that would require a working knowledge of all three tongues to accurately translate. It was dark and incredibly beautiful, speaking to something ancient deep in Oaklyn's soul.

She swallowed and forced her gaze up to his face. Yellow-green eyes glared back at her, his face a flushed combination of temper and desire, jaw clenched so tight it turned his cheekbones to blades.

Mother goddess, it was too much. With a huff of surrender, Oaklyn wrapped her tail around his waist and dragged him close. When he stumbled, she snorted a puff of fog and shifted, catching his body in the cradle of her own as it reshaped from dragon to human. They tumbled backwards to the grass, Lux's arms braced either side of her head, his body hard and his pendants draped across her throat.

"For the record," she purred, revelling in the feel of his hot skin against hers, "when you took my blood, my reactions were my own. The glamour in a vamp bite doesn't work on dragons."

Lux swallowed. "I didn't know that."

"There are lots of things about me you don't know. We've only been together two days."

"You think it's too fast?" He began to pull back, but Oaklyn wrapped her arms around his waist, smoothing her hands up the length of his spine.

"No." She shook her head. "Time is a relative concept, created by intelligent life forms as a way to rationalise the constant repetition of now. The past and the future aren't real, nor are the days and weeks and months we surround ourselves with. I've been alive a long time, gorgeous. I know what I want, and it's you. Here, in this now that we're sharing together."

Lux relaxed against her with a groan, burying his face in her hair and nipping the soft skin of her neck in a way that made Oaklyn shiver. His silken ears brushed over her cheek and he braced his weight on one arm to run a lean, long-fingered hand over her collarbone, cupping the weight of a breast on his path over her ribs to the flare of her hip.

"I'm not very good at this, am I?" He huffed a dry laugh against her ear. "Shouting and throwing things isn't very romantic."

"You sell yourself too short, kitty. I adore your passion – I adore everything about you. Trust me, those feelings you were so worried about are definitely reciprocated."

"I ..." He swallowed heavily. "Are you sure?"

Oaklyn slid her hands over his denim-covered ass and squeezed. "Very. Pants off, gorgeous."

There was only a minor hesitation before he lifted off her enough that Oaklyn could unfasten his jeans and shove them down. Working together, they wriggled the pants down his legs until Lux could kick them aside, his very healthy erection now sandwiched between them.

"Mother goddess," Oaklyn whispered, her eyes going wide as Lux began to kiss a trail along her jaw. "That is the cutest damned tail I have ever seen."

It flicked in the air overhead, curling in that almost-sentient way only a cat's tail could. Grey and black striped like Lux's tabby ears and silken hair, she couldn't resist following the curve of his spine until she found the place where it sprouted, just above the slope of his butt. When she dared to stroke her fingers along the nubile length, Lux's tail wrapped around her wrist like a bracelet and he lifted his head to catch her eyes.

"You really like it."

"Of course I do." Oaklyn stroked his tail again, grinning when he shivered. "You forget, kitty – in my dragon form, I have one too."

"I love your tail," he whispered, and then sealed his mouth to hers.

The kiss started out trembling, a press of lips that grew in both confidence and heat until Lux slipped his tongue in. Oaklyn surrendered with a sigh and he grew bolder, licking and nipping at her lips before paving a fiery path down her throat to her breasts, where he sucked a nipple into his mouth and swirled his tongue around it, fangs providing a sharply erotic counterpoint to the smooth, insistent heat building inside her.

"I'm hungry," he growled against her skin, moving to scrape his teeth over the curve of her other breast. "Gods, Oaklyn, tell me now, before I lose it, how far I can go."

"Take whatever you want," she gasped, her fingers tight in his hair. "I'm all yours."

His moan was almost a whimper, and before she quite knew what happened, lightning shot through her blood as he sank his fangs into the side of one breast. The bite was quick, barely enough for a taste before he licked over the punctures and lifted his head. "Okay?"

"Yes," she gasped, trying to shove him back down. "Don't stop."

Lux rumbled a laugh, lowering his head to lick and kiss his way down to the juncture of her thighs. His tongue swirled around her clit and slid down her centre, drawing needy cries from her throat.

"So wet," he mumbled, his voice a weapon all by itself. "So beautiful."

Tears threatened to prick the corners of her eyes, but before she could get too mushy over the sweet words, Lux sank his fangs into her inner thigh at the same time he slid a finger inside her body. Pleasure arched Oaklyn's spine, and he flattened his free hand over her abdomen to hold her down. Pressure began to build as one finger became two, curling and working in rhythm to the pull of his bite.

"Oh," she managed, tugging at his hair. "*Yes.*"

Her inner muscles began to clench and quick as a flash, Lux shifted his mouth to her clit and sucked hard. She shattered with a cry, the world coming apart in a glittering ecstasy of light and colour and sensation, the vampire between her legs the only thing anchoring her to reality. He pushed her with hands and mouth, wringing every drop of pleasure from her body and then gentling her down the other side, carefully removing his fingers and licking over the punctures on her inner thigh.

"Still okay?" He rasped, sliding up her body with slinky grace. The warmth of his erection nudged at her entrance as he bent to capture her lips, his kiss coaxing and tender. "Oaklyn?"

"Inside me," she gasped, wrapping her legs around his hips.

Lux trembled with strain above her, the tendons standing out in his neck. "I …"

"You can't knock me up," she managed, registering his reluctance through a haze. "Dragons can turn their reproductive cycles on and off at will, and there aren't any diseases that can survive the magic content in our blood – just like a vampire. So as long as your vamp blood is strong enough—"

"It is. I'm clean."

Oaklyn reached up to cup his face, her body vibrating with desperation. "Then by all you hold dear, Lux, get inside me *right now.*"

With a purring growl, he slid home. She gasped at the intrusion, so much bigger than expected but so incredibly good. Lux impaled himself to the hilt and dropped his head for a searing kiss while he waited for her to adjust, his hands moving over her skin in skilful complement to his tongue. In moments, Oaklyn was rocking helplessly against him, seeking friction – and with a shuddering groan, Lux began to move.

In all Oaklyn's years, there had never been anything like the glide of his body inside hers. Nothing like the flex of his hips, the contraction of his muscles, the sheer masculine magic of every rocking thrust.

She was one of the most powerful creatures to walk the Earth and yet she was powerless beneath him, every single part of her cracking open as they moved together, sharing pleasure until it was impossible to tell where he ended and she began.

Someone was sobbing and Oaklyn thought it might be her. Lux began to shake, his rhythm sliding from intentional to primal, inciting a deep, raw response from inside her own body. He broke their kiss on a growl, setting his fangs against the galloping pulse in her throat. For a horrifying moment she thought he was going to stop and ask for permission – then his fangs sank deep as he thrust home hard, and she came apart with a scream that wrenched from the depths of her very soul. Lux's throat worked in time with the frenzy of his body and the incredible ecstasy of their joining pushed her over into a second orgasm, this one all the more intense because he followed, their bodies shuddering in unison.

Lux collapsed on top of her, making no effort to pull out or soften his weight, and Oaklyn loved every single thing about it – about him. She wrapped her arms tight over his back and drifted, shivering in delight as he licked at her neck and then returned to her mouth for a lazy, luscious kiss that carried the tang of her own blood.

"Okay?" he whispered against her lips.

Oaklyn laughed. "Okay? My entire universe has just been rearranged and you're asking if I'm *okay?*"

"I'll take that as a yes." A smile that could only be described as pure, raw male dawned on his face. "You did say I could have whatever I wanted." His expression flickered. "I didn't intend to bite you quite so much, though. It kind of just happened."

"Don't you dare apologise, pretty kitty. There are no words to express how much I loved what we just did. I'm a predator, same as you; I like a good bite or three." Oaklyn glanced up from beneath the veil of her lashes. "Four, if you need it."

"Gods above us, I'm not a fucking piranha," Lux muttered – but he was smiling again, tension melting away so that he lay quiescent in her arms. "Also, your blood is rich and my body's in a state of flux. Too much and I'll bliss out."

He lowered his head to the crook of her neck and licked across the puncture wounds again, which were already tingling as Oaklyn's body started to heal. She smoothed her hands over his shoulders and down his spine in long, sweeping strokes, and Lux began to purr. After a few minutes, the purr softened to a rumble, and then he murmured incoherently against her skin and fell asleep. Content in a way she'd not been for a long, long time, Oaklyn continued to stroke his back, revelling in the warmth they created as she watched the sun climb slowly higher into the sky. Soon, they'd have to walk the Old Road, but for now, in this perfect, shining moment, he belonged entirely to her – and for the first time in her life, Oaklyn wondered if the only reason she'd never had a hoard was because she hadn't stumbled upon something precious enough to cherish until the end of her days.

THE OLD ROAD

LUX WOKE TO SOFT KISSES and gentle caresses as the sun approached noon. He burrowed his face into Oaklyn's hair and nipped at her neck while she laughed, soft and throaty, and gave his tail a playful tug.

"We have to get moving, gorgeous," she murmured. "If you want to walk the Old Road, you'll need to be on my back in less than ten minutes."

Lux sighed. As wonderful as it was to bask in Oaklyn's embrace, it hadn't escaped his attention that her admissions of affection had been based purely in the now, with no mention of a future. Was he … not what she wanted? Danger's perfect face floated into Lux's mind, followed swiftly by the literary mountains on the floor in Oaklyn's den. Crushing the urge to cover his ears, Lux rolled upright and began hunting down his clothes. For all it was instinct to list his own imperfections, the idea that Oaklyn had bedded him purely out of curiosity didn't sit right. She, too, was unusual, and lonely because of it. Lux dumped his recovered clothing in a pile at the base of a tree and frowned. Something else was going on, something that made his dragon reluctant to open herself up completely – and once he was done with his obligation to Ra, he was going to find out exactly what the problem was, and solve it.

Skinny ass and cat ears or not, he was going to fight for the future she'd danced around.

Bending to hide his grin, Lux sorted his clothes into some semblance of order and shook out his pants. Oaklyn had returned to her dragon form and watched him from the bank of the lake, expression fascinated as he curved his tail around one thigh, pulled on his jeans and fastened them.

"What?" Lux asked, yanking his t-shirt over his head. "I can feel your questions."

"Do you ever ..." she waved her hand at his butt.

"Let my tail out? Sometimes." Lux shrugged, sitting down to tug on his socks and shoes. "I have some pants with a hole in the back where it can poke through, but they're ... situational."

"I guess that makes sense." Oaklyn handed him their backpack and got to her feet. "Ready, then?"

"As I'll ever be. Do we have a plan?"

"Not in so many words." Oaklyn tapped a claw against her chin. "Destroying the darkhounds might have hidden our exact location from Chraxis, but he'd be an idiot not to think you're heading for Mu. If I was him, I'd be stationing a couple of people at every Old Road I could find."

"You're saying we should expect an ambush."

"No, I'm saying we stage one." Draconic lips parted as she smiled, revealing deadly teeth. "They're expecting you – or at best, you and Danger. They're not expecting me."

"True enough." He scuffed at the grass a long moment. "Do you think Danger healed up okay?"

Oaklyn's expression softened. "I'm sure of it, gorgeous. He'll be waiting for us when we get back. You'll see."

"Yeah, you're probably right." Lux blew out a soft laugh. "So ... you want me to shut up and hang on while you open a can of whoop-ass on Chraxis' cronies?"

"That's exactly what I want, gorgeous – but it will mean some fancier flying that what you've been used to so far."

"This mission has been hell on my ego, you know that?" Lux sighed. "Fine. I promise not to scream, pee or vomit."

"And you will hold on to me, kitty."

"Like a limpet."

"Excellent." Oaklyn scooped him up and settled him into place across her shoulders. Lux fisted his hands in the white fur ruff running down her spine, the action now so familiar it was hard to believe he hadn't been doing it forever. When Oaklyn's body shifted beneath him, he shifted with it, the motion reminding Lux of the way they'd moved together making love on the grass.

It had been everything he'd ever hoped for and more, stripping him bare not just to the skin but to the very depths of his being – a vulnerability he'd have found uncomfortable with anyone other than Oaklyn.

I love you. The words tingled on the tip of his tongue, but Lux bit them back. He might have poured his heart out like a crazy person in the clearing, but she'd been noticeably quiet. In fact, if he were of a gambling mind, he'd be willing to bet she'd been hurt in the past – it would certainly explain why someone so powerful, beautiful, intelligent and funny chose to live like a hermit, using those qualities to deflect attention from her gentle, loving nature.

Lux stroked his palm down the warmth of her scales, unsure whether he was soothing Oaklyn or himself. He knew all about hurt, about throwing everything you had at life and never quite stacking up. Hell, though he loved Danger like a brother, having six and a half feet of vampiric perfection by his side every day was a constant reminder of his own shortcomings.

Maybe, instead of pouting because a dragon hadn't promised him forever after two days of forced proximity, he should be grateful she'd been brave enough to lower the walls around her heart long enough to take notice of him at all.

Both the sun and moon edged higher in the sky, moving closer to noon with every passing moment. The lake at Oaklyn's feet glowed gold, the surface so still it reflected with all the brilliance of a mirror. Magic rose around them, thick and choking, and a chill wind teased Lux's hair. With her head high and her wings partially spread, Oaklyn stepped onto the lake, walking across the water's surface as though it were marble. The world shimmered, magic roiled and when next Lux blinked, they stood on the opposite shore of an identical lake in a completely different environment.

Gone was the lazy warmth of late summer, replaced by icy winds, snow-laden bushes and hunched evergreens. Lux shivered, tucking himself close to Oaklyn's warmth as she took two jerky steps and launched skyward, barely missing the whistling arrows that streaked from the thick, dark treeline.

"Looks like you were right," he shouted. "Chraxis set guards."

"Funnily enough, kitty, this isn't my first crazy vampire rodeo." Oaklyn dipped a wing, the tips of her feathers brushing the snowy ground as she executed a turn so sharp Lux's stomach dropped out through his feet.

A strong pump of dragon wings shot them in the direction the arrows had come from. Oaklyn twisted mid-air, lashing out with her tail to thwack the leading edge of the evergreens. The trees shuddered under the force of the blow, and two humanoid figures in dark cloaks tumbled from the branches. Landing in a flurry of snow, Oaklyn slammed a foreclaw flat onto each of their enemies, the rage bugling from her throat barely enough to cover the meaty squelch as the guards were pulverised into mush. Silence fell, broken only by the soft shush of settling snow.

"I think we're safe," Lux ventured at last.

"Hmmm." Oaklyn sat on her haunches, lifted one messy claw and sniffed. "Purebred Nightstalkers."

"What a surprise."

"Hah!" Shaking off the worst of the gore, she picked up a heavy crossbow. "Idiots. These take far too long to reload."

"Yeah, well, like you said, they weren't expecting dragons – and guns might work on Earth, but not in Mu."

Oaklyn crushed the crossbow in her fist, then located the second one and applied the same treatment. Dropping the splinters beside their liquidised owners, she wiped her claws on the nearby trunk of a tree and padded back down to the more open area surrounding the lake.

"I don't think we'll meet any more resistance, kitty, but I can also hear your teeth chattering. Are you happy if we hightail it to Lilith and get this over with?"

Lux pressed a kiss to her smooth scales. "That's the best thing you've said since we got here."

She threw herself into the air with a surge of muscle, the tips of her wings leaving swirly vapour trails and her body wiggling like a hyperactive belly dancer. The speed at which Oaklyn cut through the sky negated the ability for speech, so Lux buried his face in her fur, clenched his teeth and hung on for all he was worth.

Mu stretched out far below, less of a land and more a fractured collection of alternate realms scattered around the Earth like sprinkles on a cake, connected by dreams and wishes and pure, raw energy. Deserts and swamps existed side by side with gentle grasslands and wild, thick forests, the landscape rich and ever changing and entirely impossible to comprehend, no matter how long one spent there.

In what may have been an hour or perhaps only a minute, a shining gold ziggurat loomed on the skyline. Sumerian in styling with distinctly Egyptian ornamentation, it glittered in the sun from amidst a steaming, verdant jungle. Oaklyn didn't angle towards the top, where the traditional entrance was, but rather the base, where a yawning maw of a passage led into darkness. When they were almost directly overhead, she folded her wings against her back, tipped her nose downwards and fell with the sleek precision of the arrows they'd dodged earlier.

Lux's entire body shrieked, but fear and vertigo froze his jaw shut so that the sound he emitted was more like a whistling kettle than a reputation-soiling wail. He'd just finished saying silent goodbyes to his parents and wishing he'd tried that cake mix smoothie Danger dared him to make last week when Oaklyn flared her wings with a snap and landed neatly.

"Okay, kitty?"

"No," he rasped. "I'm dead. Again."

She chuckled, the sound normal enough that he lifted his head, buying time for his limbs to unclench by examining their new surroundings. The interior of the ziggurat was lit by dancing motes of light the size of his clenched fist. The floor was an intricate sunburst mosaic, in the centre of which stood an altar bearing an elegant, canopied bed. By the bed's head stood the great, golden form of Ra and the sleek, deadly shape of Lilith.

As gods went, Ra fit the bill. Tall, broad, with brown skin that shimmered gold and eyes like twin suns. Roughly handsome in worn jeans and a white t-shirt, Egypt's sun god exuded both confidence and power. By contrast, Lilith was barely five feet tall, with pale skin and black hair that hung not so much in waves as it wasn't quite straight. She was beautiful in the way an artisan knife was beautiful; all delicate lines and razor perfect edges. Her eyes were black, her lips scarlet, and she wore a simple black tunic and leggings over patent red stilettos. The couple couldn't have been more different, yet looking at them together, it was impossible to deny they were a perfect match.

Oaklyn shifted into human form without warning, leaving Lux with an arm around her shoulders and her body clothed in nothing but the lingering mist conjured by her magic. She tossed a two-fingered salute at the waiting gods then turned to face him, smoothing a hand over his chest.

"Breathe, kitty," she murmured. "We made it."

"How did you know where to come?"

She lifted a brow. "I've been here before."

"No, I meant ..." Lux drew a deep breath, tugging her closer to his body so that he could borrow just a little more of her strength. "How did you know they would be *here*?"

"Ah." Oaklyn paused, pursing her lips. "Think of it as something like a radar. I just kind of ... pinged them." She shrugged. "It's a dragon thing."

"You pinged the gods on your dragon radar."

"Yep." She caught his look and winked. "Don't worry, kitty, it only works on the gods and it only works in Mu. You're safe. Come on, now, hmm? Let's go say hi."

Oaklyn twined her fingers through his and together they mounted the steps to the altar where Ra and Lilith waited. To Lux's incredible shock, as they hit the top step, Lilith's face split into a fangy grin and she leapt forward to throw her arms around Oaklyn's neck.

"Oaklyn Airecross, as I live and breathe!" the goddess cried.

"Hello, Lil." Oaklyn returned the embrace with a laugh. "Do you actually live and breathe, or did you just eat someone from the sixteen hundreds this morning?"

Lilith stepped back with a mock-stern expression. "I thought I told you to stop spying on me with that magic mirror."

"I can't help it! You just do winged eyeliner so damned well."

"If you two are done," Ra intoned, his expression resigned, "might I be so bold as to ask what in the world is going on? Oaklyn, the last time we spoke, you were hibernating to discern a collection of, ahem, 'book boyfriends'."

"I was, but Lux and Danger ran into a few troubles trying to get your mission accomplished. When we crossed paths, I offered to help." Oaklyn glanced up at the bed, and the motionless woman in it. "You could have called me, Lil."

Lilith sighed. "I wanted to, but it all happened so fast. Bast was concerned that any damage to the curse focus could injure or even kill Solaris, so we made the call to keep things quiet and trust in Luxor's ability to get in and out undetected."

"That makes sense, I guess." Oaklyn turned to Lux and made an extravagant gesture. "Speaking of the curse focus, I think that's your cue, kitty."

The world spun and though Lux knew he was in the presence of the gods and should, in theory, be far more respectful, all he could do was gape. "You know Ra and Lilith?"

"Yes, well." Oaklyn's cheeks darkened. "A little."

"And you didn't mention this because ..."

"I didn't know you very well at the time?"

"You – you – what about -" Taking a deep, steadying breath, Lux clamped down on the tirade building in his chest and turned to face Ra and Lilith. They watched him with varying degrees of consternation, and, mindful that he'd come with a purpose, Lux ignored the dragon beside him and swept the gods an old-world bow. The chain at his neck swung free with the movement and he grasped it, carefully removing the wire-wrapped red crystal as he straightened.

"My Queen." Lux extended his hand towards Lilith. "This is for you."

The Sumerian goddess stared down at the gem for a long moment. "Is this it?"

Ra plucked the pendant from Lux's hand and held it to the light. "Bast was right. The enchantment on this crystal is a clever one."

"Ra!" Lilith kicked her mate in the ankle.

"Be calm, my love. Luxor has done exactly what he promised – this is most definitely the key to Solaris' curse." Ra approached the bed, where a woman lay unnaturally still beneath the covers.

With an elegant flourish and a mutter in his native language, the god of the sun laid the pendant on his daughter's sternum. A faint hum filled the ziggurat and Lux's skin crawled as magic crackled in the air. The cursed pendant sank into Solaris' skin, sending a cobweb of shimmering lines through her pale body before winking out entirely. A moment later, brilliant red eyes snapped open and Solaris sat bolt upright.

"Mother?" she said, her voice dusty with disuse. She looked to Ra. "Father?" Her eyes tracked to Oaklyn and went wide. "Aunt Oaklyn?"

Lux choked, and just like that, the equilibrium he'd clung to so desperately fled. "*Aunt* Oaklyn?"

"Mmm-hmmm." She inspected the floor between her feet. "I'm her fairy godmother. Well, dragon godmother, I suppose."

"And this is yet another thing you didn't think to mention *before we got here?*"

"Peace, son of Bast." Ra held up a placating hand. "Oaklyn keeps her knowledge of us quiet by request. Don't take your temper out on her for keeping a promise made over a baby's cradle long, long ago."

"That's all very well to say when you're not the one with the rug being pulled out from under his feet." Lux curled his lip far enough to show fang. "I'll accept that you and Oaklyn knowing each other personally had no impact on my involvement in this mission. I'll even go further and say reticence was probably a good move, because at the time Oaklyn offered her help, we didn't know each other very well. But now I'm going to turn right back around and say I thought I'd payed my dues since that moment. Earnt your trust."

"You did." Oaklyn blew out a long breath. "I wanted to tell you the truth, but I'd have been breaking my own word to do it – and if I don't have my word, what do I have?"

"Oh, I don't know … me, maybe? Or was that just temporary, seeing as there's no such thing as the past or the future, only a series of nows? And, clearly, in this particular now, I'm not good enough for you to treat like an equal." He paused, then narrowed his eyes. "What if I was on Chraxis' side? What would you have done then?"

Oaklyn, looking more and more mournful, snapped her teeth half-heartedly.

"Right." Lux snorted and shook his head. "Honestly, I don't even know why I'm surprised, at this point."

"Kitty—"

"Don't," he growled, claws slicing out of the ends of his fingers. "I can't think about this right now. Chraxis first, then us."

After a reluctant pause, Oaklyn nodded. "Okay."

"Chraxis," Solaris breathed, fear lacing her tone. "Mother, he—"

Lilith sat on the bed and drew her daughter into a fierce embrace. "I know. Don't worry, poppet – now that you're safe, I'm going to tear his head from his shoulders and shove it up his traitorous ass."

Solaris sniffled. "I guess we're lucky Aunt Oaklyn was there when she was."

Lux flinched from the words, fisting both hands until his claws dug into his palms. It took every ounce of his conscious will to smooth his expression rather than turn and storm away, slamming every slammable door and finding something to kick while he was at it.

"My involvement was pure luck," Oaklyn murmured, examining

the vaulted roof overhead. "I'm sure I made the job a little easier, but Lux would've seen you safe with or without Danger around to back him up."

"That's right." Lilith nodded, tossing Lux a warning glare when he made a choking noise in the back of his throat. "Now, you need to rest, recover your strength, and put Chraxis out of your mind. Papa's going to take care of you, and Mama's going to deliver some justice."

"Just make sure you're delivering justice where it's needed, rather than wreaking bloody vengeance on innocent bystanders." Oaklyn bent until she caught Lilith's gaze with her own. "I'm serious, Lil."

Lilith tsked deep in her throat. "Am I ever going to live that down?"

"No."

"It was only a little bit of vengeance."

"It was an entire city!"

Lilith made a moue. "Only the warriors were left. They made their choice."

"*Lilith.*"

"Oh, fine." The queen of all vampires rolled her black eyes. "I promise my wrath will be dispensed only to those truly guilty. Happy, now?"

"Yes." Oaklyn smiled and patted Solaris' knee under the blanket. "Now, I think we'll go. Your mother's right, Sol – you should rest."

"Are you sure you won't take refreshment before you go?" Ra asked, raising an eyebrow.

Lux shook his head. "I've got some of my own things to sort out, now that this is done with."

The god of the sun laughed and clapped Lux heartily on the back. "Very well. Thank you, Daywalker, for the risks you took on our behalf. If there's anything you need, don't hesitate to ask."

"It was my honour," Lux replied, cutting another bow. He shot Lilith a look from beneath his lashes. "A word of warning: Chraxis sent a pack of darkhounds after us. He's probably got a host of nasty surprises up his sleeve."

"Darkhounds," Lilith murmured, tapping her chin in a gesture that reminded Lux of Oaklyn. "Interesting. Once Chraxis is dealt with, I'll talk to Anubis about the state of the darker realms – but in the meantime, thanks for the warning."

"My pleasure."

Lux stood back as a round of enthusiastic goodbye hugs were exchanged, and a promise wrung from Oaklyn to visit in a few weeks' time for meatballs. As they backed down the stairs, Solaris offered a tentative smile and a finger wiggle, which Oaklyn returned with a full-armed, proud-aunt wave.

Shoving both hands in his pockets, Lux stalked out the ziggurat's impressive lower doorway and into the sunlight. He turned his face to the warmth, drawing both energy and calm from the familiar caress, and waited.

"Kitty?" Oaklyn's hand smoothed gently across his shoulders, and her face swam into view as she slipped into his line of sight. "You mad?"

"You think? I mean, I get that you had to keep the secret, but the entire time we were laughing and joking, you were secretly assessing me to work out if I warranted eating." Lux lowered his lashes and sighed. "I assumed I'd earnt better, particularly after what we shared in the clearing. I thought you cared." He huffed a laugh. "I should've known it wasn't real, I guess. After all, what would someone like me possibly have to offer someone like you? I've seen the books you read. I know I'm not your perfect idea of a man – and yet, here I am, following you around like a lost kitten and making an idiot of myself in front of the gods."

Oaklyn was quiet for a long minute, continuing to stroke his back with firm, soothing motions. When she sidled close enough to press a soft kiss to his cheek, tendrils of vapour curled under his nostrils and sank into his lungs.

"Dragons are a funny thing," she murmured, lips silky against his skin. "Made from magic and primordial chaos. Scattered through all the different universes, all the different realities, a part of and yet apart from the places we call home. Protectors, destroyers, and all shades in between, we are not gods but we also do not serve gods – or anyone else, for that matter. We birth in the frenetic folds of the universe and are as rare and mythical as the unicorn, no two ever exactly the same." Oaklyn paused, and Lux opened his eyes to see her blinking back tears. "My parents were human, you know. They said they were blessed to birth such a wild, raw, magical creature, but at the end of the day, they lived human lives and died a very human death. Lilith … helped me from a dark place. She brought me to Mu and introduced me to beings who helped me come to terms not only with my losses, but also the monumental responsibility of being a dragon. So, kitty, no matter how much I wished I could have been honest with you, I owe her my sanity. I owe her my ability to make love to you in the clearing, and my ability to stand here and beg your forgiveness right now – because without the mother of all vampires, I'd have ended my own life long, long ago."

The words struck deep, sweeping aside centuries of self-loathing and replacing it with bone-deep panic. Lux seized Oaklyn's shoulders in a bruising grip, the tips of his claws pricking her bare skin. "I refuse to contemplate a world without you in it. Don't joke about that, cream puff."

Tears breached the corners of her eyes and trickled down her cheeks. She stayed silent, and that alone was enough to chill Lux to the very core of his soul. They'd never have met, he realised. Never have had the opportunity to stand here in the sun and question what they were to each other.

"I forgive you," he whispered, and kissed her. *I love you.* "But I'm still angry. And hurt."

Oaklyn nipped at his lower lip, then kissed him again, soft and sweet. "I'm sorry, kitty. I really, really am."

"So am I." Gods, was he ever. Falling in love with a dragon? What had he been thinking? Staring up at the sky so he wasn't swallowed by her sad cornflower eyes, Lux sighed. "Would you take me back to your place? If Danger did decide to hang around, that's where he'll be."

"Sure." Oaklyn cleared her throat, stepped back and resumed her dragon form. "Climb on, and we'll be on our way."

VALENTINE'S DAY

After a long flight during which Lux interchanged chilly silence with fitful napping, Oaklyn landed in her backyard with the full understanding that there were six Nightstalker vampires waiting on the back porch. Reining in the urge to splat them en masse, she mantled her wings and bared her teeth. "You have five seconds to speak before I mince you all into pancake batter and have you for breakfast."

"Peace, Oaklyn Airecross." A female vampire in plaid capris and a slick black top minced down the porch steps. "We were sent by the queen, with news that Chraxis is dead and the North Castle is secure." She flipped blonde hair off her shoulder with perfectly manicured nails and pouted at Lux. "And we need your help."

"My help?" Lux slid down from Oaklyn's neck, his tone thick with suspicion. "What for?"

The vampire looked back at her companions, who shifted uncomfortably on their feet. "Ah. Well, when we arrived, there was another Nightstalker already here. He didn't take kindly to our presence."

"Danger." Lux passed a hand over his face. "Did he kill anyone?"

"No, but he wounded five of us before we were able to tranq him." The woman frowned prettily. "Her majesty said he'd been injured under Chraxis' rule, and that it might be better if you were present to reassure him when the sedatives wear off."

Lux muttered something under his breath, then turned to Oaklyn. "I have to go and fix this."

"I can come with you," she offered, but he was shaking his head before the words had finished forming.

"It's better if I handle this myself. There's going to be all sorts of red tape and I don't want to upset your plans any more than I already have."

"Still mad, huh?"

"A little." His cool fingers stroked over the scales of her cheek. "I told you I forgave you and I do, but I just … I need some space to get my head on straight."

"I guess I deserve that."

"Oaklyn …"

"It's okay, kitty." Though her heart was cracking, Oaklyn casually folded her wings and flopped to her belly. "I understand."

Lux sighed, leaning in to kiss the tip of her snout. When she didn't respond, he shook his head and moved to join his fellow vampires. The blonde pulled a mage stone from her pocket and the group converged as the sigils blared to life. A few moments later, they were gone.

As the sun sank below the back of the house and the stars winked to life in an obsidian sky, Oaklyn rolled onto her back and clasped her claws over her chest. Mother Goddess, she was an idiot. So sure, after so many years of life, that she was too rare, too different, to ever find a true mate. Then Lux had turned up, with his tortured soul and that cheeky smile she had to work to earn, offering her everything with those brilliant green eyes. And while she'd revelled in his attention, she'd opted to joke and protect rather than tell Lux how she really felt. For all the scorn he'd directed at himself, her kitty had been nothing but up front. He'd dared to face what a dragon had shied away from, and Oaklyn respected the hell out of his honesty and his courage. If she hadn't already fallen in love with him, she fancied she would have, in the moment he ran soft fingers over her cheek and told her he needed space.

Even if she hated that space with the fire of a thousand suns.

It was after midnight when Oaklyn shifted and went inside, making a meal out of some leftover kabana, cheese and crackers. Fatigue pulled at every movement so she stumbled straight to bed, falling into a deep, dreamless sleep amongst sheets that still carried Lux's vetiver and myrrh scent.

Valentine's Day dawned bright and clear – or at least, that's what the weather app on her phone said. Oaklyn lazed in bed staring at the ceiling, her thoughts consumed with the memory of Lux's betrayed expression when he realised she'd known Lilith all along.

Enough.

Perhaps she should have shared more of herself, given him what she could without breaking her word to Lilith, but it was done now. Oaklyn had made her mistakes, given her reasons, asked for forgiveness. All she could do was hope that when the fog of hurt cleared, Lux realised their electric connection was real and that, in spite of her many shortcomings, her hearts rested solely in his clawed kitty hands. If she ever saw him again, she'd do whatever it took to prove her feelings were genuine – and in the meantime, there was a boatload of chocolate mousse in the fridge that would make the perfect Valentine's Day breakfast.

Oaklyn rolled out of bed and stretched, then smoothed the tank and tiny shorts she slept in and made her way out to the kitchen. Stacking as many bowls of chocolate mousse into her arms as she could carry, she returned to the den and the comfort of her favourite chair. With the first of her Valentine's shortlisted books in one hand and a spoon in the other, she pushed images of Lux firmly from her mind and began to read.

By late morning, she'd finished her book and though it was an old favourite, the conclusion failed to stir her the way it usually would. Heaving a sigh, Oaklyn set her empty dishes and the book aside and retired to the bathroom for a long, scalding shower. The familiar routine of brushing her teeth, washing her hair and scrubbing herself clean helped settle her jagged edges, but as she dried off, she was forced to admit that her pre-kitty contentment was a thing of the past. Promising herself more mousse as soon as she was dressed, Oaklyn wrapped her towel tight around her body, opened the bathroom door and strode out.

"… stroked her fingers over the broad planes of his sculpted chest, revelling in the crisp hairs as they tickled her sensitive skin. He moaned and dipped his head to suckle her ear – her *ear?*" Lux looked up from the book in his hand. "Of all the things he could choose to suck on, he picks her ear?"

Oaklyn's uninvited houseguest lounged on a beanbag like he owned it, wearing a clean pair of black skinny jeans and a dusky blue t-shirt with a dragon on it. He was barefoot, his adorable kitty tail dangling down one side of the beanbag and both adorable kitty ears swivelled in her direction. The smile on his face was wide, his green-yellow eyes sparkled with welcome, and he was so fucking perfect that Oaklyn couldn't move an inch.

"Some people find the ear to be a sensitive area." She cleared her throat, found it still lumpy, tried again. "What are you doing here?"

He shot her a look from beneath lowered lashes. "I'm a burglar, remember? Robberpants McGee? Freddie Felon? Home Invader Harry? I go where I like."

"I …" Oaklyn groped for something witty to say, but the truth came out instead. "I wasn't sure I'd ever see you again."

Lux appeared in front of her in a blur of lean muscle, long-fingered hands cupping her face and the heat of his body soaking into her skin.

"I hated every minute I was away," he whispered. "I thought I wasn't good enough for you, not handsome enough or vampire enough or … anything enough. I thought you'd kept yourself apart because you knew that, deep down, I was just a loser half-breed. I was so angry that I never stopped to think that maybe you had your own demons to fight, your own insecurities to wrestle. Even after you told me that you did." Lux drew a deep breath and let it out between his teeth. "I spent so much time telling myself I'd dig out the truth and make you see that I was here, that we were *real*. Then, when the truth did come out, I threw myself a pity party and flounced."

"It wasn't just you," Oaklyn managed, swallowing around the lump in her throat. "I held back because I knew you'd be angry when you found out the truth of my friendship with Lilith. I should've told you the truth sooner, and shared my feelings rather than have you wondering if I cared at all."

"So we're both idiots?"

A watery chuckle echoed in her chest. "I guess so."

"I can work with that." Lux grinned, then his expression turned serious. "The moment that portal stone winked me out, I knew I'd made the stupidest mistake of my life. Nothing else mattered but getting back here as soon as possible." One hand dropped, and his body wriggled as he fished something from his pocket. "I know I'm not one of your book boyfriends, but ... happy Valentine's Day."

Oaklyn stared down at the folded note for a long minute before she summoned the courage to open it.

Cream Puff;
I love you. Keep me?
- your Pretty Kitty.

Her eyes blurred with tears as she nodded. "Gods, yes."

Lux kissed her, hard and deep and perfect, adorable kitty fangs scraping her lip as his tongue probed her mouth. The note was crushed between them and Oaklyn curled her fingers around it, determined to add it to the library in the shed so that she could treasure it forever.

"I brought wine," Lux gasped, tugging the towel away. "I thought we could drink it in front of the fire. Maybe you can read to me."

"Later." She pawed at his clothes until they came off, then backed him into the bedroom and the enormous, soft expanse of her bed. "Much later."

"Later works for me." He sprawled on the mattress as she set the note on her bedside table, smoothing it flat to avoid any further damage.

"I love you," Oaklyn whispered, kissing her way up his body until they shared breath. "I think I loved you from the moment you fell into that beanbag."

"Funnily enough, that's about the time I fell in love with you, too."

"Fate?"

"Nah. Just draconic perfection." Lux's grin was wicked sin and sharp fangs. "Make love to me, cream puff?"

"With pleasure, pretty kitty. With pleasure."

I HOPE you enjoyed Oaklyn and Lux's story. It was a joy to write, and I'm crossing my fingers that you all had a laugh, because I know I sure did.

So … do I write other stuff? You bet I do! Keep up to date with all the latest shenanigans at:

www.sliceofsammy.com

LOVE A FREE BOOK?

Learn to let go... or burn.

Dating Noah Acheson has always been gentle, predictable and above all, safe – but when the softly spoken foxkin breaks the rules of their carefully crafted relationship, Deanna cuts him off, retreating to her private sanctuary deep in the Australian bush.

Stinging from Deanna's rejection, Noah returns from a brief stint fighting fires in New South Wales to face an infinitely more vicious fire front in Victoria. Though his broken heart still very much belongs to Deanna Schellponte, he's determined not to chase her – until the wind changes, turning the fires towards pack land, and Deanna is reported missing.

With fire raging all around, Noah races into the bush to find the wolfkin he loves. To survive, Deanna and Noah must confront not only the fury of Mother Nature... but the ghost whose memory tore them apart.

ALSO BY SAMANTHA MARSHALL

THE WEAVER'S WAR SERIES

- Sorcery and Stardust
- Sorcery and Subterfuge
- Sorcery and Sandstorms

THE KIN CHRONICLES SERIES

- Aislinn's Shadow
- Tobias' Spark
- Deanna's Ghost

THE MERGED WORLDS SERIES

- The Heart of a Shadow
- Catnip (that's this one!)
- Headless
- Foiled

COMING SOON

- Sorcery and Sacrilege (Book four in the Weaver's War series)

To find out more about these awesome tales, check out my website:

www.sliceofsammy.com

ABOUT SAMANTHA

Hi, I'm Sam!

I've been writing my whole life, scribbling stories on anything close to hand – from the shopping list to napkins to post-it notes (don't mention post-its to hubby haha).

I grew up reading fantasy of the likes of Anne McCaffrey, Terry Pratchett, and their peers. I'm also a lifelong vampire fan, along with all things spooky. In my late teens I was introduced to paranormal romance and discovered a whole new layer of storytelling with a bit of a spicy edge! Taking what I learnt from all of the above, I devoted myself to creating full-bodied characters, meaty plots, epic adventure, and a little bit of naughty sauce on the side.

I completed a Diploma of Professional Writing and Editing after high school and spent the next several years in my writing cave, working on a novel that is now in a drawer somewhere, followed by a couple of others who shared the same fate. (What can I say? I'm a recovering perfectionist.)

I came close to debuting my novel career in 2009, then ended up pregnant and took some time off to have kids. I debuted for real in 2019 with *Sorcery and Stardust* and won ARRA's Favourite Debut Romance Author for 2019, which was extremely cool!

I write speculative fiction that is a fusion of multiple sub-genres and therefore doesn't fit particularly well into any of them, but after many years and a lot of angst, I'm okay with that. I love all my characters and their stories for different reasons, but have a soft spot for an excellent villain and a tortured protagonist.

I currently live in south east Melbourne, Victoria, with my hubby, two kids, a Golden Retriever and a turtle. I volunteer with the Romance Writers of Australia, and I'm passionate about great writing, interesting characters, chai tea and happily ever afters.

And if you want to get to know the Perfectly Paranormal Anthology authors a bit more, get sneak peeks of what's coming up for the APP Anthologies, as well as giveaways, special offers and just some PNR fun, then join our Perfectly Paranormal Paramours Facebook Group.

Find us here:

https://www.facebook.com/groups/251663560162131

ACKNOWLEDGMENTS

This book would never have happened without the wonderful friends who collaborated with me to make this anthology truly great: Hellucy Howe, Leisl Leighton, Marnie St Clair and Georgia Tingley – who, though she chose not to continue her anthology journey with us long term, once told me she'd never read a good dragon romance before. It was from this conversation that Oaklyn was born, and the first chapter written in the early hours of the evening while I was cooking (burning) dinner for the family.

Special mention goes to Mum, who always reads my chapters as I write them, and offers feedback, questions and general stamps of approval. Thanks Mum – you're amazing and I'm forever grateful we're on this journey together.

Beyond that, another special thank-you goes to Bron, who listened to me rant about the final chapters while we sat around a campfire together – and who shortly thereafter beta read this novella for me, pointing out such things as Lux taking off his beanie twice in two paragraphs without putting it back on again, and then helping me to navigate Plot Hole Swamp safely.

To my ARC readers – you're incredible. You never balk no matter what I send, and you always give the most incredibly honest feedback, which means more than I can say. Thank you.

LOVE PNR? JOIN OUR PERFECTLY PARANORMAL PARAMOURS FACEBOOK GROUP

If you want to get to know the Perfectly Paranormal Anthology authors a bit more, get sneak peeks of what's coming up as well as giveaways, special offers and just some PNR fun, then join our Perfectly Paranormal Paramours Facebook Group.

Find us here:

https://www.facebook.com/groups/251663560162131